ONE-KNIGHT STAND

BARBARA DEVLIN

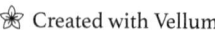 Created with Vellum

This book is dedicated to my best female friends, which includes family, whose unconditional love and support allows me to live boldly.

BFF Honor Roll (In no particular order):

Dee Rowell

Candace Castillo

Tina Castillo

Carla Castillo

Candee Tipler

Debbie Byers

Diane Gibson

Jeanne Adams

Leah Grant

Amy Barrett

Carla Chadwick

Lauren Champagne

Christi Doporto

Lyndsey Lewellen

Kathryn Le Veque

Do old friends

truly make the

best lovers?

PROLOGUE

The Ascendants
England
The Year of Our Lord 1313

"How did we come to this, brother?" Demetrius scratched his chin and frowned.

"At the pointed end of a sword." Arucard chuckled, though he knew it was not that simple. "And it is not so bad as you may think, once you accustom yourself to the idea."

"You say that now, but if memory serves, you were none too pleased when faced with similar circumstances." With a groan, Demetrius stood and paced the floor. "Eternal damnation seems an awfully high price. Surely it would have been preferable to die a warrior's death."

"Well, let us not be too dramatic." In silence, Arucard pondered his fellow knight's predicament and smiled. Had he not felt the same on the eve of his nuptials? "It just requires a period of adjustment on your part."

"Perchance this is punishment for Randulf." Demetrius shook his head. "Never should I have left him in my wake."

"Wait a minute, brother. You are no more or less to blame for his demise than any of us, and there was naught we could do to save him." He pointed for emphasis. "As it is, we barely escaped with our lives, and only five of us remain. Would you rather none survived?"

"I would have him hither." Demetrius gazed at the ceiling and sighed. "At the very least, I would trade places, as he was the better man."

"Now there I must take exception, as such comparison is as blancmange to brewets." Leaning forward, Arucard propped his elbows on his knees. "Neither you nor Randulf could claim such distinction, as you are two drastically different beasts."

"And yet I persist, and he is gone." Demetrius speared his fingers through his hair, and then he fisted his hands. "So I am resolved to consider my situation a burden and my fate one of lifelong penance."

"My friend, you are not thinking clearly, as your judgment is clouded by misplaced guilt." Of course, Arucard neglected to mention that he, too, carried their comrade's death as a stain on his conscience and invisible wounds that had not quite healed.

Of their set, Randulf had been the youngest and most good-natured Templar. Facing every day with a mischievous grin, a biting sense of humor, and a wild streak to match, Randulf was forever garnering additional weapons practice for himself and his brother knights for a wide variety of infractions. Still, the lighthearted gadling was a favored son.

"My guilt is well-founded, and I do not deserve happiness. In my rush to stem the tide, I did not realize he had yet to cast off, and it was too late when I noted my error. I abandoned him to the king's guard, and his loss is my shame." Demetrius scowled. "Mayhap it is fitting that I am required to marry."

"You equate matrimony with hell?" Arucard's ears rang with disbelief.

"Will you argue otherwise?" Demetrius mumbled.

"Well, in truth, it can at times be an abyss of suffering unique unto itself." Arucard laughed aloud and slapped his thigh. "But if you ever repeat that to Isolde, I will send you to the glorious hereafter, posthaste."

"Do you find sport in my misery?"

"I find sport in the absurdity of your logic." Arucard stood and walked to his friend. "Guilt is a powerful emotion, brother. It numbs your senses and impairs your vision, shrouding your reality in a dense cloud of regret, which further impedes your capacity to reap the rewards of life. You may as well be dead, as you have one foot in the grave, and Randulf, God rest him, would never wish that on you."

"What would you have of me? Am I to marry Athe-lyna and spend my days in connubial bliss?" With fists resting on hips, Demetrius inclined his head. "And what sort of name is that? Sounds like a rather nasty infection. Can you not hear the boys? 'Poor bastard caught the Athelyna, and his most prized protuberance shriveled and fell off.'"

"By God's bones, I will grant you that." Arucard surrendered to boisterous guffaws. "Wherefore do you not call the poor lass by a term of affection—one known only to her?"

Demetrius shifted his weight. "And wherefore would I do that?"

"To foster a true and lasting bond with your mate."

"And wherefore would I want to do that?" Demetrius shuffled his feet.

"Well, if for no other reason than to hasten conception of your heirs."

With a look of sheer terror, Demetrius turned white as a sheet and splayed his arms as he teetered precariously.

"Whoa, brother." Arucard steadied his fellow Nautionnier Knight. "Have a seat before you fall flat on your face, and the fair maiden refuses to marry you."

"Babes—I forgot about that." Demetrius cradled his head in his hands. "Back up, else I will ruin the shine on your boots, because I fear I am going to vomit."

"Is it safe to assume you didst not avail yourself of a whore, as Morgan suggested?" Arucard grimaced, as he had rejected the same notion prior to marrying Isolde. "It might have put your mind at ease for tonight."

"No, it would not. Call me a lunatic, but if I am to risk everlasting condemnation, then I would join my body only with whom I have spoken the vows, per the sacrament." With an expression of unfailing determination, Demetrius compressed his lips. "I will have no other."

"Then let us be done with it." With arms crossed, Arucard retreated a step. "So you may beget your heir, as the King commands."

"Am I to breed as a prized stallion put to pasture?" Demetrius grumbled with unveiled irritation. "Are we naught more than means to produce the next generation of mariners insane enough to undertake His Majesty's bidding?"

"You make procreation sound so romantic, brother." Arucard blanched. "Believe me, it is not a chore, though it does require some effort to master from the start, but the work is good."

"That is precisely what it is to me—drudgery."

Demetrius thrust his chin. "And I suspect we have merely exchanged one hangman's noose for another. In short, it is naught more than the trappings of duty owed to an oath ill-pledged that I shall endeavor to persevere."

"Oh, come now." Since his brother would soon learn differently, Arucard succumbed to a full-blown belly laugh. "As I have seen Athelyna, she is nice duty, if one can get it."

"Then you should take her to wife."

"Alas, I am in love with Isolde."

"Be that as it may, I am obliged not to enjoy the experience."

"You forget yourself." Arucard wiped a stray tear from his eye. "As I explained last night, you must enjoy it, to some degree, in order to conceive a child."

A knock at the door gave them pause.

"Oh hell, it is time." Demetrius paled in an instant and swallowed hard. "Come."

Morgan peered inside and cast a playful grin. "Ready to face the enemy?"

Once again, Demetrius tottered, and Arucard all but carried him to the chair. To Morgan, Arucard said, "Brother, we have a problem."

"What is this?" Morgan closed the oak panel. "Did you not pay a visit to Matild, as I instructed?"

"She has a groat-sized wart on her nose." Demetrius flinched. "And she is missing two front teeth."

"Indeed, she is, and that is what makes her proficient in her most popular service." Morgan clucked his tongue. "And wherefore would I care for a wart? Matild's reputation precedes her."

Demetrius snorted. "You must know I am not entirely comfortable with your lustful embrace of English customs."

Morgan waggled his brows. "As they say, when in Rome—"

"We are not in Rome."

"And we are no longer Templars." Levity aside, Morgan said, "Are you still going on about Randulf?"

The room was as silent as a tomb.

Morgan glanced at Arucard, and he shrugged.

"You were not there when he disappeared into the sea." Demetrius closed his eyes. "Screaming for his mother, the lad went down with his ship."

"And, apart from the screaming, he would have it no other way," Arucard stated softly. "Randulf was a fine mariner and man, albeit a young one, and your steadfast refusal to let him go does no credit to his memory."

"Arucard is correct." Morgan cocked his head. "But if you are truly unwilling to wed the lady, I shall be too happy to take your place, as the woman is handsome and the title generous."

Demetrius snapped to attention. "She is my bride—already promised."

"And I suppose the earldom means naught?" Morgan rocked on his heels.

"I would have her without it, but the King gives me no choice," Demetrius asserted without hesitation. "His Majesty seems intent on corrupting us."

"Then for what are you waiting?" Arucard inquired. "Do yourself a favor, brother, and leave the past to yesterday."

Demetrius opened and then closed his mouth. After a minute, he sighed heavily and mustered a smile. "All right. Bring on the archbishop, for I am to wed. But you must promise me something."

"Whatever you require, know ye shall have it." Arucard

slapped his longtime friend on the back. "Now, let us get you to the altar."

"Wait." Demetrius halted in his tracks. "At the first opportunity, you must help me compose a pet name, as *Athelyna* is not something I imagine myself uttering in the throes of passion."

CHAPTER ONE

The Descendants
The English Channel
September, 1812

If one had to die, now was as good a time as any, or so Lance Prescott, sixth Marquess of Raynesford, thought as his ship heeled hard a-larboard. Of course, he did not want to die, but neither did he think that, when his days were at an end, he would seriously be consulted in the matter.

Memories, bits of the past, flashed before his eyes.

His mother had died in childbirth, so he never knew her. In brief, he relived the sadness when his father had perished of a liver ailment after years of excessive drinking, although the man was, for all intents and purposes, a stranger. He revisited the sense of vulnerability when, at the age of four and ten, he struggled in vain against frigid waters to save his cousin, Thomas.

As an anchor about his neck, he considered his title, which he inherited once his guardian passed, because

Thomas, the original heir, had preceded his sire in death. Lance had always looked on the burden of the peerage as penance for his inability to rescue his beloved relation.

Triumphs. Losses. Regrets.

Things he had said and done that he wished he could take back. Accomplishments he wished he had achieved but had not attained. There were so many experiences of which he had yet to partake and places to which he had never journeyed. He had not married, and he had no heir.

They were all there.

There was a woman he admired—always had. He had known her since she was born, but he did not deserve her, never would. Long ago, he had resigned himself to marrying another. Trouble was, in his mind and his heart if truth were told, none compared with her.

Lance shook himself out of the morbid reverie that was his personal history and focused on the task at hand. Grasping the carved quarterdeck rail, he held on tight as the *Demetrius* righted herself. Frothing waves crashed over the sides, spilling onto the deck. A ravenous beast, the angry seas threatened to swallow the mighty frigate in a single gulp.

Staccato bursts of lightning pierced the turbulent skies, flashing rapid-fire glimpses of the tempest raging in all directions. In the distance, four imposing vessels belonging to the knights of the Brethren of the Coast tossed about like wooden toys in a bath, and his was the fifth ship in the line.

In his wake, he could barely make out a familiar silhouette. Trevor Marshall, the most recent addition to the infamous knighthood descended of the famed Templars, the warriors of the Crusades, struggled to steer the *Hera* through violent waters and did not appear to fare any better.

"Into the wind, Scottie," Lance yelled.

"We're tryin', Cap'n."

Scottie and the helmsman, Mr. Hazard, engaged in fierce combat for control of the craft. Lashed to the wheel to keep from falling overboard, they waged war against the tempestuous ocean.

Surrendering to a mighty gale, the *Demetrius* heeled hard a-starboard. Clutching the rail, Lance peered down and surmised he could skim the surface of the swirling sea if he fully extended his arm. With a wicked shudder, he gulped and decided not to put it to test.

"Hold her, boys!" The first mate screamed above the howling winds.

With a death-grip on the wheel, Lance braced himself as the bow rose sharply. The ship crested, lightning speared the clouds, and thunder roared in an ominous specter of doom.

In an instant, the fore topmast stay snapped, and the staysail unfurled. Lance noted the fluttering canvas and cursed, because he knew what would happen next, and it was the last thing he needed at the moment.

"No." Though he voiced the denial, it was muffled amid the bluster of the storm.

As if Mother Nature had read his thoughts, the wind caught the end, filled the sheet, and hauled the large sail into the blast.

"Bloody hell." He gritted his teeth. "Hold on!"

The bow jerked forcibly to starboard, and the relentless zephyr threatened to bring down the rigging *en masse*.

"Cap'n, we have to take in that sail before we founder."

"I know." Lance tugged at his lifeline.

It was time to dance with Death. The gnarled hand of his first mate halted him, and he glanced at the seasoned tar. The stern lamps had long ago been doused by the mountainous waves, and in the flickering light from the storm, he spied grim resolution etched in his crewman's expression.

"The *Demetrius* will swim without me, Cap'n. You're responsible for the ship and her crew." Scottie squeezed hard on his wrist. "Let me go, sir."

Despite instincts to the contrary, Lance nodded once.

In mere minutes, Lance lost sight of his first mate in the driving rain. "Can you see him?" he shouted to the helmsman.

"No, sir." Mr. Hazard wiped his brow. "He might have gone in the drink, Cap'n."

With a hand, Lance shielded his eyes from the savage deluge that pummeled his flesh, stinging like a swarm of angry bees. He did not want to think it, did not want to consider the fact that he may have sent his first mate to his death. Craning his neck, he strained to focus through the torrent. Lightning blazed across the sky, and Lance caught sight of Scottie. A tremor of fear wrenched his gut.

Off the bow, which rose as they rode the peak of the wave, the first mate dangled precariously from the larboard rail. Another thunderbolt momentarily blinded Lance.

In an instant, he was no longer aboard his ship. Instead, he found himself at Eton. It was winter, and his cousin Thomas asked him to skip Latin and go skating on a nearby frozen pond.

"Come on, Lance." Thomas waved. *"You do not always have to follow the rules."*

With clenched fists to his hips, he stopped short of reminding his errant relation that rules were put in place for a reason. And unlike his brash cousin, Lance always followed the straight and narrow path. He supposed it was that difference that made them such good friends. While he kept Thomas grounded, the fiery gadling kept Lance from being the proverbial stick in the mud.

Finally, Lance smiled and shook his head. "We are going to get into trouble," he hollered to his cousin, who was already walking away. He frowned and checked to see no one was watching before following Thomas into the field.

Nestled in a crescent of snow dusted oak trees, the little pond was almost perfectly round, and a thick, white layer of ice covered the small body of water.

Amid hoots and hollers, the young cousins, more like brothers, exactly the same age and lifelong mates, took turns running onto the ice. The air was crisp, and their expelled breath produced puffs of smoke, as they slid across the slippery surface on the smooth soles of their boots.

Lance fell flat on his bottom and scowled at Thomas, who held a hand to his belly and laughed heartily. As he tried to stand, his foot skidded on the ice. Lance ended up as he started— back on his bum.

"Is this not better than reciting a dead language no one uses anymore?" Thomas skipped on the ice, and then he splayed his arms wide for balance, as he veered in a graceful arc.

As he struggled to right himself, Lance halted when a loud cracking sound snared his attention. Beneath his feet, in the pristine veneer, jagged lines suddenly snaked in every direction. He froze.

"Thomas, do not move."

To his irritation, his disobedient cousin ignored the warning. In the process of gathering speed for another sail across the ice, Thomas tripped and disappeared below the surface. Only his arms, shoulders, and head remained visible.

"Lance. Help. Help me!" Thomas fought to pull himself up, but every time he managed to inch out of the water, another piece of ice broke away. He fell, deeper and deeper.

"Stay still, Thomas." Crawling slowly, on his palms and knees, Lance scooted toward the middle of the pond and closer to his cousin. "I am coming for you."

But as Lance neared, the ice collapsed. He sucked in a breath as the painfully cold water penetrated his clothes. Because he had not made it to the center of the pond, it was still shallow enough for his feet to reach the bottom, and the water came only to his chin.

Tilting his head back, he gasped for air.

A flicker of movement caught his attention.

Hands flailed helplessly.

Lightning flashed, and water splashed over his face as he wrenched to the present. Lance sputtered and wiped his cheeks with his oilskin rain gear. Determination welled within him. He was a man now, not a child. He might not have been able to save his cousin, but he would not let his first mate die.

He untied his lifeline, and the helmsman did the same.

"Go below and get help."

Mr. Hazard nodded. "Aye, sir."

Using a section of rope, Lance tied the wheel in place, hoping the thick twine would withstand the forces of nature until he or the helmsman returned.

The stern rose as the waves drove the ship, and then the bow crashed violently into the valley. In a burst of light, Lance spied Scottie. He had lost his grip with one hand and was swinging by the other.

After making his way down the companion ladder, he crawled along the larboard rail. The ship bucked, as would an unbroken horse. When the bow rose, he held tight to the railing. When it leveled, he moved forward as fast as possible. While it took him mere minutes to reach his first mate, it seemed an eternity.

The storm flared all around. The wind wailed, as the mournful cries of a grieving widow.

Reaching out, Lance grasped the wrist of his first mate. Scottie stared at him, and a mixture of relief and gratitude washed over his face. With one powerful tug, using his bodyweight as a counterbalance, Lance fell backward on the deck as he hauled Scottie over the rail.

"Are you injured?"

"No, Cap'n." With a balled fist, the first mate punched him in the arm. "I knew you would come for me."

Lance wiped the rain from his eyes. "Let us tuck in that sail and get back to the helm."

Moving in unison with the ship, they dragged in the slapping canvas. The laces had torn from the yardarm at one end, causing the sail to arc wildly.

Scottie lunged for the wayward corner and managed to catch it. He landed on his rear in the middle of the deck.

Lance laughed as they engaged in an awkward waltz, of sorts, gathering the unruly sheet. In a rush, he tucked the sail to the yardarm.

A loud, unnatural crack snared his senses.

An eerie premonition of *deja vu* nipped at his heels, gooseflesh covered him from top to toe, and he peered skyward. Hanging over them like the sword of Damocles, the foremast yardarm splintered in two, and it listed in the wind, back and forth, as a perilous pendulum, with one end threatening to drop on them at any moment.

"Look out." Lance waved his arms in warning. "Scottie, get out of the way."

"What?" the seaman replied.

He pointed, but the first mate did not appear cognizant of the impending danger.

And then it happened.

The yardarm broke free and came crashing down.

Without thought, he dove toward Scottie, shoving him out of the path of the large, jagged piece of wood. Lance landed, face first, on the unforgiving planks of the main deck. Pain ratcheted through his body, though it was not from his fall. It was from the crushing weight of the yardarm, as it snapped the bone of his sprawled leg.

"Captain."

Lance flinched at the shout of alarm and the panic in the voice of his first mate. It seemed as though a hundred fingers surveyed his body, and someone turned him over. He blinked his eyes and found himself in his room at Sandgate Manor, the Raynesford ancestral pile.

A single candle sat on a bedside table, and thick quilts had been tucked to his chin. A physician explained his condition to his aunt and uncle, the Marquess and Marchioness of Raynesford, who had cared for him since his father had passed.

He trained his ear as the marquess detailed how a schoolmaster spied Lance and Thomas running away from class. By the time the teacher trailed them, Thomas had drowned in the icy pond. The schoolmaster pulled a barely conscious Lance from the frigid water and carried him back to school.

He shivered.

Thomas died.

Lance moaned and twisted beneath the mountain of bedcovers. The physician ushered his guardians into the hall, so as not to disturb him. He fought sleep, because he feared if he surrendered he might never wake, and was still lucid when the door to his bedchamber creaked.

A shadowy silhouette entered the room and tiptoed to his bed. In the soft light from the candle, he studied the familiar face, committing every subtle nuance to memory. He had known the young girl since she was born.

Through half-open eyes, he gazed on her graceful form as she placed one of her wooden miniatures, a brightly painted green turtle, on the bedside table. She collected the quaint figurines, treasured them, so he was surprised she would part with one of her gems.

She glanced over her shoulder and appeared to be checking to make sure no one was there, before leaning forward and setting her mouth to his.

It was his first kiss.

"Get well, Lance." She pressed her palm, cool against his fevered skin, to his cheek. "You are my hero."

After that, he slept.

"Easy, lads!"

The concern in Scottie's words came to him through a fog of anguish and confusion.

As Lance slipped beneath the comforting blanket of unconsciousness, a name passed his lips. A bare whisper, it was lost in the blustery gale of the storm, so no one heard, but he said it just the same.

"Cara."

FAR AWAY, in a fashionable London town home, all were abed, and the household slept. The halls were silent, save the ticking of the long-case clock in the foyer at the foot of the grand staircase.

The candles were guttered, having long ago extinguished, and the hearths were cold. No shadows played on the carpets, because no moonlight filtered through the windows.

Had anyone been awake to see, the sky beyond the glass was angry.

In the dark of night, Cara Douglas shifted and frowned, and a soft moan passed her lips as she struggled somewhere between consciousness and slumber. Tucked, safe and sound, in her bedchamber, she rolled her head restlessly to one side and sighed as she pushed at the bedclothes.

The clock in the hall sounded the hour. It was late.

A flash of light and a distant rumbling provided the first warnings of the violent storm approaching the city.

Cara kicked at the sheets, which had become tangled about her legs as she tossed and turned. And she wiped the faint sheen of perspiration from her brow, as she fought imaginary wraiths in haunted repose.

"No," she murmured, ensnared in a vivid dream.

An army of visions plagued her rest, and bits and pieces of her past flashed a staccato of unsettling imagery. In a vaguely familiar surrounding, a single candle sat on a bedside table. Beneath mountains of blankets, a motionless form reclined. As she crossed the room, she stared down and realized she was a child, not the woman she was now. The young Cara set a tiny wooden figurine on the table and then claimed a kiss in payment for her willingly relinquished treasure.

Suddenly, reflections of a wild sea rocked her world. Mountainous waves of water caved in around her, burying her in an ocean grave. In her sleep, she screamed and lashed at some invisible tormenter.

Beyond the walls of her home, the wind whipped and howled. Trees swayed, rubbish and dust swirled in the air. The pitter-patter of raindrops sounded on the windowpanes, a gentle drumbeat heralding the arrival of nature's tempest.

Thunder roared through her bedchamber, and she

sobbed. Tears slipped from her still closed eyes, and though she dozed, it was neither peaceful nor comforting.

In her dreams, she pictured his face; the one she had known all her life. He did not smile, and his black hair was wet. His green eyes shimmered with determination—and uncharacteristic fear. And she was with him, sharing his emotions as though they were one entity.

Drenched in sweat, her fine cambric nightgown clung to her body. In despair, she kicked and thrashed in a snare of linens. With desperation, she searched the gloom for an escape, some way to break free from the bonds of the terror holding her captive.

Through the misery, he called her name.

And she murmured softly and reached for him.

Rain pelted her windows, as would an eager suitor beckoning her in a midnight rendezvous. Her pillow grew damp as tears streamed her temples, and she listed frantically from side to side.

Urgent. Tortured.

Cara cried out.

But still she languished, trapped in a seemingly endless vortex of nocturnal desolation.

The storm intensified, and thunder shook the walls of her home. The gentle shower escalated into a torrential downpour. Finally, on a booming clap, she bolted upright.

Liberated from the nightmare that had arrested her, Cara took a few seconds to gather her wits and discern that she remained in her chamber, safely ensconced in her family residence on Upper Brooke Street. Clutching the sheet to her chest, she shivered and rubbed the gooseflesh covering her arms. A quick glance about the room told her no one presented a threat, and nothing was amiss. But the cause of her concern remained quite tangible.

Eerily realistic.

After tossing the blankets aside, Cara swung her legs over the edge of the mattress and leapt from the bed. She walked to the windows, pulled open the drapes, and gasped at the display of raw power as nature assailed the city.

With clasped hands pressed to her bosom, she choked on a sob. An obscure but nonetheless compelling weight hung heavy in her heart. She struggled to breathe, as if from overexertion. Fear lapped at her senses and filled her with tension. She rolled her shoulders in a valiant but failed attempt to relax.

He was out there.

Coming home—to her.

Uncertain as to how she knew, she simply knew.

A shiver of dread traipsed her spine, and a wraith of gloom danced a merry jig in the recesses of her mind. Entombed in a melancholy prison, she wept. But now was not the time to cry, so she wiped her tears.

Something had gone horribly wrong.

Her hero suffered.

How she longed to go to him, to hold him in her arms and ease his torment. Operating on instinct, she sensed that he needed her, and she would have to be strong.

Pressing her brow against the cool surface of the glass, Cara closed her eyes and whispered, "Lance."

CHAPTER TWO

"*H*urry, Alex." Cara waved to the elegantly dressed young woman, who descended the stairs of her home with a not so convincing air of refined serenity she had tried but failed to project. Cara gave vent to a giggle. "Else we will be late."

Lady Alexandra Seymour, known to her family as Alex, was one of Cara's lifelong friends. Originally, there were ten in the group known only to a privileged few as the Brethren of the Coast. Lady Elaine Prescott, Caroline Marshall, Countess of Lockwood, and Sabrina Markham, Countess of Woverton and Cara's younger sister, rounded out the female half.

"What is your hurry?" Alex asked, as a footman handed her into the carriage. She glanced at the empty seat opposite Cara and looked her question. "And where is Brie?"

"With her head over a basin." Cara grimaced.

"Poor dear." Alex wrinkled her nose and settled into the squabs as the coach lurched forward. "Still no relief from the morning sickness?"

"No. And you should see Everett." Cara rolled her eyes.

"The man is completely undone, and I do not know what is worse—her wrenching heaves or his reaction."

"Well, I suppose we can take comfort in the knowledge that he loves her. And we would not have it otherwise." Alex laughed and gazed out the window. "Devil of a storm we had last night. I hope the boys are all right. What did their missive say?"

"I beg your pardon?" She winced and shifted her weight. "What missive?"

"You know." Alex checked her skirts. "The one calling us to the docks."

As nervous anticipation waltzed in her belly, Cara bit her lip and tried to form a suitable excuse for her behavior. Just as quick, she reminded herself that biting her lip was not only unladylike but also a clear violation of the edicts governing feminine deportment. And Cara was nothing if not a lady.

A brow arched, Alex inclined her head. "Cara, what are you not telling me?"

She shrugged in what she prayed was a haphazard manner, because try as she might, she could not relax. "I did not receive a notice."

"What?" Alex stared, mouth agape. "If you did not receive a summons, then why on earth do we journey to Deptford?"

"Oh, I do not know." Cara made a show of settling her cloak as she sought acceptable justification for her behavior. But what could she say? How could she explain that which she could not explain? Her actions were born of a dream and a connection that defied rhyme and reason. In the end, she opted for varnished truth. "Something is wrong—I can feel it. Call it intuition, but they will be there. Of that I am sure."

"Are you all right?" With a countenance of suspicion mixed with care, Alex studied her. "You look tired, sister."

"I did not sleep well." Hoping to avoid further examination, she flicked an imaginary speck of lint from her sleeve and then searched for the familiar lucky kerchief in her pocket. Given to her years ago by her hero, the square boasted the embroidered initials LPF, for its owner Lance Fortescue Prescott. "The storm kept me awake."

"Well, if they have not yet arrived, I suppose we could go shopping." Alex extended her kidskin-covered hands. "I need a new pair of gloves."

"That sounds lovely." She mustered a half-grin. Despite her light-hearted friend's carefree demeanor, Cara could not shake the foreboding unease that declared they would not make it to Bond Street that day.

THE HONOURABLE EAST INDIA COMPANY had built an extensive dockyard in Deptford. The East Indiamen, as the mighty ships of the fleet were known, sailed from the impressive, privately owned yard. The best and the largest merchant vessels, they were also armed as warships to guard against pirates and the French, with whom England currently waged war.

Buccaneer Trading existed not only as a lucrative business incorporated into the East India Company, but also as a well played ruse for the Brethren of the Coast, a secret order of Nautionnier Knights in service to the Crown.

Under the guise of mercantile commerce, the Brethren sailed on various missions for the national defense effort. Serving in silence, their assignments were always of utmost importance and unimaginable danger, and there were never any public acknowledgments of their achievements.

The five original Brethren comprised the membership of the much-fabled order. Blake Elliott, Duke of Rylan, and Caroline's older brother, Damian Seymour, Duke of Weston, and Alex's elder sibling, and Dirk Randolph, Viscount Wainsbrough, were the most senior at one and thirty. Lance Prescott, Marquess of Raynesford, and Elaine's cousin and guardian, was next oldest at thirty. Sir Dalton Randolph was, at nine and twenty, the youngest.

Recently, their group welcomed new additions. Trevor Marshall, Earl of Lockwood, had married Caroline and immediately accepted a knighthood in the order. A year later, Dirk had married Lady Rebecca Wentworth, as was. Then, she served as an agent of the elusive Counterintelligence Corps and had been paired with Dirk to catch a traitor. In the process, the spy and the knight fell in love.

And that spring, Sabrina married Lord Everett Markham, who later became Earl of Woverton when his elder brother perished in an accident. With a natural inclination for financial matters, Everett assumed control of the family business, with the blessing of Admiral Douglas. But that was not the only significant development.

Already, the married Brethren were busily providing for the next generation. The birth of Welton Henry Marshall, Viscount Denbury, was heralded with much fanfare. But the joy was quickly compounded with the news that all three Brethren wives were expecting.

Cara smiled as she and Alex traversed the wooden planks of Deptford Yard. As they neared the slips belonging to Buccaneer Trading, they halted in their tracks.

Images from the previous night flashed in her brain in

horrid detail. With a hand pressed to her throat, and her heart pounding in her chest, Cara whispered, "My God."

"Oh, Cara." Adopting a similar stance, Alex shook her head. "What do you suppose happened?"

Before them, the magnificent vessels belonging to the Brethren stood as mere shadows of their former selves. Splintered wood from broken yardarms jutted viciously in all directions. Dangling ropes swung in the gentle breeze and torn canvas fluttered. The once intricate, mighty rigging listed in tatters.

It was a wonder they made it home.

"Alex?" a familiar voice called. "Cara?"

"Damian?" Cara blinked. "Is that you?"

Descending the gangplank, Damian waved a welcome. Alex ran to him, threw up her arms, and affectionately hugged her brother. Cara followed on her heels.

"Oh, Damian." Alex cast a mournful glance over his shoulder. "Your lovely lady is ravaged."

"Do not worry about the *Sagremor*, sister." He cupped her cheek. "We will have her shipshape and good as new. You should see the *Intrepid*. She limped into Great Dock just behind us. Collingwood will probably be land-bound while his craft is refitted."

"Oh, dear." Alex gasped. "You do not suppose he has been injured?"

Cara understood the younger Seymour's concern and sympathized with her friend. It was common knowledge Alex harbored a wicked crush on the handsome naval captain of the *Intrepid*, Jason Collingwood.

"Do not fret, little one. Since I spied him on the quarter-deck at dawn, I am sure he is fine." Damian patted her shoulders in what appeared to be an attempt to calm his sister. "And fortunately for us, we had already delivered our cargo of munitions and supplies to the troops and were carrying nothing but ballast. It could have been much worse were we caught in the storm while still bearing explosives."

"Are you all right?" Alex pulled back and eyed him from top to foot. "Were you hurt?"

"I am fine." He placed a brotherly kiss on her forehead. "We are quite well, with the exception of Lance."

"What about Lance?" Cara flinched and swallowed hard. She prayed her dream had not foretold a grim reality beyond the damaged vessels. "What is the extent of his injuries? Is it severe?"

"I do not think so." He offered his escort to each lady and steered them toward the *Demetrius*. "By the by, where is Dr. Handley?"

Alex blinked at her brother. "Dr. Handley?"

"Yes." He nodded once. "I requested you summon him to care for Lance."

"Er, I received no such missive." With brows quirked in question, Alex peered at Cara.

"I beg your pardon?" Damian halted mid-stride. He gazed at Alex, then Cara, and then Alex again. "If you did not get my message, how did you learn of our return?"

Cara grasped at the barest threads of convincing rationale. Would anyone believe her actions had been prompted by a tortuous dream the previous night? Or perhaps a wee bird told her? After a few tense seconds, she seized on a reasonable explanation.

"Gossip," she stated, with fixed purpose. "You know how the *ton* is—nothing escapes their notice. There was rumor of several ships in the Thames estuary, from the North Forelands lighthouse." She shrugged and rocked on her heels.

"We thought we would chance it, in the event you had made it home, else we were going shopping."

"I see." Damian scratched his temple. "Perhaps Conrad will send for the doctor," he said, referring to the butler at Seymour House.

"I am sure he will." Alex smiled and patted his arm. "And Dr. Handley shall be right behind us."

"Do tell." Cara fought to calm herself and disguise the apprehension roiling within her. "What exactly is wrong with Lance? Nothing serious, I hope?"

"Well, I am not entirely certain, but I suppose time and the good doctor will put him right." As Cara tugged at his elbow, Damian stared at her. For a brief moment, he searched her gaze, but if he suspected her concern extended beyond mere friendship, he remained silent. Finally, he inclined his head. "It is only a broken leg. Once the bone is set and healed, no doubt he will be the same old Lance."

Relief showered her as a gentle mist, and Cara sighed, as it appeared she had woven unsustainable conclusions from whole cloth. When next she suffered a tempest-driven bad dream, she would chastise herself with the memory of her uncharacteristic overreaction and breach of deportment.

At the foot of the gangplank of the *Demetrius*, Lance's frigate, they lingered. On deck, Trevor, Blake, and Dirk waved an acknowledgement.

"May I suggest you two wait here?" Damian led them to a safe spot, while the crew continued to scurry about, disembarking with various items in transit. "We have Lance secured to a cot. He cannot walk, and we will have to carry him down."

"Oh, dear," Alex cried. "Poor Lance."

"We shall remain here." Cara wrapped a protective arm about Alex's shoulders. Comforting Damian's sister provided fortuitous distraction from Cara's own nagging fears.

A few minutes had passed when Dr. Handley shuffled in their direction, his physician's bag in tow. When he caught sight of them, he doffed his hat and bowed.

"Lady Alex. Miss Douglas." With a wrinkle of his nose, he narrowed his stare and peered at the gangplank. "Conrad forwarded a directive from His Grace. I understand Lord Raynesford is injured?"

"He is, indeed." Cara nodded. "They are expecting you to join them on deck, posthaste." How she longed to rush to her hero's side, to see for herself that Lance was alive and well, hale and hearty. She swallowed her frustration as the grey-haired, bespectacled doctor strolled aboard ship.

After what seemed hours, but was in reality only several minutes, the men appeared at the rail, holding a well-worn cot bearing a blanketed, motionless form. With Dr. Handley in the lead, the Brethren descended at a leisurely pace.

"Careful, gentlemen," the physician cautioned. "Do not jostle my patient."

Telling herself that her worried thoughts would cease their torment once she glimpsed Lance, Cara stepped forward with Alex at her side. But his deathly pale visage left her senses reeling and her knees buckling.

"Oh, my." Clinging to her wits by a hairsbreadth, Cara managed not to swoon. "Is there anything we can do to help?"

"My equipage can convey his lordship to Raynesford House." Dr. Handley removed his spectacles and cleaned them with a handkerchief pulled from his coat pocket, before resettling the wire frames atop his nose. "But I shall require assistance in caring for him."

"We have my coach." Cursing her moment of weakness,

and bolstered by renewed purpose, Cara lowered her chin. "I am at your service."

RAYNESFORD HOUSE OCCUPIED a venerable position in Grosvenor Square. Built in the Palladian style, with urn-topped rails and a Corinthian columned portico, it presented a grand gem among London's more fashionable residences.

As Cara and Alex entered the foyer, Elaine skipped down the main staircase and held her arms wide in welcome.

"Oh, Cara, did you see him?" The younger Prescott's lower lip trembled, and she cast a tear-filled gaze. "It is too dreadful to contemplate."

Though Elaine and Lance were cousins, they were, in actuality, more akin to brother and sister. Since their parents had passed, as had Thomas, Elaine's only sibling, Elaine and Lance were alone save the Brethren. And of the close-knit group of friends, Elaine was the most timid and delicate.

"There, there, dearest. You mustn't cry." Cara hugged Elaine and winked at Alex, as it became readily apparent that caring for Lance would be a two-fold operation. Someone would have to support Elaine, in Lance's absence. "Why do you not offer Alex a spot of tea, while I assist Dr. Handley?"

"As usual, you are right, Cara. I must be strong for Lance." Elaine withdrew and wiped her damp cheeks. As the hostess one would expect of the stately abode, she turned to the butler. "Banks, please show Miss Douglas to his lordship's chambers, and I shall see to the refreshments."

"Very good, my lady." Banks bowed, righted his coat, and faced Cara. "This way, Miss Douglas."

As she climbed the grand staircase, with her hand trailing the polished oak balustrade, Cara realized with heightened anticipation that in mere minutes she would enjoy her first glimpse of Lance's bedchamber. In an instant, she thought of the square kerchief her hero had gifted her so long ago, which rested, folded and tucked inside her bodice, near her heart.

Though it would, no doubt, be considered highly improper, even scandalous in most circles, for an unmarried woman to enter his private apartments, no one in his household would give her presence a second thought. Because they were lifelong friends, no one would ever conceive of anything untoward occurring between them. Therefore, it would not be mentioned beyond the walls of Raynesford House.

Banks approached a large, oak-paneled door, and set it wide. With an elegant sweep of his arm, he retreated a step. "After you, Miss Douglas."

"Thank you, Banks." Excitement charged every nerve, pulsed in every vein, and Cara inhaled deeply before crossing the threshold.

Wall coverings of evergreen damask sporting stamped leather inserts lent a decidedly masculine feel to the chamber, and the current occupant's signature sandalwood scent teased her nose, evoking fonder times. Cara took little note of various accouterments, other than the massive, four-poster bed at the center of the back wall. For some reason she could not fathom, that single piece of seemingly innocuous furniture captured her attention to the detriment of all else.

Sitting high atop a platform, the magnificent structure boasted a hand-carved mahogany headboard, with a canopy that kissed the ceiling, and floor-length, evergreen velvet drapery cascaded from each crowned corner. A matching counterpane of sumptuous velvet and silk sheets blanketed the mattress, and a mountain of fluffy pillows completed the tempting ensemble. Oh, what an adventure it would be to take her ease in such opulence with the man of her fantasies.

"Ahem." Cara did not realize she was staring until Dr. Handley cleared his throat. "Are you, or are you not, going to assist me, Miss Douglas?"

Masking her embarrassment, Cara closed her mouth and slowly walked to the footboard. As she ascended the impressive platform, she caught sight of the man she had often referred to as her hero since childhood.

With hair as black as her own, they might have been confused for siblings by a casual observer. Whereas she gazed on the world with vivid blue eyes, her knight looked on her with the most potent emerald stare, which often saw more than she wished to reveal, framed by thickly lashed lids she had studied for the better part of a year. An aquiline nose sat between chiseled cheekbones, and his patrician chin was strong and proud.

As was the rest of Lance.

At just over six feet tall, he had broad shoulders and a long, lithe frame. Unlike most men of his stature, Lance had an air of understated elegance about him, and he moved with the grace and ease of a gazelle mixed with the power of a jungle cat. Indeed, his was an irresistible combination. Something she knew well, as she had spent many a night in his arms, circling the dance floors of some of London's most fashionable ballrooms.

Yet, they remained nothing more than friends—much to her dissatisfaction.

"I have given his lordship another dose of laudanum. It will keep the pain at bay."

"Oh?" She blinked. "Is there anything you require?"

"I have set the bone, and the leg is splinted. See to it he remains in bed." Dr. Handley checked his timepiece. "Keep his lordship comfortable. When he wakes, make sure he eats."

Determined to do her part and aid Lance in his recovery, she composed a mental list. "Anything in particular?"

"Whatever he prefers." The physician collected the typical utensils of his trade and retrieved his bag, before stepping from the platform. "I shall stop by in the morning to check his progress."

"Thank you, doctor." Cara dipped her chin and half-curtseyed.

With a smile and patience, which should qualify her for sainthood, she stood as sentry until the door closed behind the physician. In a flash, she whirled about and examined her hero.

Unnaturally pale, and with a small scrape that showed the slightest hint of bruising above his left eye, Lance remained motionless. Sitting at the edge of the bed, she tucked the covers beneath his chin, tried not to notice his bare shoulders, and pressed a palm to his forehead. Thankfully, his flesh was cool.

"My poor darling."

Just then, he shifted, pushed away the covers, and revealed a magnificent chest. Though propriety demanded she avert her stare, she could not tear herself from the temptation he presented for her delectation, but her cheeks burned with embarrassment. With his arm, he reached as though he searched for a lifeline, and she was there for him. Clasping his hand in hers, she started when he clung to her. His brow furrowed, and the corners of his mouth curved downward.

"Lance, I am here." She did her best to reassure him. "It is I—Cara."

To her relief, his grip tightened, and his frown faded.

With their fingers still twined, she inched even closer. Leaning forward, she loomed near. For several minutes, she studied the face she knew so well, the face she always sought in a crowd.

The face that haunted her dreams.

Without thought, Cara stretched long and placed a chaste kiss on his forehead. To her delight, the furrows magically vanished at her touch. Retreating ever so slightly, she hovered, her nose mere inches from his.

As a whispery summons, his warm breath wafted over her skin. So she obeyed the come-hither caress and skimmed the tip of his nose with hers, as she wondered how Lance would react had he woke just then?

Would he be happy?

Would he be mad?

Cara chuckled. As the oldest among the Brethren women, she had been expected to marry long ago. Certainly before Caroline and Sabrina. But no one had ever turned her head, at least beyond their clique, and she was determined to wed for love.

Unlike her friends, she had never done anything to further her goal. Had never taken any aggressive action to capture the attention of the one man she had ever considered a suitable candidate.

Caroline had resorted to stowing away aboard Dalton's ship in an attempt to avoid the Season. Inadvertently, she was mistaken for a courtesan, kidnapped by Trevor, and forced into a union, which resulted in a love match. Sabrina, on the other hand, set her cap for Everett and spent a summer preparing for the chase. She, too, enjoyed a marriage based on love.

But Cara had always been known as the levelheaded one, the personification of a true English lady. A legion of admirers, none of which had captured her heart, lauded her beauty and refinement. She could always be counted on to do the right thing. The epitome of feminine deportment, her outlandish younger sister teasingly called her Miss Perfect. Though it was all in good fun, she was beginning to wonder if it was not time for a change, time to break free of her prim and proper shell.

And if she intended to follow in her sister's footsteps, however awkward, Cara needed to rethink her strategy. How many years had she waited for Lance to make his declaration, or give her some inclination he shared her devotion?

Too many to suit her.

At any rate, it was clear that if she remained a disinterested spectator in regard to her future, she would be an old maid before he ever offered for her—if at all.

Of course, she had to consider the fact that her hero might not feel for her what she felt for him. Though they had often partnered at social functions, he had never done anything more than act the perfect gentleman—it was most insulting. But what if he only looked on her as a good friend? Did that mean he would never see her as something more? And if so, what was she prepared to do to alter his position?

A hint of derring-do traversed her spine.

Cara gazed on Lance and smiled. Her quarry rested

peacefully, with no hint of the sultry offer that lay before him. Summoning every ounce of courage within her, she took her first small step toward her goal.

Slowly, deliberately, she bent her head and pressed her lips to his in an inexpressibly sweet caress, sashaying back and forth against his mouth.

In his sleep, he hummed his appreciation; a deep, husky sound she felt all the way to her toes. Instinctively, she retreated, but he freed her hand, speared his fingers through her hair, and drew her impossibly closer.

When Lance slipped his tongue between her parted lips, Cara gasped in shock, but curiosity won the day, so she did not resist. While she had pushed at his chest, in an attempt to break loose, she changed her tack. Relaxing, she splayed her fingers and sank into their kiss. As she acquiesced, he delved further, licking and suckling her flesh in a delicate invasion, and she drank him in as she would a fine wine, savoring each nuance that was uniquely his.

Fire sang in her veins, and it was a new and enticing sensation. Her heart beat a rapid salvo in her chest, and her ears rang like the bells in a Wren steeple. Virgin desire blossomed in the pit of her belly, and she moaned. Responding to the pressure of his palm at the back of her neck, she met him, measure for measure, with all she had and for all she was worth.

And then everything screeched to a halt.

Their first intimate exchange ended as quickly as it began, as Lance sighed, reclined on his pillow, and his arms fell limp. Rolling his head to the side, he shifted beneath the covers, and an elementally male smile played on his lips.

"My God," she whispered.

Cara sat upright and clutched a fist to her chest as remnants of their passion showered her in a gentle yet nonetheless potent heat. Trembling uncontrollably, she struggled to breathe. At last, she closed her eyes and rode the wave of pleasure simmering in her blood and lingering in every charged nerve, leaving no part of her unscathed. Never could she have imagined the power of such a heretofore-simple act.

And Cara wanted more.

After resettling the blanket, she descended the platform and almost shrieked when she spied her reflection in the long mirror. Wearing a pale yellow sprig muslin dress, and matching slippers, with her hair piled in artful curls atop her head, she cut the perfect picture of a proper English lady. Yet, her kiss-swollen lips and flushed cheeks contradicted the image she attempted to portray.

Given that her hero had come at her in a laudanum-induced stupor, she wondered what he could achieve when fully *compos mentis*. Cara skimmed her throat with the back of her fingers and shivered. "Oh, Lance, whatever am I to do now?"

Before that moment, physical intimacy had existed for her as the stuff of fantasy, an elusive realm, something Caroline and Sabrina had hinted at but upon which they had never truly expounded. Relations between a man and a woman were a taboo topic in which no woman of estimable station indulged. But Cara had to admit that, had they enlightened her, she would have doubted the truth.

She brushed her palms to her forearms and marveled as gooseflesh covered her uncharacteristically sensitized skin.

"Miss Perfect, indeed." She humphed.

However, neither her sister nor her dear friend had found love within the strict dictums governing their set. It was only when they threw caution to the wind and ventured beyond the limits of good society that they discovered genuine happiness and lifelong devotion. And something told her that, were she to be successful in her endeavor to catch the husband of her choosing, she would have to do the same.

And Cara had no time to lose.

Pulling the pins from her hair, she loosened her chignon in a figurative signal of rebellion. Yes, she was definitely due for change.

CHAPTER THREE

*I*f there was one person Cara could count on for the unvarnished answers to all her questions, she knew without doubt where to commence her campaign. Having spent the better part of the night considering her predicament, she decided on a daring plan of action and intended to start out as she meant to go on with Lance. In silence, she prayed she was not making a huge mistake, which could result in epic embarrassment of her family.

Standing before the entrance of a palatial Mayfair home, with Lance's kerchief tucked in its secret spot near her heart, she raised a hand, ignored the subtle tremor in her fingers, caught hold of the brass knocker, and gave it a sound pounding. With a long drawn inhale and a mental plea for luck, she rolled her shoulders in an attempt to appear relaxed.

A very proper butler opened the door. "Good morning, Miss Douglas." He bowed and retreated a step.

"And may I bid you the same, Ware." She crossed the threshold. "Is my sister in residence?"

"Indeed." He nodded. "Her ladyship is in the morning room. If you would care to follow me."

"Oh, do not bother." She brushed him aside with a casual but polite wave. "I can see to myself."

To wit he smiled and inclined his head. "As you wish, Miss Douglas."

She found Sabrina sitting on a daybed, sipping a cup of tea, chamomile no doubt, and pressing a palm to her belly. Her usually ebullient younger sister waned due to persistent symptoms of her pregnancy.

"Cara, what a lovely surprise." With an expression of unutterable joy, Sabrina stood, and just as quick her radiant smile faded to an unsteady frown. She swayed and splayed her arms. "Oh, dear."

"Sit down, Brie. You are green as a toad." Cara helped her sister recline before taking the space beside her. She removed the cup from Sabrina's unstable grasp and raised it to her sibling's lips. "Here, dearest, finish your tea. It will settle your stomach."

"I swear, that blasted Eve did us all a woeful turn." Sabrina closed her eyes and took a drink. "This is so unfair. The wife tosses her breakfast, grows round as a pumpkin, and suffers miserably in the birthing, while the man gets his jollies and an heir."

Cara laughed and patted Sabrina's cheek. "You do have a way with words, my darling sister." After returning the porcelain cup to its saucer, she wet a napkin and pressed it to Sabrina's brow.

"Oh, that feels delightful." Her lids fluttered, and Sabrina opened her eyes. "What brings you for a visit—not that you require a reason? But I gather it must be important, because you did not send a formal notice of your arrival."

"Well—"

Just then, the door opened, and Everett peered around the edge of the oak panel. "Darling—" He spied Cara and entered. To his wife, he said, "I am sorry. Did not know you had a visitor, love." With a smile and a nod he addressed her. "Morning, Cara."

"Hello, Everett."

"I am going out, but I shall return in time for lunch." He crossed the room and bent to place a tender kiss on his wife's forehead. "And I will dine at home, tonight, as well."

"What is this I hear?" With brows arched, Sabrina inclined her head. "Not going to your club?"

"No." Everett stood with hands on hips. "I do not fancy the idea of leaving you alone when you are ill."

"But I am not alone, as we have a full compliment of servants in residence, and I am feeling better. And I daresay the worst is yet to come." Sabrina chuckled. "So you had best maintain your usual schedule while I am still of a mind to allow it."

"Do not say such things—even in jest. And I can do whatever I please. If *I* choose to stay home with *my wife*, then so be it." Everett frowned and then nipped the tip of her nose in play. "Has the sickness truly eased, my saucy Sabrina?"

"It has, at least, for today." Sabrina shrugged and then wound her arms about his neck and pulled her husband close. "But you may soothe any lingering malaise with your special brand of medicine, my shameless lord."

As they shared an amazingly thorough kiss, Cara cursed the searing heat of a blush in her cheeks and averted her gaze. In an instant, images of the similar tryst she had enjoyed with Lance flooded her mind, and the room grew unseasonably warm.

Still, it was comforting to know the possibilities in a

marriage when both hearts were engaged. Their charming exchange reinforced her position and strengthened her resolve anew, as did the kerchief bearing Lance's initials, which she clutched to her breast as invisible armor.

"Dearest, I would gladly shoulder your burden to spare you any pain." Everett withdrew from his wife and lifted her hand to his lips before standing upright. "I swear I can bear anything but your suffering."

"I know, and I adore you for the mere sentiment." Sabrina cast him a lopsided grin and hugged her protruding belly. "But we both know it is not possible, as this is mine to carry."

"Then pray indulge me," he said softly, as he traced the curve of her cheek with his finger. "Allow me to support you as I see fit, else this will be our first and last child."

"As you wish." She waved dismissively as he made for the door. "And I shall look for you at lunch. Perhaps you would care to join me for a nap?"

Everett came to an abrupt halt, cast her a devilish smile and winked. "My lady wife, you may depend upon it."

Sabrina giggled as Everett exited the morning room, and then she leveled her gaze on Cara. "Out with it, sister mine. Just what are you about?"

Though she had no personal experience on which to base her suspicions, Cara felt sure that Sabrina and Everett's idea of a nap had little to do with sleep or rest, of any nature. And in that second, she realized she envied her sibling—not for the man, though she was very fond of her brother-in-law, but for the match. And she was more deter- mined than ever to launch her war of hearts. "You seem so happy, Brie."

"I am a vast deal more than that." Sabrina positively glowed. She reached for Cara's hand and squeezed in emphasis. "I am content beyond my wildest dreams, beyond my fondest fantasies, as Everett is the love of my life." She paused for a moment and then asked, "How is Lance?"

"As well as can be expected." Cara frowned as she sought refuge in polite conversation. "He has a fever this morning, but Dr. Handley says it is not too serious."

"Poor Lance." With an expression of curiosity, Sabrina studied Cara. "Do tell, what brings you by?"

Cara considered her words carefully. "Well, I have been thinking of getting married—"

"*What?*"

"Wait a minute, Brie." Judging from her sister's reaction, she had chosen the wrong words. "Remember the babe. Do not work yourself into a state."

"Forget my state. Who is he?" Sabrina asked, with a narrow gaze and arms folded imperiously in front of her. "What is his profession? Is he in trade? Will I approve of him?"

"He is the best of men." Cara peered at her hands clasped properly in her lap. "And I believe you already approve." Amid the sudden quiet, she lifted her chin and stared her sister straight in the eye.

After a few tense seconds, Sabrina's mouth fell agape, and she blinked.

Cara waited for her to say something—anything. But Sabrina remained frustratingly silent, and Cara wondered if her younger sister suspected the identity of Cara's intended target. If so, Sabrina gave no hint of her conjecture.

Instead, she simply asked, "What has this to do with me?"

Cara summoned every ounce of courage and declared without hesitation, "I need your help."

"Me?" Sabrina looked her surprise. "What can I do?"

Once again, Cara carefully considered her words. She had not a clue as to how she should proceed; because it was not every day she asked her baby sister how to entice a man. "I need the benefit of your...expertise."

"I beg your pardon?" Sabrina opened and then closed her mouth. "My expertise in—what?"

"I need to know how to attract a man." In case Sabrina had not fully comprehended her meaning, Cara added, "How to seduce him."

"Attract or seduce?" Shock briefly invested her features, but Sabrina recovered in a scarce second. She resituated her morning dress and sighed. "Trust me, Cara, those are two vastly different things."

"I know, and yet I do not know." For the umpteenth time, she told herself that the hurdle separating her and Lance from a glorious future was not insurmountable. Determined to stay her course, and refusing to retreat, Cara forged ahead without shame or reticence. "I need you to teach me how to do both."

"I do not understand." With her brow a mass of furrows, Sabrina traced the damask pattern on the daybed coverlet. "Is he a reluctant suitor or just an ignorant one?"

Cara pondered the question, mulling various past interactions with Lance. "I am not sure."

"Oh, dear." Sabrina tapped a finger to her chin in a familiar affectation of deep thought. "That is a problem."

"Yes." Cara nodded once. "And I am afraid he may view me as a friend and nothing exceeding a polite acquaintance."

"I see." Again, Sabrina scrutinized her, and Cara was positive recognition had dawned when her little sister gasped. "Oh, I say. You are in a tricky spot."

"I believe you get my meaning." In that instant, Cara feared Sabrina saw everything in vivid detail. "And I must venture beyond the conventional if I am to claim him as my own."

"Bloody hell." Sabrina whistled in monotone. "So you plan to seduce him into accepting you as something else?"

Once more, Cara nodded. "That is the general idea."

Sabrina bit her lip, which was her habit when weighing her prospects and plan of attack. "Does he love you?"

The answer to that seemingly innocuous query presented the crux of the conundrum. "As a friend, I am assured of his regard."

"It is not the same, Cara." Sabrina appeared skeptical. "When it comes to women, men can be very fickle. I would not have you end up with a broken heart, and papa will kill me if I help you do something foolish."

"That never stopped you before." With her plan in peril at the onset, Cara hoped to sway her with a pout. "Since when do you err on the side of caution?"

"That was different." Her sister snatched a square of shortbread from a plate and nibbled on the corner. "My posterior was the only one at risk. You cry at the mere threat of a spanking."

"Whereas you always dared father to make you weep and then steadfastly refused to yield." Counting on her wayward younger sister as a staunch ally, Sabrina's unusual, unwelcome, and inconvenient constraint stunned Cara. Leaning forward, she caught hold of her sibling's wrist. "Believe me, I am more than willing to accept the repercussions from my actions."

"I do not know." Sabrina sighed heavily. "This is not like you. You have always been so perfect."

"Do you not see?" Cara squeezed her fingers. "That is

why I have to do something. If I do not take control of my destiny, if I do not make a stand for the man I want, papa will marry me off to some very proper, well-heeled English gentleman."

"Perhaps." Sabrina clucked her tongue. "But that sounds just the thing for you."

"And you could not be more wrong, as nothing could be further from the truth." Decrying years of obeisance of societal strictures, Cara emitted a self-mocking snort. "I want what you, Caroline, and Dirk enjoy. You have found real love, true devotion, and I want the same. Is that too much to ask?"

"Of course not." With a dreamy expression, Sabrina stretched her feet. "And you think the man for whom you have set your cap is capable of such a match?"

"I know he is." For a scarce second, Cara considered otherwise. Revisiting fonder times and countless memories, a single nagging doubt plagued her campaign. While Lance danced attendance on her without fail, his attentions had never breached the limits of polite decorum. Then again, the same could be said for her actions toward him. With renewed determination, Cara lowered her voice. "He just needs someone to believe in him."

"And you are that person?" her younger sibling inquired softly.

"I know I am."

"Are you absolutely certain?" Sabrina seemed perplexed.

"Help me, Brie." Cara pressed her suit. "I promise, I will not do anything reckless. And if I do, I will bear up, whatever the consequences." For good measure, she added, "Please, you are my only hope."

"But why begin with seduction?" With a countenance of

pure confusion, Sabrina cast a questioning glance. "Why not take the normal route? You know, a courtship?"

Having expected her sister to leap at the opportunity to aid her cause, Cara was again stumped at how to explain herself. Would Sabrina understand that Cara had been waiting all her life for Lance to make a move? Unlike the other Brethren females, what she felt for him far surpassed the bounds of friendship. In fact, it was their lifelong companionship that settled her mind and gave her the confidence to act. Were he a stranger, never would she ponder such bold endeavors.

But Lance was...well, Lance.

In the end, Cara opted for what she thought the most logical answer. "I do not have the time to wait for him to come to me. We both know I am not getting any younger. And if I am going to take a chance on love, I had best start out as I mean to go on."

"And are your affections engaged?" Sabrina asked, much to Cara's consternation.

"I will have no other."

"And you are sure it is more than an infatuation or girlish crush?"

Now Cara was certain Sabrina had discerned the identity of her elder sister's intended target, yet she could muster no shame, because she knew her aim was true.

"He is the love of my life, a fact of which I suspect you are well aware."

"Oh, my." For a while, Sabrina studied her. A few tense minutes passed. At last, she said, "I have always wondered, but—well, I suppose it might work—if you promise to be careful."

"You have my word."

"And do nothing rash. Love does not come easy, espe-

cially for men, and I would have you settle for nothing less."
All of a sudden, Sabrina grinned mischievously and slapped
her thigh. "So you want to duel with the Jolly Roger?"

"Great heavens, is t-that what you call it?" In her embarrassment, Cara stuttered.

"Indubitably." Sabrina laughed and nodded with
newfound vigor. "And you will understand, soon enough."

Dreading the answer, but too fascinated to restrain
herself, Cara asked, "Why?"

"Because." Sabrina shrugged. "Standing upright, perky
and proud, looking at me with its one good eye, it reminds
me of a pirate."

For a moment, both sisters simply stared at each other.
Finally, they collapsed in laughter.

THE FOLLOWING MORNING, as she ascended the stairs at
Raynesford House, Cara spared a glance below as Alex shuffled Elaine into the drawing room. The youngest and most
painfully shy member of their family, the poor dear was
beside herself with worry for her cousin.

Thankfully, Cara had convinced Alex to accompany her
to the Prescott home and keep Elaine occupied, while Cara
tended Lance. And although some might question her
motives in securing the services of Lady Alex, Cara
comforted herself in the knowledge that Elaine required
reassurance and support. After all, how could Elaine nurse
Lance, when she could not manage herself? And everyone
relied on Cara in difficult circumstances.

Because she could always be depended upon in a pinch.

After a restful first night, Lance developed a nasty fever,
which left him fitful and hallucinating. What began as an

occasional incoherent shout soon morphed into an eerie audial tapestry of angry cries that reverberated off the walls and cast a mournful pall on the grand residence. Unwilling to abandon her hero in his hour of need, she resolved to sit with him every day, reading poetry or the latest copy of *The Times*.

Standing before the door to his bedchamber, she turned the knob and peered inside before entering. Dr. Handley paused beside the four-poster, and when she crossed the threshold, he smiled.

"Hello, Miss Douglas."

"Dr. Handley." She dipped her chin in acknowledgement, as would any proper young lady, and then gave her attention to the motionless form in the middle of the mattress. As Lance slept, she spoke in hushed tones. "How is he today?"

"Much better. The fever broke sometime overnight." The gray-haired physician scratched his temple. "His lordship had a light breakfast and another dose of laudanum. I want him to rest as much as possible."

"Oh, that is wonderful news." Cara could have danced a jig. "How long should he remain in bed?"

"Daresay the worst is behind us, but he must continue in a reclined state until the bone heals to some extent— perhaps, three weeks." Dr. Handley removed his spectacles, pulled a handkerchief from his coat pocket, and wiped the smudged lenses. "After that, he must limit his movement and shall require the use of a cane. Once his lordship is completely recovered, he will be as before."

"And how much time might that require?" In silence, she calculated, because if she were to succeed, she had to avail herself of every moment spent exclusively in Lance's company. Given that her intended was at present, for all intents and purposes, unconscious, she could hardly persuade him to marry her. "I ask only because the marquess does so love Christmas."

"Well, one never knows with these things." He returned his spectacles to his nose and shrugged. "So it is difficult to predict. But, as his lordship is in excellent physical condition, I would wager he will be up and about, hale and whole, by the holidays."

Lady luck shone on Cara, because she had months to capture Lance's heart. It was too perfect, and she bit her tongue to keep from shouting for joy. If she could not seduce Lance by then, with no competition, she did not deserve him.

The physician pulled his timepiece from his waistcoat pocket and consulted it before returning it to the fold. "Well now, must be off. Have two more calls to make before lunch." He reached for his hat, plopped it on his head, and bowed.

"Good day, Miss Douglas."

"And the same to you, Dr. Handley."

Once they were alone, Cara retrieved the kerchief from her bodice and smoothed the initials. "Oh, Lance. I do love you."

Then she stepped on the platform, took a long look at her personal sleeping beauty, of a sort, sunk a knee into the downy mattress, and touched her lips to his. To her inexpressible disappointment, he did not move.

How on earth was she supposed to entice an unconscious suitor?

Nagging skepticism nipped at her heels, and she stomped a foot in insouciant salute. She would not quit the field before the battle commenced. Visions of her wedding day, as well as her honeymoon, quieted the troubling doubts plaguing her conscience.

"I brought a new book today." She pushed a stray lock of hair from his face and cast a side-glance at the leather bound collection of sonnets. "I hope you like Shakespeare. And papa sent today's edition of *The Times*."

With a frown, she slid from the mattress. Assuming a familiar position in a chair beside the bed, she picked up the diminutive work and flipped through the pages. The words came to life before her eyes, rose-colored images danced merrily in her head, and a chorus of fanciful cherubs sang a rollicking ditty of love. She imagined Lance reading aloud the romantic poetry and stifled a giggle.

Just as quick, she recalled the advice imparted at her request, illicit instructions on how to seduce the stronger sex. To her embarrassment, her sister had spared no detail. Sabrina had even summoned a maid to bring them a banana, so she could demonstrate as she described various techniques. But, Cara reminded herself, she had asked for it.

Now was not the time to be squeamish.

Before she knew it, she once again perched beside Lance on the bed. Sabrina said that for a woman to tackle the understandable and quite common fear of the male body, and one part in particular, she had to dive in—headlong.

Take the bull by the horns—or horn, so to speak.

Determined to stay her course, she had composed a mental list as a guide, of sorts. Cara was certain that, when the moment was right, she would turn the situation to her advantage. With that in mind, she gave her attention to the front page of *The Times*.

"Oh, dear. It says Napoleon marches on Moscow. How tragic." After summarizing the main points of the story, she peered at another article. "And Wellington closes in on Burgos, where it is estimated that some two-thousand French troops defend the fortress. Sounds as though our redcoats are in for a difficult battle."

In that instant, she spied something unusual from the corner of her eye. Cara folded the newspaper and tossed it to the chair, and then studied a rather curious protrusion from beneath the covers.

"What on earth is that?" With a narrow stare, she searched her memory. Had the odd bulge been present when she arrived? If so, how could she have missed it? And then it hit her—Dr. Handley must have misplaced a tool of his trade during his examination of Lance. With a finger, she poked the mysterious lump, which felt rather firm. What if the unknown item caused further injury to her hero? From her vantage, the utensil appeared quite large, so she could not simply ignore it.

But as she suspected Lance remained nude during his convalescence, she could not bring herself to lift the sheet. Yet she had to retrieve the object before it harmed her intended bridegroom. She spared a brief peek toward the door, checking to make sure no one witnessed her questionable foray. Biting her lip, Cara scooted to the edge of the mattress and then slipped her hand under the blanket.

"Fear not, my darling." She smiled at her future husband. Grasping fistfuls of the sheet, she inched forward. "No harm shall befall you on my watch, and I shall—*oh.*"

The first touch, the initial contact with his most male member had her gasping for air, because it was not as Sabrina had said—soft and mushy. Far more threatening than she could have anticipated or imagined, his miracle of flesh was as forged steel encased in the softest velvet. But why had it roused? According to Sabrina, men required stimulation to achieve an erection, with the exception of the early morning hours.

Yet Cara had only read to Lance and nothing more.

Was it possible—had her mere presence inspired his reaction? Could it be that he was not so indifferent as she had thought?

She made to retreat, but Lance grabbed her by the wrist and drew her hand to the soft pouch at the base. He shifted his hips and moaned his appreciation.

Cara nearly jumped out of her skin.

She told herself she should not touch him, at least, not without his permission. Taking a man unaware had to be the greatest breach in etiquette, and no doubt an unforgivable abuse of hospitality, but he gave her no quarter. In her defense, she made an honest mistake, and even in slumber Lance directed her movements. When she tried to break free, he tightened his grip, refusing to release her.

The ever-hardening protuberance snared her attention, as he pressed her palm to his length. Again, she tried but failed to wrestle loose, but he merely smiled and initiated a repetitive rhythm. Cara marveled at her ability to provoke him. She felt powerful. She felt...naughty.

And naughty never felt so good.

A deep longing, an unfamiliar hunger fluttered in her belly, and gooseflesh covered her from top to toe. Closing her eyes, she relaxed and let him have his way. Soaring as a sensate being, she operated wholly on instinct, with her senses commanded by their point of skin-to-skin contact. With her heart beating wildly in her chest, Cara sighed.

Almost as quickly, Cara snorted as Sabrina's words of warning filled her ears: *Just do not put your teeth to it. Tried that once and poor Everett was out of commission for a week.*

Until that moment, Cara would never have conceived of

putting into her mouth what she now held in her tenuous clutch.

Such behavior did not seem acceptable.

But she was prepared to shed her prim and proper shell if it meant gaining Lance as a husband. And if she could not be comfortable with him, a man she had known since she was born, with whom could she be comfortable?

And so she yielded. Let him have his way. She scrutinized his face, searching for any sign of discomfit, as his hips rocked in concert with his instruction. When his brow creased, a faint trace of a grin fell on his lips, lifting the corners of his mouth. He moved her hand faster and lauded her efforts with another husky groan.

"I believe I left my bag in his lordship's chambers." The voice of Dr. Handley reverberated through the house.

Sheer panic replaced virgin passion.

With a violent flinch and a gasp of horror, Cara at last wrenched free and spared a glance at the door. "Oh, dear."

After resituating the covers, she pushed away from the bed. Just as she was about to take her seat, she spied the telltale hump beneath the bedclothes, which all but proclaimed her however unintended risqué dalliance.

"Oh, no."

Conscious of the footfalls growing near, she launched herself at the bed. Pulling back the blanket and sheet, she found herself face-to-face—so to speak, with the marvel she had held in her tremulous clasp. Jutting flagrantly in the air from its nest of black curls danced the dreaded Jolly Roger.

"Put it away, dearest." Cara rued the fact that Sabrina hadn't disclosed how to reverse the arousal process. "You must."

When Lance failed to respond to her plea, she fanned at

his unruly appendage with her hand, as she would a dish that had been served too hot to consume. "Go down."

Largely ignorant of the mysteries of the male form and fearing discovery, she leaned forward and blew on his erection in an attempt to extinguish him like the burning flame of a candle. To her abject terror, the Jolly Roger seemed to thicken and grow even more animated.

"I will only be a minute," the doctor declared. "I know exactly where I left it."

The door to the bedchamber opened, and the grey-haired physician crossed the threshold.

"It says Wellington's troops have—oh, Dr. Handley. What are you doing here?" Sitting in the chair, Cara struggled to portray an image of cherubic innocence and smiled. She set aside the copy of *The Times* and prayed he did not note her trembling fingers. "I thought you had calls to make."

"Sorry to disturb you, Miss Douglas, but I left my bag." He motioned to the table. "Got halfway to the Hogart's and had to turn around."

She peered to her right. There, on the bedside table, sat her undoing—the black leather satchel of his trade. "Here it is."

The good doctor accepted the bag she held for him and then stepped to the platform to check his patient. At his back, Cara held her breath, her ears rang, and her knees buckled. Painful minutes ticked past as a tortuous death knell, and she was just about to confess her offense when the doctor stood upright.

He turned and assessed her with a stern expression.

She gulped and thought she would surely swoon, as the physician must have discerned her illicit activity.

"He seems to be faring well." He smiled. "You are doing a fine job, Miss Douglas."

Though her legs weakened, she managed a not-so-graceful curtsey. "Thank you, Dr. Handley."

"I shall drop by tomorrow to check his progress."

"I will see you then," she said with a curt nod.

With an awkward prayer of thanks, she held her position until the door closed. Despite the urge to flee, she remained stock-still until the clip-clop of his footsteps dissipated.

Quiet returned to the household.

With a shriek, she shot forward. Wrenching the bedclothes from Lance, she spied the copy of Shakespeare's sonnets covering her intended's crotch and whisked the tome from his body.

The Jolly Roger sprang forth in a stout salute.

Proud. Formidable. Mocking her with its one good eye.

With nary a gaze at her future groom, Cara shrieked again and threw the covers over him. With the book in hand, and heedless of everything save her desire to be gone from his chamber, she ran.

Vowing never to return again.

CHAPTER FOUR

*T*hrough a haze of pain a familiar voice came to him, and how well he knew its owner. How many hours he had passed listening to her gentle lilt he could not estimate. As fond memories warmed his heart, he smiled. Fluttering his lids, Lance opened his eyes.

In a bedside chair Cara sat, picture-perfect and poised, reading some heart-rending tale of love lost and never found. For a moment, he savored the smoothness of her elegant inflection. Gowned in pale blue muslin, with her black curls piled high atop her head, she was a fantasy, an ethereal vision powerful enough to make him doubt his consciousness and his sanity.

How he loved watching her, a habit that reigned supreme for the better portion of his life.

With a pair of crystal blue eyes, a delicate, heart-shaped face, a neck like a swan, and the body of a sylph, she was the sort of lady every young man dreamed of marrying. But at five and twenty, she had yet to take a husband, and for a woman her age, society considered her on the shelf.

Every year, as the Season came to a close and betrothals

were announced, he held his breath in anticipation of the dreaded news of her impending nuptials. And to his begrudged relief, no such pronouncement presented itself.

He knew one day she would speak the vows, and it had to happen at some point soon, as Admiral Douglas would not allow her to waste away. So Lance prepared for the inevitable and knew exactly how he would react. He wanted the best for her and would not settle for any less than what she deserved. Neither would he accept just anyone wedding his Cara.

And she was *his* Cara.

They had been the closest of friends for as long as he could remember, and whomever she married would have to understand and tolerate their friendship, because they would always share a special bond. Never would he give her up, and it would take a confident man to live with their relationship.

Once she was safely wed, and his youthful fantasies dashed, perhaps then he, too, would find a spouse.

She turned the page and rubbed the back of her neck. When her hand again rested in her lap, he focused his gaze on the rise and fall of her bodice. To the creamy skin, soft as silk, he knew continued beneath the edge.

As children, they had spent many afternoons swimming naked in the pond at Pembroke, the Elliott ancestral home. Of course, their other friends were there, as well. But somehow he had, without fail, managed to accidentally swim next to Cara, and when their wet flesh came together for however brief an instant, she always gasped with charming shyness and pulled away.

For his part, it was an innocent maneuver, with no ulterior motive other than an immature desire to be near her. For as long as Lance could remember, he considered Cara the most fascinating creature of his existence. There was something special about their friendship. Some indiscernible but very real entity joined them, and whatever it was, the mysterious connection was noticeably absent in his familial ties with the other Brethren.

With good humor, he recalled the first time in his life he fell victim to a rampant erection. On a particularly hot summer day, Blake ran from the pond shouting that he had seen a snake. Though it had been nothing more than a mischievous prank, Cara had thrown herself into Lance's arms.

Having a naked female, more specifically one he had often pretended was his wife whenever they played lord of the manor, pressed against him had sent unsettling sensations soaring through his loins. Lance had been terrified and curious at once. The only problem was that in the time it took his exuberant new friend to calm down, the rest of him resembled a prune.

For some reason after that, he had always looked on Cara as something more than a harmless playmate, more than a friend. But he had never told her, or anyone else for that matter, otherwise. And he had no intention of doing so, because he was not worthy of her.

Lance closed his eyes, and salacious imagery assailed his senses.

Cara kissing him.

Cara touching him.

Cara arousing him.

In a flash, he responded, as would any red-blooded male.

Since the accident aboard his ship, he had enjoyed some pretty odd dreams involving his childhood friend. Must've been the laudanum that damn Dr. Handley kept shoving down his throat.

Thankfully, Cara was an innocent. He comforted himself in the knowledge she would not notice the fast rising bulge south of his belly. Or, if she did, she would not know what it was, much less the cause.

But the force of his reaction perplexed him. It had been years since he had suffered an erection in her presence. As a man, he had learned to marshal his thoughts and his body —especially where Cara was concerned.

Then he reminded himself it had been a long time since he'd had a woman, because his last importuning conquest had left him a tad battle shy. Surely that was sufficient cause to garner such a response? Yes, given his current state, a ripping release would feel good about now. Were Cara not present, he would take care of the deed himself. After all, there was nothing wrong with his hands.

The mere thought elicited an involuntary groan.

In an instant, Cara glanced at him.

He caught her gaze and smiled.

"Lance?" Immediately, she stood, closed the book, set it on the seat, and approached him. "You are awake."

"Aye." His heart warmed at her enthusiasm.

She drew a wet cloth from the basin and stepped on the platform. Leaning forward, she wiped his brow, and a hint of lilac teased his nose. Unbeknownst to Cara, when she stretched long, the bodice of her dress puckered, providing him an ample display of her bosom.

While only a cad would take advantage of the situation, Lance was in no mood to be noble, so he dipped his chin, affording himself a better view. How he ached to taste her, to cover a pebbled nipple with his mouth as he palmed the other tempting peak.

Painfully erect, he bit back another groan.

Almost instantly, Lance chided himself, as she was a friend—nothing more. He had known her since she was born. They had grown up together. They had played together.

And he wanted to play now, but not the games to which she was accustomed.

And not with her.

In sheer desperation, he summoned pure thoughts as she bathed his face and neck. Tried to remember her as a child, at Christmas, opening packages. The time he taught her to ride a horse. He envisioned her fat with another man's heir.

But nothing erased the erotic image of Cara, leaning over him, stroking his mainmast.

"Lance, are you in pain?"

"No." He clenched his jaw. "No, I am not."

"Are you sure?" Cara moved closer, and her breasts pressed against his chest. "You do not have to be brave for me. I can give you another dose of laudanum."

That is not what I need. "Actually, I am a bit hungry."

She inclined her head. "Shall I ring for a tray?"

"I was hoping you would bring me something with your own sweet hands." In a valiant attempt to disguise his discomfit, because he was well nigh near to exploding, he grinned. "Surely it will taste all the more delicious."

"Are you not the charmer?" With a flirty giggle, which scored a direct hit to his Jolly Roger, she withdrew. "You must be feeling better."

Not yet, but he was going to be much improved before she returned. And after enduring the blissful weight of her bosom against him, it was not going to take long.

"Oh, could you leave the cloth on my forehead?" He half-closed his eyes and sighed. "It is quite soothing."

"Certainly." Cara nodded. "Here, let me refresh it for you."

He stopped short of telling her that was not necessary—not for what he had in mind. Instead, he waited patiently while she re-wet the rag. He bit his tongue as she squeezed out the excess water. He stifled another groan when she folded the cloth neatly into a square and settled it on his forehead. To further his torment, she pressed herself against him once more and bent to kiss his cheek.

On the verge of eruption, Lance thought he would go insane before she ever exited his chambers.

"I SHALL BE RIGHT BACK." Cara turned and grinned.

The ever-tempestuous Jolly Roger had awakened, and it had not escaped her notice. The telltale bulge caught her attention as she read poetry to Lance, but she was too wise to tangle with it, and twice she had stumbled over her words. Despite doubts to the contrary, it seemed entirely possible her hero was not impervious to her, as one might expect of a friend.

Purposefully leaning against him, pressing her breasts to his chest, was the maiden test of her theory. And to her unutterable delight, it was impossible to ignore the hitch in his breath and the revealing tension of muscles beneath her. According to Sabrina, such behavior served as undeni-able indications of attraction.

In short, Lance was not indifferent to her.

She recalled her scandalized flight from his apartments

the previous day. It had taken all night to muster the courage to return to the scene of the crime. Steadfastly committed to her goal, to make him her husband, to marry for love, she had swallowed her pride, and more than a little fear if truth were told, and forced herself to resume her bedside vigil. In light of recent events, it was worth the effort.

She smiled, quite pleased with herself as she approached the butler in the foyer. "Banks, his lordship would like a tray."

"I believe Cook has prepared something in anticipation of such request." He bowed. "I will have the meal sent immediately, Miss Douglas."

"I beg your pardon." She stayed him with an upraised hand. "His lordship asked me to convey it personally."

"Very good, Miss Douglas. If you would wait in the drawing room, I shall see to it at once."

Cara stepped into the elegantly appointed chamber and grinned as Alex and Elaine faced her and stood.

"How is he?" Alex inquired.

"Awake and hungry." Cara shrugged. "I suppose that bodes well for his recovery."

"Oh, Cara." Elaine sniffed. "How can I ever thank you?"

She stared quizzically at Elaine. "For what?"

"For all your help. You are so strong. How I wish I could be more like you." With tears welling, Elaine frowned. "When I think of losing Lance—"

"Dearest, you mustn't say such things." Cara encircled the youngest Brethren in her arms. "And do not cry, else you will make your eyes puffy. With the Little Season set to commence in only a few weeks, you do not want to spoil your lovely complexion."

As she hugged Elaine, Cara envisioned a grand future, whirling about the ton's dance floors in Lance's embrace, standing at his side as they were announced to the crowds, and waving from the docks at Deptford, filled with pride, as he departed on missions for the Crown, safe in the knowledge that he would come home to her. Her duties would be many as the marchioness of Raynesford, though she cared naught for the title but for the man who came with it.

"I beg your pardon, my lady." Banks stood in the doorway, bearing a tray laden with covered dishes. "Miss Douglas, if you will allow me, I shall convey the meal to his lordship's chamber, wherein you may deliver it, per his wishes."

"Let us go with her, Alex." Elaine caught the younger Seymour by the wrist. "If he is awake, I should very much like to see my cousin."

"All right." With a conspiratorial grin, Alex nodded. "We can provide divertissement and give Cara a deserved rest."

Arm in arm, trailing the venerable butler, the three friends skipped their way upstairs. At the entrance to Lance's bedchamber, Banks passed the elegant salver to Cara and bowed before opening the door.

In the pale saffron hue peeking from a separation in the drawn drapes, she walked to the bed, set the tray on a side table, and then stepped on the platform. To her surprise, Lance slept with a smug smile dancing on his lips.

"I do not understand it," she remarked quietly. "Only a minute ago, he was wide awake and clamoring for food."

Alex peered at the man in question and whispered, "Well, he seems to have decided otherwise. If you prefer, Elaine and I can return the meal to the kitchen, so you may resume your watch."

"All right." Cara bent and pressed her palm to his cool flesh and came up short. For a moment, she simply stared at her perplexing patient, revisiting their earlier conversation. Confused, she searched his pillow and then the folds of the sheet and blanket, before sparing a glance at the empty basin. "What happened to it?"

"To—what?" Elaine inquired. "Is something wrong, sister?"

"I know I left a cold compress on his forehead, but it is missing." She searched the floor and under the bed skirt but failed to locate the curiously absent item.

"Do you suppose he shifted in his sleep, and the cloth fell between the covers?" Alex asked.

"I am unsure." Cara shrugged. "But perhaps it did."

"So, DEAR SISTER, DO TELL." Sabrina stuck her tongue in her cheek and grinned. "How goes it with the reluctant suitor?"

"Well, I have definitely enjoyed some improvement in my campaign of hearts." Sitting beside her sibling on a daybed in the morning room at Woverton House, Cara sipped her tea and averted her gaze. "Thanks to your insight and tutelage, I believe I can say, without doubt, he is attracted to me in the physical sense."

"Really? You are wasting no time. It was only a fortnight when last we spoke." Sabrina set her cup on a tray and eased to the pillows. "What is your hurry?"

"Suffice it to say his current situation lends itself to my endeavor, but that will not always be so. Therefore, I must act quickly if I am to secure his affection—"

"And a proposal," Sabrina interjected. "Trust me, Cara. For your sake and my sanity, not to mention our posteriors should papa discover our conspiracy, before you skin his rabbit, make sure you have his declaration and a betrothal agreement."

"My darling Brie, if you will recall, of we two, I am the eldest." How Cara wished she could stave off the pesky blush burning in her cheeks. Why she was uncomfortable she did not know. Had she not already confronted the most curious aspect of the male body? What else was there of which to be afraid? "You, of all people, know I never venture into the fray without a well-devised plan."

"In that I will not argue, sister." Her incorrigible partner in nefarious enterprises did not have the decency to appear contrite. "But I am married to the Jolly Roger I salute."

"*Sabrina,*" Cara hissed. "Must you purposefully be so crude?"

"Yes." Sabrina nodded once. "Your vexation with my choice of terms and topic tells me you have not thought things through clearly. You see, Everett curls my toes at every opportunity, and there is nothing embarrassing or shameful about what occurs in our marriage bed, or the chair in his study, or the—"

"I get your meaning."

"Sorry." Sabrina shifted her weight. "I daresay I love my husband all the more with each passing day and night. And I would wager that were you to ask Caroline, she would say the same about Trevor, as would Rebecca of Dirk. If you truly want a love match, then make sure you have engaged his heart before his ship weighs anchor in your harbor."

"You shame me." Cara frowned. "But you would believe otherwise if you knew of my intended's identity."

"I am not so sure that is the case." Folding her arms, Sabrina humphed. "Do you want to tell me, in the event you are correct?"

"Oh, dear." Wringing her fingers, Cara blanched. "Must I divulge my secret to secure your guidance?"

"No, of course not." Sabrina shook her head and stretched her legs. "I think I can guess for myself, so I will not press you for answers you are reluctant to impart. But I will say this—the identity of your mystery suitor makes no difference in the grand scheme. Whether you have known him all your life, or met him on the night of your come-out, giving yourself to a man is the most intimate adventure you will ever experience. And despite mama's rather awkward but enlightening discussion prior to my wedding, I was not so prepared for the reality, as I had thought, when the time came to consummate my vows."

It was the height of unfairness that her baby sister had correctly surmised the root of Cara's quandary. "How so?"

"Before I married, I thought ladies made too much of their virtue, as I considered a maidenhead nothing more than a purse, of sorts, auctioned to the highest bidder." With a dreamy expression, Sabrina sighed. "But as I have shared myself with my husband, I now understand why some women seek to remain chaste. Virginity is a gift you owe to yourself. Do not sell your honor cheap, and do not surrender it on a girlish whim. Is your mystery suitor worthy of your love? If he is who I think he is, of that I have no doubt. At issue is whether or not he welcomes your regard. If he does not, then he does not deserve your prize."

"Oh, Brie." Through a tear-filled gaze, Cara studied the once immature gadling. "Since when did you become an expert in the ways of love?"

"Though Everett would not appreciate my candor, and you are sworn to silence, I must admit I made some mistakes early in my marriage, which could have doomed my union were his affections not firmly planted in my garden. My advice is well intended, as I only seek to spare you similar torment." Sabrina's eyes were now equally swimming. "Promise you will be careful?"

"I promise." Cara sniffed.

At that very instant, the door to the morning room opened.

"Darling, I am—Good heavens! Sabrina, what is the matter?" Everett all but ran to his wife, knelt at her feet, and drew her into his arms. "Why are you crying, sweet?"

"I do not know." Over his shoulder, she waved goodbye to Cara, and then smiled and winked. "I cannot help myself."

Just before she exited, Cara risked a quick glance and stifled a giggle as Everett settled Sabrina in his lap.

"There, there, dearest." He kissed Sabrina's forehead and then tipped her chin. "Perhaps I have the cure for what ails you, love."

Not for a second did Cara doubt her brother-in-law's abilities, and her devilish little sister would enjoy every minute of his attention. With a smile and renewed resolve, Cara secured the oak panel, patted the secreted kerchief nestled to her breast, and set course for Raynesford House.

Where she would win her hero's heart.

"*Lance!* What on earth are you doing?" Cara rushed inside and wrapped her arms about his waist. "You are not supposed to be on your feet. Dr. Handley says you must give the bone ample time to heal."

"Like bloody hell." With a mighty grimace, and his good leg bearing his weight, he leaned against the side of the bed. "No longer can I tolerate being locked in my room while we are at war. I belong on my ship."

"You belong in bed." Swift and sure, she assessed his appearance and condition. Aside from the heavy splint on his right leg, he was garbed only in a black silk robe. "And who gave permission to dress you?"

"I clothed myself." With his brow a mass of furrows, he raised his chin. "One of the servants was kind enough to fetch it for me."

"Thank you for apprising me of a weakness in my care." Cara humphed. "It is obvious I need to speak with Banks, as you are to remain abed, per Dr. Handley's instructions. I daresay that is why the physician had you stripped naked. No doubt your propensity to wander off would be sufficiently stifled without clothing."

"Damn you, Cara." Lance emitted a feral growl and raked a hand through his hair. "This is my house and my staff. They follow my orders—not yours."

"In that I will not argue." Despite his ire, Cara moved with unimpaired aplomb as she helped him ascend the platform. "But while you convalesce, you will obey my orders—not yours."

"Oh?" He stopped short. "Is that so?"

"It is." Wrestling the urge to smile, and thus risk invoking further fury, she narrowed her stare. "Now give me that robe."

"No," he said with a boyish pout.

"Lance, I am not in jest." She tapped her foot. "The robe—now."

"You want it?" With a sly smile, he lowered his chin. "Come and take it."

Cara blinked, as she did not misunderstand the challenge in his words. Was he testing her fortitude? In her, he would find his challenge well met. And then she noted her rapidly beating heart and the gooseflesh covering her arms. With a deep breath and a silent prayer for composure, she faced her future husband.

They stood with shoulders squared like two opponents on the battlefield. How long she peered into his green eyes she did not know or care.

After an interminable silence, Lance arched a brow. "Well?"

For good or ill, she had to act, and do so wisely, because she suspected he anticipated a retreat on her part. Or perhaps he expected her to flee. But Cara had other plans, as it was high time to show her lifelong companion that she could be more than a friend.

She could be his wife.

Without a word, she entered the arena. Summoning every ounce of intestinal fortitude she could muster, she neared her connubial conquest. Trapping his gaze, she reached for the belt, grasped the ends, and untied the knot. At her bold maneuver, he parted his lips and emitted a soft gasp, but it pealed in her ears.

Skimming the edges of fabric with her palms, she intentionally traced the curves of his bare chest with the pad of her thumbs, before pushing the silk from his shoulders and whisking the flimsy garment from his body.

With a nasty scowl, Lance loomed before her naked as the day he was born. Once again, they simply stared at each other, and she desperately struggled to ignore a particularly animated protuberant of his anatomy, even as it impressively saluted her. Resisting the urge to run, she held her ground.

After a few tense minutes, his smug smile faltered, and a charming red hue shaded his cheeks and spread to his neck. He swallowed hard. "Are you going to tuck me in, too?"

Oh, he was sporting for a fight.

Although she knew he was not serious, Cara considered his offer. For a hairsbreadth of a second, she thought of pushing him to the down mattress and stretching alongside him. Of setting her lips to his, of spearing her fingers through his hair, of trailing her hand over his masculine curves and sinewy muscles. It would be so easy, for how could he resist?

What man, sane or otherwise, would reject a willing partner? According to the Nautionnier Knights, not many. But did he love her? Would he marry her? It was a well-known fact, however antiquated, the Brethren married for love.

As if on cue, Sabrina's words of warning echoed in Cara's brain.

Make sure you have engaged his heart before his ship weighs anchor in your harbor.

Until she had the requisite answers to her questions, Cara had to be vigilant in her cause. Mirroring his rigid stance, she said, "You got yourself out of bed, you can bloody well put yourself back in it."

With that, she turned on her heel and made for a temporary safe haven in the form of his dressing room. Sandalwood, his signature scent, teased her nose as she searched for an empty peg on which to hang the garment. In his chamber, Lance grunted and groaned, and her mind supplied vivid images as he let fly a colorful string of invective. The urge to rush to his aid overwhelmed her. Closing her eyes, she inhaled deeply and attempted to marshal her thoughts and senses into some semblance of order, which proved a difficult task, because desire was a powerful intoxicant.

Just being near him sent delicious shivers up her spine. And in that instant, she realized it was not the first time she had experienced similar sensations, albeit in lesser amounts, when they shared a dance, when they strolled arm in arm through the park, when he lifted her to the saddle of her favorite mount, and when—

"What are you doing in there?" Lance called out with unmasked irritation. "I swear, if you take one stitch of my belongings from this house, I shall call the Runners."

Jolted to reality, Cara laughed and re-entered his suite. Sitting in the middle of the bed, with blankets pulled to his waist, arms folded in front of him, and a wicked glower marring his handsome features, he averted his gaze.

"My, my, but we are quite the curmudgeon today."

"If you do not like it, do not let the door strike you in the arse."

Standing at the footboard, she planted hands on hips and inclined her head. "Trying to get rid of me?"

"Damn willful woman." Lance snorted. "Why do you not get yourself a husband and leave me alone?"

She gasped at the rapier retort but recovered just as fast. "Why do you not get yourself a wife? Then I would not have to take care of you."

"I am not the old maid in this room," he replied acerbically. "I can marry whenever it suits me."

Had he not been injured, Cara might have been hurt by his insult. She may have even walked out on him, given his callous exchange. But she reminded herself of his condition and, as a knight of the Brethren, he would naturally be frustrated by his affliction. Still, she could not resist rising to the occasion and spiking his guns.

"Do not fret, my dear friend." She paused for effect. "I have a prime prospect for a husband."

"What?" Lance snapped to attention, which gave her food for thought. "Who is he? Am I acquainted with him? Is he solvent? Is he a military man? You know he must pass inspection, else I do not consent to the match—not by a long chalk."

His excited reaction and avid interest served as a balm to her injured pride, both restoring her flagging confidence and encouraging her to stay the course. Cara managed a coy smile and trailed her hand along the foot of the bed. Drawing out the suspense, she moved to the chair she often occupied.

"I would say you know him very well, and the rest is none of your concern."

"And your father approves?" Lance grimaced. "He has blessed the match?"

"More or less." She studied her fingernails. "Papa will be overjoyed."

"Wait a minute. The Admiral *will be* overjoyed?" Unadulterated confusion invested his expression. "The mystery bounder has not asked for your hand?"

Was that relief she detected in his voice?

"Not yet." Cara shrugged. "But I am confident of his regard."

"You are lying." He cast her a narrow stare. "Now why would you weave such falsehood for me, dear friend? Given our longstanding relationship, I had thought us above the usual games men and women play."

"Which is why I share my secret with you, alone." Ignoring the implication of his affirmation, and the nagging doubts once again plaguing her spirit, she smoothed the blankets and chuckled. "And I can assure

CHAPTER FIVE

"*I want out of this bed!*"

"Lance, you know what Dr. Handley said." Cara pressed her palms to his shoulders and stayed him. "Only a week or two more, and we can get you up and about —slowly." Though he resisted, she managed to push him into the pillows. "If you try to do too much, too soon, you risk re-injuring yourself and prolonging your convalescence. Is that what you want?"

No." With a grimace, he speared his fingers through his hair. "But I will go insane if I am locked in here, another week. You do not know what this is like. You get to go outside"

"I am sorry you are so unhappy." She sat on the edge of the bed and clasped his hand in hers. "What can I do to make it better?"

Lance carefully considered the question innocently posed by the girl of his dreams. With his right leg firmly set in a splint, his lap remained in fine form, and a soft female rider would do quite nicely. In truth, there was much Cara could provide to alleviate his misery, given that he craved release, so there was nothing he preferred more than to offer her a salacious proposal, or two. Yet he could not proposition the gently reared object of his fantasies, because she merited more than a broken wreck of a man.

Still, he wondered why so many hours spent in her company, alone, left him more randy than a lad who had just discovered a new use for four fingers and a thumb. No giddy virgin, he'd honed his skills in the arms of some of London's most notorious courtesans. His experiences involved superficial attachments, base desire of the flesh, and professional paramours. Cara was in another class, all by herself. Perhaps that was why he could not resist her—not that he ever could.

"Lance?" The raven-haired beauty nudged him. "Where are you, my hero?"

He cocked his head to the side and cast a lopsided grin that never failed to bend her to his will. "Read to me?" He patted the spot beside him on the mattress. "Like you used to when we were young."

As children, whenever their families gathered, Cara had always sought his attention, but, where she was concerned, he was an easy mark. Snuggled to his side with the current novel she favored, and she was always reading something, they passed many lazy afternoons. And though he would deny it to his grave, as she focused on the pages, he availed himself of the opportunity to revel in her lilac scented hair. Such were his fondest memories, as were his fanciful illusions of marrying her.

But those illusions died with his cousin.

While some might think him foolish, he believed himself undeserving of happiness, because he had not saved the gadling. The estate, fortune, and title once destined for Thomas now belonged to Lance. Were they not enough? Yet he would surrender the lot in exchange for Cara.

As he could not rewrite history, he had spent his life endeavoring to atone for the mistake of his past. Guilt, he learned, was a powerful inducement. In memory of his brash relation, he had dedicated his life, volunteering for the most dangerous missions and assuming the most unimaginable risks as a Nautionnier Knight of the Brethren of the Coast. A warrior's death would do his cousin proud.

"I do not know." Cara bit her lip and hesitated. "What if someone should find us?"

He blinked. "Well, you could tell me more of your mystery suitor. And no one enters my chambers without first knocking—except you."

"Stuff and nonsense." She giggled.

"Please." He did his best to pout. "Pretty please?"

"Oh, all right." She cast him a shy smile. "But you are shameless."

"And what is new about that?" Lance fluffed a pillow and situated the covers.

"Nothing, now that you mention it." After kicking off her slippers, Cara inched alongside him, book in hand, and settled the skirts of her pale blue dress.

Without thought, he snaked his arm about her shoulders and brushed his fingertips to her velvety skin bared by her short sleeves. As was her custom, she scooted close, affording him a view of the pages from over her shoulder.

As well as a healthy glimpse of her ample bosom.

"Are you comfortable?" She peered at him.

"Fine." Lance averted his gaze, shifted, and swallowed hard. Perhaps his grand idea was not so grand. "Never better."

"You must tell me if you grow tired." With a cherubic

smile she gave her attention to the old tome, flipping the crisp parchment until she located a folded corner. "Ah, here we are."

Reading in the lilting voice that seemed to melt over him like honey on a hot scone, she commanded his senses, and he leaned to the side and inhaled. The subtle lilac fragrance, uniquely hers, wafted through his nostrils. Some things never changed, and he sighed in inexpressible content.

The gentle crest of her ear snared his interest, and he imagined her reaction as he suckled her fleshy lobe. In an erotic flash, he envisioned her lying beneath him as he claimed her lips, certain in the belief that she tasted as sweet as marzipan. He studied the swanlike curve of her neck and contemplated a trail of feathery nips leading to the sumptuous valley of her breasts, and beyond.

Despite his heretofore-vaunted self-control, he fought in vain to suppress a fast rising erection. Clearing his throat, Lance forced himself to focus on the printed words as Cara continued to read.

However, her mere presence seduced him. Immersed in her task, she remained oblivious to his tremulous state and the threat he presented. Incapable of rational thought, Lance closed his eyes and yielded to her unintended but nonetheless potent summons. Tracing feathery circles on her skin, he shuddered, and a surge of triumph mixed with lust roared through his veins as gooseflesh signaled her undeniable response.

It was then he noted the deafening silence.

Lifting his lids, Lance discovered Cara perched perilously near, their noses scarce inches apart. He met her gaze, trapping it with his own. After a few tense seconds, she ran her pink tongue along her lower lip and inhaled a shivery breath. Thousands of pulse points blazed to life, and his heart beat a rapid volley in his chest. Clutching her waist, he pulled her close.

Before things got out of hand, and with Cara that was a definite possibility, he grasped the reins. She was his friend, nothing more. Convinced his momentary lapse of control was born of a brush with death, an injury, an unscheduled and unappreciated period of celibacy, and an over-reliance on laudanum, Lance comforted himself in the knowledge that he could cease their harmless play—right up until she kissed him.

CARA HAD ONLY MEANT to offer comfort with what she deemed a small, seemingly inconsequential gesture. But when her future groom came at her with a force she could never have anticipated or imagined, licking her flesh and engaging her tongue in a frisky little contest, she sang a chorus of triumph in her head. How she managed to hold a firm grip on reality beneath her hero's amorous assault she neither knew nor cared. But she scored a victory in her heart, because, at long last, she had broken a very real, albeit invisible, barrier between them.

Now if only she could secure his declaration.

On the thought, she turned her attention to the man currently devouring her with his lips and sank into him. In the minuscule part of her brain still clinging to coherent reflection, she hardly registered the subtle but enticing shift of her bodice or the illicit caress of her chemise as he swept it aside. But when his palm made contact with her bare breast, she prayed he did not discover the kerchief, and then she cried with pleasure.

Taunting and teasing, he explored her with naughty fingers in long, questing strokes. Fire and desire burned in her veins, and a powerful hunger blossomed in her belly. Arching her back, Cara invited the love of her life to take— to claim. Aching to intensify their intimate connection, she skimmed his muscled chest with her hand and then moved lower, to playfully prod his naval before blazing a mischievous trail to his Jolly Roger, which she found hot, hard, and breathtakingly jolly.

In that instant Lance broke their kiss. For a few frustrating seconds, he ceased all action and stared at her, jaw agape, eyes wide, and stunned but obviously delighted, given his healthy erection.

"Cara—"

"Shh," she whispered. "Do not think. Just feel."

With renewed vigor, Cara worked his length, eliciting guttural grunts in concert with her movements, and a husky groan further betrayed his appreciation. When Lance rested his forehead to hers and gritted his teeth, she feared she had hurt him and halted her play. In a flash, he grabbed her wrist, pumped once, and then twice. With his mouth open in a silent scream, and his brow a mass of furrows, he climaxed in powerful staccato bursts, which left her senses reeling.

Cara shivered with passion.

Because she enjoyed no such release. Recalling her sister's tutelage, she knew with certainty that she had not reached completion, and she craved it. Bending her leg at the knee, she bumped the splint. Lance flinched, drew a sharp breath, and pulled from her embrace.

"Oh, dearest, I am so sorry." Still shaken from the effects of their tryst, she carefully eased from his side and righted her clothes. "How clumsy of me. Do you think I did any damage?"

To her dismay, he remained eerily silent.

"Lance, are you all right?"

"Leave me." To her dismay, he recoiled. "Go home."

"I am not abandoning you in pain." She slipped from the edge of the bed. "Let me administer a dose of laudanum."

"I do not want it, and I do not want you," he spat. He hunkered and pressed his fists to his forehead. "Go away. Leave me—*now.*"

"I do not understand." Confused by his unmasked hostility, Cara halted in her tracks, with the bottle of medicine in one hand and a spoon in the other. "Are you angry with me? Is this about—"

"Say no more. I do not wish to discuss it." He scowled. "Just get out."

"Lance, please." She ascended the platform. "Do not turn from me. There was nothing wrong with what we did. If you would only—"

"Cara, so help me, if you do not depart, this instant, I am going to get out of this bed, hop to the bellpull, and have you forcibly removed from my sight," he said through gritted teeth.

With a gasp of shock, she jerked as if she had been slapped. In truth, her hero could not have hurt her more had he physically struck her, and she would die before she told him. However late, Cara realized she had celebrated a premature victory over her intended. And as the situation now stood, her objective seemed impossible to attain.

Despite attempts to portray herself otherwise, it appeared Lance viewed her as nothing more than a friend. Rejection nipped at her heels, and anger rode in its wake. How could she have been so foolish? Humiliated, she set the bottle and spoon on the bedside table and walked to the door. Clothed in her trusty armor of feminine deportment, without a word, without so much as a backward glance, she exited the bedchamber.

But her broken heart remained in pieces, scattered at the foot of his bed as a casualty of her ill-fated campaign.

CARA SAT in the morning room of her parent's town home desperately trying to concentrate on her embroidery. Needlework was a skill in which she had always excelled, and such endeavor had never failed to soothe frazzled nerves. However, that morning she could not seem to sew a straight stitch.

Gowned in pale yellow muslin, her raven hair artfully arranged in curls atop her head, her legs crossed and discreetly tucked to the side, she cut the perfect picture of a gently bred English lady partaking of an activity that was expected of her. It was no surprise she had earned high marks in deportment at finishing school. Her calm façade betrayed no hint of the conflict waging war within her.

It had been two days since Cara had seen Lance.

Two days since they had shared a kiss and subsequent heated exchange.

Two days, and still she had no intention of visiting her somewhat battle worn hero, until she reassessed her strategy. And although he remained atop his white charger, her knight in shining armor no longer sat so tall in the saddle.

How dare he ruthlessly seduce her and then toss her aside?

Then again, had she not seduced him? They were

supposed to be friends, lifelong companions. Their tryst had turned her world on its end, and yet Lance remained unaffected. Worse, he seemed rather put out, had threatened to have her removed from his presence. She clung to her anger at the unfairness of it all, because if she did not, the heartbreak would surely devastate her.

Cara had pinned all her hopes on that kiss.

And what she had thought would happen shortly thereafter, a proposal and pledge of eternal love, had not occurred. Instead, she had been banished—exiled from his life. And while she remained entrenched in her belief that he was destined to be hers, she was no longer certain of her tack. Disappointment was a bitter pill, as was pride. She pondered his kerchief, tucked inside her chemise, near her heart, and sighed. Staring at her work, she spied a wayward stitch, frowned, and reached for the scissors.

A knock on the oak panel gave her pause. "Come."

"I beg your pardon." The butler cleared his throat. "Lady Alexandra to see you, Miss Cara."

"Thank you, Milton." She smiled and nodded. "Please, show her in, at once." Setting aside her silks, she composed herself, stood, and smoothed her skirts.

When next the door opened, Alex entered with what Cara recognized as a strained expression. In an instant, she feared the worst. Her chest constricted, as though an invisible band stretched taut across her torso, and she almost choked on a lump in her throat. "What is it? What is wrong?"

Alex huffed and stomped a foot. "Am I that transparent?"

"Afraid so."

"It is Lance." Pulling at the ribbons of her bonnet, she sighed heavily. "I have assumed your duties while you nurse your headache." Her brow furrowed. "Tell me you are feeling better."

Cara successfully suppressed her reaction to the mere mention of her tormentor's name. "I am much improved."

"Wonderful." Alex settled in an overstuffed chair and rolled her eyes. "I simply can't endure another day with His Grouchiness. Really, Cara, you must have the patience of Job to put up with him. I know it is difficult for him, being bedridden and all, but he has been downright boorish." She paused to inhale. "And he asks for you, every day. I swear, as soon as I inform him you are not coming, he turns into a fork-tongued dragon of the orneriest sort."

"Oh, dear." Cara hugged herself and paced the floor. What could Lance possibly want? Not for a minute would she allow him to chastise her further for her behavior, because she was not entirely at fault for what had occurred between them. As far as she was concerned, he'd had a hand in the cherry compote, too. Had he wanted to cease their play, he had but to protest. Instead, he had encouraged her.

"I had thought he was growing tired of me." She lied in a feeble excuse to explain why she would not journey to Raynesford House. "Surely one of the boys can help you. I have cared for him since they returned."

"No." Alex shook her head. "They are busy overseeing repairs to their ships."

"Elaine?"

"You know how fragile she is."

Cara stared at her properly clasped hands.

She searched for a justifiable reason to delay what she knew was her duty. And though she tried to convince herself otherwise, she had to admit Alex was not to blame for her injured heart and, therefore, should not suffer as a result. And if she did not have to be alone with Lance, she was certain she could bear his company.

"I suppose I could come with you, as long as you are willing to help me. Perhaps, between the two of us, we can handle him and his temper."

"Oh, thank you, Cara." With an easy smile, Alex hugged her affectionately. "I was positive I could depend on you."

The next thing she knew, Cara found herself ensconced in the Weston town coach, barreling up the lane for Raynesford House. She inhaled a shivery breath at the thought of seeing Lance again. Already, her cheeks burned with embarrassment. In an instant, she told herself he had just as much to be ashamed of, as had she.

When they pulled beneath the portico, she swallowed the fast rising panic in her throat. The door to the coach opened, and a footman handed them down. As they neared the entrance stairs, a familiar call brought them to a halt.

"Alex! Cara!" Wearing a teal wool riding habit, with a crop tucked under her arm, Elaine waved a greeting and tugged off her gloves. "I have been to the park this morning. It is such a lovely day, and the winter chill will be upon us soon enough." She welcomed them with a kiss on the cheek before turning to Cara. "I am so happy to see you are feeling better. And I know Lance will be pleased, too. He has asked for you every day, sometimes at breakfast and lunch. He has missed you so."

"Really?" Cara tried not to be excited that he had shown some interest in her welfare. Had she been mistaken? Had he altered his thinking? Perhaps he wanted to apologize. "Then my presence will reassure him that I am quite well."

The friends ascended the entrance stairs and crossed the threshold, pausing in the marbled foyer to doff their outwear.

"Ladies, this is an unexpected treat." A booming baritone snared Cara's interest.

On the grand staircase stood Jason Collingwood, captain of the H.M.S. *Intrepid*, a warship of the Royal Navy. Dressed in a rich blue uniform festooned with gold epaulets, the impressive giant loomed at well over six feet tall. With wavy blond hair and a conqueror's smile, he conjured images of a hero in a Greek tragedy. Immediately, his heated gaze settled on Alex, and Cara bit her tongue to stifle a giggle.

"Captain Collingwood, what a wonderful surprise." Slowly, Alex approached the foot of the stairs, cocked her head, and peered at him through her long lashes. With what Cara would characterize as a flirty pucker, Alex lowered her chin. "It has been too long since you last graced my company, and I would have you rectify said deficiency."

"The pleasure is mine, Lady Alex. You are stunning, as always." He held her stare as he descended the steps. When they met, toe-to-toe, Alex brazenly offered her hand, which the captain caught in his grasp, before bringing her gloved knuckles to his lips. "A thousand apologies if I have neglected you so, but I am afraid duty calls. Were I a gentleman of leisure, know that your every happiness would be my first priority."

The intimate interplay between the obviously smitten couple left Cara breathless, and she cast Elaine a questioning glance. "Perhaps—tea?"

"Oh, yes," Elaine blurted. "What a marvelous idea."

To Cara's astonishment, neither the handsome naval captain nor her good friend seemed to notice them. Still, she spoke softly. "Why do we not adjourn to the drawing room and leave them to enjoy their reunion?" She slipped her arm about the younger woman's shoulders and steered her to the left.

"My lady?" Banks positioned a vase, filled to overflow with a mix of red and white roses, on a table. "I did not know you had returned from your ride."

"I let myself in." Elaine grinned. "And we would like tea, Banks."

The stodgy butler nodded once. "Yes, my lady."

Arm in arm, Alex and Captain Collingwood strolled into the sumptuously appointed chamber. "Captain, you do recall Miss Cara Douglas and Lady Elaine Prescott?"

"Of course." With a warm smile, he bowed. "How do you do, ladies?"

Cara smoothed the folds of her skirt. "Fine, thank you."

"Have you visited Lance?" Elaine inquired.

The seaman shifted his weight and winked at Alex. "I have, indeed."

"How fares he this morning?" Alex tugged on his elbow, and the naval man blushed.

"He seemed much improved when I left him."

At that moment Banks appeared, bearing a tray loaded with a pot of tea and a plate of shortbread.

"Will you join us, Captain?" Elaine asked.

Cara sighed in relief when the younger Prescott assumed the position of hostess. As the youngest and most reserved of the Brethren women, Elaine had yet to find her footing, and Cara often worried that her friend was destined for a permanent position on the shelf.

"While there is nothing I would rather do than pass the afternoon in your estimable company, I must decline your gracious offer." With a mighty frown, Captain Collingwood stared at Alex. "To my infinite disappointment, I must away, as I am due at Deptford."

"May I show you to the door," Alex offered in an unabashed manner.

Elaine picked up the pot. "Tea, Cara?"

"No, thank you." She wrinkled her nose, because it was time to face the music. "I believe I shall see how Lance progresses."

As she crossed the foyer, Cara spied Alex and Captain Collingwood at the entrance stairs, with their heads together, dallying shamelessly, and deep in conversation. Though propriety demanded she part the couple, Cara could not bring herself to intercede, because she could only imagine having her affection returned. And she was in no hurry to meet her fate at Lance's bedside.

Still, with resolve as a shield, she ascended the steps and navigated the hall leading to the family apartments. Wiping her uncharacteristically damp palms on her dress, she mulled recent events and vowed never to surrender her cause. Her future groom might not realize it, but he would be hers.

At last, she paused before what she had recently come to consider the door to her doom, because she had shown her hand and lost. But a first round loss did not equate defeat, from her perspective. Yet she had not constructed a suitable flanking maneuver. She glanced over her shoulder and thought of retreat. Forcing the memory of that horrible afternoon from her mind, Cara decided her best course of action was to ignore the past. Pretend nothing had happened between them.

They were friends—nothing more.

Without knocking, she opened the door and crossed the threshold.

"Morning Lance. I hear you are doing much better—"

Cara froze.

Her lifelong friend, the husband of her dreams, the man she had lovingly called her hero reclined in the middle of his bed, with the covers gathered at his waist. With one arm draped across his lap, in an obvious attempt to gain his attention—and more—Lady Moreton, a beautiful young widow quite popular with gentlemen of the *ton*, sat beside him.

"Cara?"

She could not miss the shock in his tone as she averted her gaze. "My lord, pray, forgive me. I did not know you had company. I thought...that is to say...I labored under the mistaken impression that you were alone. Had I known you were otherwise occupied, I should never have trespassed on your privacy. I shall leave you now."

"Cara, *wait*!"

Ignoring his plea, she hauled the door open and fled his suite.

And ran straight into Alex.

"Oh, dear." Her friend was out of breath. "Oh, dear. Jason told me Lance had a visitor. When I returned to the drawing room, Elaine informed me you had come up. I had hoped to catch you before you discovered them."

With a crushing pain permeating her chest, Cara gasped for air. Tears welled in her eyes, and unimaginable humiliation stole her voice.

"Cara, what is it?" Alex shook her by the shoulders. "What did you see?"

Just then, Lady Moreton emerged from the bedchamber, wearing a sultry smile to which Cara would have taken exception under better circumstances.

"Good day, ladies." Her head held high, she continued down the hall as if she owned the place. "The marquess is all yours."

"*Cara!*" Lance roared, and she feared she might be ill.

"I can't go in there," she whispered. "Please, Alex, take me home. I beg you."

"Cara!"

"Wait here." Alex grasped Cara's hand and squeezed her fingers. "I will make our excuses."

She disappeared into Lance's bedchamber and, to Cara's relief, returned a minute later.

"Let us go." Wrapping a protective arm about Cara's shoulders, Alex lent unshakeable support as they descended the stairs.

"Miss Douglas?" Banks caught Cara just as her knees buckled. "Are you unwell?"

"Please, help me secure Miss Douglas in my coach," Alex stated with the authority of a highborn daughter of a duke. "And give our apologies to Lady Elaine."

As the Weston equipage lurched forward, Alex asked, "Do you want to tell me what happened?"

With a soft sob, she unleashed her tears, and misery flowed as a rushing river, completely out of control. In a flash, the world as she knew it tilted precariously. Cara sank into the squabs and fainted.

CHAPTER SIX

*W*hen next Cara woke, she found herself in an unfamiliar place, until she regained her wits and realized she reclined in Alex's bedchamber at Seymour House. As a child, she had spent many a night in that room, telling spooky stories by candlelight. As they grew and matured, the tales had focused decidedly on one tantalizing topic.

Men.

The elegant suite had also undergone a transformation, indicative of the changing tastes of its occupant. At one point, everything had been decorated in a very feminine pale pink, with lace accents. Now, the drapery, the counterpane, the canopy, and trimmings boasted rich burgundy velvet.

"How do you feel?"

She blinked rapidly and turned her head. In a bedside chair, Alex sat with an open book on her lap.

"Much improved." Cara stretched, shifted, rolled on her side, propped an elbow on the mattress, and rested her cheek in her palm. "Why did you bring me here?"

"Because I did not know how to explain your sudden illness." After setting aside the volume, Alex moved to sit on the edge of the bed. "Something tells me you do not wish to share the details of what transpired in Lance's chamber." She paused for a moment and rested a hand on Cara's shoulder. "Do you want to enlighten me? I shall carry it to my grave, I swear on the Brethren oath."

Invoking the Brethren oath was tantamount to a vow of eternal silence undertaken by the most devoted monk upon entering the monastery, and no member of the Brethren could idly dismiss such a promise.

With a heavy sigh, Cara shuddered as images of the day flashed through her mind. She would rather keep the extent of her humiliation to herself, but as Alex had seen fit to protect her secret, she felt honor-bound to confide in her friend.

"Oh, Alex." She closed her eyes. "I fear I have made a dreadful mistake."

"Come now, it could not have been that bad. Jason said she had only just arrived."

"I am not referring to Lady Moreton." Cara groaned and stared at the younger Seymour. "Would that it were so simple."

With her brow a mass of furrows, Alex inclined her head. "I do not understand, because you are talking stuff and nonsense. If interrupting Lance and Lady Moreton did not upset you, then what did?"

"I can't believe what I am about to impart." Sitting upright, Cara clutched Alex's fingers and squeezed. "You see I care for Lance."

"Of course, you do. We all do." Alex chuckled. "There is nothing new or wrong with that."

"You do not comprehend the full weight of my declaration." Cara lifted her chin and looked her straight in the eye. "I care for him—*deeply*."

At first, Alex cast an expression of pure confusion.

To emphasize her point, Cara added, "As you care for Captain Collingwood."

After a few painful seconds, the smile on Alex's face faltered, and Cara knew the precise moment that realization dawned, because Alex gasped. She opened and then closed her mouth.

"What?" A chill of unease traipsed her spine, and Cara leaned forward. "What is it?"

"Nothing." Alex averted her stare.

"You know something," Cara remarked, and it was a statement, not a question.

"No." Never one to avoid controversy, Alex remained uncharacteristically evasive. "I know nothing."

"You are not being truthful." Her well founded instincts piqued, and Cara pressed her suit. "Look at me, Alex, and tell me otherwise."

"It is nothing, really." With a piteous countenance, Alex frowned. "You see, I have always wondered if there were something more than friendship between you and Lance."

"You knew?" Cara inhaled sharply, because discovery equated her worst fear. "Does anyone else suspect me? Has anyone said anything?" she asked in rapid succession, praying no one had stumbled upon her secret.

"I had an inkling." Alex sighed. "And I believe there are none the wiser."

"But—what gave me away?"

"I am not sure." She shrugged. "It was just a feeling."

"Oh, no." Cara could have cried, because her carefully constructed demeanor, her invisible armor, possessed a glaring chink. "Do you think anyone knows?"

"No, I am certain they do not." Alex paused, as though searching her memory. "It has never been mentioned."

"Oh, dear. Whatever am I to do?" Cara scooted to the edge of the bed and dangled her legs from the side. "How will I ever be able to face Lance again? How can we ever go back to being nothing more than friends?"

"Come now, Cara." Alex draped a supportive arm about her shoulders. "You do not think Lance will let something as trivial as your intrusion on his private audience with Lady Moreton come between you? Yours was a harmless mistake."

"There is rather more to it than that."

"Does this have something to do with your mysterious ailment of late?" Alex arched a brow. "Is that why you have been avoiding him?"

Incapable of speech, Cara nodded an affirmative.

"Out with it," Alex said, with a friendly nudge. "What happened between you two?"

Cara considered lying for a scarce second. She had already told Sabrina of her plans and rued burdening her sister, given her pregnancy. But she desperately wanted to share her anguish. Wanted to divulge the pain threatening to suffocate her, as if acknowledgement would somehow lessen her suffering. She knew without doubt that Alex would not betray her secret.

Summoning courage, she said, "We kissed."

"You kissed?" Alex asked in a whisper.

Once again rendered mute, Cara nodded.

"Was it a friendly little buss?" Alex inquired indifferently —before leaning in to add, "Or was it the kind with your lips parted, which curls your toes?"

"Alex."

"What?" Her smile was pure devil. "It is an honest question."

Cara humphed. "It might be honest, but it is certainly indelicate."

"Was his kiss?"

"What?"

"Indelicate?"

"Alex." She flung herself, face first, into the pillows. "I never should have told you."

"Oh, come now. Do not be hesitant with me, sister." Alex clucked her tongue. "Sometimes, when Jason takes after me, I feel as though I could rip his uniform off with my teeth."

"I beg your pardon?" She peeked at her friend and blinked.

"Did you not experience similar sensations? Wait." Alex flinched. "I just pictured that in my mind."

"Pictured—what?" Cara shivered with unease, because the depth of their conversation was a vast deal more than she was prepared to digest.

"You with Lance." Now she had the nerve to grimace. "He is as much my brother as Damian."

"Would you say the same of Captain Collingwood?"

"Good heavens, no."

"Well, I have never considered Lance a sibling." Cara wrung her fingers. "He is, altogether, quite special."

"All right. I will make you a bargain." In jest, Alex tugged a wayward lock of hair. "I will tell you of Jason's kisses, if you will tell me of Lance's."

In shock, Cara covered her mouth. "You have kissed Captain Collingwood?"

With a smirk, Alex appeared quite proud.

"Is he courting you?"

"I rather hope he will, if this blasted war ever ends." Alex cast her a narrow-eyed stare. "Now, stop stalling. Do we or do we not have a deal?"

"I suppose." Cara sat upright and settled her skirts. "But you first."

"Well, he has held me close on more occasions than I can count. We have kissed more than a few times, and that is not all. Twice, he used his tongue," Alex proclaimed with unabashed enthusiasm and a breathy sigh. "I get shivers just thinking of it."

"It sounds wonderful," she murmured, as sumptuous visions assailed her senses.

In a flash, Alex gave her attention to Cara. "Now it is your turn."

"Well, we kissed only once." Suddenly shy, Cara lowered her chin. "But it went on for several minutes."

"I know exactly what you mean."

"Are you going to let me tell this?"

"My apologies. Pray, continue."

"As I said, it lasted for some time. But while he kissed me, he—he touched my—" Cara was not sure she could admit the length of her ruin. Finally, she leaned over, cupped a hand to Alex's ear, and whispered in confidence.

With an expression of shock and awe, Alex gasped. "He touched your breast?" She flew from the bed. "I do not believe it. Jason has never done that to me, and it is the height of insult."

"Alex, please. Someone might hear you."

"Do not worry, there is no cause for concern. I had a footman carry you up, because Damian is at Deptford." Alex paced before lashing out in unveiled anger. "And I thought the man wanted me. *Haa!*"

"Dearest, I am sure Captain Collingwood has too much respect for you—"

"Respect?" She halted and humphed in unmistakable disgust. "What care I for that? I have the respect of many men, and I have the respect of my staff." With hands on hips, Alex stomped a foot. "I want passion. The damn fool sailor has played me false."

With a chuckle, Cara walked to her lifelong friend and grasped her shoulders. "You are being silly, and you should not compare my situation with Lance to yours with Captain Collingwood. Besides, you have only just met. What more can you expect from a man of his station?"

"That is precisely the point." Alex raised a finger in argument. "I made him free with my name. Surely he knows that includes the rest of me."

"Not so, dearest." Cara shook her head. "A gentleman would never assume such a thing."

"I do not want gentlemanly love." With a countenance of unbridled determination, which Cara could only envy, Alex folded her arms in front of her. "I want what my parents enjoyed. I want true love."

"As do we all." In her brain, she revisited the horrific scene in Lance's bedchamber, as well as the embroidered kerchief the remained tucked close to her heart. Until that instant, she'd clung to hope for the future she desperately desired with her hero. "But, perhaps, for some of us, it is not possible."

"Why do you say that? Because of Lady Moreton?" Alex frowned. "Lance could not be interested in her. Half the men in the *ton* have already had her, and I daresay she will run through both houses of Parliament before her death. The woman will probably expire on her back."

"Alex." Cara cursed the telltale heat of a blush at the improper, unladylike comment. "Must you be so crass?"

"But it is true. She makes a play for every man in the *ton*. Sabrina said that harridan tried to turn Everett's head more than once—even after they married."

"But Everett loves Sabrina." Cara smiled, recalling the unspoken but nonetheless powerful devotion her sister and brother-in-law shared. "He would never break his marriage vows."

"Well, Lance loves you," Alex countered. "What is the difference?"

"How can you be sure?"

"I have seen how he looks at you."

"And just how is that?"

"I am not certain I can describe it." Alex tapped a finger to her chin in an affectation of deep thought. "It is as though he is discomfited."

"That could be nothing more than poor digestion."

"Oh, you are sporting for an argument," Alex replied with an upturned nose.

"No. It is quite simple, really. Lance loves me as a friend, nothing more." Cara shrugged. "After our kiss, he threatened to have me bodily thrown out of his room."

"He did not." Alex looked her shock. "You must be exaggerating."

"Trust me, he did." Oh, the agony of remembrance. "And I am afraid to return to Raynesford House, lest I be crudely and physically ejected from his residence."

"Well, there you are. Lance loves you," Alex proclaimed with conviction.

"He ordered me from his chambers, from his sight, because he loves me?" Cara gave vent to a snort of skepticism. "Pull my other leg."

"Hear me out." Alex grasped Cara by her wrists. "Had the kiss meant nothing, had he viewed you only as a friend, then he would not have been angry. Surely, his reaction means something."

"It does," Cara stated flatly. "He sees me as a friend, nothing more. He is angry because that kiss never should have happened."

"I prefer my interpretation." Alex frowned. "It bodes better for you."

"I prefer the truth."

For a pregnant moment, both stood mute.

Suddenly, Alex snapped her fingers. "I have got it."

Cara jumped. "What?"

"The answer to your dilemma."

"Alex, I have no dilemma." She sighed impatiently. "Lance most assuredly does not love me, so nothing more need be said."

"Cara, I love you as a sister, but I propose, where Lance is concerned, you are afraid to discover the extent of his feelings."

It was her turn to frown. "Go on."

"Come back to Raynesford House—"

"No—"

"Let me finish." Alex stared at the ceiling and squeezed her fingers. "I am asking you to help me tend Lance. You will never be alone with him."

Cara mulled the possibility. "To what purpose?"

"It will show us how he feels about you."

"How so?" In silence, Cara pondered the situation, because, however disastrous her predicament, she remained firmly entrenched in her belief that Lance was destined to be hers. "I do not follow."

"It is simple, really." Alex grinned her cat that ate the

canary grin. "We shall both take care of him, and if he needs something, you shall fetch it. While it matters not that I am alone with him, we shall take great pains to be certain that the two of you never enjoy a private audience. At best, we might discover he harbors a deep and abiding devotion for you. At the very least, you may mend fences and be friends again." She shrugged. "Surely that counts for something?"

"I do not know." What if their efforts resulted in further disillusionment?

"Come on, Cara." Alex elbowed her ribs. "Give it a go."

Against her better judgment, Cara acquiesced. "All right."

THE DOOR to Lance's bedchamber fast approached, and Cara swayed and splayed her arms for balance, while her ears pealed a carillon of warning. In a reflexive gesture, she placed her palm over her heart and, thereby, the embroidered kerchief. Any minute, she was certain she would swoon.

"Come on, you can do it," Alex whispered in her ear.

"Oh, dear." Cara grimaced and bit back the bitter nausea welling in her throat. "I think I am going to be unwell."

It had taken four days to muster the nerve to return to Raynesford House, and now she reconsidered her decision. Why had she let Alex talk her into their foolhardy plan, which had her standing outside the door of the room she looked on as a torture chamber?

The answer was simple.

As much as she tried to deny it, to herself and Alex, Cara

held tight to the smallest bit of hope that her friend was right. That Lance considered her something more than a childhood companion. And perhaps, with a little luck, he would one day call her wife.

"Be strong, Cara. Just as you always are, and I promise I will not leave you alone with him."

"I must be insane to hatch this scheme." Cara inhaled a deep breath and rolled her shoulders. "Where is Elaine?"

"I sent her to Sabrina's." Alex gazed at the floor. "The poor dear is suffering nightmares."

"If memory serves, she endured the same after Thomas passed, too."

"I know. I thought it best to get her out of the house for a while." Alex cast a lopsided grin. "And Brie can make the sun shine on a cloudy day."

"All right." Cara chuckled, and the tension gripping the whole of her frame abated. "I can do this."

Determined to stay the course, she turned the knob and marched across the threshold as a soldier going into battle.

"Morning, Miss Douglas. Lady Alexandra." Dr. Handley dipped his chin and set his hat atop his head.

Call her a coward, but Cara refused to look at Lance, preferring instead to focus her attention on the doctor's amiable, decidedly unthreatening expression of welcome.

"Morning, Dr. Handley." She composed a proper curtsey. "How fares our patient this day?"

"Very well, Miss Douglas. Due in no small measure to your fine care, he should be able to get out of bed in a sennight. Though the splint will remain, we can put a little weight on the leg. I shall give you further instructions for his recovery, Monday next." Picking up his familiar black leather bag, the grey-haired physician bowed. "Good day, ladies."

"Alex, why do not you show Dr. Handley to the door?" Lance suggested, and Cara flinched.

Inwardly, she cursed herself. It was obvious her hero wanted to speak with her in private, and she had no intention of allowing that to occur, at least, not yet.

"By all means, permit me the pleasure." Poised to perfection, Cara inclined her head and smiled.

"How very kind of you, Miss Douglas." Dr. Handley paused and offered his arm in escort. "But it is not necessary, I assure you."

"It would be my honor," she responded, as she clutched the crook of his elbow.

As soon as they entered the hall, Cara swore the weight of the world had been lifted from her shoulders, and, in some respects, it had, because despite the fact that she had not so much as peeked at Lance, his interest in her attendance had not escaped her notice. She imagined his potent green gaze focused in her direction, and it threw her off balance. Perhaps she required additional days of preparation in order to withstand his presence?

While the doctor chatted about nothing, Cara concentrated on putting one foot in front of the other, lest she trip. How ridiculous was it that a man who, as a child, had begged her to read to him on stormy nights, because he feared thunder, now intimidated her. Of course, he had long since gotten over his anxiety.

She wished she had gotten over him.

"Thank you for the joy of your company, Miss Douglas." Dr. Handley bowed. "I shall see you Monday."

After shutting the door, Cara whirled about and stared at the second floor landing. At a turtle's pace, she crossed the foyer and set her palm to the polished oak balustrade.

For a long while, she gazed at the first step of the grand staircase and revisited her strategy.

When she embarked on her quest to claim Lance's heart, she had not considered the effect such endeavors might have on their friendship. In truth, her efforts had jeopardized, if not destroyed, their lifelong rapport. Now, common sense demanded she confront the risks.

In the carriage, en route to Raynesford House, Alex had encouraged Cara to remain strong. The younger Seymour had extended no words of caution, leaving Cara alone to contemplate the permanent alteration, for good or ill, in her relationship with Lance.

In brief, she examined her options. She could flee, but was that really a choice? Alex would be disappointed, but she would understand. As for Lance, the implication would be unmistakable. She could no longer bear his company, much less the sight of him, especially once he took a wife.

But how would the Brethren, as a whole, react to the sudden division in their ranks? To her knowledge, none in their group had ever commingled. In light of her current situation, she understood why.

Though she had but one sister on which to base her opinion, Cara regarded the knights of the Brethren as something akin to brothers, in truth. They were, for all intents and purposes, big, lovable, sometimes heavy-handed, but with the best intentions, older male siblings.

Except for Lance.

What she harbored for him was different. Indescribable.

With her hero she experienced an undeniable connection of the intimate sort, one that stirred an unfamiliar fluttering in the pit of her belly, a bond that reduced her legs to mush and set her heart pounding in her chest at the mere sight of him. When their hands touched, oh, what she felt. Delicious heat coursed her veins, setting her skin alight.

And she had thought he felt it, too.

It physically hurt her to think that he had not shared what she considered a compelling attachment, which had long ago breached the limits of harmless child play. That it had been an illusion. A mistake. One she had made and was honor-bound to correct.

However unpleasant, that was the other alternative.

She could return to the scene of the crime, so to speak, help Alex care for Lance, and do her best to repair the damage she had done to their friendship. In the dark recesses of her brain, where she was always honest with herself, she worried that they would never be the same, would never share the companionable silences, the comfortable dances, the easy conversation. Cara was positive those days were gone, and she was more than a little sad at their passing. She remained haunted by what might have been had he given her a chance.

But she quickly reminded herself she was entirely to blame for her predicament.

I never should have kissed you.

"May I be of service, Miss Douglas?"

In surprise, Cara gasped, flinched, and, without hesitation, took the first step. Clutching the balustrade, she gazed over her shoulder. "No, thank you, Banks. I was just showing Dr. Handley to the door." With a dip of her chin, she turned. "I shall return to his lordship."

"Very good, Miss Douglas."

As she ascended the stairs, she counted her reasons for embarking on her campaign. Never had she wavered in her belief that Lance was destined to be her husband, as her indecision lay in how to achieve her dream. After all, they had known each other since they wore christening gowns. She had nothing to fear of him, because he would never hurt her, at least, not intentionally. And she owed it to her friends to resolve their differences, to bridge the gap she had inadvertently created with her ill-fated pursuit.

Standing before the door to Lance's bedchamber, she prayed for strength, adjusted the embroidered kerchief tucked in her bodice, turned the knob, and entered the fray.

To her relief, Lance remained where he had been since the accident, in the middle of the great bed. Valiantly, she forced the unwelcome visions of Lady Moreton from her head. Alex smiled and dipped her chin. Cara located a chair on the opposite side of the room, near a large window.

With the grace and elegance borne of years of practice, Cara perched on the edge of the seat. Hoping her face portrayed the essence of serenity, and her posture personified unflinching confidence, she swallowed hard. And although she inclined her head in his direction, she averted her gaze.

"And how are you today, Lance?"

CHAPTER SEVEN

"*W*hat a lovely tray," Lance replied, as Alex set his noon meal before him. Briefly, he scanned the fare before wrinkling his nose. "May I have some salt for my chicken?"

"I will get it," Cara offered and sped from the room.

Surreptitiously, he cursed as she departed. When she returned, minutes later, she handed a silver shaker to Alex, who passed it to him.

He frowned. After a pause, he asked, "Where is my latest edition of the *Mariner's Mirror*? I should like to peruse it while I dine."

"I believe I saw it downstairs, in the drawing room." Alex gazed uneasily at Cara. "Blake and Damian took it with them when they visited earlier."

Cara all but leaped from her chair. "Then I shall retrieve it, at once."

Again, Lance swore as she withdrew.

In truth he had no interest in the quarterly journal of nautical life, he just wanted to see how many more concocted errands Cara could endure before swooning from exhaustion. To his infinite frustration, she seemed to possess the enviable stamina of a young lad. Since returning to aid Alex in his recovery, she had done everything she could to avoid his unreserved and exclusive company. And he had seized upon every conceivable excuse to get her alone.

All he wanted to do was talk to her. The tension between them was palpable, and he simply could not bear it any longer. Why? Because Lance missed his lifelong friend, though he would deny it should anyone dare ask. An invisible but nonetheless excruciating chasm had sliced through him, and he ached with an arduous emptiness.

He wanted to set things right, wanted to atone for the stolen kiss and his unforgivable reaction. And he needed to explain the visit from Lady Moreton. Needed to assure Cara there was nothing between him and the attractive but importuning ace of spades. Why? Now that was a question for which he had no answer.

Just then the door opened, and Cara reappeared with the requested item. "Here it is," she called out in a cheery little singsong.

Once again, in a ridiculous practice, she passed the journal to Alex, who gave it to him. Bloody hell, he had a broken leg—not the plague. Would she have no direct contact with him? Absently, he scanned the cover and stifled a groan of delight.

"This is the July issue." He sniffed and set aside the periodical. "I have read it."

"Oh?" Cara bit her lip, and he fought uncharacteristic humor. "It is the most recent."

"No, it is not." He shook his head. "The latest quarterly just arrived. The October issue is most current."

"Could you not have said as much before I went in

search of it?" She slumped, and her shoulders drooped visibly. "You did not specify."

"I do not mean to be an imposition." He thrust his lower lip and set his chin firm in an affectation she had never been able to resist. "If I could get it myself, I would."

"Have you any idea where it might be?" she asked tentatively.

"Perhaps, my study." He wrinkled his nose. "I had Damian set some correspondence on my desk."

"All right." Cara huffed, took two steps, and then came to an abrupt halt. "Is there anything else you require?"

Lance pretended to give due consideration to her question, before responding, "No." Of course, he would conjure another errand of dire importance before she returned.

"I shall be right back." Cara stomped to the door.

Was it his imagination, or were her footfalls decidedly heavy? For a woman who prided herself on poised perfection, her innate feminine deportment had all but abandoned her. Inwardly, he laughed.

Shortly thereafter, an out of breath Miss Douglas appeared, huffing and puffing like a mare that had just completed a race.

"Found it." In a repeat performance of her previous inane routine, Cara gave the journal to Alex, who handed it to him. "It was on your desk."

Lance clenched his jaw and gritted his teeth. He'd had just about enough of her evasive maneuvers. As his mind raced, he tapped his fingers in an impatient rhythm on the edge of the tray.

"May I have some tea?"

Cara sighed audibly, and he barely managed to swallow a snort.

"My lord, I asked if there was anything else you required

when I went in search of the journal." She marched to the foot of the bed. "You indicated you wanted nothing."

Craning his neck, he lifted his head and for the first time caught her eye. "I thought you meant from the study."

"I meant in general." Cara quickly averted her stare and bit her lip, choking on a rapier retort, no doubt.

"I am sorry." Lance shrugged and smiled, as it was nice to catch a glimpse, however brief, of *his* Cara. "It was an honest mistake."

"I thought you preferred coffee," she murmured.

"Normally, I do." In vain he studied her, desperately trying to snare her attention, but she stood distant and aloof. It bothered him that she would not meet his gaze. "But today I feel like tea. If it is too much trouble, perhaps Alex—"

"Oh, no," Cara interrupted. "It is no trouble. I will see to it, at once."

She scurried in pursuit of the tea he did not want.

Lance turned his thoughts to Alex, who currently favored him with a cherubic smile. She was a dear friend. Like Cara, he had known her all her life. He adored her, truly he did. But if he had to suffer one more discourse on the heroics of one Captain Jason Collingwood, he would hang himself from the canopy of his bed.

Minutes later, a withering Cara shuffled ungracefully to the fore, and he bit his tongue to keep from laughing. Balancing a small tray, bearing a single cup and saucer and a small pot, she approached and handed the tray to Alex. Cara pressed a hand to her cheek, and it was then he spied a faint sheen of perspiration on her brow.

While Cara returned to her chair on the opposite side of the room, Alex poured the steaming brew and then handed him the tiny porcelain cup.

For a hairsbreadth of a second, he moved to accept her offering but stopped short. With a grimace of distaste he asked, "But where is my cinnamon stick?"

A plaintive cry reverberated from Cara's direction.

Alex blinked. "Cinnamon?"

"Yes." He pouted. "I much prefer it to lemon."

"I see." Alex frowned and stared at Cara.

"Would you be so kind, Alex?" Lance grinned the grin of the innocent. "Poor Cara has worked herself to the bone."

Just when he thought Alex would finally relent and give them a moment's peace, she refused to budge from his side. He seriously wondered if she had taken root.

"No, I have not," Cara chimed.

"Are you sure?" Lance swallowed a curse.

"Of course." She stood, avoiding him entirely.

"Come now, Cara. You must be exhausted." To his amazement, and begrudging admiration, she exited his company, with nary a complaint, and made for the kitchen.

Frustrated beyond belief, Lance decided that, barring insanity, he would enjoy a private audience with Cara. They could do it his way or the hard way. If she continued to be stubborn, so be it. It was time to take off the gloves.

"Lance is trying to kill me."

Cara kicked her slippers to the floor in a manner that could be described as anything but ladylike, dragged herself to the *chaise* in her bedchamber, and collapsed, face down, into the cushions.

"He is doing no such thing. He is just very needy right now." Alex giggled and sat beside her. "Our plan is working perfectly."

"You must be joking." Cara rolled over and snorted. "Our plan is a disaster." She stared at her toes and groaned. "My feet ache, my back hurts, and my legs are sore from running up and down the stairs. From where I stand, I would say our plan is a miserable failure. Lance is on to us."

"How could he possibly know?" Her brow a mass of furrows, Alex frowned. "You are imagining things."

"Am I? Yesterday, Cook served him coffee, and he wanted tea—with cinnamon, at that. Today, I ordered tea, and he asked for coffee—with cream. Lance never takes cream. Not only that, but when I anticipated a request for sugar, and brought the bowl, he asked for honey. Whoever heard of putting honey in coffee?" Cara flung a pillow across the room. "Oh, I can't take it any longer. I am not going back."

"Do not quit, Cara." Alex grasped her forearms. "Can you not see what is happening?" She shook her gently. "Lance desperately wants to be alone with you."

Cara narrowed her stare. "You know no such thing."

Alex lifted her chin. "I do, too."

"How?" She arched a brow in question. "Did you read his mind?"

"I did not have to resort to such inferior tactics." Alex smiled smugly. "Because he told me so."

Surprise shivered down her spine, and hope welled anew, as Cara bit back a joyful cry. "He did?"

"Yes," Alex replied with a definite nod.

"When?"

"Today, when you went for honey."

With grim skepticism, Cara mulled the development. "What exactly did he say?"

"That he needed to speak with you in private." Alex clucked her tongue and rocked on her heels. "He said he had treated you abominably, early in his recovery, and owed you an apology. He begged me to give him an audience with you, alone."

It seemed too good to be true, and Cara shook her head in disbelief. Still, she doubted her friend, because, like her, Alex was an eternal optimist.

"I am certain he did not beg."

"'I beg you, Alex. Please, let me speak with Cara'." The younger Seymour humphed. "Now do you believe me?"

She snapped to attention. "Is that what he said?"

Alex nodded. "His exact words."

Cara bit her lip. "Oh, dear."

"Give him a chance, Cara. This could be it, the moment for which you have been waiting."

She studied the damask pattern on the *chaise*. "I rather doubt it."

Alex cupped her chin, trapping her stare. "But how will you know if you do not talk to him?"

Cara shrugged and bemoaned her precarious position. "Perhaps I do not want to know."

"You have been taking the stairs like a fox with a hound on its tail, and you want me to believe you indifferent?" Alex emitted a snort of disbelief. "Forgive me, dear friend, but as you once said to me, pull my other leg."

"I am serious." Cara pressed a clenched fist to her bosom, considered the embroidered kerchief tucked in her bodice, and tried to remain calm. "I am not convinced Lance intends to profess an undying devotion for me."

"Must you be so negative?" Alex hugged a pillow. "What do you suspect are his motives?"

"I think he sincerely wants to apologize and return to the way things were between us."

"Indeed." Alex appeared perplexed. "Would that be so bad?"

Her insides twisted and turned with tension, and Cara compressed her lips. "It would not be, if I thought it possible."

"I do not understand."

"I am not certain I can revert to the way we were."

THE FOLLOWING MORNING, Cara sat in the chair opposite the massive bed belonging to the master of Raynesford House, pretending to read a book. Thankfully, Dr. Handley and Captain Collingwood, with Alex hanging on his every word, kept His Lordship occupied. At that moment, she would welcome Napoleon, himself, if he would hold Lance's attention and, thus, spare her toes at least one round-trip on the stairs.

"Well now, let us get you on your feet, Lord Raynesford." Dr. Handley glanced at her. "Miss Douglas, if you would be so kind as to fetch us a robe."

"Right away, Doctor." Marking her page, Cara closed the volume and set it aside. She stepped into the dressing room and retrieved the black silk gown Lance wore the day she found him trying to walk on his own. As she pulled it from the peg on the wall, she smiled. That afternoon had been the one time, as a grown woman, that Cara ever pretended to be his wife. And, if memory served, she had handled him quite well.

Returning to the bedchamber, she quickly crossed the room and handed the garment to Dr. Handley. "Lady Alex and I will wait in the hall while his lordship dresses."

"Very good, Miss Douglas." The physician bowed. "But

as you are charged with his care, I should like you to practice supporting him while I am here."

"Please, allow me to assist you, Dr. Handley," Captain Collingwood offered. "I daresay I am a bit stronger than our Miss Douglas." The last was said with a wink.

"That may be, young man, but you are not here every day, as is Miss Douglas. I need someone I can rely upon to supervise his recovery in my absence." The grey-haired physician wrinkled his nose and eyed Cara. "Is there a problem?"

"Of course not." Resisting the urge to argue, she shook her head. "I am at your service, Doctor."

After a brief respite in the hall, Cara found herself standing aside Lance, tucked in the crook of his arm, as he grasped her shoulder. For added stability, she held him at his waist, as the crusty old physician directed.

"Excellent." Dr. Handley beamed at his patient. "Now, gently, take a step."

Lance thrust his good leg forward, letting his injured, splinted limb bear his weight. Immediately, he winced, and his body tensed as he leaned on Cara. Instinctively, she squeezed his fingers in silent reassurance, and Lance clung to her. Still, she resisted the urge to look at him, until he inched out his injured leg and moaned.

Without thought, she peered at him—and barely stifled a sob. Pain invested his unnaturally pale face. He gritted his teeth, the muscles in his neck stretched taut, and unshed tears welled in his emerald eyes. Lance stared at her, agony mixed with fear. While her initial thought had been to guard her heart by maintaining a comfortable distance, Cara could not ignore the fact that, at that moment, he needed her.

Releasing her grip on his hand, she twined her fingers

with his in a more intimate hold and mustered a smile. "Come now, my hero, it is a walk in the park," she whispered.

Searching her gaze, Lance inhaled a shaky breath and appeared to relax. After a few tenuous seconds, he nodded. "All right. Let us have a go, my girl."

With Dr. Handley offering instruction, Lance and Cara traversed the length of the cavernous bedchamber, step by interminable step. Though he endured admirably, grunting and groaning at a snail's pace, Cara suffered every gut-wrenching grumble as a dagger to her heart. How she wished she could absorb some measure of his anguish.

After they completed one lap, the physician removed his spectacles and wiped his lenses. "Excellent effort, your lord-ship. Make two more rounds and rest." He set a piece of paper on the bedside table. "Here is my prescribed course of exercise. See to it he completes the suggested activity for each day, Miss Douglas."

"Are you leaving?" Alex inquired from the corner she occupied with Captain Collingwood.

"Must be off." Dr. Handley settled his hat on his noggin and picked up his physician's bag. "Other calls to make, you know."

"And I am afraid I must away, as well," Captain Colling-wood added.

"So soon?" Alex pouted.

"But I am due at the docks." Captain Collingwood offered his arm in escort. "Though it pains me to depart your company, Lady Alex."

"I share your sentiment, Captain." Alex placed her hand in the crook of his elbow. "Allow me to show you to the door." With a side-glance for her wary friend, she shuttled the physician and navy man into the hall.

Leaving Cara alone with Lance.

For a few minutes, they stood there in uncomfortable and uncharacteristic silence.

Cara stared at her slippered feet and searched for something to say.

"Cara."

She bit her lip. "Yes?"

"You have my solemn vow, there is nothing untoward between myself and Lady Moreton. Despite what you may or may not have seen, I rebuffed her advances."

"I am sure it is none of my business." She shrugged and carefully considered her words. "Daresay it is long past the time for you to consider marriage. There is the marquessate to consider, you know."

"Perish the thought." Lance heaved a sigh. "And you mean more to me than she ever could, as does your good opinion. It is important you know the truth, because I would not have you mistake what you witnessed the day you interrupted us."

Cara paused to compose a suitable response, because she could ill afford to court more trouble. She took a minute to calm herself, determined to betray no hint of panic—or pain—in her voice.

"Worry not, my friend, for I never gave it another thought. I was simply embarrassed by my breach of decorum, for which I owe you an apology. Let me assure you, such an egregious infraction of etiquette will not happen again. In future, I will always knock before entering your suite."

"I preferred it when you did not." Lance placed a brotherly kiss atop her head. "You are always welcome in my bedchamber."

Cara gasped. Without conscious thought, she snapped

to attention. With mouth agape, she rued the telltale heat of a blush burning her cheeks.

Wide-eyed, Lance sputtered. "I meant...that is to say...that did not come out as I had intended."

"Say no more," Cara cautioned. "I get your meaning, and it is sufficient. Now, shall we continue your exercise?"

She tried to step forward, but Lance stayed her.

"Wait. I want you to know how special your friendship is to me. Please, you must believe me when I say that I would never purposefully do anything to jeopardize what we have." He cast her a lopsided grin. "Do you understand?"

She knew only too well.

In his own words, Lance was telling her he wanted to go back to the way things were—before the kiss. When they were nothing more than friends.

Though inside her heart shattered beneath his embroidered kerchief, she summoned all her years of training, all her skills, and shielded herself in polite gentility.

He would never know how much he hurt her.

"Nothing more need be said, my hero." With a forced smile, Cara squeezed his hand. "Now, stop dallying."

She took a tentative step, and that time, Lance was with her.

TWO DAYS LATER, Lance and Cara assumed a familiar pose after completing a rotation.

"Do we really have to go around again?" He grimaced. "Can we not skip it, and say we did it?"

"Absolutely not." Clutching his hand tightly, she glared at him and shook her head. "Dr. Handley prescribed this physical regimen for your benefit, and we are going to get it done, one way or another."

"Quite the taskmaster, are we not? And I love it when you use that governessy tone. Tell me, what will you do if I refuse?" Lance stuck his tongue in his cheek and grinned. "Spank me?"

"Don't tempt me." With a charming blush coloring her cheeks, Cara's eyes flared. "Now, stop stalling and start walking."

With a hearty chuckle, he stepped out and immediately swallowed a groan. "Bloody hell, it hurts."

"Perhaps if you put more into your routine you would not be whining like a newborn pup." Cara steadfastly refused to meet his gaze. But despite her reproach he could not miss her smile, and it was comforting, given the disquietude of their relations.

"It is not as it was before, is it?" He asked the question before he realized what he'd said.

"No."

In silence, he suffered her response as a death knell to their friendship. In fact, nothing remained as it was once, prior to the incident, but until that moment Lance had been confident their rift would heal with the passage of time. As was her custom, Cara betrayed no hesitance in her enthusiasm for his convalescence.

Elegance personified, she arrived every morning, bright and early, with a cheery expression investing her delicate features, to assist him with his exercises, not that he expected anything less. With an arm about his waist, she anchored him as he stumbled, limped, and cursed the perimeter of his bedchamber. And while she often referred to him as her hero, he ached to proclaim that, in truth, she was his hero.

"A newborn pup, am I?" Though he groused, it was in jest. "I take issue, my dear. Is there a tail attached to my bum?"

"No." Now she cast him a flirty grin. "But, now that you mention it, you are a bit droopy about the ears."

"Droopy?" Lance thrust his chin in mock offense. "We shall see about that. Prepare to defend yourself, madam." With a titillating touch, he brushed his fingertips to the highly sensitized flesh at the base of her neck.

"Oh, Lance." In an instant, Cara shrieked and flinched. "I beg you, do not tickle me."

When she jerked hard, in a pitiful attempt to escape, she threw him off balance, and he teetered precariously. Just as quick, she reversed course in an awkward dance, of sorts, hugging him close to keep him from falling, which brought them toe-to-toe.

For inexpressibly sweet minutes, he melted in her cerulean eyes.

The walls of his suite collapsed, the world tilted beneath his feet, and the air sizzled with incomparable desire, enveloping them in a sensuous cocoon. An uncontrollable salute from his Jolly Roger took him by surprise, because his tempestuous Roger was dangerously jolly. But it was the raw anguish she tried but failed to hide that brought him back to reality and stayed the beast below his belly button.

Lance cupped her cheek and sighed. "Cara, tell me truly, did I hurt you?"

"Of course not." She swallowed hard and shifted in his embrace. "You did not so much as step on me."

Lance frowned. "That is not what I refer to, and you know it."

Her lower lip trembled, and again she averted her stare. "Perhaps we have worked you too hard today."

"Cara—"

"Dr. Handley cautioned you not to overtire yourself." She moved to his side. "Let me put you to bed."

"We have to talk—"

"What is there to say?" She gave him a gentle nudge. "It is a tempest in a teacup."

"I know you too well—"

"You know nothing," she snapped, and he knew without doubt a gaping wound remained in their friendship.

Though he desperately wanted to discuss their kiss, the one that stood as a very real barrier between them, Lance was reluctant to press the issue for fear she'd turn tail and run, and he was in no condition to give chase. He needed to reassure her it had been an aberration, an unforgivable blunder, a rare moment of weakness brought about by his injury and subsequent isolation. He wanted her to know she had nothing to fear from him. It wouldn't happen again, because he would not risk their friendship on a whim.

As Lance perched on the edge of the mattress, he dared ask, "Will you come tomorrow?"

"Of course, I will, silly man." Cara draped the blanket over his splinted leg. "It is my duty."

CHAPTER EIGHT

*D*r. Handley removed the splint, on a blustery morning, which Cara thought appropriate, because the weather matched the turmoil roiling within her. Free of the heavy restraint, Lance would no longer require her assistance. In no time, he would be on his feet, and life would return to normal. Everything would be as it was—before that kiss.

To her surprise, she was horribly mistaken.

In the weeks his leg had been immobilized, it had become weak and stiff. Or as the doctor put it, atrophy had set in with a vengeance. To stand tall and proud as he once had, her hero would need to work doubly hard to strengthen his leg, and the process would be neither easy nor painless. Each passing day was a test of endurance, physically and mentally.

With good humor he trudged forth admirably, gritting his teeth in a desperate attempt to stifle the agony, but his awkward gait belied a cumbersome and uncooperative limb. As Lance struggled to walk, a black, desperate mood invested his frame, eating at his spirit and further hampering his progress. And Cara bled for him.

As a single entity they suffered, each from their own wounds, his physical injury and her emotional trauma. Yet she remained resolute in her belief that Lance was fated to be hers, if only her strategy were as fixed. And although they'd not spoken of that brief but blissful interlude, she revisited it every night in her dreams.

But in her visions Lance stood hale and whole.

"Whoa." He tottered and splayed his arms wide for balance. Absent the splint, he was considerably more vulnerable.

"I am sorry, my hero." She clutched him close. "I did not pay attention."

"It is not your fault. This is insanity," he growled. "I am a bloody cripple."

"Do not say such things," she chastised him.

"It is true." Just then, he lost his footing and flapped furiously, as if to take flight. "Look at me, hobbling as an old woman."

"But Dr. Handley says it is to be expected. You were stationary for several weeks, and it will work itself out." Cara half-hugged him and rested her head on his shoulder. "You must have hope."

"Hope?" In an instant, his expression softened. "Ever the optimist, my girl."

"Always, where you are concerned." When he pressed his lips to her forehead, she gasped.

"What say we forget this nonsense?" he whispered. "We can recline amid the pillows, as we did when we were children, and you can read that god awful book of poetry, if you wish."

Desire flickered as a slow-burning flame, and hope

bloomed anew, yet she tempered her response. "But—you have not completed your exercise."

"My dear, I can't negotiate the room without this infernal walking stick." He squeezed her ever so gently. "What is the point?"

"Lance, you have only just begun." Despite his tempting offer, not for a minute would she place his needs above her wants. And she much preferred his grouchy demeanor to outright surrender. In order to improve, he had to fight. "It is a temporary condition. You must believe that."

"What you believe and what I know are two different things. I am useless." He scowled. "I could not even command my ship."

"That is ridiculous." Now Cara had him. If she could raise his ire, she might be able to inspire him to continue his therapy. "You are still captain of the *Demetrius*."

"How long do you think I will last when the men get an eyeful of me? The crippled captain." Lance snorted. "They will hoist me over the rail and make off with my rig, and then what would I do? I would wager I could not stay afloat, and I would end up in the belly of a shark."

"Stuff and nonsense." She tried to get him to take another step, but he resisted. "If you will only—"

"No more, Cara." He wrenched free and shifted his weight to his good leg. "It is past due for me to accept the reality of my situation."

"Stop this rubbish at once." In unchecked frustration, she stomped the carpeted floor. How could she motivate him? "What is wrong with you? Never have I known you to give up or quit anything."

"I speak the truth," he said, with a wicked grimace. "You would not understand, given that you live in the world of perfume and petticoats."

"Perfume and petticoats, indeed." Oh, he was sporting for an argument, and in her he would find his challenge well met. And on the wings of high dudgeon, they would succeed. Unabashed and undaunted, she pinned his stare. "But I know myself, and I would not be cowed by the hardship. And I had thought the same of you, as never would I have figured you a coward—"

"A coward?" He clenched his jaw. "Tread lightly, friend. I have run through bigger men for lesser insult."

"That may be, but you recall a different Lance." She giggled, and he bared his teeth. "As you have one foot in the grave, what have I to fear?"

She prompted him to move, but he wouldn't budge.

"My wrath." He lowered his chin. "And my belt."

"Ooh, that is tough talk for an invalid." Cara cast him a flirty pout, as she sharpened her tongue and aimed. "You know, we could hire a nanny and put you in towels. Then you need never leave your bed."

For a scarce second, Lance said nothing. But she could sense the barely restrained anger simmering beneath his quiet façade.

"How easy it is to parody my pain." He wiped perspiration from his brow. "As for you, ignorance is bliss."

"On the contrary. I know it hurts, and I know it has been difficult, but you must not yield." She cupped his cheek, but he jerked, as if repulsed by her touch. "You have to fight to get back on your feet."

"I will not fool myself into believing something that is not going to happen." He speared his fingers through his hair, and it spiked. "I am tired."

"Come now, is this my hero? Is this the friend with whom I have shared so much?" She smiled and tried to cajole him into resuming his exercise. "Is this the brave one who saved me from the snakes in the pond at Pembroke?"

"Grow up, Cara." His expression sobered. "We are no longer a boy and a girl. We are man and woman, and I am no more your hero than you are a queen. And there were no snakes. Blake was joking because he knew I—"

"He knew—what?"

"It does not signify." His jaw muscles flexed as he clamped his mouth shut.

"All right. Now you have tarried long enough." Reminding herself to stay focused, she prodded him. "Are you quite finished feeling sorry for yourself, or should I invite the rest of the Brethren to your pity party?"

In a flash, he snapped to attention. "Go to hell."

"I should wish you the same." For each successive affront, she paid in the coin of self-control, yet she persevered. Cara rocked on her heels and smirked. "Then again, you would have to crawl to get there."

"Get out!"

"What a bad bargain." Unfazed, she shrugged and looked him up and down. "Is that the best you can do?"

At long last, Lance stepped in her direction. "Leave me, you buttock and tongue!"

And then he took another.

"You should be so fortunate. And who is going to make me?" Withdrawing, she grinned, arched a brow, and innocently touched a finger to her cheek. "You?"

With the walking stick as a counterbalance, he closed the distance between them. "Cara, so help me, when I get my hands on you, I am going to baste some manners into your backside."

"You will have to catch me first." To incite him further, she stuck out her tongue and retreated once more.

"Cara!"

"Poor bantling." She flicked her fingers in entreaty. "Come and get me."

Methodically, but at a conservative pace, she steered him in a merry chase about the room.

"I am not in leading strings, and I mean what I say." With sweat trickling his temples, Lance glared at her. "I am going to bend you over my knees, and you will not sit comfortably for a sennight."

"Oh, I am quaking in my slippers." As a damsel in distress, she rested the back of her hand to her forehead. Just as quick, she lowered her chin and snickered. "Wait a minute. Do you not mean knee? According to you, the one serves no purpose."

His eyes flared. "I *am* going to beat you."

"Those are big words for the chicken-hearted." She yawned. "An idle threat."

"You will not think so." He inched forward.

"Careful, else you might fall arsy yarsey." She favored him with a rich, throaty laugh and withdrew again. "You can't capture me."

With a bestial growl, he swung wide and lashed out, but she jumped, and he missed her. "I am going to heat your posterior."

"Oops." She smacked her lips and rolled her eyes. "You missed."

"Come here."

"Not a chance."

"No, I mean it." Lance posed in his best little boy lost impersonation, which she knew too well. "I need your help."

"You are not going to get me that easy. I am rather more than seven." She paused for effect. "Or is it eight?"

"*Cara!*"

Again, he reached for her, and again she eluded his grasp.

"You are getting closer," she said in a flirty singsong before skipping away.

It was unfortunate for Cara that in her attempt to provoke her friend, she hadn't realized she'd backed herself into a corner—right beside the bed.

She smiled—and hit the wall.

All of a sudden, he extended the walking stick, which pinned her to the spot. He grinned, as the cat that ate the canary, dropped the cane, sidled near, and planted his hands at either side of her head. "I have you now, my lady."

Cara remained steadfast. "Lance, look around you."

He quirked his brows and peered over his shoulder.

"You did it, my hero," she proclaimed, bursting with inexpressible joy. "You made it all by yourself."

Lance faced her with tear-filled eyes and then hugged her, resting his chin to her hair. "Never could I have done it without you. We did it together, my girl."

"*You* did it." She wound her arms about his waist. "And I am so proud of you. I hope you understand that I did not doubt you."

"I think I know that now," he said with a heavy sigh.

She bit her lip. "So you are not going to beat me?"

"I should." His chest shook when he chuckled, and she squeezed him. "But I will not."

Instead, Lance did something completely out of character. He grasped her by the back of the neck, lowered his head, and set his mouth to hers in a much prayed for but unexpected assault of a sumptuous sort.

The first tantalizing touch, the first tempting taste set her skin on fire. Passion simmered in her veins, and victory echoed in her ears. When Lance engaged her tongue in a lively little duel, licking and suckling her flesh, Cara moaned, and he groaned. In a slow, sensuous grind, he shifted his hips against her, the Jolly Roger beckoned, and her knees buckled. He wanted her, and the knowledge worked on her in ways she could not have foreseen, because never had Lance been so hungry or so bold.

And, oh, what she felt.

Without thought, she slipped her hands beneath the edges of his silk robe and skimmed his chest with her palms. Arching her back, she brazenly offered herself to him.

And then he withdrew from her arms.

Struck by a tortuous desire she could neither understand nor manage, Cara shivered, and Lance swore under his breath.

"We should not be doing this." He ran his fingers through his hair and then righted his robe. "As we are friends, I have no right to force my attentions on you. In my defense, I was overcome by the achievement in my convalescence. My apologies."

"Do not be ridiculous." She reached for him, and he recoiled in an odd reversal of their respective, previous positions. "Do I appear offended?"

"Look at me." He attempted to gain his four-poster, but since he'd dropped the cane, he could not negotiate the platform on his own. "I am broken, Cara. I am no good, to you or anyone else."

"Balderdash. The sum of your worth is defined by more than a limb." She bent and retrieved the walking stick. "Here, let me help you."

"Do you see what I mean?" Lance angrily snatched the

rod from her grip. "I can't even get into my own bed without assistance. I am an old woman."

"It is only temporary, and you are not an old woman." She laughed, searching for a bit of levity to lighten his mood. "Though you certainly complain like one. But you remain, now and forever, my hero—"

"Stop calling me that." He sank to the mattress.

"Oh, no." She fluffed a pillow and adjusted his wayward robe, which bared a chiseled shoulder. "Are we back to the same tired tune?"

"Do not touch me." He slapped her wrist. "You should not be here. It is improper for you to tend me without a chaperone, and I have no need of your services."

"Shall I hire a violinist? Surely your piteous diatribe would benefit greatly from background music." Cara rolled her eyes. "And no one suspects anything nefarious."

"What does your father think?" Lance folded his arms and pouted. "He would suspect plenty were I to apprise him of our inappropriate behavior."

"What inappropriate behavior?" Cara perched on the edge of the mattress. "And if you suggest otherwise, papa will force you to marry me. I gather you are referring to a few harmless kisses?"

"I mentioned your father in abstract." Lance frowned. "And friends do not kiss."

"But we always have," she replied, recalling the pleasantly chaste endearments the Brethren shared in welcome and farewell.

"Not like that." Lance impaled her with a heated stare. "And not with tongues."

"And who is complaining." She winked. "I certainly am not. Do you regret it?"

Lance averted his gaze before answering, "Aye."

Bullet to the heart deadly precision.

"But—why?"

"Because I do not deserve you."

"What?" His was not the response she expected. "You cannot mean that."

"But I do." With his brow a mass of furrows, and his chin granite-like, at last Lance faced her. "I have taken liberties and unfairly impinged on our friendship. I sincerely apologize, Cara. It will never happen again."

Not if I can help it.

"What if I told you I was not averse to your advances?" She inclined her head and covered his hand with her own. "What if I encouraged you?"

"You are an innocent." He scoffed. "You are far too naïve to know what you want."

"And if I said I want you?" The words fell from her lips before she realized she had spoken, and it was too late to retreat. Embarrassed by her unplanned admission, Cara cursed the warmth of a blush in her cheeks.

For a brief moment, she thought she spied surprise in his green depths, but Lance recovered quickly. "You feel sorry for me, nothing more."

"And if I confessed I have felt this way for as long as I can remember?" Stung by his rejection, but refusing to concede defeat, Cara pressed her suit. "That I have admired you from afar since we were children?"

"You confuse emotions born of friendship for something more." Lance snickered. "An arena in which you have little, if any, experience."

"Such as physical relations?" she stated with an air of indifference, as if she discussed the intimate topic with regularity.

"It is called lovemaking, Cara." His frown deepened.

"And yes, my knowledge far surpasses yours. Unless you have secretly served as ladybird to some anonymous nobleman with a very voluptuous appetite."

"You know I have not." Just as she knew without doubt he intended to shock her with his scandalous statement, and she was equally certain that it was time to abandon the remaining vestiges of her prim and proper shell. "But I am willing to learn, if you are prepared to educate me."

Nonplussed, his brows nearly met his hairline. "No."

"Why not?" she asked in a small voice.

"Because you are not meant for me."

She blinked. "How can you be sure?"

"Because I said so." Lance gave vent to a groan of frustration. "And what of your mystery suitor? Were you mine, I would brook no dalliances with other men."

"Oh?" She stood and rested hands on hips. "Let me worry about my suitor."

"If he truly exists." His narrowed his stare. "I should dearly love to know his name."

"I think not."

"Cara..."

"Lance..." she mocked his sigh.

"I refuse to discuss the situation further."

"I am afraid your protests fall a tad late."

He exhaled audibly. "Then I am ceasing it this instant."

Lowering her chin, she inclined her head. "But I am not satisfied."

"You are now." Lance pointed to the door. "Leave me."

"Ah, throwing me out again?" She smiled and remained rooted to the floor.

"This is my home, my bedchamber." With a curt nod, he said, "I decide who stays or goes."

"Not this time," quick as a wink she replied.

"*Cara.*"

"No."

"You are so stubborn." He pounded a pillow. "God help me, you have always been the most intractable woman of my unfortunate acquaintance."

"Then my behavior should come as no surprise. Now, tell me why you think my regard is misplaced?"

"Because I am no good for you."

Had he denied his affection, outright and unprompted, she would have considered resigning her cause. Instead, his concerns focused only on his assessment of her supposed reaction to his advances, which she found rather curious. Yet she had not achieved victory, and she would settle for nothing less than his declaration.

"You have to give me a better reason than that."

"I do not have to do anything." His dour demeanor spoke volumes, none of which he would appreciate were he aware of her conclusions. "Take my word for it."

"I will not walk away from you." Cara paused and reconsidered her tack. If she let him, he would shut her out entirely, barring her from his company. How on earth could she entice him? "I do not know what you see when you look in the mirror, but let me tell you—"

"I am not interested."

Goodness, it was bad enough to surmount the barrier their lifelong friendship presented, but now she had to deal with his low opinion of himself. "Well, as you are a captive audience, you will just have to listen."

He glanced at the length of polished oak propped within reach. In a scarce second, she snatched the cane just as he reached for it.

"Give me the walking stick," he groused.

She thrust her chin in the air and clutched the rod to her bosom. "Not until you hear me out."

Folding his arms in front of him, Lance stared straight ahead. And he thought *she* was stubborn? Cara shook her head.

"Aside from being my dearest friend for as long as I can remember, you are trustworthy and loyal."

"So is my best hound."

"If you are going to interrupt me, this is going to take longer." She tapped her foot.

"By all means, please proceed." He gazed at the canopy.

"You are also one of the bravest men of my acquaintance. You take the worst missions for the Brethren. I know, because papa told me." She wanted to hold him, to soothe his aches, and to reassure him that all would be well in due course. "There is not a thing I could ask of you that you would not do. You are kind, noble, and generous to a fault. You would make an excellent father—"

"Father? You think I am going to marry you?" Lance laughed sarcastically. "Cara, I hate to disappoint you, but I will *never* be your husband."

"You are titled, and you must have an heir, so you must take a wife." She spread her arms wide. "Why not me?"

"Do you really have to ask? Look at me. I am half the man I used to be. Though I must wed, I will not burden you with such commitment. You mean too much to me." He halted her protest with an upraised hand. "I value our friendship, and I will not jeopardize that."

"Dearest, your condition is only temporary." Once again, it did not escape her notice that he made no denial of an attachment to her. His rejection had everything to do with his newfound handicap and nothing to do with her.

"Dr. Handley says there is every hope to believe you will be as you were. But it will not happen overnight."

"And what if he is wrong?"

"He is not wrong." She shrugged. "But neither does it matter to me."

"It matters to me," he spat in anger. "I will not saddle you with an invalid. And, if must needs, the marquessate can pass to an obscure relation, for all I care."

Was Cara mistaken, or had he just declared that, if he could not marry her, then he would never wed? How could she convince him that her devotion was unshakeable—rock solid? The answer, when it came to her, seemed so simple, yet the bold maneuver necessitated unwavering gumption. No mere kiss would suffice, as she recalled a particularly poignant exchange with Sabrina.

According to her younger sister, it was only after she bestowed upon Everett her most intimate gift that Sabrina truly considered herself Lady Markham. So it seemed only logical that, for Lance to view Cara as his wife, the circumstance required similar sacrifice. Without a word, she walked to the door.

"Finally, you have come to your senses." Lance snorted behind her. "Run away, Cara. Flee. Why should you not? You are not the cripple in this room."

The raw anguish in his voice almost halted her in her tracks, and she yearned to console him, but she remained strong and stayed her course. Appraising the weaknesses in her hastily sketched plan, she propped the cane against the wall, well beyond his reach. In her chest, her heart beat an anxious accompaniment to her padded footfalls, as she crossed the elegant master bedchamber she hoped to share some day.

All too soon, she stood before the door. With her hand

on the knob, she stared at the oak panels. She had one chance to make her play. One opportunity to stand for the man she intended to marry and the life of which she dreamed.

It was now or never.

Do or die.

In that moment, she found the key in the lock—and twisted. The bolt slid home with a definitive click. At her back, the bedchamber fell conspicuously silent, as she withdrew the embroidered kerchief from its hiding place.

Cara turned on her heel and strolled to the foot of the bed, mustering courage with each successive step. She caught his gaze, and trapped it with her own, because she required his full attention.

"So you believe yourself unworthy?"

With his brow a mass of furrows, Lance nodded once.

With trembling hands, she slipped free the top button of her bodice and then moved her nimble fingers to the second, as she smiled with hard won confidence. The kerchief dislodged from her grip and dropped to the floor, with his embroidered initials face-up, and she considered it a good omen.

"All right, my hero. Now let me show you what I think."

CHAPTER NINE

*W*ith her bodice unbuttoned, Cara inhaled a deep breath, crossed her arms, grasped the folds of her skirts, and pulled her dress over her head. It was a scene Lance had lived countless times in his dreams. But the half naked woman that stood before him was no vision, at least, in the metaphorical sense. In truth, she defined his reality and captivated his senses, in every way possible.

As he sat in bed, composing myriad protests, none of which he possessed sufficient strength to deliver, he studied every feminine curve and each subtle nuance that was uniquely Cara's. Although warnings bells pealed in his brain, and polite decorum demanded he avert his stare, he simply could not resist her allure, because the societal ingénue most of the *ton* referred to as Miss Perfect was temptation personified.

Conveying an air of unutterably endearing derring-do, she boldly met his gaze, all but challenging him to deny her, as she strolled to the side of the bed and kicked off her slippers. With a feminine smile and a charming blush, she bent a knee and rested her dainty foot on the bedside chair. When she unfastened her garter, he could have wept. But it was the slow, tortuous removal of her stockings, baring inch by glorious inch of her creamy flesh, which brought him to the brink of insanity.

At last, clad only in a sheer chemise, which left nothing to his imagination, Cara loomed at the edge of the mattress.

"Lie to me—to my face, if you dare." Then she whisked the flimsy slip of lawn from her body and stood before him as God fashioned her. "Tell me you do not want me."

A relentless tug of war raged within him, and his insides twisted and churned, as he devised one objection after another. But the beast below his belly button successfully flanked every suitable rejoinder on the limits of propriety, rendering him mute. Bloody hell, he had a broken leg—he was not dead.

"Turn around," he commanded, through a haze of raw lust, scarcely recognizing his own voice.

Whatever he had thought to say, that was not it. She did as he bade, rotating in full, leaving nothing unseen, and he committed everything about that single fragment of time to memory.

With skin of pure alabaster, ruche-tipped breasts, a trim waist, generous hips, and a sumptuously rounded bottom, Cara was indeed exquisite.

"You are so beautiful." His mouth watered.

"As are you, my hero." She favored him with a flirty grin and then bit her lip when her gaze fell on a particularly protuberant six inches of his anatomy, which stretched the confines of his silk robe and could, no doubt, support the weight of the most cumbersome sheet of canvas from his ship's rigging. But it was her next move that sent him spiraling to dangerous heights of passion.

With nary a hint of fear or hesitation, she stepped to the platform and eased to the mattress. On all fours, she crawled to him, and then she tucked her legs beneath her and sat on her ankles.

The triangle of black curls at the juncture of her thighs manifested an inexorable lure, and Lance closed his eyes. "Cara, I do not know what—"

"Shh." She slipped her hand through the opening of his robe and touched him where he wanted it most. "Please, do not fight me."

"Hell and the Reaper." Reclining in the pillows, he groaned in admiration of her decadent massage, before shifting his hips in concert with her rhythm to extend the luscious slip and slide. "How did you know?"

"Sabrina taught me," she whispered.

"She did *what*?" He caught her wrist and halted her play. "Tell me Brie's tutelage did not involve Everett."

"Of course not." She scoffed. "We used a banana. It was very educational."

"I can imagine." In his mind Lance composed a bawdy picture of the Douglas sisters engaged in their licentious labors, and he chuckled. "And I never knew you were so resourceful."

Then it struck him.

None other than Cara Felicity Douglas, the subject of his youthful fantasies, perched nude in his bed.

That singular realization worked on him in ways he could never have anticipated. As always, he recalled his failures and his guilt and mentally defined his current predicament a betrayal of his cousin's memory.

"I do not think—" All protest died in his throat when she straddled him and sank to his lap.

"Then do not think," Cara murmured against his lips.

In that instant, something inside him fractured.

The cold, dull pain of the past yielded to soothing, seductive warmth unlike any Lance had ever known. The tide turned, and in a swift move, he wrapped his arms about her waist and hauled her against him. Summoning the finesse of a lifetime, he seized control of their kiss, plundering her lips, and then laid siege to her mouth.

Given his ardent attack, he expected a modicum of resistance from the gently bred, soon-to-be ex-virgin, but she flayed the last vestiges of his defenses with her sultry surrender, and in his arms an erotic enchantress was born.

When Cara scored her nails to the back of his neck and thrust her hips in time with his movements, he groaned in appreciation of her efforts. And while he would have preferred to take his time and school her in the art of lovemaking, heaven help him, he was hungry.

"Lance, please." She sighed and then nipped his shoulder. "I am hurting."

"Come closer, sweet Cara." He cupped her bottom and guided her in preparation for his intimate invasion. "Are you sure about this? You do understand that, once I take you, I will be your only option?"

"You have always been my only option—" She gasped when he slipped a finger inside her.

"Ah, you are already wet for me." Reveling in the undeniable knowledge that she wanted him, he plumbed her moist flesh. "But what about your mystery suitor?"

"I am yours, my hero." Cara bit her lip and gave vent to a plaintive cry when he pushed deeper still. "Now and forever, I am yours."

That simple statement, six elementary words when considered on their own, but taken together as a whole a

powerful promise that set his course for a voluptuous journey. Without further equivocation, he said, "Kiss me."

In that instant, the girl of his dreams came at Lance with
an appetite that startled even him, and she would have
toppled them to the floor had they not been safely
ensconced in his bed. As their tongues met and dueled in a
fiery battle, he feared he might melt into the mattress.
Searing heat poured through his veins and pooled in his
loins, as she all but devoured him. Availing himself of the
intentional distraction, he grasped her hips and pushed her
down as he thrust, and his Jolly Roger sailed into her honey
harbor.

Cara broke their kiss and stared him straight in the eye.
For a second, he thought she might scream. Instead, she
inhaled a shaky breath and then favored him with the
loveliest smile he had ever seen.

"No going back?" she inquired, with a charming blush in
her cheeks.

He shook his head. "No going back, my lady."

"Then I am truly yours."

Her unabashedly happy expression rendered him inexpressibly bewitched. "So it seems."

With his arm as an anchor, he leaned over her and
suckled her breasts, teasing her pert nipples with playful
bites, before burying his face in the cleft of her bosom. And
Cara applauded his talents with a chorus of lusty exhala-
tions that he savored as a priceless treasure.

"You like that, do you not?" He repeated the illicit caress.

"Yes. It is—*oh*." He covered her mouth with his hand,
smothering what promised to be quite a roof-rattling
scream.

"You know, I have always wondered how you might
communicate your pleasure." He nudged her in the deca-

dent dance as old as time. "Most women either shout their exultation or convey their desire through quiet sighs."

"Indeed?" His Cara proved a fast learner, as she assumed control of their coupling, alternating between awkward pumping motions and a delicious bump and grind that left him gritting his teeth against a raucous affirmation of her abilities.

"But you present an irresistible combination of both." He brought her arms to rest on his shoulders and growled when she hugged him close.

"Is that bad?" she asked, as he rubbed his nose to hers.

"No." He clenched his jaw when she rose on her knees and then reversed her tack, slowly welcoming him anew, until his flesh seated deep within hers. "But as much as I covet your screams, today, that cannot be, as you would no doubt raise the household. Once we are wed, you may bring the walls down about us."

With something between a sob and a sigh, Cara framed his face, set her lips to his, and rode him hell bent for leather into heretofore-unrivaled bliss. And although he longed to extend the experience, because her precious gift of maidenhood was a rare jewel not to be rushed, he could not contain the emotions raging within him. When he thought he could take no more, and completion beckoned, Miss Perfect gave her cry of release into his mouth, as he surrendered to wave upon wave of pure, unadulterated pleasure.

For several unguarded minutes, they held each other, as remnants of their passion shimmered in the air as a gentle spring shower. Unwilling to relinquish his heaven on earth, he replayed their first union, again and again, in his mind. It had been fire and ice, sultry but sweet, torrid yet tender.

Indeed, their joining had been superb, exceptional enough to astonish even him.

An unholy crash reverberated from the hall, just beyond his suite, and Lance came alert in an instant.

In his lap, Cara started. "What—"

"Shh." He cradled her head, and nuzzled her, as she rested her cheek to his shoulder.

"Perhaps I should dress, before we are discovered." She shifted, rousing his still very healthy, unusually stubborn erection.

"I think not." He tilted his hips, rocking her in more ways than one, as evidenced by her uncharacteristically robust moan. "Because I want you again."

Wide-eyed, she met his stare. "Is it permissible?"

"Quite so, my dear. And I think it a tad late for concern." He could not help but chuckle at the naïveté of her query. "Trust me, you are well and thoroughly compromised, but I am fully prepared to make amends."

"Then who am I to object?" Covered in gooseflesh, Cara cast him a lopsided grin.

"Will you do something for me?" He kissed the corner of her mouth.

"My hero, you have but to ask."

"Keep your eyes open and watch us, Cara."

"I beg your pardon?" She looked her question.

"For countless nights I have envisioned you like this." With gentle prodding, he led her in a conservative cadence. "I imagined the taste of you, the softness of your body beneath mine, and the feminine cries heralding your release. And now that I have you, I want it all."

"You have dreamed of me?" she inquired with a shudder.

"For as long as I can remember." He skimmed her belly with the backs of his knuckles and then walked his fingers in a naughty path to the point of their coupling. At his first touch of the core of her desire, she dropped her head back. "Eyes open, Cara."

"Oh, Lance." Immediately, she acquiesced. "You make this very difficult for me to comply with your wishes."

"Indulge me, just this once, love."

"All right." Innumerable emotions flickered in her gaze, and she swallowed hard. "What exactly would you have of me?"

"As I said, I want you to watch us, as our bodies come together."

"You mean—where you enter me?" Her eyes flared.

"Aye."

"Is it proper?" Cara licked her lips. "Is it done?"

"You little hypocrite." For some reason Lance could not fathom, he laughed. "After your improvised but nonetheless powerful Dance of the Seven Veils, and subsequent command of my bed, you want to see us. You want to know my body as you know your own; else you would not be here. So scoot back and look your fill."

"Like this?" She shuffled her hips but did not disengage him.

"Perfect." Lance studied her face as she examined their elemental connection with unmasked enthusiasm, and in her reaction he found paradise and well nigh spilt his seed. "My flesh glistens with the proof of your arousal, Cara. You want me, as I want you. Now ride me, sugar kisses."

Slowly, methodically, he steered her into uncharted waters, nipping, sucking, licking, and stroking as he mapped her curves. Maintaining ruthless control of his own hedonistic appetite, he stoked her flame to a blazing pinnacle, only to temper his sensuous assault until the intensity abated. Again and again he repeated the tactic, and tension built in epic proportions, as he wrenched from her the affirmation he required.

Whispering praise and encouragement, he told her what she did to him—what he felt. And, oh, what he felt.

Lance was undone.

With his arms at his sides, he surrendered, stunned by the power she wielded over him. Cara framed his face with her hands and kissed him, as she seduced him with a repetitive roll of her hips. It was at once the most exquisite pleasure and the most intense frustration.

Eager to meet his fate, he clutched her hips and drove her, harder and faster, and she met him, measure for measure. As he neared the glorious peak of their union, he pressed his fingertips to the cleft of her backside and anchored her in place. With his other hand, he grasped the hair at the nape of her neck and covered her mouth with his.

Swept away in a tidal wave of passion, they rode the current. Once again, his lady lauded his expertise with a smothered shriek. As euphoria claimed him, Lance declared, "Oh, Cara, we will get on well, you and I."

WE WILL GET ON WELL?

Cara traced the wood grain of the headboard and considered Lance's statement. In truth, it was not the affirmation she had sought after a rigorous round of coitus. Given what had just occurred between them, she had anticipated a vow of eternal love and devotion—as well as a proposal of marriage.

Could the situation get any worse?

"You know, we must marry and soon." Lance rubbed her

lower back. "As I have compromised your character, I feel it is the least I can do to restore your honor."

It had just gotten worse.

"You have wide-set hips, which are excellent for begetting heirs." He stroked her hair. "And you have always possessed a healthy constitution, so we will have few concerns in regard to the birthing process."

He considered the growing of their family a birthing process? And what next would he assess, her teeth?

"In retrospect, you have done me a favor, as I shall escape the morose lunacy of courtship." He shifted beneath her. "I know you require no roses, scented handkerchiefs, or chocolates, as you are a sensible sort."

His words echoed in her ears, mocking her, and Cara shuddered and clamped her mouth shut against fast rising nausea.

"As it stands, the deed is done, and we shall have to make the best of it. We will wed as soon as I can procure a special license. As a marquess, I must uphold the social strictures governing my title and place among the peerage. It is my duty, and I vow I will not fail you."

As Lance continued his impromptu diatribe, it barely registered with Cara.

After all they had shared she expected a grand overture, though not the flowery sort delivered on bended knee, given her hero's injury. Yet, in light of their long history, she had thought he would make some mention of love. And she considered her assumptions logical and reasonable. But never had she anticipated an offer more akin to a discussion of the latest troop movements on The Continent.

His declaration, though well spoken, was born of societal ideals, gallantry, and obligation. It was the cruelest insult.

I gift you my virginity—my body, and you speak to me of providence?

Gathering her wits, and swallowing the last vestiges of her pride, she pressed her palms to his bare chest for stability, as she rose on her knees and disengaged herself from his body. A rush of warm wetness seeped from between her legs, and she cursed the telltale sting of a blush in her cheeks.

"Your connections are impeccable, and I daresay we shall be a force to be reckoned with when Parliament is in session," he stated with unimpaired aplomb.

For a while, she sat beside him, staring at his face. With indefatigable sangfroid, he laid out his case, counting the reasons on his fingers, which necessitated their hasty nuptials. Indeed, he presented his rationale with polite decorum and common sense.

Yet what they enjoyed had been the most incredible, beautiful, intimate experience of her life. Nothing about the joining of their bodies had been proper or sensible. It had been an act of love—at least, for her.

To Cara's chagrin, all too familiar words of warning sounded in her brain: *If you truly want a love match, then make sure you have engaged his heart before his ship weighs anchor in your harbor.*

At the time, her sister's admonishment had seemed uncharacteristically cautious and a tad overprotective. In the aftermath of her amorous tangle in Lance's sheets, Cara could not deny the irony of Brie's sage advice. Despite her carefully crafted plan, she had erred in her judgment. And because she refused to settle for less than her fondest hopes, she could not accept her hero's offer.

Inside, her heart shattered, scattering in invisible pieces at her feet. If she could not marry Lance, then she would forever remain a spinster, always wondering what might have been had she listened to Sabrina.

In ear-splitting silence, she retrieved her clothes and his kerchief. Donning the chemise as armor, she shielded herself from the agony of his pragmatic proposition. After slipping into her stockings, she cinched her garters and then pulled her dress over her head. Mustering the signature deportment that had never failed her, she walked to the long mirror and smoothed her wayward locks. Once fortified with her prim and proper facade, which manifested a lie of the cruelest sort, she faced him.

"So, it is agreed. We will marry in two weeks," Lance stated with grim acceptance, which almost brought her to tears. "I shall send a directive to your father requesting an immediate audience. My solicitor can have the contracts drawn in a matter of hours, and the announcement will be sent to *The Times*, tomorrow."

For good or ill, Cara set a new course. "No."

He blinked. "I beg your pardon?"

The picture of serenity, she strolled to the middle of the bedchamber. "I said no."

"To what?" With an arched brow, he cleared his throat. "Have I missed something of importance?"

"You might be surprised." Gazing at the floor, she mulled her circumstances. How could she make him understand her position without revealing her reasons? "I cannot marry you."

"What?" His mouth fell agape, but he quickly snapped it shut. "You must be joking."

"Actually, I am quite serious." She lowered her chin and inclined her head. "As it is, I do not comprehend the fuss."

"Cara, there is no time for a proper courtship. If there were, I would gladly do the pretty for all to see." Lance belted his robe and eased to the edge of the mattress. "Given our exercise for the better part of the afternoon, you could very well be carrying my heir. I will brook no doubts to its legitimacy."

"Stuff and nonsense." She managed a giggle. "You make too much of the situation, but that is your nature. I am sure there is no cause for alarm, because we did it only once."

"Twice." He held up two fingers, as if she could not count. "And once is enough."

"I grant you that." She shuffled her feet. "But it is still no reason to marry."

"How can you be so obtuse?" He speared his fingers through his hair. "I have ruined you. Do you not recall my admonition prior to claiming your maidenhead? You cannot take another to the altar. I am your only option."

"Perhaps I do not wish to wed, and I did not require such commitment to give myself to you." She shrugged. "If I indicated otherwise, I am sorry."

"Then you should not have come to my bed." He stood, leaning on the mattress for support. "You are mine."

"I am my own person." Cara clutched a fist to her bosom. "And I will not marry you."

"You will do as I say." He clung to the footboard.

"I will not." She retreated, nearing the door to the chamber. "What we did was pass a pleasant afternoon in each other's company. Nothing more."

"Excuse me?" Grasping the frame of the four-poster, Lance limped to the corner of the platform. "We made love, Cara. I breached you."

"Yes, we did. And I thank you for the enlightenment." She drew herself up with the noble hauteur of the daughter of an admiral. "I learned a good deal today." *More than I wanted to know.*

"My dear, you must be in shock, as you are clearly not thinking."

"But I am." She had to remain calm. "Furthermore, I impinged on our friendship. For that, I am truly sorry. It will not happen again."

"Why do you not ring for tea, my girl?" Lance reached for her. "Let us discuss our future, at length."

"That is not necessary, as I believe I see the situation better than you, old friend." She smiled, as she had to stay strong. "And your actions do you great credit."

"Cara, there are consequences to our actions." He sighed, and she fought the urge to console him. "If you refuse to accept my terms, then you leave me little choice. I will have to speak with your father."

"Go ahead." She picked a speck of lint from her dress. "He will not force me to marry you."

"Oh, no?" He frowned. "How can you be sure?"

"When Lord Markham compromised Sabrina, my father did not compel her to wed," she explained. "He left the decision to her. It serves to reason he will afford me the same courtesy."

"I would wager Everett's infraction was nowhere near egregious as mine." Lance's stare fixed on the walking stick, which rested on the floor. "Would you be so kind as to hand me my cane?"

"But I must away." She shook her head and palmed the doorknob. "It has been an eventful day, and you should sleep, as you missed your nap."

"Cara, stay—please." He flicked his fingers in entreaty, and she gave him her back before she weakened. "Come, let us talk things over."

"I must go—now." If she went to him, if she allowed him to touch her, she would never have the courage to do what needed to be done. "And given your improvement, you no longer have need of my assistance. My presence will only impede your progress, so I wish you well with your continued recovery, Lance."

With that, Cara exited the chamber—but not his life.

She would retrench. And when the time was right, she would stand for her man. She may have lost the opening battle, but she would win the war.

CHAPTER TEN

"*D*earest, you have callers."

Engrossed in her embroidery, Cara flinched, pricked her finger, and then peered at her mother. "I am still not feeling quite myself. Could you explain that I am not at present receiving callers, and convey my regrets?"

"Of course."

Cara returned her attention to her needlework and, for the third time, pierced her flesh. "Ouch."

It had been a week since the incident, as she privately referred to her encounter with Lance. On pain of a cold, which she faked admirably with a sniff here and a sneeze there, she had been excused from the few galas and dinners that signaled the beginning of the Little Season. With Parliament in session, London once again bustled with *tonnish* activity.

And uncharacteristically, she wanted nothing to do with it.

Instead, Cara secluded herself in her bedchamber. Alex

had visited once, Sabrina twice. Cara pled fear of exposing them to her illness and refused to grant an audience.

Call her a coward, but she could not face her sister or her friend with such shame. And given that she had confided in both, concerning her campaign to win Lance, she fretted they would have a litany of questions, for which she had no answer. When she was certain she could meet their inquiries with unreserved equanimity, she would welcome their company.

Never would she divulge the truth.

Her love had been unrequited and her affection denied. Nor would she admit the extent of her ruin. They would not know she had resorted to seduction in a desperate attempt to claim the man she loved.

On the thought, Cara closed her eyes, lowered her head, and tamped the ever-encroaching tears. Crying had benefited her greatly, rendering her nose red and puffy, and her parents mistook her malady for the cold of which she complained. When the door opened, she reached for her handkerchief to maintain the pretense.

"Why are you avoiding us?" With a frown, Sabrina tapped her foot.

Cara was positive she would swoon.

Poised behind her younger sister, Alex adopted a similar stance, along with Caroline and Rebecca, and Cara knew her goose was well and truly cooked.

"I do not know what you mean." Inwardly, Cara cursed herself and her shaky voice. "I was concerned for your health. With the babe coming, I did not want to risk infecting you and my future niece or nephew."

With the door secured, Sabrina, Alex, Caroline, and Rebecca stood before Cara as immovable sentries, with arms folded imperiously in front of them.

"And I see no reason to contaminate Alex, Caroline, or Rebecca." Suspicious in an instant, and with nerves on edge, Cara babbled. "How fares the weather?"

Her sisters remained silent.

"Mama told me you called." She set aside her silks and smoothed her skirts. "And I am grateful for your regard, but it is not necessary, as I improve every day."

They uttered not a word.

"So, how are you?" Cara wrung her fingers in front of her, and her heart beat a rapid salvo in her chest. "Heard any gossip? Any new on-dits?"

The chamber remained quiet as a tomb.

"No? Well, you need not worry about me." Cara thought the room unseasonably warm, and she searched the immediate vicinity for her fan. "I assure you I am quite at my leisure."

A pin drop would have reverberated throughout her quarters.

"This has nothing to do with Lance," she blurted.

"Ah-ha!" Sabrina waddled to the *chaise* and plopped to the cushion. "I knew it. What happened? Did he propose? When are you getting married?"

"Did everything go as planned?" Alex bounced with giddy excitement. "Did he declare himself?"

Caroline and Rebecca exchanged a surreptitious glance, and gooseflesh covered Cara from head to toe. Did they suspect her? Did they discern her shame? To calm her trembling, she clasped her hands in her lap.

"Sister, what did you do?" Sabrina offered a half-hug of support. "Tell us the latest developments."

For a few desperate seconds, Cara considered her predicament and Lance's rejection. Despite efforts to conceal the truth, a traitorous tear belied her tremulous state, and she sniffed.

"Oh, dear." Sabrina caressed her round belly. "Alex, would you ask Mama to send us a tray? I, for one, would love some shortbread. And perhaps some chamomile tea?"

"All right." Alex paused before the door. "But do not say anything interesting until I return."

"You have my word." Sabrina waved. When the hinges creaked and the latch clicked, she turned to Cara. "Now, out with it."

"Why did you invite Caroline and Rebecca?" To her life-long friends, Cara said, "I mean no insult, but this is such a personal matter, and I had hoped to keep it secret."

"Of course, it is." Caroline pouted. "But we understand your situation, as we have been there, ourselves."

"And you need the reinforcements," Brie stated.

"You made love to him," Rebecca declared.

It was a statement, not a question.

Caroline gasped.

For a scarce second, denial traipsed her tongue, but Cara desperately needed their help. So she nodded an affirmative, and then doubled over, buried her face in her hands, and succumbed to inestimable grief, which gushed as a roaring river of tears. "Oh, do not tell Alex. I cannot bear it."

"We will say nothing, I promise." Sabrina stroked Cara's hair. "She could not comprehend the intimacy involved."

"So the deed is done?" Caroline inquired in a small voice.

"Physical relations complicate everything," Rebecca stated grimly.

"Yes, and you should have heard him. After all that we shared, he proposed marriage." She sobbed. "It was awful."

"Wait a minute." Sabrina sat upright. "Lance proposed?"

Cara dipped her chin.

"Then why are you crying?" With unabashed enthusiasm, Sabrina chucked Cara on the shoulder. "That is wonderful news. We must begin wedding preparations, posthaste."

Though well intended, her younger sister's words only compounded Cara's sorrow. Drowning in misery, she wailed even louder.

"Hold hard, Brie." Caroline frowned. "Cara, what are you not telling us?"

Dragging her sleeve across her eyes, in an unforgivable breach of decorum, Cara hiccuped. "After we—you know—he said we *had* to get married. He said he compromised me and *owed* it to me."

"Damn fool." Rebecca humphed. "He is no different than the rest."

"You know, men are not stupid." Caroline grimaced. "They just behave very stupidly."

"Which makes us want to kill them," Sabrina added.

"With an ax," Rebecca chimed.

"Oh, good one, Becca." Caroline stretched her legs, as the Brethren wives giggled in concert.

"Ladies, focus, please." Cara wiped her nose. "I am in a terrible fix."

"Of course, you are." Sabrina huffed a breath. "After I warned you not to skin his rabbit before you secured his declaration, you ignored my advice."

"Easy, Brie. We are none of us perfect." Rebecca hugged a pillow. "Who are we to judge, given our own mistakes?"

"And just what do you infer?" Sabrina narrowed her stare. "Everett did not weigh anchor in my harbor until we were properly wed, and I presume the same can be said for both of you."

Rebecca peered at Caroline. In unison, they blinked.

"I do not believe it." Sabrina stood and stomped a foot. "Am I to understand that I, alone, waited until the vows were spoken to surrender my maidenhead? Sisters, I am disappointed in you."

"Well, in all fairness, Trevor kidnapped me." Caroline snapped her fingers. "And he thought me a courtesan, so he chased my skirts from when first we met. How could I resist?"

"And what is your excuse?" Sabrina arched a brow.

To wit Rebecca shrugged and stated, "I was a spy."

"You dare call me a rebel." Brie shook her head. "And I am the only one who observed all strictures in obeisance of societal expectations."

"Well, mine was a precarious position, as I pursued a lethal traitor, you know." Rebecca fidgeted in her chair. "So I had no choice but to seduce Dirk, else I might have forever lost my chance."

Again, an appreciable ensemble of shock filled the air, and Cara was grateful for the distraction.

The door to the chamber opened, and Alex made a grand entry, with the butler in tow bearing a tray laden with plates of shortbread, teacakes, and a small pot. After the manservant quit the room, Alex lifted the delicate porcelain and poured the hot tea.

As she passed a cup to Cara, the younger Seymour frowned. "You started without me."

"No, we did not." Sabrina swiped a square of shortbread from the plate. "She is just upset."

"Sorry, Alex." Cara examined the steaming liquid. "I suppose I am a tad emotional."

"Do not apologize." Alex settled in a Hepplewhite chair. "Now then, tell us what happened with Lance."

"Where should I begin?" Cara bit her lip and glanced at Sabrina. "Well, things did not turn out quite as I had hoped."

"I believe I guessed that." With elbows resting on her thighs, Alex leaned forward. "Did you kiss him again?" she asked with a wistful expression.

"Again?" Sabrina inquired, her countenance one of surprise.

"Oh, dear." Cara averted her gaze and tried not to spill her tea. Never had she intended to share her humiliation with the full compliment of the Brethren women, save Elaine.

"Oops." Alex covered her mouth with her hand. "I had assumed you told Sabrina."

"Told me—what? You confided in her and not me?" Sabrina snorted. "But I am your sister."

"She is my sister, too," Alex argued.

"But she is mine by birth," Sabrina responded, quick as a wink.

"Ladies, please." Rebecca scooted to the edge of her seat. "We are here for Cara's sake and to bring another man low."

"Becca is right." Caroline pointed for emphasis. "We must not fight each other, as we are not the enemy."

"Precisely." Rebecca smacked a fist to a palm. "Our adversary is the male sex, a being of superior physical strength but a vast deal inferior mental acumen."

"This is dreadful." Cara closed her eyes and rubbed her temples. "I should have kept my feelings to myself. Or perhaps I should concede defeat."

"What?"

"You can't mean that."

"Do not give up."

"Lance is a dolt."

"You must keep at him."

Her sisters fired one rebuttal after another.

"*Enough!*" Cara cursed the burn of a blush in her cheeks. "I cannot think straight."

"Dearest, now I know you are truly out of sorts, as never have I seen you so discomposed." Sabrina returned her cup to the tray. "How, exactly, did Lance propose?"

Alex shot out of her chair. "He proposed!"

Sabrina silenced her with a glare of reproach.

"Forgive my outburst." With lips pursed, Alex sat. "Pray, continue."

"Well, let me explain." Cara inhaled deeply. "After we...kissed, he said he had compromised me and would marry me to restore my honor. He called it his duty."

"Men." Sabrina snickered. "They are always the last to know they are in love. Why, I had to abandon my Everett to make him realize how much he adored me. Now he can't live without me. Blasted idiots, the lot of them."

"I could not agree more, because it took my near-drowning for Trevor to declare himself," Caroline added with a sympathetic expression.

Then Cara gazed at Rebecca, who seemed atypically reticent. At last, Dirk's wife sighed and said, "My no-nonsense captain professed his love on our wedding night."

Sabrina's mouth fell agape. "The devil, you say."

"How wonderful," Alex replied.

"And I am positive we can induce Lance to make his testimonial in similar fashion, if not before the vows have been spoken. You know, what we need is a diversion."

Rebecca tapped a finger to her chin. "Something dramatic to force Lance to commit his heart and proclaim his devotion."

A dark sense of foreboding blanketed her in impenetrable gloom, and Cara shuddered. How she coveted hope, yet she had stood at that precipice and lost. So she was a tad battle shy, and with good reason. "I beg your pardon?"

"Precisely." Sabrina slapped her thigh. "But what?"

"Excuse me." Cara tried but failed to intervene.

"I do not know." Alex stared at the ceiling. "But it has to grab his attention. We must find a way to center his regard unreservedly on Cara."

"Bring him to his knees." Caroline wrinkled her nose. "It serves him right, as the silly fool knows no other way."

"Caroline is correct," Sabrina said with a curt nod. "We must rip out his heart."

"Rip out his heart?" Cara gulped. "But I do not want to hurt—"

"I have got it!" Rebecca exclaimed.

"What?" Caroline, Alex, and Sabrina inquired in unison. Cara was not sure she wanted to know their plan.

Rebecca smiled, a cat that ate the canary smile, and lowered her chin. "What we need is competition."

"You can't be serious." Cara thought she might swoon. "You must be joking."

"Gather round, my pretty friends." With a flick of her wrist, Rebecca drew them near. "What is the one thing guaranteed to bring a hesitant suitor to the altar?"

"Another man," Caroline answered with confidence. "You are a bloody genius, Becca."

"Exactly," Sabrina said with a cluck of her tongue. "All we need do is secure another candidate for Cara's hand."

"I have never heard such nonsense." Cara sipped her tea and feigned disinterest. "And where would we find someone to aid our cause? The only males of our acquaintance are Brethren. The married ones are out of the question, and Lance would not believe for a minute that Blake, Damian, or Dalton had suddenly developed a tendre for me."

Recognition dawned in Alex's expression, and she snapped to attention. "I know a contender we could enlist."

"Who?" Sabrina inclined her head.

"Captain Collingwood," Alex stated with unchecked enthusiasm.

"Do you think he will help us?" Rebecca queried.

"Indeed." With a sly smile, Alex boldly pronounced, "He will if I ask him."

"Now, you wait in here until I send Conrad for you." Alex shuffled Cara into the study at Seymour House.

"If you insist." In a flash, Cara whirled about and gasped. "Do you really believe this is going to work?"

"Indubitably. Be brave, my dear. Remember, you are doing this for love." Alex placed a sisterly kiss on Cara's cheek and gave her a hug. "And ours is a sound scheme—we cannot fail. I mean, what could go wrong?"

"Alex, if he is unwilling, do not press him." Cara clenched and unclenched her fists. "I cannot bear further embarrassment."

"Do not worry." She winked. "I predict that with my special brand of persuasion, he will be very cooperative."

Alex pulled the door shut behind her, leaving Cara quite alone with her thoughts, none of which brought her comfort. Resolved to make the best of her situation, she perched in one of the high-back chairs arranged in a half-circle before the large desk, sat upright, crossed her legs, and tucked her feet as she'd been taught. It had been a long time since she'd ventured into the man's domain of the great home.

As children, whenever their parents gathered at Seymour House, her generation of Brethren had cloistered amid the leather wall coverings and faint smell of cigar smoke. Of course, the boys had taken turns sitting behind the impressive, hand-tooled appointment, pretending to be lord of the manor, to which the girls played chatelaine.

For some reason, whenever Lance positioned himself in the formidable chair at the head of the room, Cara always portrayed his lady. She had no idea when the child's fancy had ended, and love—true love, had blossomed.

She'd tried to talk some sense into herself once Alex, Sabrina, Caroline, and Rebecca had departed her home. Their plan seemed foolhardy at best and a useless humiliation at worst. Regardless of her feelings, and her Brethren sister's good intentions, Lance might never see her as anything more than a friend.

She drew the embroidered kerchief from her bodice, kissed the initials, and spread the linen square in her lap.

For her fifteenth birthday, her father had purchased a lovely mare, and Lance taught her to ride. On their first outing in the park, the wind had unexpectedly blown from the west, and a speck of dust brought a tear to her eye. Ever the knight of her dreams, her gallant hero had sidled close, offered her the embroidered swatch, and bent his head to tend her. What she had not expected was the briefest brush of his lips to hers. Indeed, that moment reigned supreme as the most precious birthday present of her life.

Even then, in her heart and mind, she conjured the power of his touch, his gentle caresses, as a permanent brand on her consciousness. As long as she lived, no man would ever supplant Lance. She belonged to him.

And he belonged to her.

"I beg your pardon, Miss Douglas." Conrad, the butler, interrupted her thoughts. "Lady Alex awaits you in the drawing room."

Trembling with excitement mixed with fear, Cara strolled the long hallway, navigated the cavernous foyer, and waited with the patience of a saint as a footman opened the door. Well nigh suffocating in anxiety, she stepped into the sea green colored room.

Captain Collingwood cast Cara a furtive glance. From their position, it was evident what form of persuasion Alex had chosen to sway her admirer. With flushed cheeks and kiss-swollen lips, Alex batted her lashes and giggled, as Captain Collingwood whispered in her ear.

Standing stock-still, Cara bit her lip. "If I am interrupting, I can come back."

"Nonsense." Alex smiled brilliantly and gazed at her captain. "I was just telling Jason about your dilemma, and he has gallantly offered to come to your rescue."

"Well," Captain Collingwood said, as he shifted his weight, "I am not entirely sure how I may be of use, but I shall be too happy to provide assistance."

"Oh, Jason." Alex nudged the naval man in a manner that breached the limits of acceptable deportment for a lady of character, but Cara held her tongue against reproach. "As I explained, our poor Miss Douglas was ill-treated by a fickle suitor who availed himself of her affections and then refused to marry her."

"Oh, I say." Captain Collingwood canted his head. "Am I to call out the blackguard?"

"*No.*" Cara clutched her throat and swallowed hard, certain she would faint at any moment. In truth, she did not know what shocked her more—their hastily sketched plot or Alex's behavior.

"My dearest Captain, what a credit you are to your sex." Alex cupped his cheek, commanding his attention. "But such a grand gesture is unnecessary, as we believe the man worthy of her hand and therefore redeemable. He simply lacks proper motivation."

"Indeed." He arched a brow. "I gather that is the part I am to play?"

"We need you to dance attendance upon Cara, and escort her to dinner. It is our hope that her wayward suitor would be inclined to make an offer were he in competition with another." Alex averted her gaze. "After all, what would you do in similar circumstances?"

"You mean, if some bloody aristocrat spent too much time sniffing your skirts?" His expression sobered, and his features were granite-like. "I would rip out his noble throat with my teeth."

Alex gasped but quickly regained her composure, and Cara stifled a snort.

"I would consider it a personal favor, Jason," the younger Seymour said in a hushed tone. "Of course, I require your utmost discretion."

He nodded once. "You shall have it, my lady."

Their exchange simmered with sensuous undertones, and Cara thought of Lance. Why could he not have shown similar amorous fervor after they made love? Cara was certain that, had Damian's sister asked, the impressive

Collingwood would have fallen at Alex's feet and kissed her toes.

Alex favored Jason with a heated glance. "I will be *very* grateful."

Captain Collingwood smiled, and although he spoke to Cara, his stare remained fixed on Alex. "Miss Douglas, I am at your service."

AS HIS CARRIAGE approached the entrance to the stately townhouse on Upper Brook Street, Lance scrutinized his appearance. Unwilling to admit to himself or anyone else that he was more than a little nervous at the prospect of attending his first social function since his injury, he sighed and sank into the squabs.

To his relief, the occasion was a private dinner party at the home of his mentor, Admiral Douglas. The Brethren, his lifelong friends, were among the invited guests, as well as a few elders. Of course, the opportunity to see Cara figured heavily in his decision to accept the invitation.

She had not graced his home with her presence since the afternoon they shared his bed. In a flash, vivid memories flooded his mind, and his skin tingled, as delicious heat poured through his loins. A sumptuous chorus of feminine cries filled his ears, sugar kisses teased his tongue, and his fingertips itched as he recalled Cara's velvety soft flesh. How he longed to take her in his arms and—

"Are you in pain, Lance?"

He came alert in an instant. Seated across from him, Elaine pouted, with a look of concern on her face. He cleared his throat and tugged at his cravat. "I am fine. Why do you ask?"

"From your expression, I thought you discomfited." His young cousin shook her head and cast him a lopsided grin. "Perhaps it is too soon for you to socialize."

"Nonsense." He clutched the walking stick at his side and mustered a smile. "I can't stay locked in my bedchamber for the remainder of my days."

The carriage halted suddenly.

"We are here." Elaine bubbled with excitement as the footman handed her to the pavement.

Much to his displeasure, Lance required assistance as he descended his equipage. In the doorway, Admiral Douglas stood with arms outstretched in welcome.

"Well, well, what have we here?" The venerable naval legend gave Elaine a fatherly hug, bent to receive her peck on his cheek, and then he turned to Lance. "Good to see you up and about, my boy."

As they exchanged a hearty back slap, Lance chuckled. "I must say it is good to be seen, Sir."

"The ladies are in the drawing room." The admiral retreated a step. "We will join them in a moment, but we have some business to conduct before we commence our celebration of your return."

Following years of engrained custom as a member of the Brethren of the Coast, Lance veered to the right and limped down the hall, as he mulled the reason for the impromptu meeting. Still, it was comforting to resume some semblance of normalcy in his life. At the door to the study, he rapped softly before entering the strategic headquarters of the Nautionnier Knights descended of the Templars. In the familiar half-circle of matching high-back chairs sat his brothers.

With one unexpected addition.

Captain Jason Collingwood, of the Royal Navy, occupied

Lance's usual seat. The tall, blonde, burly man stood as Lance and Admiral Douglas approached. Collingwood greeted Lance with an outstretched hand and a smile, which for some reason he could not discern he did not trust. "Lord Raynesford, I am pleased to see you making such a speedy recovery."

To his annoyance, Lance tried but failed to stave off the unease dancing a merry jig down his spine. Why had Captain Collingwood been invited into the private domain of the Brethren?

"Lance, why do you not sit here?" Blake stood. "It will serve me well to stretch my legs."

"My apologies," Captain Collingwood replied. "I believe I unfairly usurped your place."

"No, do not bother." Lance shuffled to the rear. "I assure you, I am fit stand."

"Don't be ridiculous, Lance." Admiral Douglas patted him on the shoulder. "Assume your position, as the good captain will be on his knees soon enough."

"I beg your pardon?" The world shifted beneath his feet, as Lance divined the implication of the admiral's statement. The Brethren of the Coast were about to induct a new member into the notorious, much-rumored band of Nautionnier Knights.

But why?

That was not to suggest Lance harbored ill will toward the estimable mariner, because he had nothing but admiration for the naval man's acumen. Rather, he did not comprehend the need to increase the number of Brethren.

As the knights assumed their usual formation, Captain Collingwood reclined on the sofa, and Admiral Douglas situated himself behind his formidable desk and steepled his hands on the leather blotter.

"Gentlemen, as you know, the tide has turned in our war with France. Wellington enjoyed marked success with victories at Ciudad Rodrigo, Badajoz, and Salamanca." The admiral compressed his lips. "However, those campaigns exacted a high cost to His Majesty's troops, so it is imperative we continue to feed reinforcements into Wellington's army. That being said, the injury to one of our own could not have come at a more inopportune moment, thus the Lord High Admiral has decided that we are in dire need of an addition to our ranks."

A collective of agreement graced every face—save two.

Lance swallowed the bitter pill of pride as he realized his was the weakest link in their heretofore-impenetrable chain of defense.

And Captain Collingwood shifted, his visage invested with more than vague curiosity as he asked, "An addition to —what?"

As Admiral Douglas launched into the history of the notorious but noble order, Lance drowned in a sea of apprehension and incompetence. How he wanted to refute the impression that he lacked the ability to command his ship, yet he recalled his conversation with Cara and his assertions to that effect. In his mind he revisited her counter-arguments and drew strength from her, even then.

At that instant, Captain Collingwood accepted the seal of the order. The impressive badge, fashioned of gold, bore the familiar shape of an eight-point wind-star, the compass of ancient seafarers. A large, ocean-blue diamond twinkled at the center, and beneath was inscribed the Latin phrase *Nulli Secundus*, Second to None.

With a large ceremonial sword in his grasp, the same magnificent weapon used to inaugurate Lance into the exclusive knighthood, Admiral Douglas rounded his desk.

Collingwood knelt, and the admiral tapped the flat of the blade to either shoulder. In mere seconds, Sir Jason Collingwood was born. Uttering a silent rebuke for wallowing in self-pity, Lance mustered a smile and mentally sketched a hastily composed reception for his new brother mariner.

"You do realize that your maiden undertaking is to gift us a case of your finest brandy?" Lance extended a hand in fraternal kinship.

"Correction," Blake interrupted. "That would be a case for each of us."

"And a box of your best cigars," Damian added.

"Bloody hell, am I to sell my rig to finance the order?" Jason asked with a chuckle.

"Oh, nothing so grand." Dalton tossed his lucky coin. "Heads. You are most fortunate, as your mistress will suffice or, perhaps, your heir."

"You should know they tried to abscond with my son." Trevor grimaced. "They took him just after the christening."

"Given that you kidnapped my sister, be glad you retain the ability to sire children," Blake chimed with a wink. "And it was only to conduct our own ceremony, of sorts, to herald the next generation of Brethren."

"Blister it, Rylan, are we sailing that route again?" Trevor elbowed Blake in the ribs. "And it was not so much the initiation with which I took issue but Caroline's wrath upon our return, as you placed responsibility for the prank squarely on my shoulders."

"Is that not what marriage is all about?" Blake snorted. "One row after another?"

"Heed my warning, Collingwood." Dirk arched a brow. "If you take their lip now, there will be no end to your torment."

"Gentlemen, you do me great honor, and I can only hope to fulfill your expectations. But how can I help?" Collingwood inquired. "The *Intrepid* is dry-docked for refitting."

"Ah, yes. That is a problem." Admiral Douglas caught Lance in his sights. "Given repairs to the *Demetrius* are almost complete, I had wondered if you would consent to let us borrow her—until you are able to resume command."

Once again, the world shifted beneath his feet, and Lance shuddered. Let another man captain his ship? Everything inside him screamed against it, because that was akin to surrendering his woman for a night. And, Brethren or not, he shared Cara with no man.

But just as quick, he reminded himself that he would not so much as blink were it Blake, Damian, Dirk, Dalton, or Trevor posing the request to borrow his vessel. How could he balk? The answer was simple. He could not refuse the newest entrant of the order.

"Do me a favor." Lance shifted his weight and turned to Jason. "Take care of her."

"Lord Raynesford, you have my word as a gentleman, I shall sail her as if she were my own," Collingwood responded.

"There are no titles here, brother." Lance compressed his lips and rued the stress investing his frame. After all, it was not as if the blonde giant had asked to court Cara. "When we gather as family—and the badge marks you as such, it is Lance."

"Lance, it is." Jason smiled and nodded once.

After a rousing bit of ribald toasts, the knights joined the ladies in the drawing room, and it could not have happened soon enough for Lance, because that always meant the same thing. He alone enjoyed the undivided attention of one Miss Douglas. As he limped into the elegantly appointed chamber, he held his breath until he found the object of his quest. And as usual, his heart skipped a beat at the first sight of Cara.

Gowned in rich navy satin, with her hair piled in countless curls atop her head, she cut the perfect picture of feminine sensuality, and familiar heat pooled in his loins. But in that moment he seemed powerless to move, as he knew well what sumptuous treasure hid beneath the polite façade and polished veneer.

At the far end of an emerald damask sofa she sat in graceful repose, and he paused in anticipation of her acknowledgement. Painful seconds ticked past as he awaited the ebullient greeting she never failed to bestow upon him, but none came.

Instead, to his exasperation, she leaped into the arms of Collingwood, after her father announced, "Distinguished guests, we have a new knight in our midst."

Just what was she about? Lance frowned, as a green-eyed monster of an unfamiliar and altogether unpleasant sort reared its ugly head, and then he muttered a silent curse at the blasted cane in his left hand.

"I beg your pardon." The butler loomed in the doorway. "Dinner is served."

At last, things would return to normal. Lance stepped forward and opened his mouth, and then clamped it shut, when the dark blue of a navy uniform passed before him in a flash, cutting short his approach.

"May I have the honor of escorting you, Miss Douglas?"

The words came to him as though from afar, which seemed quite odd, as Lance had uttered them on occasions too numerous to count. The only problem was he was not the one who had spoken.

With the effervescence Cara typically reserved for

Lance, she proclaimed, "I assure you, Captain Collingwood, the honor is mine."

Paralyzed by a lethal combination of anger, uncertainty and, dare he think it, fear, Lance clenched his jaw as Jason availed himself of Cara's company. The man had taken Lance's position among the Brethren, command of his ship, and worst of all, his lady.

CHAPTER ELEVEN

*L*ost in a seemingly endless chasm of self-pity, Lance was the last to enter the elegant dining room. Without thought, he hobbled to his customary place at Cara's side. But to his infinite irritation, he discovered his seat already occupied.

"Hope you do not mind." Jason grinned. "We switched name cards and put you down there." He pointed to the far end of the table. "You are beside Dalton."

Wonderful. Lance forced a smile, limped to his chair, and spent the better part of the meal enduring the explicit tales of Dalton's latest conquest. As the gadling launched into his most recent escapade, which stretched the limits of believability, Lance afforded the younger Randolph the occasional nod and chuckled in concert to maintain the illusion that he listened to every bawdy detail, because every fiber of Lance's being focused on Cara.

The soft lilt of her voice, and her rich, unfeigned laughter called to him as a sultry summons impossible to deny. With furtive glances he sought her regard, yearning for some indication or affirmation, however slight, that he remained her hero. But it was as if he no longer existed, and that hurt.

Sadness and despair shrouded his world in cold darkness, as he realized how making love to Cara had impacted their relationship, but never could he have predicted utter indifference. It was like losing Thomas, all over again. Only now he would have to reconstruct his life without Cara if he could not induce her to accept his proposal. Had what occurred between them meant nothing to her?

As the elders withdrew to the drawing room, which was their custom, the Brethren reshuffled themselves at the center of the large table. Spying a vacant seat at Cara's left, Lance made a beeline for it.

The topic of conversation centered on the new addition to the Brethren. Acting completely out of character, Lance participated with profuse enthusiasm in the animated discourse. To his inexpressible frustration, Cara managed to keep her back to him, as she favored Jason with her face and attention.

Unable to bear her apathy any longer, Lance searched for some excuse to initiate a conversation. He supposed he could tickle her, but that would garner an audience of all present. And then he noted her clasped hands resting in her lap, which the tablecloth partially shielded. Assuming an air of nonchalance, he skimmed her clothed thigh and then set his palm to her gloved knuckles.

Cara didn't so much as flinch.

So next he squeezed her fingers, and at length she turned to him. For a fleeting moment, he spied pain in her blue gaze, but she masked it in polite gentility.

At long last, she smiled. "How are you?"

Once again, Lance was taken aback. The warmth, the unabashed fervor noticeably absent in her voice and demeanor, it was as though she conversed with a stranger. Shocked by the emptiness of her response, he could muster only a one-word reply. "Fine."

"Delighted to hear it," she stated with a blank stare.

"So..." He fumbled for something to say—anything to hold her interest. "H-how are you?"

"Quite well, thank you." She maintained the same unremarkable expression.

"Cara, please, talk to me." He wiped his suddenly damp palms on his napkin and reminded himself he was no dandy fop or shy schoolboy. He had bedded enough sophisticated women in his life that no barely ex-virgin debutante should bring him to his knees. "We must settle our situation."

"There is nothing to discuss," she whispered. Then, in a brilliant flanking maneuver, she nudged Jason. "I am so looking forward to the events of the Little Season, Captain Collingwood."

"Please, call me Jason." The fledgling Nautionnier Knight canted his head. "And may I be so bold as to address you as Cara?"

No, you most certainly may not, Lance thought.

"Of course." She giggled, and Lance wanted to puke.

Again relegated to the position of spectator, he fought to remain calm and at least appear to enjoy the evening. But inside he wanted to kill someone.

Specifically, Captain Jason Collingwood.

So he sat, without ceremony, simmering and seething in silence, until the Brethren gathered with the elders in the drawing room. But if he thought the situation in the dining room had been an exercise in futility, what awaited Lance brought him to the brink of insanity.

Engaging Cara in an awkward game of cat and mouse,

he literally chased her in circles about the sofa. Of course, due to his injury, he rarely neared her skirts before she skittered beyond reach. And in the singular instance he caught his prey, Alex and Sabrina loomed at either side, as though rooted to the bloody floor. Gnashing his teeth and leashing his temper, he joined the ladies, suffering such titillating topics as stain removal and teething remedies.

"You know, I am honor bound to save you from yourself," Everett stated in a low voice and then chuckled. "If for no other reason than to spare myself the painful performance of your prurient pursuit."

"I beg your pardon?" Lance sniffed and ignored the inference. "I know of no such prurient pursuit."

"And you deny it." Markham had the nerve to wink. "A sure sign that another man has been felled by perfume and petticoats."

"Blister it, Everett—"

"Oh, give over." Sabrina's husband rocked on his heels and smirked. "Come. You need a drink."

"In that I will not argue." In Everett's wake, Lance devised a rebuttal and hobbled to the back wall. "Brother, I believe you have woven unsupported conclusions from whole cloth."

"Of course, I have." Everett offered a brandy.

"No, I mean it." He gulped a healthy portion of liquid courage. "You have mistaken lifelong friendship for something of greater importance."

"My apologies." Everett arched a brow. "So tell me, how long have you harbored undying devotion for the elder Miss Douglas?"

Lance opened and then closed his mouth.

Everett burst into laughter.

"You are sworn to secrecy, else you will never gaze on your firstborn."

"Now I resent that, Lance. Really, I do."

"And you may not divulge my confidence to Sabrina."

"Do I look like a brainless nincompoop?"

"Bloody hell. How did you know?" Lance scratched his temple. "What gave me away?"

"You can't be serious."

"Am I that obvious?"

"Indubitably."

"Hell and the Reaper." His head spun, and Lance swayed.

"Whoa, friend." Everett provided much needed support and kept Lance upright. "May I impart a bit of sage advice? Mind you, I speak as the veteran of three wicked tours of duty."

"Three?"

"The Battles of Caroline, Rebecca, and my own darling Sabrina." Everett shuffled his feet. "Brother, I could tell you stories that would turn your hair white. Instead, I would share the secret guaranteed to solve all your problems."

"And that would be—what?"

"Tell her you love her," Trevor inserted into the conversation.

Lance choked on his brandy. "Does everyone suspect me?"

"Sorry Raynesford." Trevor chortled. "Did not intend to startle you, but I could not help but overhear your exchange, and as I am only too familiar with that delicate but nonetheless volatile brand of warfare genteel society has the unmitigated audacity to refer to as courtship, I know the signs, which you manifest in spades."

"Oh, I say." Again, Lance teetered. "Beware, I fear I am going to vomit."

"None of that, now." Trevor peered over his shoulder. "You would never live down the embarrassment, and I would prefer you not grant our women such ammunition. By the by, Everett is correct in his assertion."

"Ooh, I like that." Everett snorted and said to Trevor, "Would you mind repeating it?"

"Will you shut up?" Trevor grumbled. "We are here to save another man from a fate worse than death."

"Brothers, if that is an attempt to inspire confidence, you failed miserably." Lance sighed and repositioned his cane. "And is there not an easier way?"

"You would think so." Everett compressed his lips. "But—no."

"Then it appears I am sailing into rough seas."

"And committing a dire err in judgment for which I suspect you shall pay dearly, friend." Trevor paused and then added, "You know, I almost lost my wife when I refused to declare myself, because I actually thought I could avoid it."

"And my similar exercise in lunacy resulted in an overnight horseback ride to London, from which my arse still smarts on occasion, in hot pursuit of my wayward bride, because she inaccurately presumed I sought another." At that moment, Everett cast Sabrina a heated stare to which Lance would have taken exception were they not married. "Gentlemen, I believe I am neglecting my lady, an aberration I would correct, posthaste. Whatever you decide, happy hunting, Raynesford."

Everett's salutation struck Lance as the icy waters of the Baltic.

Of course.

The solution to his quandary, when it dawned, seemed so elementary. Cara viewed Lance as nothing more than a friend because he had never behaved otherwise, with the exception of that glorious afternoon spent in his bed. And while that, alone, should have sufficed, it was evident she demanded something else, entirely.

"Uh-oh." Trevor snickered. "I know that look."

"To what do you refer?" Lance admired the gentle curve of Cara's neck, the creamy velvet flesh of her bosom, and invoked the memory of her lusty cries in the throes of passion.

"Brother, you are sporting for incalculable grief." Trevor adjusted his cravat and appeared to snare his wife's regard. "I, for one, cannot bear to watch, so I shall borrow a page from Everett's log and seek delectable divertissement in the arms of my Caroline. But I would have you note, before I depart your company, that the beauty of a declaration lies in its ability to soothe the most heinous infraction upon mere utterance. And, indeed, its efficacy never wanes. In short, as a whole, they are the three most powerful words ever spoken, and you would do well to make use of them—the sooner the better."

With that, Trevor sketched a bow, all but ran to his wife, and steered her toward a dark corner. Lance stifled a hearty guffaw when his friend extinguished a nearby candle and eased his bride to a *chaise*. And then Lance gave his attention to his intended target. Slowly, he smiled.

Oh, yes.

Thus far, Cara had successfully evaded Lance—her old pal—because he hadn't deviated from the tried and true. To his detriment, he remained a comfortable, predictable childhood chum. But things were different now, because they had made love, a point of fact in his strategy he had woefully discounted.

As such, he had to rethink his tack, had to consider Cara his conquest. She was no longer just an afternoon reading buddy—she was his quarry, his prey. And he would hunt her to the ends of the earth if necessary. Employing all his skills, drawing on his considerable expertise, his vast cache of knowledge in the sensuous arena, he would stalk her.

Cara would never know what hit her.

In that instant, he sincerely anticipated the chase because, despite his injury, everything else was in prime working order, so he was definitely up to the challenge. The end result, to make Cara his bride, would be the sweetest victory of all. And he did not doubt for a hairsbreadth of a second his eventual triumph, because once Lance set his sights on female game, he never lost.

Adopting his best swagger, and with a bad leg that was no idle feat, he grasped the crystal decanter of brandy, poured another portion of the amber intoxicant, and raised his glass in insouciant salute.

Let the games begin.

"WELL, I believe last night was a smashing success." Sabrina thrust her chin and sipped her tea.

"I could not agree more." Alex nodded with enthusiasm. "It was simply stupendous."

"Yes, I concur." Rebecca tapped a finger to her chin. "Our plot appears to be working."

"Do you really think so?" Cara furrowed her brow and stared at her clasped hands, as doubt nagged her conscience. "Lance looked so sad."

"As he should." Sabrina leaned forward and swiped a square of shortbread from a tray. "You must stay the course."

"I, for one, would very much like to know what our husbands were discussing with Lance," Caroline said to Brie. "They had their heads together for quite some time, and Trevor skillfully evaded my inquiry regarding the topic of their conversation."

The friends gathered in the morning room at the Markham's Park Lane town home. They had decided in advance to meet and discuss each successive event of their plan, but Cara already second-guessed her ability to carry out their scheme. After tossing and turning all night, she had arrived at the requisite hour, fully intending to end their foolhardy endeavor.

"Do you think they suspect us?" Cara asked Caroline, who merely shrugged, and then frowned and shook her head at Brie. "And I do not want to hurt him."

"My dear, need I remind you that men do not come easily to love, as I grow weary of repeating myself." Sabrina wrinkled her nose and sighed. "Must I again explain that we have to rip out their heart and stomp it flat before they realize how precious it is?"

"But I do not wish to rip out his heart." A haunting image flashed in her brain, of Lance with a bloody hole in his chest, and Cara gulped. "I only want to be his wife."

"Hmm." Sabrina narrowed her stare. "I am not so sure it is possible to distinguish between the two."

"Then you must be strong." Waving a fist in the air, Alex rallied the troops. "Yours is a noble cause. In the end, he will thank you."

"I daresay you would believe otherwise were it Jason who spent the evening moping as if he had just lost his best friend." Mulling her circumstances, Cara snatched an open-faced cherry tart. "Would you relish the prospect of causing him torment?"

"Well, I should think I would do whatever necessary to secure his affection, but it is of no concern." With a smug smile, Alex stuck her tongue in her cheek. "Jason has already gifted me his heart—on a silver platter, no less."

"The man must have been a woman in another life." Rebecca nudged Caroline, who giggled.

"What makes you say that?" Alex looked her question. "I assure you, Jason is every inch a man."

"Because a male with uncommonly good sense is a rare creature, indeed." Rebecca hugged a pillow to her belly. "How else could you explain it but that he is in touch with his feminine nature?"

In concert, the women shared a hearty laugh, and Cara shed the tension investing her shoulders.

"Tell me something, Alex," Cara inquired, as she wiped a stray tear from her eye. "Just how did you persuade the estimable captain to help us?"

Alex averted her gaze and bit her lip.

"Come now." In the process of taking another bite of shortbread, Sabrina paused. "Do tell."

"Why do I get the impression we will not like what we hear?" Rebecca stated with a grimace.

"Oh, no." Caroline swallowed hard. "What did you do?"

"Well." Alex paused, squirmed in her chair, and glanced at Sabrina, then Cara, then Rebecca, and back to Cara. With a flick of her wrist she drew them near. In a low voice, she said, "I put his hand on my breast."

Sabrina's eyes grew wide as she dropped the remainder of her shortbread.

Rebecca and Caroline gasped in unison.

In horror, Cara almost sent her cup and saucer to the floor. After a few seconds of impenetrable silence, she blinked. "Alex, you quite take my breath away."

"Are you out of your mind?" Caroline inquired with a countenance of disapproval. "Whatever possessed you to do such a thing?"

"Cara let Lance do it to her—*oh*." Alex covered her mouth with a clenched fist.

The room spun on end, and Cara slumped in her seat. A chorus of male grunts, groans, and whispered praise filled her ears as she relived the memory of Lance touching her, kissing her, loving her.

Sabrina folded her arms and snickered. "Well that is a charming image."

"Oh, it was a vast deal more than charming." With a dreamy expression, Alex clasped her hands to her bosom and closed her eyes. "It was divine."

"Spare me the details." Sabrina pressed a napkin to her brow. "Else the morning malaise will surely revisit me."

With a nervous chuckle, Cara lifted the pot and sought distraction in polite decorum. "May I pour you more tea, sister?"

"No, thank you." Sabrina favored Alex and Cara with an icy glare of reproach. "But you would do well to heed my advice. If you want to secure a husband, hold your favors until after you are wed. With the exception of Trevor and Dirk, why on earth would any man buy a cow when it freely bestows the milk?"

Duly chastised, Alex dipped her chin. "Yes, Brie."

"I do not understand." Cara considered her little sister's instruction but could make no sense of it. "What has this to do with cows?"

"What she means to say is that you may talk to Lance.

Walk with Lance. Dance with Lance." Caroline pointed for emphasis. "But for heaven's sake, Cara, keep his hands off your breasts."

LIKE A WOLF SCENTING ITS MEAL, he spied her as soon as she entered the ballroom. When the invitation arrived, Lance had not intended to grace the halls of Hogart House, but he decided it was time to enact his grand plan to win his lady.

Gowned in crimson velvet, with her raven hair coifed in her usual style, Cara silently beckoned him as she descended the main staircase. And as a bull in the ring, he prepared to charge.

But he lurked in the shadows, hugging the sidewall. Patient and deliberate, he loomed as an apparition of doom for his competition, because he would make his move soon enough.

As he had expected, Jason lingered at the foot of the steps and offered to escort Cara into the gala, which she accepted without hesitation. To his satisfaction, the blonde Adonis led Miss Perfect to the back corner where the Brethren gathered.

Lance would join them—eventually.

Focused on a wealth of tempting ebony curls, he navigated the throng, winding his way across the cavernous ballroom. At his leisure, he nabbed a glass of champagne from a passing servant. Sipping the cool refreshment, he strolled along the edge of the dance floor, relaxed and unhurried, nodding a casual acknowledgement here and a modest greeting there, just enough to feign interest.

When he reached his lifelong friends, he eased into the group, paying particular attention to the male dominated conversation, and ignored Cara completely. As anticipated, the men congregated to one side, and the women to the other, and he positioned himself behind his intended target.

As Dalton laughed aloud at some audacious comment, Lance cut loose with boisterous mirth and simultaneously seized the opportunity to trail the curves of Cara's bottom with his fingertips. She rewarded his efforts with a feminine gasp of surprise.

Round one: Advantage, the Marquess of Raynesford.

With a tight lid on burgeoning confidence, he adopted a demeanor that he hoped conveyed unutterable passivity, half-turned, and stared at Cara.

With her lips parted, her cheeks flushed a charming red, which almost matched her gown. Shock and something he could not quite define danced as shadows in her blue eyes.

Cara blinked and murmured, "I beg your pardon."

Without a word, he arched a brow, nodded once, and gave her his back. His smile came easy as he engaged in the vigorous banter between seamen.

The familiar strains of the first waltz sliced through the air, and prospective suitors jockeyed for a fair partner. With calm deliberation, Lance hobbled aside as Jason claimed Cara.

As couples whirled about the marble floor, he relocated to a position of serviceable concealment provided by a bust sitting atop a pedestal, which suited his purpose. From his vantage, he studied his prey.

Every time his lady neared the locale in which the Brethren assembled, Cara cast a surreptitious glance in that direction. As certain was he of his name, Lance surmised she searched for him. When the dance ended, he tarried in the shelter of the statuette.

Watching Cara watching for him.

To her detriment, she retreated to the corner, and he decided it was past due to tweak her again. With his walking stick for support, Lance limped to her vicinity. Engrossed in some female occupation with Elaine, Cara did not spy him.

Persisting in her wake, he bent his head, pretended to consider the toe of his shoe, and expelled his warm breath across the nape of her neck. She flinched ever so slightly, and gooseflesh covered her in a flash, only to be concealed by her gloved hand, but he saw it just the same.

Victory: The Marquess of Raynesford.

CARA SHIVERED, peered over her shoulder, and stared Lance straight in the eye. His answering smile was pure wolf and did nothing to soothe her frazzled nerves. She expected him to say something—anything, but he abandoned her to her thoughts, which ran amok at his bold and curious behavior.

Just what was her hero about?

For the next hour, her world rocked on end, and Cara teetered beyond her control as a familiar-faced incubus haunted and taunted her. Every time she recollected her faculties, Lance caught her in another sneak attack, rendering her befuddled and weak-kneed.

If only he would declare his love.

She would accept his proposal, and anything else, for that matter. Regardless of his endeavor and aim, which she speculated had everything to do with righting his perceived wrong and nothing to do with undying devotion, she had no idea how to counter his licentious offensive. Worse, she suspected her conspiracy had unwittingly pricked the pride of a past master of passionate pursuits, resulting in her perilous predicament.

"May I escort you to dinner, Cara?" Jason stood tall and winked. Then he bent and whispered, "Have we caught the attention of your errant suitor?"

She glanced from side to side, and then nodded once and gulped. "Oh, I would say we definitely have caught his attention."

"Then we should toast to your future happiness," stated the affable captain.

When Collingwood settled at her right, she had thought to find refuge in his company. How quickly she realized her error when her tormentor appeared as if from nowhere and claimed the seat to her immediate left.

"Is this a private party?" Lance inquired with cherubic innocence, which didn't fool her for a second.

"Not at all," Jason replied. "Pull up a chair, Raynesford."

Almost at once, her not-so-gallant hero brushed the bare skin of her inner arm, and she shivered.

"You are chilled, my dear. Allow me to fetch you a glass of ratafia." To Lance, Captain Collingwood said, "Would you guard our fair Miss Douglas until I return?"

"Oh, it would be my pleasure." And that is when Lance really went to work on her nerves.

No sooner had Jason disappeared than her nemesis rubbed his leg to hers in an illicit rhythm that left her in no doubt of his meaning and the memories he intended to provoke. And the energy she expended to maintain her prim and proper façade, else she risked exposure and further ruin, exhausted her resolve. Indeed, nothing her finishing governess had taught her prepared Cara for his onslaught.

Just then, she spotted Jason and Alex deep in conversation and realized she was truly on her own.

"Will you not look at me, Cara?" Lance asked in a low voice, which gave her gooseflesh. "Or are you afraid of what you might reveal?"

"I beg your pardon? Of what should I be afraid?" Against her trusty intuition, Cara met her tormentor's gaze. "After all, there is nothing to see."

"Ah-ha."

"Lance—"

"Cara," he mocked her sigh as she had done to him in his bedchamber. "And it is just as I predicted."

"What is?"

"Lovely lying eyes, sugar kisses." He leaned near. "You could never keep secrets from me."

"Your ratafia, Miss Douglas." Jason placed a cup of the noxious brew before her, and she jumped. "I apologize for the delay, but I became distracted."

"No worries." At his charming admission, she couldn't help but laugh. "And I had Lance to—" When she peered over shoulder, she discovered her mischievous hero gone. "Well, he was here a minute ago."

Just then the music resumed, and the revelers cued to return to the ballroom.

"Shall we, Miss Douglas?" Jason offered his arm in escort.

"No, thank you." Desperate for a moment's peace, Cara shook her head. "Given the success of this evening's enterprise, perhaps you should ask Alex. I know she would love to indulge you in a country dance, and it is not fair of me to monopolize your company."

"Well, if you insist." Jason favored her with a boyish grin. "I shall seek my lady as a boon for my efforts."

The handsome naval captain waggled his brows and approached Alex from behind. With a gentle tap on the shoulder he gained her attention, and she cast a wide smile. How Cara envied the palpable emotional undercurrent they shared, and she yearned for the same connection, the unspoken communication. Their attachment reflected what she thought she had found with Lance.

An imaginary darkness shrouded her in impenetrable melancholy, and the misery of her situation loomed as storm clouds on the horizon. Disappointed hopes played agonizing vignettes, which only intensified her heartache. The room seemed unseasonably hot, and she almost suffocated from the heat. In dire need of fresh air, she searched the vicinity, navigated the throng, and located a small alcove. Standing before a pair of French doors, she grasped the knob but paused to check for Lance. To her relief, he was nowhere to be found.

A full moon cast a silvery glow on the crisp November night. Wrapping her arms about herself, Cara walked to the rail of the diminutive terrace, which overlooked a small topiary garden. A pebbled path led to an orangery tucked amid a cluster of rose bushes, and their gentle fragrance teased her nose as she inhaled deeply. At length, she relaxed, closed her eyes, and shivered.

Arms encircled her waist, and welcoming warmth enveloped her.

Lance chuckled. "Alone at last."

CHAPTER TWELVE

*I*t was just her luck to walk straight into the devil's embrace. When Lance cupped the undersides of her breasts, Cara conjured all manner of protests to his inappropriate behavior. But given what had already transpired between them, how could she object? And though she would deny it were he to ask, she hadn't realized how much she needed him until that instant. So she leaned back her head and sighed, as he blazed a fiery path along the curve of her neck with his lips.

"I miss you, my hero." She gasped with pleasure when he nipped the crest of her ear with his teeth. "I miss you so much."

"But I am right here, sugar kisses." His new term of endearment thrilled her to her toes, as his hands seemed to be everywhere at once, caressing, massaging, tickling ever so teasingly, and she was grateful for his expertise and what he made her feel.

And, oh, what she felt.

"Yet it is not the same with us, is it?" She turned—right into his kiss.

From the first, their lips met in calm and gentle communion, as he brushed and sashayed his mouth to hers. Then, in a flash, everything exploded in a fevered pitch, and without shame, she opened to her man, licking and suckling his tongue, as she wound her arms beneath his formal coat and pressed herself to his body. Sumptuous fire sang in her veins and charged every nerve, stealing every scrap of rational thought. Dizzy with desire, she ground her pelvis to his and hummed in appreciation when his impressive erection jutted against her belly.

"I want you, Cara," he whispered.

Drunk with passion, and seduced by the addictive power he wielded over her, she craved more, and Lance did not disappoint. A subtle shift provided the slightest warning of the dazzling enticement on the horizon, before he slipped a hand between them. For a scarce second she held her breath, and she emitted a plaintive cry as he delved beneath her velvet bodice and lightly pinched a nipple. To her frustration, words of warning rang in her head.

Keep his hands off your breasts.

And she recalled something about cows.

In that instant, Cara jolted alert and broke their kiss. Breathing heavily, she struggled for composure and retreated to the rail, before sparing a glance at him.

"I apologize, Lance." She tucked a stray tendril behind her ear and shifted her dress.

"For what?" His features were obscured in the dark, but she detected surprise in his voice.

"For making improper advances on your person." She shook her head. "I do not know what came over me."

"Do you not?" He chuckled. "You want me, despite actions to the contrary. And you may make improper advances on my person, any time."

"Have I ever claimed otherwise?"

"Then marry me."

The words served as both a balm and an irritant to her conscience. She found solace in his proposal, because nothing would give her greater joy than to be his wife, yet she could not accept a commitment born of obligation, however well intended. So she steeled herself to pose the question foremost on her mind, the answer to which would determine her response.

"Why?"

"Because it is the right thing to do," Lance stated without hesitation.

Wrong rebuttal.

Her heart plummeted. "That is not sufficient justification to compel me to wed."

"And what of my heir? You could be pregnant."

"I am not."

"How can you be sure?"

"Do not play the fool."

"I get your meaning." Lance shrugged. "Marry me, regardless. After all, what gentleman of character would have a soiled dove, when I have staked my undeniable claim?"

"That can be managed with strategically placed chicken blood."

"But we are friends and well suited in bed." Lance shrugged. "And you were determined to have me, until the deed was done. What happened, Cara? How did I fail you?"

"I have my requirements."

"And they are—what?"

To her discontent, Cara perched on the banks of her own private Rubicon. And from where she stood, she had only two choices. She could surrender her principles, confess her prerequisite, and forever wonder if her hero genuinely loved her as something more than a friend. The unpalatable prospect prompted her to consider the second option.

Biding her time, she could hold her tongue and pray that Captain Collingwood's spurious courtship provoked the prize she sought. She could hold out for her dream, to wed for true love.

With renewed determination she lowered her chin. "My reasons are my own."

"Am I to guess?" He reached for her, and she skittered to the doors.

Pausing at the threshold, she said, "Do as you will."

IT WAS ANOTHER NIGHT AND, to his frustration, yet another garish fete epitomizing the gross opulence that was the Little Season. As had become his custom, Lance lurked amid the shadows in Lady Richmond's ballroom, studying his quarry from a distance.

Gowned in teal silk, with a thick, flirty curl caressing her throat, Cara manifested his own private princess. If not for his limp, he would don the gleaming suit of armor that had belonged to his ancestors, which held pride of place in his study, and charge forth on a white stallion to claim her for all of London society to witness.

In silence, he cursed his injury. While he no longer required the use of a cane, he wobbled as a newborn taking its first steps. No matter what he did, no matter how hard he exercised, his leg remained unresponsive and inflexible to the physical therapy Dr. Handley prescribed. As a man, he was accustomed to a little stiffness in the morning, just not in that particular body part.

With a gloved hand, Cara rubbed the back of her neck, and his mouth watered. Despite her assertions to the contrary, they remained connected by some invisible force, a nameless entity, and her movements belied the fact that she sensed his presence. For as long as he could remember, they shared some transparent yet nonetheless potent attachment.

Regardless of his travels, whether at school or at sea, Lance existed as some mystical extension of Cara. And he believed, without doubt, she felt it too. He did not know why or how he knew—he just did. Which begged the question: Why had she refused his offer of marriage when he had well and truly compromised her?

As he wound his way through the crush, he kept his gaze fixed on a thick mass of hair, black as a crow's feather. When he neared, Cara faced him. For a scant second, he glimpsed agony in her blue eyes, before the pain disappeared behind a mask of polite decorum, which she usually reserved for strangers. That she sought to conceal her natural state from him, the one person with whom she had shared everything, cut like the sharpest knife.

She dipped her chin and smiled, but it was not the effervescent sort with which she always welcomed him. "Good evening, Lance."

"My lady." In a single swift move, he took her hand in his, raised it to his lips, and then pressed her gloved palm to the crook of his arm. "Take a turn about the room with me."

To his surprise, she acquiesced without argument.

As they strolled, he nodded acknowledgments to various members of society. "Have you given any more thought to my proposal?"

She flinched, and he cursed.

"Cara, I must confess I am at a loss." Lance sighed and forced himself to remain patient. "Please know it is not my intent to cause you discomfort. I merely seek to understand your motives."

"My motives for—what?" She nodded once and smiled at Lord Albemarle, and he mirrored her movements.

"For your actions both before and after I claimed the proof of your virtue." Lance scanned the area for a venue to suit his purpose. "You were quite insistent in your desire to become my marchioness, and made a passionate argument to that effect, until you consummated the bargain. I believe you have confused the situation, as most women operate in reverse, holding their favors hostage in exchange for a marriage contract."

"How dare you." Cara halted so suddenly that he tripped. "Do you believe I planned to trap you?"

"Easy, sugar kisses." Conscious of the multitude of stares cast in their direction, and the rush of whispers, Lance steered her toward a nearby terrace. "Else you risk further ruin, which you will not escape so easily, given our esteemed audience."

As he expected, she checked her demeanor and assumed a cordial expression. "Just what do you imply?" she inquired through gritted teeth.

"I imply nothing." They weaved right, then left, and then right again. "I merely state the facts of our predicament, as they have occurred, and urge you to proceed with caution."

"That sounds like a threat." Her eyes flared.

"No, not a threat but a friendly suggestion." Then, for the benefit of those within earshot, he stated rather loudly,

"You look a bit flushed, Miss Douglas. Perhaps some fresh air will improve your disposition."

"How very thoughtful, my lord." Again, she followed his lead. "And perhaps you will explain your insistence on discussing personal matters in such a public forum."

"You give me no choice, as you refuse to answer my summons to my satisfaction and decline to receive me when I call." Lance opened the terrace door and handed her over the threshold to the flagged surface.

When he secured their privacy, she whirled on a heel. "Are you planning to make advances?"

"No." He could not help but laugh. "Trust me, when I makes advances, I shall be far more direct, and you will have no doubt of my resolve."

"Then why are we here?"

"To settle our situation."

"I will not yield." She raised her chin. "Nothing you can do will sway me."

"Nothing?" Someday soon he was sincerely going to enjoy proving otherwise. "You talk a bold game, sugar kisses. I wonder if you are prepared to accept the consequences of your actions?"

Cara opened her mouth and then snapped it shut. "That was not a challenge."

"Really?" Lance smirked. "You do not sound too certain of yourself."

"I was simply making a statement." She shivered and crossed her arms. "It was not a dare."

He remained silent but grasped her by the waist and hugged her close.

"Lance—"

"Relax." He nuzzled her hair and kissed her forehead. "I only want to talk, Cara."

"I can't see anything," she said in a small voice, offering the slightest resistance, before resting her cheek to his shoulder.

"Then you may rely on me." Having traversed the grounds on occasions too numerous to count, in past illicit endeavors, he could navigate the Richmond's garden with his eyes closed.

Their locale, situated far off the well-traveled path, afforded the perfect place for a tryst, had he been so inclined. The moonless night reinforced their concealment, for which he was grateful because Cara would have taken umbrage with his supremely male countenance were their sufficient light to illuminate him.

"All right." She sighed. "Just what are you about?"

"I thought it obvious." He rubbed her lower back. "And why are you whispering?"

"Your motives for bringing me here can't be proper."

"Miss Douglas, how uncharacteristically unladylike of you." He thrust his hips and grinned when her breath hitched. "I must confess my motives are honorable, for me. But let us not abandon your idea."

"Do not play coy with me." Though her words bespoke rebuke, her tone hinted at amusement.

"I do not think I have ever been accused of being coy."

"Lance, we are not here to smell the roses."

"Would you be disappointed if I told you my intent was as gallant? And why are you whispering? Have you something to hide? Are you afraid to be seen with me?"

"We do not have to hide, as it is pitch black out here." She wound her arms about his waist. "And of course I am not ashamed of you."

Lance stiffened in her embrace. "I said *afraid*."

"As did I."

"No, you said *ashamed*."

"Well, you know what I meant."

"Are you ashamed of me? Has my injury altered your good opinion of me?" Was that why she would not marry him?

"Lance, I could never be ashamed of you, and I apologize if I indicated otherwise." She shifted in his hold, just enough to frame his face. "I believe your injury is temporary, and you will one day walk as you did before. But if it does not come to pass, you will never be anything less than the man you have always been. In short, you are now, and forever, my hero."

And then Cara kissed him.

Hers was not the most polished or ardent of expressions, but its effects were certainly the most potent. Instead of coming at him as a practiced seraph, with a twenty-one-gun assault, which he could have easily resisted, she lured him with seemingly harmless but flirty flicks of her tongue and achingly sweet caresses. Indeed, the moment reigned supreme as a stealth attack of the gentlest sort, which built momentum with each successive nip of his flesh, as a poignant affirmation to prove her point.

"Why will you not have me, Cara?" He clung to her as a drowning man and she his only lifeline. "You wanted me. You told me and showed me, as much."

"And you turned me away," she whispered.

"It appears we have changed positions." He caught the crest of her ear in his teeth. "Is that your aim—to teach me a lesson?"

"Would that I were that clever." She withdrew from his embrace. "Rather, I submit that you and I are on the same page."

"How so?" Were she correct, he would be planning a wedding.

"Do you recall your objections to our union?" Cara inquired.

"No." Lance lied, because he cursed his miserable hide every waking hour for having argued with her.

"Well, I do. And one counterpoint, in particular, has merit."

"And that would be—what?"

"I do not deserve you," she replied in a grave tone.

In a flash, his blood ran cold. "When did I ever make such an asinine statement?"

"While you were abed, just before we—"

"Made love?"

"Yes."

"But you misunderstood, as I do not deserve you."

"Oh, I beg to disagree, my hero."

"Cara, you are not making sense." She could not have shocked him more had she physically struck him. "I insist you explain yourself, this instant."

"I cannot."

"So you reject my offer of marriage, and you refuse to tell me why?" The world tilted beneath his feet.

"Yes."

"For the love of all creation, why?"

"Lance, I do not expect you to comprehend my position, but if I confess my reason, then I can never wed you."

What in bloody hell did she mean? He scratched his temple and replayed her words. Had she clearly defined the impediments to their union, he could have dissected each obstacle, one by one. But her intransigence narrowed his options. In essence, to win Cara, he had to fight Cara.

Incredulous, he shifted his weight. "You must be joking."

"Actually, I am quite serious." In that second, he would have given his ship for a full moon, as he could glean nothing from her demeanor and would dearly love to study her face.

"Then I am to guess?" He settled hands on hips.

"Well, in a manner of speaking—yes."

"And you can give me no hint of your requirements?"

"I am not sure," she stated with an air of indecision.

"Then allow me to bring some semblance of sanity to this exercise in lunacy." For good or ill, he had to charge her position; else he might never understand her view.

"By all means."

"Since, for whatever logic, you reject me, then I have no choice but to chart my own course."

"Why do I get the feeling I am not going to like this?" Cara queried with more than a hint of skepticism.

Lance laughed. "Suffice it to say, for better or worse, I will propose once more, and only once more. If your response remains unchanged, I will never again offer for you."

"However you dress it, that is a threat."

"Not a threat but a promise." He hated to be stern, but he had to do something, as they could not indefinitely maintain their current heading. "Now have you any clues to impart regarding your inexplicable behavior?"

"I have but one."

"And that would be?"

"I am sworn to uphold the Brethren oath."

"As am I." He considered the ancient pledge and pictured the words in his mind.

"Yet you set your sights on a lesser goal when it comes to your bride."

"What is that supposed to mean?" Now she well and truly befuddled him.

"Therein lies the answer, Lance."

"So he will propose only once more?" Sabrina humphed and set her cup on the table. "I do not care what Lance calls it, that is an ultimatum pure and simple."

"How dare he resort to such bully tactics." Caroline slapped a fist to an open palm. "Brethren or not, the man ought to be horsewhipped."

"And when did he have the opportunity to deliver this not so gracious overture?" Rebecca inquired with an arched brow.

"Last night." Cara averted her gaze and cursed the sting of a blush in her cheeks. Although she would have preferred not to disclose recent events surrounding her scheme of hearts, she relied on their aid, and they could not offer guidance without knowledge of current developments. "At the Richmond's ball."

"You were alone with him." Sabrina compressed her lips.

"How exciting." Alex gasped and perched on the edge of her chair. "Did you kiss?"

"Well—yes." Cara shifted her weight. "But I had to do it."

Sabrina, Caroline, and Rebecca gave vent to simultaneous snorts of skepticism. Alex bounced with unchecked enthusiasm, clapped her hands, and squealed with delight.

"I did, I swear." Cara stretched her feet and studied her slippers. "He required reassurance, and I could not resist."

Sabrina rolled her eyes. "If I did not know any better, I would say you are deliberately undermining our mission."

Cara blinked. "Mission?"

"Indeed," Sabrina replied with a nod. "If we are to succeed, then you must consider Lance your adversary in a war of love."

"And is that all you did? Remember, you promised to divulge every detail in our little endeavor." Alex leaned forward and lowered her chin. "And I will tell you of my rendezvous with Jason in the orangery."

"Alex." Caroline folded her arms. "Might I suggest you heed my advice where men are concerned?"

"Why should I?" Alex pouted. "I foresee no impediments in marrying Jason. He has but to declare himself."

"A rather important step you would do well not to concede," Rebecca added, with a countenance of disapproval.

"Are you out of your mind?" Sabrina frowned. "Have I taught you nothing? Why should he offer for you, when you already make him free of your favors?"

"Dear sisters, I see no reason to deny my own desires." Alex scoffed. "I will not lie to him or myself and pretend I am something I am not."

"But you have already deceived him," Cara stated in a small voice. A knock at the door brought her up short.

"Come," Brie responded.

If Cara had thought her situation dire, what followed sent her plummeting to new depths of despair.

"Just as I suspected." Elaine loomed with a dour visage of gloom. "I had thought to pay call but found everyone curiously absent. And what are you ladies about?"

"My darling Elaine." Cara leapt to her feet. "How are you? Will you not join us?" She cleared her throat. "Would you care for tea?"

"Actually, I am in no mood for tea, and I am quite displeased." Elaine drew herself up with the noble superiority one would expect of the daughter of a marquess. "I should very much like to know what is going on and your reasons for excluding me."

"Come and sit, dearest." Caroline stood and offered her place to the youngest member of the Brethren. "I will take the ottoman."

An uncomfortable silence cast a pall on the gathering, and Cara mulled the situation, which had gone from critical to worse in a hairsbreadth of a second. "I owe you an apology. I have a problem, and our sisters have provided their assistance. Given your cousin's injury, and your delicate emotional state, I did not wish to compound your misery by burdening you with my predicament."

"Because you are in love with Lance?" Elaine queried with cherubic innocence.

In the process of sipping her tea, Alex choked violently. Caroline examined the hem of her sleeve, while Rebecca gazed at the ceiling, and Brie whistled in monotone. Yes, Cara's goose was well and truly cooked.

"How did you know?" Cara whispered.

"Do you think me ignorant?" Elaine shrugged. "I may not possess Caroline's adventurous derring-do, Sabrina's carefree spirit, Alex's inestimable charm, Rebecca's unfailing courage, or your inner strength, but neither am I blind. Although I prefer the comfort of shadows, and shall always shelter in the background, I see more than you realize, and I have known for a time that something more than friendship binds you to Lance."

In that instant, Cara discovered she had woefully under-estimated Elaine. "My friend, I am more sorry than I can say for not including you in our plan. My only excuse is that, since you must share his home, I did not wish to put you in a difficult position. I did not believe you could tolerate my confidence."

"And yet I can provide invaluable insight, because I live with him." Elaine shook her head. "I thought you knew me better than that."

In mere minutes, Sabrina assumed command of their meeting and catalogued the events for Elaine, as they had occurred, but omitted any reference to Cara's loss of virginity.

"Again, my apologies, as I never intended to offend you." Cara thought of the embroidered kerchief nestled to her breast, which Lance had gifted her so long ago. Made of crisp white lawn, it had signified the purity of their commit-ment, in her estimation, but how could that be, given a scheme based on prevarication? "As things stand, I must reassess my course of action."

"Because of me?" Elaine appeared hurt by the implica-tion. "On the Brethren oath, I vow never to betray your secret."

"This is not an issue of secrecy," Cara explained. "It is a matter of honor, and in that we are none of us innocent. We were not honest with Captain Collingwood when we solicited his assistance. I must confess, I am no longer certain of my path, and I wonder if do more harm by refusing Lance's proposal."

"Are you mad?"

"You mustn't surrender."

"Do not falter."

"You can't give up."

"All men are dolts."

They plead in concert.

"I love Lance." Cara stared at her clasped hands. "And because I do, I cannot, in good conscience, forge a union with him built upon a foundation of lies. If I cannot bring him to the altar, dignity intact, then I shall not wed him."

"But Lance loves you, too." Elaine inclined her head. "Would you deny him out of pride? Would you have him marry what he does not love?"

"On the contrary, I would have him no other way." With renewed purpose, Cara pressed a clenched fist to her bosom. "I will have his declaration, or I will not have him."

"Pray, indulge me." Elaine tapped a finger to her chin. "My cousin is a rather stubborn sort, so you will have to be strong for both your sakes. Our sisters are correct in that you must stay the course."

"You truly believe so?" In her mind, Cara revisited the kiss from the previous night.

"Elaine is right." Sabrina waved a clenched fist. "You must hold out for love."

"But, if memory serves, you did not." Cara pointed for emphasis. "You enjoyed no such security."

"I beg your pardon?" Sabrina faltered before squaring her shoulders. "I have always loved Everett."

"But you were not equally assured of his devotion when you spoke the vows." Cara reminisced. "In fact, as I recall, his pledge came much later, after you ran away."

"What of it?" Sabrina glared accusingly. "He adores me to distraction, and I am ensured of his affection in all enterprises."

"Then tell me, my dear sister." Cara sighed. "Have you informed Everett of our little charade?"

"No." Sabrina bowed her head.

"And why not?" Cara inquired.

"Because he is a man." Sabrina wrinkled her nose and glanced at the door to her parlor, as if expecting her husband to appear at any second. "He would not comprehend the gravity of the situation."

"I think you compound your falsehood by lying to yourself, my resourceful sister." The world seemed to spin beyond her control, and Cara clutched the armrest of her chair.

"Hang it all, Cara." Brie slapped a hand to her thigh. "If I told Everett of our escapade, he would turn me over his knee and heat my posterior."

"The truth, at last." Cara leveled her gaze on Alex, who smoothed her skirts. "And how would our estimable captain feel about being duped into aiding our none-too-virtuous cause?"

Alex gulped. "I see no reason to enlighten him."

"So you never plan on telling him the facts?"

Alex folded her arms in front of her. "It sounds awfully treacherous when you put it that way."

"But that is the situation."

"I know, but can we not call it something else?" Alex fidgeted.

The answer, when it struck her, seemed so simple that Cara grew irritated with herself. "Bloody hell."

"Oh." Caroline covered her mouth.

"Upon my word." Alex dropped her cup. "Hell hath frozen."

"Oh, I say." Sabrina hugged a pillow to her swollen belly. "You are distressed, as never have I known you to use foul language. But you must practice your delivery, as you will never survive the marital state if you cannot convincingly swear at your husband."

"Let that be a lesson for another time," Rebecca suggested with a giggle.

"Ladies, I am not proud of what I have done." Cara paced the floor. "I must take full responsibility for this farce. But Elaine has reminded me of our philosophy as Brethren women, and I am ashamed to say I forgot from whence we came."

"What are you going to do?" Sabrina and Caroline asked in unison.

"What I should have done in the beginning."

"And that would be—what?" Elaine asked.

"Think of the oath." Cara exhaled. "It is the same advice I gave Lance, last night. As I am no hypocrite, I shall heed my own counsel."

After a pregnant silence, recognition dawned in five lovely expressions.

"Of course." Caroline nodded once.

"How could we have overlooked the obvious?" Rebecca asked.

"Gather near, sisters." Cara extended her hand, and the friends piled theirs atop, one after another, in a delicate but nonetheless powerful bond forged of blood, flesh, and bone.

"For love and comradeship we live," Cara proclaimed. "And when next Lance proposes, I shall accept."

CHAPTER THIRTEEN

*T*herein lies the answer.

What exactly had she meant by that cryptic statement? For the better part of his waking hours, he had replayed his last encounter with Cara, over and over, in his head. Still the solution to his conundrum eluded him, and she caused him no end of torment.

"Lance, is something bothering you?" Admiral Douglas arched a brow. "Are you all right, my boy?"

"Uh, no." He tugged at the starched folds of his cravat and cleared his throat. "That is to say, I am fine, sir."

Standing on the dock at Deptford, Lance seethed in silence as the Brethren of the Coast prepared to cast off without him but found comfort in the familiar scent of brine mixed with kelp.

"Then you are in agreement with my temporary command of your ship?" Collingwood asked with a wry smile.

"Of course." Lance nodded once. "Take care of my crew and the *Demetrius*, and sail her with my blessing." *While I steer Cara into my bed.*

"You are an awfully good sport, brother." Jason shook his head and snickered. "It is doubtful I would be as magnanimous were I in your shoes."

The blonde Adonis might not be so congenial when he returned to find Cara nestled deep in Lance's pocket. "On the contrary, I am sure were our positions reversed, you would do exactly the same as I."

"On that note, I bid you farewell, as the tide awaits no man." Collingwood glanced at Cara, dipped his chin, and then he took Alex's hand in his and pressed a chaste kiss to her gloved knuckles, which Lance considered quite peculiar behavior, given his fellow knight's fledgling courtship of Miss Douglas.

"Fair winds and following seas." Lance sketched a mock salute and then gave his attention to the other lady in his life.

Gowned in lavender with a matching cloak, and a hat that featured a flirty feather, she personified understated elegance. But it was what lay beneath the tailored attire that snared his senses. Indeed, she manifested pure unadulterated temptation, which had driven him to foolishly force her hand at the Richmond's gala.

Now, thanks to his grand ultimatum, Lance had no viable retreat should she reject his offer of marriage. So how could he solve his conundrum to his satisfaction?

"And how are you this morning, my hero?" Pretty as a picture, Cara quite stole his breath.

"I am well, sugar kisses." He shuffled his weight to his good leg and winced as pain shot through his injured limb. "Shall we depart for London?"

"Oh, no." She compressed her lips and peered at Caroline. "I should stay, as my sisters may have need of me."

At that moment, Caroline burst into tears, and Trevor

hugged her close. "Darling, please do not cry, as I can bear anything but your sorrow."

"But I shall miss you terribly." His wife gave vent to a plaintive sob.

And then Rebecca, in similar fashion, collapsed in Dirk's embrace. "Becca, my love, do not weep, as I would carry only happy memories of your charming face to sea."

"Promise me you will be careful." The former spy sniffed and clutched fistfuls of his many-caped greatcoat. "Come home to me, in one piece, else I swear I shall never forgive you, and I will name our firstborn for your brother."

As the husbands struggled to reassure their wives, Lance realized he envied them. It seemed selfish to think it, and he would deny it to his death were he asked, but he wanted someone to pine for him, when he embarked on journeys for His Majesty.

Wanted someone to cry for him.

Wanted someone to reminisce of him while he was away.

Wanted someone to come home to when he completed his mission.

And that someone was Cara.

As usual, pangs of guilt plagued his conscience, and he thought of Thomas. Courting the exquisite Miss Douglas seemed the ultimate betrayal of the cousin he had failed to save. Yet he could not dishonor the family name and title, and claiming Cara's maidenhead required recompense in the form of a wedding ceremony.

As he waved a bittersweet goodbye to his lifelong friends, he remained stock-still while a chorus of orders rang through the air, and sailors scrambled into the ratlines. One by one, the ships of the Brethren of the Coast cast off—for the first time without him, and something inside him fractured.

"Oh, Lance." Awash with worry, Caroline foundered against him. "What will I do if something happens to Trevor?"

"There, there, Caroline." Startled by a compelling urge to comfort his friend, he cradled her head to his chest and held her, as would her elder sibling Blake. "The Brethren have made the run on occasions too numerous to count—"

"Have they been compromised?" In a flash, she jerked and pinned him with a fearful gaze. "Will the French be looking for them?"

"No." Lance attempted to soothe her frazzled nerves. "I only meant they are well acquainted with the route—"

"Do you think General Bonaparte will be lying in wait, prepared to attack?" With an expression of sheer terror, Rebecca rested a palm to her protruding belly. "Is Dirk in danger?"

He scratched his temple. "Well, all missions involve danger—"

Caroline and Rebecca sobbed in concert.

It was too late when he discovered he had only increased their distress. "But I did not intend to imply—"

"Dearest, do not fret." Cara shot him a glance of reproach, and he clamped his mouth shut. "Our brave knights know well the course and, as such, can anticipate anything the French throw at our men. Is that not correct, Lance?"

On an exhale he replied, "I could not have said it better."

"Perhaps we should escort you home, sisters." Cara wiped Rebecca's cheeks, and then tended Caroline. "Lance, will you convey as much to Papa?"

"Of course." He leapt at the chance to escape two weepy

women, as he simply did not do tears. "If you will wait here, I shall summon my coach."

After an unutterably painful ride to the city, during which Caroline and Rebecca cried the entire journey, he delivered the Brethren wives to their respective residences with one regret. To his surprise, the married ladies opted to huddle together in their misery, leaving him to share a bench with Cara. But with Dirk's bride deposited on her doorstep, the always-polite Miss Douglas settled into the squabs opposite him and smoothed her skirts.

"Does this happen every time we embark on a mission?" Lance rolled his shoulders to dispel the tension investing his frame.

"Yes, though not usually to this degree. I daresay their pregnancies have something to do with the deluge we confronted." She peered out the window. "Mama says that is a common characteristic of a mother-to-be. Indeed I have witnessed the same of Sabrina, and we both know she is no water pot."

"Bloody hell." He shook his head and studied her with renewed appreciation. "How do you do it, Cara?"

"How do I do—what?" She blinked.

Lance grimaced as he searched for the proper phrasing to convey his discomfit. "How do you deal with the gross profundity of emotions?"

With an owlish expression, she gasped—before bursting into laughter.

"What is so funny?" He folded his arms.

"You." She wiped her eyes and giggled. "Only you could describe and diminish the love and devotion of a woman as a *gross profundity of emotions*."

"That was rather unforgivable, was it not?" Given her

reaction, he could not help but grin. "Yet I would not miss the opportunity to enjoy your company, unreservedly."

"Lance." All trace of levity vanished from her charming countenance, and she averted her stare. "You must not say such things."

"Why?" He perched on the edge of his seat. "We are rather more than friends, are we not, sugar kisses?"

The coach lurched violently, Cara toppled into the corner, and he availed himself of the favorable circumstance to claim the empty space beside her. Before she could protest, he hauled her into his lap and covered her mouth with his.

Soul-stirring passion ignited the instant their lips met, and pleasure rode in its wake. Unsure of his welcome, he hummed low in his throat when she speared her fingers in his hair and teased his tongue with hers. It seemed ages since he last kissed her.

How he longed to unleash the sultry seraph lurking amid the polite decorum, wanted to lose himself in the raw desire masked by the proper façade, wanted to taste the sweet honey of the lady beneath the elegant attire. And though she might deny it were he to inquire, Lance realized with certainty that Cara wanted him as he wanted her.

So he would bide his time, do things right, and woo her, as he should have pursued an innocent young woman. He would gauge her demeanor, and when he suspected she would be more receptive to his proposal, then and only then would he make his move.

IT WAS another night and another ball. To his infinite thanks, Caroline and Rebecca chose to forgo the evening's events, which afforded Lance the opportunity to dance unfettered attendance upon Cara and advance their courtship. But much to his dismay, Alex and Sabrina seemed to be everywhere at once. Even Elaine, who always sheltered in the shadows, acted in competition with him for his lady's company.

A sennight had lapsed since the Brethren departed without him, and the first few days passed without incident, as he and his bride-to-be commenced their daily ritual of comforting the wives while their husbands remained at sea. Given his knowledge of the supply runs and routes, along with Wellington's latest troop movements, Lance surmised he had approximately two days to woo Cara before Colling-wood anchored at Deptford.

Desperate to gain ground, and after much consideration and effort on his part, he arranged a delightful surprise and decided to throw caution to the wind at the Chomley's gala, which had filled to overflow when he arrived. After a quick scan of the ballroom, he targeted the object of his affection and frowned. Looming as nettlesome sentries at either side of his ladylove stood Sabrina and Alex, and he suspected Elaine circled nearby.

"Bloody everlasting hell," he cursed under his breath.

A chill of unease traipsed his spine, and he shuddered. For some reason Lance could not fathom, a single terrifying thought danced in his brain. Dare he contemplate it? Was it possible? Had Cara confided in their friends? And if she had confessed, to what extent and purpose had she divulged their secrets? Without doubt, his plan necessitated a new tack, with a concerted siege on multiple fronts, were he to reign supreme, and he paused to consider his options.

Just then, Alex glanced in his direction. When she whispered in Cara's ear, and his ladylove gave him her back, he mentally tucked his halo in his pocket with devilish delight. Diverting to the card room, he sought three unwitting but effective accomplices.

"Everett." He chucked Sabrina's husband on the shoulder. "So good to see you and your countess out and about tonight, given her delicate condition. Tell me, how do you do it?"

"Evening, Raynesford." Markham's welcoming smile faltered. "How do I do—what?"

"How do you sit here without care?" Lance shrugged. "Daresay, were it me, I would be on pins and needles. Probably would not let my wife, if I had one, out of my sight."

"Ah, well, Brie is pregnant, and she is the last person I would ever describe as *delicate*." With a chuckle, Everett sipped his brandy. "I can't keep her under lock and key, as if she were a criminal. You will understand when it is your time."

"Yes, I am aware of her characteristic tenacity, as I have known her all her life, which is why I am worried." Braced for a lightning strike, Lance frowned and prepared to deliver his first attack. "Mind you, I would not interfere in your personal affairs, but never have I seen her so peaked." For added effect, he glanced from side to side before leaning close to impart the final blow. "Are there complications?"

"Sabrina is peaked? Do you believe she is ill?" His expression sobered, Everett jumped from his chair, spilling the remaining contents of his glass, which he thrust at Lance. "I told her we should have stayed in tonight, but no —she insisted on attending the ball. Well, enough is enough. I am putting my foot down, and we are going home."

While he hated to torture a fellow knight, Lance made a mental note to send a case of his best brandy to the overwrought man in recompense for the untenable but necessary breach of the brotherly code. Poor Sabrina had no idea that a wicked storm loomed on the horizon.

One down, two to go.

Upon re-entering the grand ballroom, he scanned the vicinity, located his next apprenticed allies, and wrinkled his nose. The Kleinfeld brothers, known throughout the ton for their ghastly attire and none too graceful ability on the dance floor, engaged in a rousing discourse on men's fashions. As much as he regretted his actions, he could devise no other solution to his quandary. Simply put, he would deliver Elaine and Alex into the gawky, clumsy embrace—and hope the Brethren women survived unscathed.

"Gentlemen, how are you faring this evening?"

The elder Kleinfeld cast a toothy grin. "Lord Raynesford, do join us." He thumbed the lapel of a garish red coat trimmed with bright gold buttons. "We were just debating the latest trend in men's apparel."

The younger Kleinfeld, sporting a hideous purple version of his brother's equally offensive garb, proudly proclaimed, "I say it is past due for us to indulge ourselves as the ladies have done for so long."

"I concur with your assessment." Lance examined his own conservative black formalwear. "I only wish I were not the provincial that I might take such daring liberties with my wardrobe."

"You could do it, Raynesford." The Elder smacked him on the shoulder. "You must be bold. Perhaps orange would suit you?"

"I will speak with my tailor, first thing." Lance forced a smile, averted his gaze, and adopted what he hoped was a convincingly forlorn expression.

"Forgive me, Raynesford." The Younger neared. "But you seem a bit out of sorts."

"Alas, I am at a loss." Lance sighed dramatically. "I am in need of assistance in a delicate matter and too proud to ask for aid."

Both brothers clicked their heels and stood at attention.

"Whatever it is, Raynesford, we are at your service," the Elder offered.

"I do not know." He tapped a finger to his chin and feigned hesitance. "You see Lady Elaine and Lady Alexandra, two of my charges for the evening, are most desirous of a dance. But in my current state, I am unable to accommodate them."

"Say nothing more, as it would be our honor." The Elder glanced at his brother and waggled his bushy brows. "Perhaps a twirl about the ballroom in the arms of two dashing rakes will lift their spirits."

"Well, if you are certain it is not too great an imposition." It was all he could do not to laugh.

"Think nothing of it." The Younger waved dismissively. "You may rely on us."

Lance strolled at a close but discreet distance from the two dandy peacocks. He bit his lip as each gangly buffoon made his request and subsequently led an unsuspecting Elaine and a wary Alex into the crush.

Which left Cara at his mercy.

With a narrow stare, she asked, "Was that your doing?"

"I beg your pardon?" he replied with angelic innocence.

"How could you be so cruel to Alex and Elaine?" And then realization dawned. "Oh, no. And you set Everett on my sister, too."

It was a statement, not a question.

Lance adjusted the lace trim of his sleeve and rued the

fact that she read him so well, yet even his future bride could not anticipate the surprise he had struggled in earnest to prepare. "I do not know what—"

"Shame on you." Cara elbowed him in the ribs. "That was neither nice nor heroic, much in opposition to your namesake. My poor brother-in-law was beside himself with worry, and he did not allow Sabrina the opportunity to say goodbye before he all but carried her home."

"And if I know Brie, she will compensate admirably for any discomfit I have caused." He shuffled his feet and arched a brow. "But I am not sorry because I long for your company without hindrance."

"I am not certain I like the sound of that." Nevertheless, Cara rested her palm in the crook of his arm. "And if the ladies ever discover the depths of your unscrupulous behavior, they will never forgive you."

"Nonsense, they are Brethren." He bent and whispered in her ear, "Trust me?"

"Not by a long chalk."

"Smart lady." He grinned. "Come away with me, sugar kisses."

"Oh?" She averted her stare and appeared disinterested, but the pressure of her fingers declared otherwise. "Where?"

"Some place more private." He steered her toward his intended destination and chuckled when she arched a brow. "I have a surprise for you, and you will enjoy it."

"Indeed?" With nervous agitation, she glanced about and bit her lip, as he led her down a side hall. "How can you be so sure?"

"Because I know you as well as you know me." Myriad emotions danced in her expression. Curiosity, anticipation, and, dare he think it, excitement. Lost amid the dim light of the cavernous mansion, he sighed in relief when he discovered the door for which he searched. Retreating, he peered from side to side, because he would brook no interruptions, and set the oak panel wide. "Ladies first."

She took a single step and jerked to a halt. "It is dark in there."

"We have a fire in the hearth, and that will suffice."

"For what?" She frowned.

"Patience is a virtue, lady mine." He tapped her nose and handed her over the threshold. Feeling his way, he fumbled with the key in the lock, waited until the music from the ballroom reached a crescendo, which he hoped would mask the telltale click, and set the bolt.

In an instant, Cara whirled and stomped a foot. "Lance, what are you about?"

"I promise, my motives are honorable." With palms raised in mock surrender, he prowled in a half-circle, but she remained fixed, as he shuffled two chairs, creating the open space he required. "On my word as a gentleman, I want only to share something special."

"I gather this is Lord Chomley's study?" she inquired in a bare whisper.

"Aye." He kissed the crest of her ear as he hugged her from behind.

"Do you think Dorothea Chomley will appreciate your relocating the furniture?" She inhaled a shaky breath.

"I will return everything to its proper place before we depart, if it pleases you." He rotated her in his grasp. "But for now, I should very much like you to close your eyes."

"What for?" She furrowed her brow.

"Indulge me, dearest and loveliest Cara." Lance rubbed his nose to hers. "Just for tonight."

"All right." She acquiesced and inclined her head. "Now

what?"

"Listen carefully," he said in a low voice. "Can you hear the music?"

"Yes." She shivered in his embrace, and desire charged the field.

How Lance ached to claim her, to push Cara to the Aubusson rug and lose himself in the lush paradise of her body. In a momentary lapse of judgment, a proposal traipsed the tip of his tongue. In the nick of time, he drew rein, as he had sworn he would not broach a betrothal until he was assured of victory.

Clutching her wrist, he situated her palm on his shoulder. Snaking an arm about her waist, he pulled her near and took her other hand in his, twining their fingers. Replaying the past fortnight in his mind, he envisioned the requisite movements and prayed that his efforts had not failed him.

Summoning courage, he asked, "May I have this dance, sugar kisses?"

She flinched, almost sending them to the floor. "What?"

He chuckled and steered her in a less-than-graceful, somewhat stilted waltz.

"How is it possible?" Cara clung to him as they completed a full rotation. "You are dancing."

"Yes." Lance grinned. "Well, it is a poor imitation, but it is the best I can do at present."

"But—your leg." And then she did something he never would have predicted. Collapsing against him, she buried her face in his chest and burst into tears.

"Easy, love." He cradled her head. "I had thought you would be pleased with my progress. I never meant to make you cry."

"Oh, but I am happy." She sobbed and clutched fistfuls

of his lapels. "I always believed you would get better, and we just had to be patient. But to see you like this, as my hero, I am overjoyed."

"Tell me truly, am I still your hero?" Even as Lance uttered the words, he cursed himself, yet he remained in desperate need of her validation.

"How could you even ask such a question?" Cara met his gaze, and he shuddered. "How could you ever doubt your importance in my life? Do you think me some fickle female, that my admiration should wane due to an injured limb?"

"No, my girl. You are, as always, the eternal optimist." With newfound respect he studied her, in awe as he uncovered a new layer of her persona, and he caressed her cheek. "And you are the strongest woman of my acquaintance. Thanks to your diligence, unwavering support, and a lot of practice, I seem to be improving."

"So who did you partner while preparing for this night?" She shifted and snuggled closer. "Perhaps Captain Collingwood?"

"Perish the thought." He grimaced at the mere suggestion. "Elaine stood in your place."

"And you thanked her by delivering her into the arms of Archibald Kleinfeld?" Cara clucked her tongue. "Shame on you."

"Fear not, as I shall make amends." At that moment, they resumed their waltz, and his confidence grew with each successful turn about the room. "I will buy her a new bonnet."

"One would think dancing with a Kleinfeld merits two bonnets, at least." Cara giggled. "Can you reverse course?"

"Indeed." Although he stumbled when he executed the maneuver and cursed in silence. "Sorry."

"Do not apologize." As they found their stride, she sighed. "This is heaven on earth."

"I could not agree more." Lance brought her gloved knuckles to his lips and held her tighter about the waist.

When the music stopped, his lady hummed the tune, the name of which he could not recall, and they continued to whirl in concert. And then for some reason he could not fathom, various images flashed in his brain.

A mischievous grin.

A snowy afternoon.

An ice-covered pond nestled amid a crescent of oaks.

A desperate plea for help.

A pair of flailing hands.

The nagging guilt that plagued his existence had resurfaced with a vengeance, and a cold chill permeated his chest. A sea of Prescotts materialized, haunting and taunting, reminding him that he did not deserve the woman in his arms, because he had failed to save the true heir to the Raynesford marquessate.

A morbid visage of Thomas materialized as an apparition of failure, wagging his finger in reproach. Lance had ruined Cara, so honor demanded he marry her. Yet what little happiness he gleaned from that revelation lay in pieces, scattered at his feet as so many hopes and dreams, when it dawned on him that he had let his cousin drown, and still he claimed the girl.

Swimming in a miasma of shame and regret, he caught the toe of his shoe on the edge of the rug and lurched forward.

"Are you all right, my hero?"

He came alert in an instant and jerked, which threw him off balance. "Bloody hell."

Together, they crashed to the floor.

CHAPTER FOURTEEN

"*L*ance, are you injured?" Cara rolled onto her back and sat upright. After settling her skirts, she stood.

"I am so sorry." He propped on his elbows and frowned. "What a clumsy oaf I have become. Did I hurt you?"

"I am unscathed but worried about you." She offered him a hand, which he pointedly ignored. "Here, let me help you."

"I have no need of your assistance," he barked. "I can do for myself."

"Do not be stubborn." She rested palms on hips. "It is no crime to accept aid."

"You think me stubborn?" He snorted as he teetered and perched on his good knee. "That is rich coming from you."

She humphed and again reached for him. "Please be reasonable."

"*I said I can manage.*" Lance scooted to the desk and used it as an anchor, as he stood.

"Do not be cross, my hero." At his terse reply, Cara checked her tone and tempered her response, because she refused to be baited when they had so much to celebrate. "Else you will spoil our special night."

"What is so special about my hurtling you to the floor?" He snickered with unmasked disgust. "I am a bungling idiot —no better than a Kleinfeld."

"You are not a bungling idiot." She adjusted his cravat, and even in the faint light from the hearth she noted his scowl. Framing his face with her hands, she said, "And I take issue with your comparison, as neither are you clumsy. You recover from a serious injury, and I know many men would not fare half so well."

Lance snorted. "Spare me the motivational speech, as I—"

Cara set her lips to his in a soul-stealing kiss intended to leave him in no doubt of her regard. Flicking her tongue, she engaged him in an energetic little duel designed to entice, to arouse. When he grasped her hips and pressed her to his fast-rising erection, she moaned in appreciation. While she had meant to soothe his discomfit with a tender balm, her simple gesture soon exploded into a firestorm of passion she could no longer deny or control. With a plaintive cry, she reached for the fastenings of his trousers.

"Cara, no." He grabbed her wrists.

"But I want you." She fought to break free, yet he refused to relent. With desire burning in her veins, she nipped his chin. "Please, I need you."

"You are going to kill me." Resting his forehead to hers, Lance sighed. "Darling, we should not risk it. As things stand, you could be carrying my heir."

"I told you already that I am not pregnant."

"How can you be certain?"

"You can't be serious."

"I see." He averted his gaze. "All the more reason not to chance it, given our current dilemma."

"You refer to your proposal of—"

"Shh." He quieted her with a hand to her mouth. "Not tonight, love. We may be lifelong friends, but I cannot guarantee I could be magnanimous in the face of another rejection."

"But I—"

"No, Cara." He rubbed his nose to hers and then scanned the room. "Besides, I did not bring you in here to seduce you."

"I know." She scored her nails to the back of his neck. "But you will not let that stop you."

He chuckled. "Here?"

"Now." She nodded once. Then they could discuss marriage, fix a date, and plan their future. At that very second, however, she wanted nothing more than a bit of pre-engagement felicitations of a carnal nature, but the furnishings provided a conundrum, as there was nary a bed in sight. "How will we manage?"

Lance smiled, all wolf. "Do I look like a giddy schoolboy?"

"No." She trailed her tongue along his jawline. "In fact, I would describe your present demeanor as deliciously rakish."

"Deliciously rakish? You have become quite the temptress, sugar kisses." He navigated her in reverse, until she bumped a solid surface. "The Cara I know once refused to swim in the pond at Pembroke without benefit of a nightgown."

"I was a young child then, and I have long since shed such youthful reserve." He lifted her to the desktop, and she slid the inkstand to the opposite end of the blotter. "What are you doing?"

"I would argue you have shed much more than youthful reserve, but I am not complaining." Lance unbuttoned his coat and then freed the hooks of his breeches. "And given our accommodations, or lack thereof, and my injury, I must improvise to satisfy my lady's demands."

"Oh, I love the sound of that." She gasped in delight as he hiked her skirts and nudged her legs, which she spread without hesitation. "Am I your lady?"

"When have you existed as anything else?" With his palms he skimmed the sensitive insides of her thighs, before slipping a finger into the folds of her most intimate flesh. "Ah, sweet Cara, you are always ready for me."

"Is that good?"

"It is very good." Just as Lance positioned himself, he paused. "That was the dinner bell. Perhaps we should return to the ballroom."

"What is your hurry? We will make it in time for supper, I think." Not for a minute would Cara surrender what she deemed a golden opportunity, as she anticipated a post-coital proposal, which she intended to accept.

"WHAT DO you mean he did not propose?" Sabrina reclined amid the pillows on the *chaise* in her morning room, dubbed the war room because it served as the primary locale for the Brethren women to gather, strategize, and debrief developments in Cara's quest to claim her errant knight. "Could you not get him alone?"

"More or less." Cara twiddled her thumbs and then

shrugged, as her calm façade fractured. "But Lance did not offer for my hand. What more can I say?"

Given that she had spent the better part of the night, tossing and turning in bed, pondering the answer to the same question, and still could discern no solution to her predicament, Cara remained befuddled.

"So what did you two do after Everett dragged me home? And what do you imagine set him off? Never have I seen the man so discomposed." Sabrina cast her a narrow stare. "Alex said you disappeared for quite some time while she endured the unwanted attentions of Sir Archibald Kleinfeld."

"Oh, Cara." Alex rolled her eyes. "It was dreadful."

Should Cara divulge the truth? Of course not. After a rigorous round of lovemaking, she had prepared to entertain and accept a proposal of marriage, for which she had composed a gracious speech in honor of the momentous occasion. As it turned out, she need not have concerned herself with such niceties.

Once their clothes had been righted, Lance had escorted her to the dining room, whereupon they assumed an air of unreserved equanimity designed to thwart any suspicion of inappropriate activity, which they portrayed to perfection for the benefit of the raucous but importuning crowd. To compound her disappointment, if it were possible, he had remained a consummate gentleman for the rest of the evening, which she considered an insult of the cruelest sort.

How dare her hero make passionate love to her and then behave himself? It was if they had done nothing more than engage in a polite game of whist in Lord Chomley's study.

"You think you had it bad?" Elaine snorted. "I danced with the Younger. Daresay I have at least one broken toe to show for it."

The world tilted as Cara reflected on Lance's machinations, which had landed two of her dearest friends in the clumsy clutches of the brothers Kleinfeld, which some might describe as a fate worse than death.

"What rotten luck for you both," Caroline chimed with a mighty frown.

"I find it rather suspicious that the Kleinfelds sought your estimable company." Rebecca gazed at the floor. "And Sabrina was conveniently removed from the premises by an uncharacteristically distraught husband."

Cara feared she might swoon, because her hero's stratagem had piqued Rebecca's spy instincts.

"That is the understatement of the year." Brie shook her head and grimaced. "Poor Everett was on the verge of hysteria. It took almost the entire night to calm him, as he thought me in a delicate state, and I expended considerable energy to prove otherwise, hence I've had little sleep and am now exhausted, in truth."

Thank heavens for her wayward younger sister, who always spoke with unvarnished honesty, as her bold statement redirected their focus.

"Oh, do tell." Alex bounced on the edge of her seat. "Just how does a wife please a husband? Mind you, spare no detail."

"Alex, you must not ask such things." In that instant, vivid images flashed through Cara's mind. Lance tugging her gown from her shoulders, kissing her bare breasts, and then guiding his most protuberant part to her secret entrance. "It is not proper."

And then Cara bit her tongue against further admonition, because the point of convergence had just shifted in her favor.

"Stuff and nonsense." The younger Seymour huffed a

breath. "What good is a marriage license if it does not grant a lady permission to be improper with her spouse?"

"Well, there you have me, but I am unsure just how much to share." Sabrina glanced at Rebecca and then Caroline. "Do either of you have anything to contribute to this discussion?"

"I never kiss and tell," Becca replied.

"You are no fun," Elaine whispered, with a look of awe. "As Alex and I are alone but for you, how else shall we learn what is expected of us on our wedding night?"

"She has a point." Caroline fidgeted and then peered at Brie. "And although my mother explained the physical act when my courses first flowed, nothing she imparted could have prepared me for Trevor. From what I gather, he is an altogether different animal from my father."

"I know just what you mean." Sabrina refilled her cup. "Mama was very forthcoming on the eve of my marriage ceremony, yet I considered myself ignorant in the midst of the actual deflowering. It was a vast deal more personal than I had imagined, and my shameless lord's behavior extended beyond the pale. The man howls, mid-coitus, as a wolf bays at the moon."

"How frightening." Elaine gulped and hugged a pillow.

"Is that normal?" Alex asked with unmasked fascination.

"Who knows, but I do not care, as I rather fancy it. In fact, I almost expect his lascivious exultations now." With a naughty grin, Sabrina giggled. "You see I view his unconventional enthusiasm as a reflection of my skills in the bedchamber."

"Very good assumption, Brie. And I concur with your logic." Caroline nodded once. "Trevor calls to his maker, again and again, with unrestrained fervor. He makes me feel so invincible and a regular seductress."

All eyes centered on Rebecca, who shifted and then said, "Dirk roars like a lion."

Caroline gasped. "He doesn't."

"Our stodgy Dirk?" Sabrina pressed a hand to her throat.

"Indeed, he does. Must confess I found the initial instance very startling, until I realized his effusive bellow served to indicate he had reached a particular pinnacle of our joining. And on occasion, he has bitten my shoulder, though I would deem it more a love nip, but what it does to me—I can't describe, as there are no adequate words." Becca assessed her fingernails and then lowered her chin. "Sisters, you are sworn to secrecy, as my man would neither understand nor forgive my candor, regardless of our familial affiliations."

"Of course." Sabrina passed a plate filled with short-bread to Caroline. "I am no traitor, Becca."

"We vow on the Brethren oath never to betray your confidence." Caroline dabbed the corner of her mouth with a napkin. "As it stands, polite society would disapprove of our topic of conversation, as gently bred ladies are not supposed to discuss physical relations between the sexes. It simply is not done."

"Well, what the *ton* does not know will not hurt it." Alex gazed at the ceiling and sighed. "And we can't possibly learn all that is required of us from our brother's collection of Rowlandson's etchings."

A choral tapestry of gasps filled the air, but just as fast a knock at the door silenced the female faction.

Carrying a silver tray, the butler entered the room. "I beg your pardon, your ladyship, but a missive has just arrived for you."

"Thank you, Ware." Sabrina swiped a folded note from

the salver. "That will be all." In mere seconds, she scanned the correspondence. "It is from Damian. Our brothers have docked."

"Jason's home." Alex leapt from her chair, assessed her attire, and frowned. "I must change into something more presentable for my knight. Elaine, will you come with me? I need your opinion."

"I should be delighted." Elaine stood at attention. "Cara, will you join us?"

"Of course. I shall give you a half hour and follow in my carriage." Cara smiled and shook her head, knowing her friend intended to don something more provocative than the simple yellow day dress she currently sported. "We can travel to Deptford together."

"Wonderful." Alex, with Elaine in tow, rushed to bestow on each lady a quick peck on the cheek, before she all but ran to the door, reached for the knob, and then glanced over her shoulder. "I want Jason to fall to his knees when he sees me."

Cara couldn't help but laugh at the younger Seymour's bawdy statement, but she sobered when she met Brie's stern gaze, after Alex and Elaine departed.

"That one is in for trouble if we do not check her behavior." Sabrina wrinkled her nose. "And she sets a poor example for Elaine."

"I could not agree more." Rebecca inclined her head and frowned. "Where Collingwood is concerned, Alex has already stretched the limits of propriety to dangerous lengths."

"She only wants to look pretty for her beau." Cara neglected to mention she had thought of doing the same thing, because Lance would have received a similar summons to the docks. "Where is the harm?"

"As long as that is all she does." Caroline folded her arms. "But you should watch her, as she is far too caught up in the romance of your situation. Damian will kill her and Collingwood if they do something stupid."

"Sisters, you make too much of nothing. To borrow Alex's favorite phrase, stuff and nonsense." Cara studied the lace trim of her sleeve and sought a change of subject. "By the by, never have I seen Elaine so curious. Her queries evidence newfound confidence even I could not have predicted."

"That reminds me, we shared our deepest secrets with you." Caroline pointed for emphasis. "Now you must share yours."

"Ah, yes." Rebecca arched a brow. "It is your turn, dear sister."

"My turn for—what?" Cara swallowed hard and feigned ignorance, but she understood their demands.

"Do not play the fool." Sabrina snuffled. "Tell us of Lance and his naughty habits."

"*Sabrina.*" Cara shifted and smoothed her skirts. "As I am not married, I have not your extensive experience—"

"Now." Brie shuffled the pillows and resituated herself.

"Oh, all right." Cara bit her lip and revisited her most intense moments with Lance. And on second thought, she realized the Brethren wives offered her a golden opportunity to examine and, perhaps, interpret her future husband's salacious tendencies. "Lance is not as vocal as are your spouses."

"How dreadful." Caroline cast a sympathetic smile. "But it is early in your relationship. Give him time. He may yet be a screamer."

In unison, the wives burst into laughter.

"I am so happy to provide you with afternoon entertainment." Cara sniffed.

"Sorry, my dear friend." Rebecca dabbed a stray tear. "Perhaps your intended's quiescent response is related to his injury."

"Actually, I believe it may be due to the fact that we have had to temper our couplings for fear of discovery." Cara recalled the instance when Lance covered her mouth with his hand. "There is something, however, but I am unsure how to describe it."

"Try making a comparison," Becca suggested.

"Well, it really is difficult to convey." Cara envisioned the somewhat frightening habit. "As Lance nears—you know, he makes the oddest expressions. When first it happened, I thought he had suffered a violent paroxysm, and it bloody well scared me to death."

"Like this?" Just then, Sabrina scooted to the edge of her seat and contorted her face.

"Oh, I have one." Caroline mimicked a tortured visage.

"That is nothing. What about mine?" Rebecca scrunched her cheeks and twisted her lips.

"Well this is what I confronted." Cara did her best to mock Lance's convoluted countenance.

Once again, silence fell over the room. And then a peal of laughter exploded into gales of unrestrained mirth, shattering the peaceful solitude.

"And they call us dramatic." Rebecca giggled and hugged her belly. "Worry not, Cara. For that is an excellent sign."

"So it seems, but it is altogether terrifying when you have no warning," Cara explained. "I thought I harmed his leg."

"It is a pain of a different sort." Caroline elbowed Rebecca. "And it hurts so good."

"Oh, I like that," Becca responded with zeal.

"Is that what happened last night?" Brie inquired.

"In a manner of speaking—" Cara clamped her mouth shut, because she had not planned to confess her transgression from the previous evening.

"Just as I suspected." In a flash, the mood changed from one of lighthearted banter to somber intensity, as Rebecca pinned Cara with a lethal stare. "You are courting disaster, sister. Have we taught you nothing? Do you wish to become pregnant?"

"And if that occurs, you leave yourself no retreat." Caroline stretched her feet. "Then you must wed amid indecision and self-doubt, beneath the unforgiving scrutiny of so-called polite society, which is anything but, and I would not wish that on my worst enemy."

"You speak as though you—"

"—Comprehend the reason for your vacillation?" Caroline sniffed. "Only too well, I am afraid. Given the circumstances surrounding my own wedding, at the pointed end of Blake's best sword, I apprehend the various difficulties of a forced union, and I would spare you such torment. You second-guess every move and word, wondering if you will ever enjoy a love match, if you are worthy of such a prize, and if it would not have been better to die an old maid."

"You pray that your husband will express his devotion but grow weary with each successive day that the much anticipated declaration eludes you." Sabrina gazed at Cara with tear-filled eyes. "You recount the events compelling you to marry and grasp at the minutest glimmer of hope, analyzing his most trivial actions for some sign of affection that extends beyond the physical, seizing upon anything, however insignificant, to deflect the *ton's* harsh criticism and protect yourself."

"But every time he takes you in his arms, whispering praise and encouragement, you tell yourself it is enough to know that he desires you, above all else, even though you believe otherwise. Yet at night, when no one watches, you study your reflection in a mirror and judge each imagined flaw as the cause of his indifference, as if his rationale were so pedestrian." Rebecca inhaled a shaky breath. "And just as you prepare to surrender the fight, accepting what is instead of longing for what might have been, he utters that simple phrase, sets the world at your feet, and your heart soars to new heights."

"Indeed, it is a priceless treasure unlike any other, a shield of impenetrable strength, and an alliance of formidable power." Caroline wiped her damp cheeks and hiccuped. "And then you truly learn what it means to exist as something more than yourself, as the love you had thought reached the limits of capacity grows by heretofore immeasurable, inconceivable amounts, filling your life with inexpressible joy."

"And if I have learned anything from my experience, it is that our men endure their own special brand of hell, albeit mostly of their making, on the road to self-discovery and a declaration." Becca fumbled for a handkerchief. "It is a small consolation, yet important to note, because it belies the fact that they, too, must bleed with despair to know the value and pleasure of true love. So you should know you are not alone in your misery."

"And in the end, the goal, once attained, will be all the more sweet because of the preceding bitterness." Caroline reached for Cara and Rebecca. "In short, the gift is worth the price you pay."

"She is right." Brie clutched Cara's hand and squeezed her fingers. "And I want that for you and Lance."

"We would have you join our most happy trio." Rebecca glanced at Caroline and then Sabrina. "And we would toast your felicitous future and a rounding belly with a cup of chamomile tea."

"I will drink to that." Cara laughed, as she formed a circle of support with the Brethren wives. And in that moment of clarity, she knew what she had to do to win her hero. "Ladies, I am certain I can make Lance see me as something more than a friend once we wed, as never have I wavered in my conviction that he is destined to be mine. In time, he will grow to love me as his wife, and I will secure his declaration."

"So you are determined to change your tack?" Sabrina inquired. "Knowing the battle that awaits, and everything it entails, you are willing to settle for less than his most ardent devotion when you speak the vows?"

"Yes." Cara nodded with renewed confidence. "With your invaluable tutelage, I will survive, come what may."

"Then you must stand firm, dearest, for both your sakes." Sabrina bowed her head and peered at the floor. "And as much as it distresses me to admit it, I will no longer be around to assist you."

"What do you mean?" Cara flinched in shock. "You cannot abandon me now, when I need you most."

"But it is not my choice, as Everett has forbidden me to attend further events of the Little Season for the duration of my pregnancy, with the exception of your birthday celebration and the family holiday gathering. For whatever reason, something inside him snapped, and my husband watches over me like a hawk." Adopting a shy smile, Sabrina glanced at Cara. "If I so much as sneeze, he sends for Dr.

Handley. Yet I can't be angry, as my shameless lord dotes on me to excess, and I am quite enamored of him, anew."

"And on that note, I should excuse myself." Rebecca scooted to the edge of her seat. "To borrow a page from Alex's book, I should change into something more appealing to welcome my gallant knight."

"Given that we share your carriage, I must away for the same purpose." Caroline stood and smirked. "Something about a mission stimulates my husband's appetites to unrivaled heights, upon his return, and I am loathe to disappoint him."

"Did you not remark that he admires your navy blue traveling coat?" Becca asked with a conspiratorial giggle.

"Perhaps I shall wear that with nothing beneath it." Caroline tapped a finger to her chin. "What say you, sister? Will he be shocked?"

"Yes." Rebecca waved a farewell. "But in a good way, I think. And you must help me select something equally appealing to rouse Dirk."

"Did he not declare your burgundy coat his favorite?" Caroline winked and blew a kiss to Cara. "What about that and a smile? After all, there is nothing like a quick and easy strip to inspire our men."

"Caroline, you are a bloody genius," Becca replied as they exited the room.

"Shall I escort you to the door, sister?" Sabrina rubbed the small of her back and yawned. "No doubt you wish to primp and preen for Lance, as well."

"Would you blame me if I said you were correct?" Arm in arm, Cara and her younger sister strolled into the hall. "Yet I am at sea. Is Everett serious, regarding his edict?"

For the first time in her life, she relied on Sabrina. As children, she had always tended Brie's countless scrapes and bruises. When Sabrina broke her wrist after a particularly nasty tumble from a tree, Cara had nursed her wayward sister back to health. And when Sabrina grew frightened from the scary stories the boys used to tell late at night, she sought Cara's bed and comfort. Now their respective positions were reversed, and Cara desperately needed Sabrina.

"But he is," Brie stated with grim finality. "I am afraid you are on your own in the ballrooms, until I give birth, and you must be vigilant, as Alex requires your counsel. I foresee breakers ahead, as she grows bolder by the minute, and the cost to her reputation will impact her marriage prospects before she realizes it."

"Wherever did you gain such uncommonly good sense?" Cara paused in the foyer.

"From my uncommonly level-headed elder sister." Sabrina cupped Cara's cheek. "I love you."

"And I you." Cara swallowed the lump in her throat. "Worry not, little gadling. I intend to cease the charade with Collingwood, before anyone gets hurt, and I will do so today. Never should I have embarked on such a foolhardy endeavor, but the fault is mine. I can only hope to manage the betrothal better than the courtship."

"Oh, that is rather elementary, as spouses are easily maneuvered by a singular part of their anatomy, just as a rudder steers a ship." Sabrina compressed her lips. "Watch and learn." Cupping her hands to her mouth, she shouted, *"Everett."*

"What are you—"

"Shh. One, two, three." Brie counted on her fingers.

At that very moment, Everett ran into the foyer and slid to a halt. "Darling, is something wrong? Are you unwell?"

Without warning, Sabrina grabbed her husband and kissed him, in full view of Cara. Then her younger sister whispered in Everett's ear, and the poor man blushed beet-root red.

"My lady, you need rest." In a flash, Everett bent and swept Sabrina into his arms. Then he cleared his throat. "Good afternoon, Cara. Brie has overtired herself, and I must see to her welfare. Please, convey our regard to our brothers, as we shall forgo the journey to Deptford for my wife's health."

"Of course." Cara averted her gaze, as the happy couple ascended the stairs.

Stepping into the sunlight, Cara lifted her chin and basked in the warmth of nature's kiss, which evoked deli-cious memories of the previous night and the heat of passion she shared with Lance. But the depth of her attach-ment extended a vast deal beyond the physical realm. What if her hero never responded, in kind?

Would the fiery blaze in her heart reduce her to ashes, if Lance did not stoke the flames of love? It was a quandary for which she had no answer. It was a gamble of the worst sort, just as her sisters had warned. Glancing left and then right, she shivered, as the lonely solitude of her situation struck as a wintery gale and chilled her to the marrow.

Thus far she had wagered her maidenhead in the quest to win a husband. She had rolled the dice and lost. So she could retreat and hope for the best, or she could bet it all in one final venture. Recalling the embroidered handkerchief nestled in her bodice, she smiled. Indeed, Cara had plans of her own and required a change of attire and attitude.

It was time to claim her knight.

CHAPTER FIFTEEN

*I*t was time to claim his lady.

As he stood on the docks at Deptford, Lance resolved not to leave Cara alone with Jason. Under the guise of concern for his ship, he loomed in the wake of his competitor. To his infinite relief, Alex and Elaine remained entrenched at Cara's side. For a scarce second, he mulled the possibility that Alex courted the blonde captain, but just as fast he vanquished the thought.

Then again, it made perfect sense to presume Alex simply performed her duties as official escort, in obeisance of societal dictates. Regardless of Collingwood's fledgling affiliations and title, the brief duration of his acquaintance with Miss Douglas rendered a private audience in gross breach of polite decorum. Lance, on the other hand, enjoyed the luxury of a lifelong liaison, sanctioned by their familial ties. Their friendship, his and Cara's, was well known throughout the ton, so no one would dare conceive of a courtship blossoming between two members of the Brethren.

How he looked forward to raising some eyebrows.

"I believe you will find everything shipshape, my friend." Jason stood tall, almost as if he were trying to impress Lance. "The *Demetrius* is a fine vessel, and she swims like a dream."

"Indeed, everything appears to be in excellent order." As he ascended the gangplank, Lance surveyed the rigging in hopes of finding something amiss. As much as he hated to admit it, a fluttering canvas or loose rope would have pleased him. To his disappointment, he found nothing awry. "I commend you, brother."

"Your praise is misplaced, as it is your crew I must compliment." Jason smiled. "They are entirely responsible for the success of my first mission as a member of the Brethren. You run a tight ship, Raynesford."

"I employ only experienced sailors." Lance waved to familiar faces and grinned as a proud parent. "They are the finest seamen I have ever commanded during my naval career."

"You should know I have nothing but good things to report." Then Collingwood turned to Cara and said, "Perhaps Miss Douglas would appreciate a full account of my mission?"

Any affinity Lance might have developed for his rival evaporated with that singular suggestion, as Cara favored Jason with her attention. "I should love to hear your tale, Captain."

Lance frowned and clenched his fists. Just what was she about? Never before had she asked of his charges. Of course, it had not been necessary, because he always cornered her upon his return and regaled her with his daring adventures at sea, in a pathetic attempt to thrill his lady. As she fussed over another man, Lance seethed in silence.

"Oh, do tell, Captain." Alex pressed her clenched hands to her dangerously low-cut bodice, of which Lance had scarcely taken note until that instant. "Did you tangle with the French?"

And although the risqué décolletage had not registered with Lance beyond a reminder to speak with Damian about her questionable behavior, it had not escaped Collingwood, who seemed quite entranced by her bold attire, as did the rest of the crew. But it was Jason's open admiration that first raised Lance's suspicions, because his adversary had been steadfast in his courtship of Cara prior to sailing. Did the man believe he could woo two Brethren women at once? That was akin to suicide.

"In all truth, Lady Alexandra, we saw little action while at sea." Jason snapped his fingers. "That reminds me, I forgot the log and report in my cabin."

"May I accompany you to retrieve it?" Cara inquired with a sweetness no man could resist, and Lance swore under his breath.

"I will get it." Without hesitation, Lance stepped to the fore. "This is, after all, my ship."

"Can I come, too?" Alex batted her lashes at Collingwood, and Lance was certain there were games afoot.

"Oh, I would dearly love to see the *Demetrius*, as never have I explored her decks." Elaine rocked on her heels, and Lance stumbled. "My cousin is a tad overprotective."

"Given that I have spent the past few weeks aboard this rig, I am familiar with the location of the captain's cabin." With an owlish expression, Jason cleared his throat. "But who am I to deprive myself of such estimable company?"

"Perhaps Lance could give you and Alex a tour," Cara said to Elaine. "While Jason and I retrieve the log?"

"But I wish to see the captain's quarters, and why should

I stay here?" Alex pouted. "Lance can amuse himself. Besides, he is injured and may not feel up to the walk."

"I am not an invalid." Like bloody hell would he allow Jason to escort Cara. How he managed to restrain his fast rising anger he didn't know or care. "Given this is my ship, I shall collect the log."

"Wait." Jason chuckled and scratched his temple. "Why do we not journey to my cabin, as a group?"

"You mean my cabin," Lance inserted with an acid tongue.

"Indubitably." Jason retreated and bowed with an exaggerated flourish. "Ladies first."

Neither Cara nor Alex moved.

"You forget yourself, brother." Lance pressed a clenched fist to his lips and shifted his weight. "They have never visited my stateroom. Perhaps you can lead the way."

"I should be delighted," Jason replied. With Cara at his left, and Alex at his right, Collingwood proceeded across the waist, steering the ladies to the correct portal.

With Elaine at his side, Lance hobbled in their wake, nodding an acknowledgment to the cook as he passed the galley.

As soon as he entered his domain, his home away from home, bawdy images filled his brain. Thoughts of Cara, naked and spread for his delectation, assailed his senses, and he tripped. Ever since Trevor confessed to spending his wedding night with Caroline aboard the *Hera*, and Dirk divulged that he had followed suit with Rebecca on the *Gawain*, Lance had fantasized about making love to Cara in the one place he had always considered a man's sanctuary—his quarters on the *Demetrius*. Despite his injury, he did not doubt his ability to rock the boat.

And although another captain had taken the *Demetrius*

to sea, the first thing Lance noticed was that Jason had changed nothing. Indeed, Lance's personal belongings remained tucked in their respective places, and not a single book or lantern had been relocated. Why it was comforting he did not know, but standing in his cabin, amid the faint smell of cigar smoke mixed with brine and the gentle roll of the Thames port, Lance felt whole again.

"I did my best to leave everything as I found it." Jason grinned and chucked Lance on the shoulder. "I am well aware my command of the *Demetrius* is a temporary commission, brother."

Unnerved that a brief acquaintance could read him with the accuracy and ease of an old friend, Lance shrugged. "I assure you, I did not give it the slightest thought."

"So you say." Jason laughed and strode to the large desk holding pride of place before the stern windows, whereupon he picked up a leather-bound log. "Are we ready?"

"So this is where you slept?" Alex stood beside the over-sized bunk, inclined her head, and held Collingwood's stare as she then perched on the edge of the down mattress. Bouncing in a flirty manner, she bit her lip. "It seems comfortable enough."

"For what?" Lance choked and sputtered. Had his friend lost her wits? Had the musty air molded her mind?

Purposely baiting a seaman who had just returned from a mission was neither smart nor safe, because running French patrols aground stirred the blood, which pooled in a particular six inches of the male anatomy. Alex treaded dangerous waters, and Lance wanted to know why.

"I refer to slumber." She favored Jason with a wide-eyed stare. "What else would you do here?"

"Alex," Cara hissed.

A red tone spread from beneath Jason's starched white

cravat, coloring his neck, his cheeks—hell, his entire face. Lance recognized the telltale, lustful male flush, and it was no surprise. With Alex dangling herself as a carrot before the horse, Jason displayed the natural reaction of an aroused sailor, so Lance could not blame his rival.

"Perhaps we should return to the docks." Lance ushered Elaine and Cara to the door. "Admiral Douglas will be expecting your report."

Cara glanced over her shoulder. "Coming, Alex?"

"We are right behind you," Jason replied.

Lance led Cara and Elaine down the short hall. She peered at him and favored him with a charming smile, which warmed him to his toes. But when she glanced back, no doubt to check Alex's behavior, the pressure of her fingers in the crook of his arm underscored some internal unrest.

"What is it?" He paused. "Is something wrong?"

"Nothing." Though Cara attempted to convey an air of serenity, she did not fool him for a second.

"Will you show me the kitchen, Lance?" Elaine tugged his wrist. "I should dearly love to know how the cook plans and provides meals at sea."

"As you wish, dear cousin." While on the surface, Lance was lighthearted and enthusiastic as he explained the intricacies of food preparation aboard ship, in reality, curiosity and angst gnawed at his nerves. What had caused the sudden change in Cara's demeanor?

Skittish and abrupt, adjectives he would never have used to describe her, she feigned interest as he provided a brief education on sea fare. To his chagrin, Lance sensed an underlying preoccupation as Cara paced.

But what had upset her? Could it be Jason's burgeoning fascination with Alex? Did Cara possess a depth of feeling for Collingwood that even Lance had underestimated? He shuddered at the mere thought. It couldn't be true. He would not allow himself to believe it.

"Well, what are we doing here?" Jason inquired. "Raiding the pantry?"

"Cara and Elaine requested a tour of the galley." Lance shot him a casual glance—and just stopped himself from gawking. Later, there would be time enough to dissect what he had just witnessed. "I had not the heart to refuse them."

"Are our fair ladies considering a career in the culinary arts, or have they acquired a taste for dried beef and stale bread?" Jason chuckled and pulled Alex, who held a death grip on his arm, even closer, which breached the limits of polite decorum for mixed company. "As you stand fast for Miss Douglas and Lady Elaine, I shall escort Lady Alex to her carriage. And then I must away, as Admiral Douglas awaits my report."

"And I should accompany you, for the debriefing," Lance added. He glanced at Elaine and winked and then turned to discover Cara staring at her feet. With a gentle nudge, he gained her attention. "What say you, dearest Cara? Are you ready?"

"Indeed," she responded with a curt nod. And then she leaned near to whisper in his ear. "I had hoped we would speak in private, but this is not the best venue. Perhaps tonight you might grant me an audience?"

"It would be my honor," he replied in a low voice.

At the fore, Alex and Jason strolled, head to head, like a couple of besotted sweethearts, which left Lance with a sick feeling in his stomach. Something about the scenario did not set right with him, as his adversary lavished his affection on Alex.

And what of the younger Seymour? It could not have

escaped her that Jason had paid call on Cara. So why would
Alex make free her favors to her friend's potential suitor?
And not for a minute did Lance doubt that Alex had
allowed Jason to compromise her. Because try as she might,
Alex could not disguise the signature flush in her cheeks
and her kiss-swollen lips.

Somewhere, somehow, someone had played his lady
false.

Before the night was over, Lance vowed to discover the
turncoat and the depth of their treachery.

BEFORE THE NIGHT WAS OVER, Cara vowed to locate Captain
Collingwood and end their arrangement. As she surveyed
the ballroom in search of Alex's blonde suitor, Cara cursed
under her breath. Having failed miserably in her attempt to
engage Jason aboard the *Demetrius* and cease her hare-
brained scheme, she had come to the Hayward Ball determined to corner her partner in nefarious enterprises and be
done with the whole miserable plot.

"And how are you this fine evening, Miss Douglas?"
Jason approached from behind, and Cara almost jumped
out of her skin.

"Captain Collingwood, it is so good to see you." She
sighed with relief. "We must talk—"

"My, but you look splendid in your formal attire, Captain
Collingwood." Draped in a gown of rich crimson, which
featured a body-hugging cut that left little to the imagination, Alex inclined her head and smiled. "And I dressed in
this old rag."

Poor Jason went up in flames, and Cara replayed the
afternoon scene aboard the *Demetrius*, which had left her

scrambling to divert Lance's attention, else Collingwood may have ended his mission with a walk on the plank.

Elaine's request to tour the galley had been a subtle attempt to cover Alex's bold behavior, which had resulted in a sneak attack of a male sort. In short, one minute Alex had stood in the hall, just outside the captain's cabin, and in the next Jason had snaked his arm about her waist, and she disappeared.

"Lady Alex." Jason bowed and then claimed her hand. "You would be a vision in a chimney sweep's togs."

"Oh, Captain Collingwood, talk like that could sweep a lady off her feet." Alex giggled, and Cara could have strangled her friend.

"Alex, if you do not mind, perhaps I could have a word with the Captain?" Cara clenched her teeth and cast a stern stare. "It is imperative."

"Oh, dear." Alex's smile faltered. "I forgot—that is, of course, as I have reserved the waltz for our esteemed Captain."

"I believe this dance is mine, Miss Douglas." Lance stood at attention, and Cara almost swooned.

"Can you manage, Raynesford?" Jason arched a brow. "It would be my honor to indulge our fair Miss Douglas in your stead."

"And I have saved the very same waltz for you, my lord." Cara swallowed hard as she gazed at Lance. "Would you not prefer that?"

Without a word, her hero frowned and dipped his chin.

As Cara assumed her proper position opposite Jason, she mentally rehearsed her carefully composed speech. When they joined hands, she said, "Captain, I—"

"Is my Alex not beautiful tonight?" He grinned like a

giddy schoolboy. "Not that she is not always beautiful, but this evening, she is exceptionally so."

"Yes, she is lovely, as always." They parted, and Cara switched partners with the lady to her left, before she again met Jason. "Captain, I had hoped—"

"Tell me, Miss Douglas, did she wear that fantasy creation just for me?" At that instant, he pinned Alex, who loomed at the edge of the dance floor, with a heated stare that made Cara blush. "Or do I presume too much?"

"Without doubt, Captain, Alex turns herself out for you, and you alone." Cara swallowed ungracious invective, as she swapped places with the woman to her right. At last she resumed the spot beside Collingwood and said, "Be that as it may—"

"I knew it." When he smiled, he bared his teeth. "Forgive my candor, Miss Douglas, but Alex boils my blood."

"I am pleased to hear it." Cara laughed. "Because I believe you have the same effect on her."

"Does she speak of me?" In a flash, Jason shook his head. "Forget I inquired, as such request is unworthy of a gentleman. I apologize for asking you to betray a confidence."

"Do not fret." Cara squeezed his hand. "I am sure she would not object to a tiny indiscretion. The answer is yes, Alex speaks of little else but her heroic Captain Collingwood."

"Oh, I say." She wouldn't have thought it possible, but his smile broadened to impressive lengths. "May I entrust you with a secret, Miss Douglas?"

"By all means, Captain." Cara nodded and summoned patience, as she had done nothing to advance her goal. "You may rely on me."

"When this infernal war is over, I intend to offer for

Alex." With an expression of trepidation, he compressed his lips and twirled Cara. "If she will have me."

"Captain, I daresay you would face far greater danger than anything General Bonaparte could pose were you to return to our shores and not propose to Alex."

"Miss Douglas, your words are music to my ears." Jason came to a halt, and she circled him. "I am in your debt."

"But I am already in yours, Captain." Cara curtseyed and thought that the perfect opportunity to initiate her discussion. "You see I no longer require—"

The dinner bell pealed, and it was then she noticed the quartet had quieted. Various couples veered toward the main hall, and Cara cursed, because she had squandered her chance.

"I believe it is time for supper." Jason bowed.

"Yes, but—"

"If I may, I would appreciate the honor of escorting Miss Douglas." Lance extended his arm, and she rested her palm in the crook of his elbow.

"Thank you, my hero." As Jason sought Alex's company, Cara's mind raced with possibilities to end their arrangement.

And then it struck her. A new idea dawned, a solution she had discounted prior to that moment. She realized that once she accepted Lance's proposal, they would make their happy announcement, and she needed only to thank Collingwood for his cooperation with none the wiser.

"Is there a particular spot you prefer, my lady?" Lance ushered her into the crowded venue. "Near the dessert trolley, perhaps?"

"How about a place that affords us a modicum of privacy, as I would share you with no one." When her future husband came to an abrupt halt, she almost tripped. "Did I say something wrong?"

"On the contrary, I like the way you think, sugar kisses." The look with which he favored her would have melted butter, and he scanned the area. "How about the dimly lit corner, near the terrace doors?"

"Perfect." They weaved left, and Cara acknowledged numerous notable members of society. "Later you might show me the Hayward's gardens."

His answering smile was pure wolf. "Now that is a request I dare not refuse."

Ah, the heretofore-unexpected benefits of table linens played right into Cara's plans, as a seemingly innocuous swath of cloth provided concealment for Lance's exuberant games. While on the surface all appeared proper, beneath the elegant shield of cream damask trimmed in old gold, Lance availed himself of every opportunity to touch her.

The heat of his caress penetrated her lavender silk gown to kiss her thigh, as he grazed the toe of his shoe along the back of her ankle. And on occasion, after a quick check of the immediate vicinity, he pinched her bottom. By the time she had consumed the main entrée of chicken fricassee, Cara was hungry.

"So, should I fetch you a cookie or some pudding?"

"Might I persuade you to forego dessert in favor of a sweet of a different sort?"

"An inspiring suggestion, sugar kisses."

"I love it when you call me that."

"Do you?" Lance winked. "Appropriate to my lady."

"And I am your lady." Cara met his gaze, held it with her own. "Never doubt me."

She knew the precise moment he understood the full meaning of her declaration, because he stood and led her outside, to the flagged surface of the terrace. In the silvery glow of moonlight, he strode to a side path.

"Where are we—"

"Shh." In a low voice, he said, "Come with me."

The cool November air rushed beneath her skirts, and Cara shivered as she scurried in his wake. "It is chilly tonight."

"Do not worry, sugar kisses. I will warm you as soon as we get where we are going." The promise in his statement conveyed the glow of passion, and again she shuddered.

Just ahead she spied a tiny gazebo, nestled amid a cluster of formidable oaks. No sooner had they entered the small structure than a rapacious marauder charged her, and without care for her own safety, she flung herself into his path, their lips met, and desire exploded at the point of contact.

For a long while Cara held him, shedding her prim façade, layer by layer, which had served her so well, and she said with her mouth, hands, and body what she was afraid to utter aloud. And then a warning from the past intruded on her delightful interlude: *But every time he takes you in his arms, whispering praise and encouragement, you tell yourself it is enough to know that he desires you, above all else, even though you believe otherwise.*

In an instant, she flinched and retreated as the words echoed a taunting refrain. How correct her sisters had been with their sage counsel, as a dull emptiness settled in her gut.

"What is wrong?" Lance asked.

"Nothing." She braced herself against his chest and considered her next move. "But there is something I would say, and I would do so without interruption."

"Now?"

"Yes."

"All right, lady mine." He kissed her forehead, which did much to soothe her frazzled nerves. "If it is that important, I yield."

"Indeed, it is of utmost urgency." Cara inhaled a deep breath and rolled her shoulders. "Do you recall the afternoon we spent at Sandgate, huddled beneath the desk in your uncle's study?"

"You were seven, and I was twelve, and a winter storm whipped up a howling gale from the west, off the Channel, and frightened you."

"The very same." What fond memories Cara had of their childhood.

"How could I forget?" He grinned the boyish grin that never failed to quicken her pulse. "For it was the first time you referred to me as your hero, as you sheltered in my lap for two hours, and I swear I grew ten feet tall in an instant, if only to fulfill your requirements."

"But you did, Lance. In every way possible." She cupped his cheek. "The truth is you were my hero long before that day, just as I have ever been your steadfast lady. And you must know that when I sit at the pianoforte, be it at our family gatherings or one of the *ton's* supper parties, I sing and play for you, alone. I want—"

Voices sounded, and Lance pressed a finger to her lips, lest they be discovered, as the unwelcome interlopers neared. But he held her so tight Cara knew not where she ended and he began. In the shadows of their hideaway, he stared into her eyes. Then he bent his head and with the jut of his nose he teased hers, his warm breath a gentle caress of her sensitized skin. Gooseflesh covered her from top to toe, and she shivered.

Lance shifted, unbuttoned his coat, and enveloped her

within the warm folds of his formalwear. Wrapping her arms about his waist, she rested her head to his shoulder, snuggled close, and sighed. In a hushed tone, she inquired, "Are we found?"

"No," he responded in kind. "But a gentleman would seek an alternate accommodation once he noted our silhouettes, so we should give it another minute."

"You will hear no complaints from me, as I should be happy to remain here, with you, like this, forever." Beneath her palms, his muscles tensed.

"Dearest and loveliest Cara, I do not pretend to understand why you rejected my previous offers of marriage, but I hope we have moved past any prior difficulties," he whispered. "Were it not for my injury, I would kneel for the occasion, my darling."

"An unnecessary gesture, my lord, as you and I have never stood on formality." At last, she would seize her prize. And while she anticipated no declaration, she vowed to fight for his heart. Just as her sisters claimed the love of their respective husbands, so, too, would she reign supreme over her Nautionnier Knight. As she considered the monogrammed handkerchief tucked inside her bodice, she smiled.

For Cara, everything progressed to perfection.

For Lance, everything progressed to perfection.

"May I presume you welcome my suit?" He held his breath.

"You may."

"Oh, Cara." He exhaled in relief, as never could he have foreseen the fervent reversal of her position. "There is so much I want for us. I want to build a family with you, to hold you as your belly swells with my heir, to comfort you when you ache, to celebrate the miracle of birth, and to grow old with you."

"I want that, too."

"But I am not a good man." Lance thought of Thomas, of his failure to save his cousin, and acknowledged the gut-wrenching guilt, which had resurfaced with a vengeance. "I fear I will never deserve you."

"Nonsense." She framed his face. "And I will have no other."

"Then have me." Rolling the dice one last time, he took her hands in his and pressed a kiss to her knuckles. "My most beautiful Miss Douglas, will—"

A feminine giggle pierced the serendipitous moment.

"Bloody hell." Again, he pulled Cara close, cursing the unknown persons who had just cut short his proposal before he could deliver it and secure her answer. "Never knew the Hayward's garden saw so much action."

Unlike the prior interruption, the most recent intruders tarried in the immediate vicinity, which placed his lady's honor in peril. Even had they announced their betrothal, the late night dalliance could mar Cara's reputation even after the vows were spoken, and society could be quite cruel.

"Oh, dear," she whispered. "What should we do now?"

"Return to the ball." Lance glanced left and then right. "Take the path by which we came, and enter from the terrace."

"But what will you do?"

"I shall return via the side door of the Hayward's library and join you for our waltz."

"Dare I ask how you possess such knowledge of their residence?"

"No." He set her at arm's length. "And you should go, before our absence is noted."

"But, we did not—"

A decidedly male chuckle hung in the air.

"Shh." Lance tucked a stray curl behind her ear and kissed her. "We will finish what we started here, I promise."

"All right, my hero." Cara descended the shelter of the gazebo and navigated the pebbled walk. As she stepped into the moonlight, she glanced over her shoulder and cast him a shy smile. Did she not know what she did to him when she looked like that?

At that very instant, the lilting singsong of lovers snared his trained ear, and he dipped his chin in insouciant salute at whichever rake inspired such impressive feminine moans.

Unwilling to enact an unforgivable breach of the unwritten but nonetheless potent male code of honor and disturb the heated tryst, he jumped the railing and bit his tongue when he snapped a fallen branch beneath his feet. The telltale rush of alert had him stifling laughter, and he held his position.

When peaceful calm fell on the garden, Lance retreated, step by cautious step—and backed straight into what he guessed was the unfortunate Romeo.

"Oh, I say." Jason Collingwood clutched a hand to his chest. "My apologies, brother, but you gave me a powerful fright."

Lance opened and then closed his mouth. Before he could reply, none other than Alexandra Seymour wandered into a clearing, and the silvery light from the moon above illuminated her face. As Alex retraced the same path that Cara had taken, Lance grabbed Jason by the lapels.

"Tell me, Collingwood, and be quick about it, if you

value your life." Lance jerked hard on his adversary. "At what games are you playing?"

"From the look of things, I would assert the same in which you engage, given your presence." Jason wrenched free and resituated his coat. "Are you mad, Raynesford?"

"I could ask the same of you." Burning with unrestrained fury, Lance rested hands on hips. "Out with it, Collingwood, else I will see you at dawn. Why do you dance attendance on Cara Douglas in the Hayward's ballroom, for all the *ton* to see, and kiss Lady Alexandra in the bushes?"

"Easy, Raynesford." The scoundrel splayed his palms. "Do not jump to conclusions, because I am innocent."

"As the devil." Lance snorted. "You have five seconds to tell me the whole of it."

"But I gave my word as a gentleman to keep their secret." Collingwood shifted his weight and scratched the back of his head. "And I am loathe to betray my Alex's confidence."

"*Your* Alex?" Brimming with ire, Lance could have throttled the newest Nautionnier Knight, right then and there. "Would you prefer to breakfast on lead shot? Or perhaps you favor swords? In either case, I shall indulge you."

"By Jove, I believe you are serious," Jason replied with palpable shock. "Yet you misjudge me, Lance. And I resent that, really I do, as I am in earnest."

"Drop the pleasantries and explain yourself, or you will not live to see the morn." Lance folded his arms and summoned patience that should qualify him for sainthood. "I am waiting."

"Hell and the Reaper, you leave me no choice. Yet I do not suppose there is any real harm if I reveal their predicament." Jason peered from side to side. "Given your lifelong acquaintance with Miss Douglas, I presume you know the identity of the blackguard who used her without regard for her reputation, availed himself of her love, and then did not make her an honorable offer. And perhaps you can solve a conundrum for which I can glean no solution. Why did she not seek the assistance of the Brethren?"

The world tilted beneath his feet, and a shiver of dread traipsed his spine. "I beg your pardon?"

"What so-called man refuses to marry Cara?" Jason clucked his tongue. "While I have never claimed to possess above average intelligence, from my perspective, Miss Douglas seems a very fine lady. Were my affection not firmly planted in Alex's garden, to the detriment of all others, I would consider Miss Douglas a suitable candidate for a wife."

"Who spun such a fantastic yarn?" Lance asked with unchecked incredulity.

"Why, Alex did, of course. But it is no yarn." Jason inclined his head. "Yet you appear surprised by my revelation."

"More than you know." Lance chucked his brother knight's shoulder and said, "Follow me."

With Collingwood in his wake, Lance located the side doors of the Hayward's library. In the confines of the impressive athenaeum, which featured countless shelves of books encompassing all manner of fiction and reality, myriad emotions attacked Lance. "All right. Start at the beginning, and spare no detail."

"Why do I suspect I have been duped?" Jason frowned and exhaled. "At the onset of the Little Season, Alex engaged my services on Cara's behalf."

"To what purpose?" His ears rang and his temples throbbed.

"It is elementary, really. They—Alex and Cara, asked me

to feign an interest and enact a mock courtship designed to bring our errant suitor, though I would argue reprobate is more apropos to the circumstance, to the fore and secure a proposal." Jason shrugged. "While I am not in full agreement with their logic, I find it difficult to deny Alex anything, as she is my lady."

In that moment, Lance closed his eyes and sighed, as something within him fractured. Double-dealing mixed with heretofore-unimaginable disappointment, which well nigh brought him to his knees, and he leaned on a nearby desk for support.

Although Lance would have loved to deny the truth, Collingwood's confession made such delusion inconceivable. That the one person Lance had always trusted, without question or doubt, had committed such unforgivable behavior left him reeling, especially in light of the devotion he had just shared with her. Had she found sport in his adoration?

"I understand your rationale for embarking on the foolhardy endeavor." In silence, he pondered Cara's possible motives for trickery. What had driven her false pretense? Why had she lied to him? "Faced with similar proposition, I would have acted the same."

"Would you?" Collingwood adjusted his cravat.

"Aye." Lance extended a hand in friendship and was relieved when Jason accepted the gesture without hesitation. "My apologies for my prior outburst."

"None necessary, as I can imagine I appeared the worst sort of villain to the uninformed party." Jason furrowed his brow. "So tell me, who is the bastard that played fast and loose with Cara's reputation?"

Lost amid the confusion, and downright hurt, though he would claim otherwise were he asked, Lance grasped at the minutest shreds of comportment, because his course necessitated recalculation. Given he had compromised Cara, he had to marry her, so his goal remained fixed. But her duplicity had destroyed the veil of fantasy and childhood innocence with which he had always viewed her.

"I am the man you seek." The pain in his chest threatened to overwhelm him. "But I disagree with your characterization, as I have not earned it."

"What?" Jason tugged on Lance's arm. "You must be joking."

"Would that I were," he replied with calm solemnity. "Let me assure you, I am serious."

"But—you?" With an owlish expression, Collingwood blinked and sputtered. "This makes no sense."

"Indeed, I concur." Were he a child, Lance would surrender to a violent spate of tears, as despair was a bitter pill, and Cara had grievously wounded him. "And it may interest you to know that I have proposed to Cara on a number of occasions, all of which she has refused."

"Then why would they tell me otherwise?" Jason asked.

"Now that is the question for which I have no answer, brother." Lance mulled the situation, and his mind raced in various directions, none of which seemed plausible excuses. "I do not pretend to comprehend Cara's actions, but I do require privacy to further explore our predicament. And there is one aspect in which my certainty is absolute."

"And that would be—what?" the blameless pawn queried.

"I need an ally." Lance lowered his chin. "And you and I need to strategize."

CHAPTER SIXTEEN

"*I* do not believe it, Alex lied to me. Women." Jason pounded a fist on the armrest of an overstuffed chair, snatched the glass of brandy Lance offered him, downed the contents in a single gulp, and scowled. "Never should I have trusted one."

"Do not be too hard on Lady Alexandra." Lance settled behind his desk and reclined. "As I do not believe deception is the solitary objective, where you are concerned."

The carriage ride from the Hayward Ball had given him ample opportunity to reflect and retrench—and tamp the anger surging within him. Tugging at the precise folds of linen at his neck, he loosened his cravat, drew it free from his collar, and tossed the yard-length swath atop the leather blotter.

"And that matters?" Jason fetched the crystal decanter and refilled his brandy balloon.

"It does to me." For Lance, of utmost importance were Cara's underlying reasons for enacting such daring fraud.

Why had she allowed him to compromise her—on more than one occasion, and yet she rebuffed his offers of marriage? And why, at the very same moment she rejected his proposals, had she deliberately set out to draw his attention? Given that the primary aim of such schemes typically centered on securing a betrothal, nothing about her actions made sense.

"Shall I confess how they bamboozled me?" Jason stretched his legs, batted his lashes, and in a high-pitched voice said, "Our poor Miss Douglas was ill-treated by a fickle suitor who availed himself of her affections and then refused to marry her."

"And the chivalrous Captain Collingwood came to their aid." In the face of such absurdity, Lance could not help but chuckle. "There is no shame in that, brother."

"Yes, if Miss Douglas had been slighted, in truth, I would have no cause." Collingwood speared his fingers through his hair. "But Alex and Cara played me false, and I should very much like to know why."

"As to their ultimate goal, I can only speculate." Lance stared into the hearth and studied the flames. "The fact that they enlisted your support suggests Cara intended to make me jealous, and however much I regret admitting it, she succeeded."

But she could not have anticipated inciting his temper, which she had done in epic proportions. Still, what had she hoped to achieve, despite his multiple proposals? What remained that he had not addressed to her satisfaction?

"I care not about Alex's reasons for deceiving me." Jason leaned forward, propped his elbows on his knees, and rested his chin in his hands. "There is no justification for double-dealing. I ought to heat her posterior."

"Well, it may not be a bad idea, but her brother might protest." Lance searched his memory for some sensible clarification to decipher Cara's plot. "I am sure Alex was motivated by a genuine desire, however misplaced, to help Miss Douglas."

"It does not signify." Jason scratched his temple and frowned. "I thought Alex unique, so different from society's witless chits. Now I see she is the same as all the other faithless jades parading through the *ton's* ballrooms."

"Easy, friend." Lance pointed in emphasis. "Regardless of her infractions, you cannot disparage the reputation of one of my dearest childhood companions. To me, Alex is my sister and I her brother. One mistake will not sever a lifelong alliance."

"How can you be so obtuse?" Jason leapt from his chair and paced before the desk. "They lied to us."

"Yes, and I should like to know why, as much as you." Lance swirled the amber liquor in his glass. "But first I must identify the incentive for the ill-conceived charade."

"Is that really of consequence?" Jason arched a brow. "Or are you just an easy mark?"

"I am no one's pawn, but as the target of this plot, their grounds are of vital importance to me." Lance doffed his coat and unhooked the collar of his shirt, as he sought a balm to soothe his injured pride. And then a brilliant flanking maneuver formed in his brain. "However, I am not opposed to a little retribution, if you are so inclined."

"Count me in for revenge." Jason came to an abrupt halt. "How shall we punish our errant ladies?"

"Well therein lies the rub." Lance considered the logistics of his scheme and grimaced. "After all is said and done, Alex is a cherished friend. And regardless of her denials, Cara will be my wife."

"You still mean to marry her?" The blonde knight opened and then closed his mouth. "Even after her deception?"

"I do—no pun intended"

"Are you out of your mind?"

"Perhaps." Fortified with his best liquid courage, Lance was more intrigued than irate. "Right now I am at sea. But, as I said, let us not rush to judgment."

There would be time enough for that in the privacy of his bedchamber, wherein he planned to dissect every bit of communication, examine each encounter, and form a suitable counterattack. So he maintained his calm façade, because no one riled Lance Prescott unless he chose to allow it.

"Blister it, Raynesford, you are a better man than I, because you are being a hell of a sport. As God is my witness, were they men, I would want blood in recompense for their folly." Jason planted his feet wide and bared his teeth. "I did Alex a personal favor, and she made an arse of me."

"You overreact, as Alex did no such thing. Given we have yet to determine their prize, had their venture succeeded, with none the wiser, you would have lost nothing. It is only because we inadvertently discovered their game that you seek vengeance, but you remain unharmed and your honor intact."

"Oh, really?" Jason shot him a glance of pure skepticism and snorted. "You were ready to call me out."

"There you have me." Lance nodded once. "When I thought you had abused Miss Douglas, I could have ripped your throat out with my teeth."

"If you are attempting to inspire confidence, you failed miserably," Collingwood replied, as he yanked on his collar. "Why not confront her?"

"I thought of that, but if this conundrum could have been resolved with a candid conversation, Cara would have told me, as she has had ample opportunity." Somewhere, Lance had missed something, and never had he felt more conflicted in his life. His original plan required extensive revisions, because his was no longer a simple matter of seduction. "That she has not done so speaks volumes, only I know not how to interpret her perplexing conduct."

"Well whatever we do, we cannot let their grievous infraction go unpunished." Jason narrowed his stare. "And I do not want you going soft on me."

"After tonight, not a chance, brother." Lance seethed in silence. "And I have an idea, but I am not sure of its virtue."

"What care I for virtue? It must possess a certain flair and be dramatic." Furrowing his brow, Jason untied his cravat. "As women know no other condition."

"We must be careful not to alienate them." Lance rubbed his chin. "However, if you no longer have a personal interest in Lady Alex, I suppose you need not concern yourself with that minor complication."

"What?" Jason snapped to attention. "Who said I am not interested in Alex?"

"Well you seem awfully put out, Collingwood." Lance had deliberately baited his fellow knight, because he needed to gauge the depth of his regard for Alex. "And I cannot deliver my friend into the clutches of a disgruntled suitor intent on hurting her."

"I would never harm Alex." Jason's eyes flared. "She needs a firm hand to manage her, because Damian coddles her to excess."

"And you presume to be the man for the task?"

Jason lowered his chin. "Believe it."

"All right." Lance chuckled. "Then how do we go about teaching our women a much-needed lesson?"

"I vote for confrontation." Jason slammed a fist to his palm. "Get it all in the open."

"And have Alex reduce you to plum pudding with her tears?" He snickered.

"I resent that, Raynesford, really I do." Jason glanced left and then right, located his brandy balloon, and again downed the contents. "Besides, I have seen Cara play you like a violin. She knows how to pluck your strings, and I am almost embarrassed for you."

"Go to the devil," Lance responded. "In this house I am lord and master."

"At least you will be whenever Cara allows it," Jason added with an air of insult.

"I ought to smite your costard." Lance flew from his chair and rounded the desk. "And I may call you out, yet."

"I shall see you at dawn, Raynesford." Jason lunged and stood toe-to-toe with Lance. "As I demand satisfaction."

"Paddington Green!" Lance shouted, at last succumbing to his simmering anger. "Be there, or I will hunt you down."

Without a word, Jason turned on a heel and stomped the door.

"Collingwood—"

"Raynesford—"

Jason grinned.

Lance smiled and shook his head. "You first."

"After you." Jason rubbed the back of his neck. "As you have rank."

"That was too close for comfort." Lance whistled in monotone. "We are fighting each other, and we are not the enemy."

"You know, this is what happens when women take the helm." Jason shifted his weight and sighed. "We drown in a lethal mix of perfume and petticoats."

"May I suggest we return our attention to the business at hand?" Once again, Lance settled in the high back chair behind his desk.

"Aye." Jason reclaimed his seat. "Have you any ideas?"

"Indeed, I do, brother." Lance compressed his lips. "What is the one thing guaranteed to bring out the green-eyed monster in a woman?"

"Competition." And then Jason's jaw dropped. "Lance, you are a bloody genius. But who will help us? I suppose we could ask the widow Moreton."

"Do you want to get us killed?" Lance recalled Cara's reaction when she discovered the sultry Ace of Spades in his bedchamber. "The mere suggestion gives me collywobbles."

"Sorry." Jason swallowed hard.

For a few minutes the study grew silent. The long case clock in the hall sounded the hour, as Lance assessed various options at his disposal. The solution, when it came to him, seemed elementary. "You know, we need not involve other ladies in our scheme. We need only switch positions to give our prey a dose of their own medicine."

"MAY I have the pleasure of your company?"

"Why, of course, Captain Collingwood." Alex smiled, extended an arm, and stepped forward. "I should be too happy to partner you."

"I apologize, Lady Alex, for the confusion." Jason hesitated, inclined his head, and, to Cara's surprise, gazed at her. "But I was asking our lovely Miss Douglas for the honor of a waltz."

Alex peered at Cara, and in unison their jaws dropped.

"But we have already shared the country-dance, Captain." Cara gulped, because everything about her mock-suitor's demeanor bespoke the unmistakable heat of passion. And then she recalled their charade, and the fact that she had yet to end it, so she gathered her wits and mentally replayed her composed speech. "I should be delighted."

"But—what about me?" Alex pouted. "Am I to be neglected?"

"Allow me to act in the estimable captain's stead, Lady Alex." Lance sketched an impressive bow. "If you are so inclined."

For a scarce second, Cara had expected her hero to protest Jason's invitation, and she swallowed the bitter pill of disappointment as Collingwood, with nary a challenge from Lance, led her into a sea of elegantly dressed ladies and gentlemen. As soon as Jason took her in his arms, Cara knew something was amiss. "Um, Captain?"

"Yes, my dear Cara?" he whispered in her ear, and she shuddered with alarm. "You look positively stunning, tonight."

"Thank you, Captain. But do you not think you are holding me a bit too close?" In an instant, she chided herself, as he no doubt continued to play the part of love-struck suitor at her request. She smiled, rolled her shoulders, and joined the masquerade. "You are liable to set the gossipmongers afire with this waltz."

"Excellent, as that is our aim, is it not?" He leaned close. "Have I ever told you how enchanting I find your eyes, Miss Douglas?"

"I beg your pardon?" She blinked.

"Oh, indeed. They are as blue as the crystal waters of the Mediterranean." Jason bent his head, and their noses were mere inches apart. "Daresay I could lose myself in your shimmering depths."

"Captain—"

"How come you never call me Jason?" he asked in a husky baritone. "I should think our understanding would leave us on more informal terms. Do you not like me, Cara?"

Warning bells pealed a distress signal in her brain. Given Collingwood's swoon-worthy looks and lethal charm, she now understood how Alex had fallen so deeply beneath his spell. Yet in Cara he stirred nothing more than trepidation and, dare she admit it, nausea.

"Of course, I do," she blurted. "But polite decorum requires I show proper respect for your station, Captain."

"Need I point out I was not to the manor born, so I have no use for polite decorum?" With a rakish gaze Jason surveyed her, leaving her in little doubt of his regard. "And I am not interested in your respect, Miss Douglas."

With a call for retreat echoing in her ears, Cara fought the desire to flee, because she had to terminate their scheme.

"Captain—"

"Jason."

Cara gritted her teeth, biting back frustration and, though it annoyed her to concede it, abiding fear. "Jason—"

"Now, was that not easy?" he queried in a tone as smooth as well-churned butter.

"You quite take my breath away, Sir." A foreboding sense of gloom shrouded her in imaginary darkness, and a chill of unease traipsed her spine. "Pray, indulge me, as I must speak with absolute candor about our arrangement."

"You refer, of course, to our scheme to bring your potential bridegroom to the altar?" he declared with a sly smile, which gave her goose flesh.

"Yes."

"What of it?"

"I wish to end the matter, posthaste."

"Why?"

Did he have to ask the lone question guaranteed to prick her nerves? Could he not just accept she had changed her mind and wanted nothing more than to wash her hands of the whole miserable affair? And how could she answer him?

Should she opt for the truth and explain, however late, that though her goal remained the same, she regretted to inform him that she enlisted his services based on prevarication? Then again, such frankness could land Alex in hot water, which further complicated the situation.

Cara sighed. "Because it was a foolish endeavor, from the first."

Jason narrowed his stare. "I disagree."

"You do?" The man could have knocked her over with a feather. "I did not realize you had formed an opinion on the topic."

"But I have, my charming Miss Douglas." He twirled her with dramatic flair, before tightening his arm at her waist. "And you should not surrender the field before the day is won."

"But, I must protest." Panic settled as chief resident in her belly. "What have I to gain?"

"Am I to understand you have secured your proposal and are now betrothed?" Alex's beau arched a brow. "Why have you not made your happy announcement?"

"You mistake my meaning, Captain." Stumped, Cara bit her lip. At that point, she could not bring herself to dissemble and intensify her shame. "Whether or not I achieve my goal, I simply cannot build my future on a foundation of deceit, however well intended. And I fear your assistance has been ill-used. I do apologize if I have caused offense."

"Miss Douglas, you are everything gentle and good." Right there on the dance floor, in full view of society, Captain Collingwood pressed on her gloved knuckles a chaste kiss. "And I believe your heart is in the right place, so I encourage you to persevere a tad longer, as you shall receive your just reward."

"But—why?" It was her luck that her attempt to end their arrangement met impenetrable resistance.

"Rules of attraction, my dear." In that instant, he reversed course, and in an uncharacteristic move she tripped. "Are you all right, Miss Douglas?"

"Yes." She cursed her clumsy behavior, as it belied heretofore-unshakeable deportment.

"And, as I was saying, the one thing guaranteed to make a man take notice is another man."

"That is just what Sabrina said." The words were uttered before she realized she had spoken.

"Really?" Beneath her palms, the captain tensed his muscles. "The Countess of Woverton is aware of our scheme of hearts?"

"Well, I might have discussed it with her." Cara bemoaned her loose lips. "She is, after all, my sister, and we have always been close."

"But, of course." He steered her left, then right, and then left again, without missing a beat. "And her reasoning is remarkably sound, so I cannot argue with her counsel."

"Then you are not vexed that I sought Brie's opinion?"

The dance ended, and Jason tucked her hand in the crook of his elbow and led her to the back wall.

"How could I be vexed, when I agreed to aid your most noble cause?" He inclined his head. "And you were so unfairly treated that no gentlemen worthy of such distinction could refuse your request."

"Indeed." Struck by the force of her duplicity, so simply stated by the unwitting dupe in her game, Cara counted herself the worst sort of fiend. Fighting tears of shame, she searched in vain for an adequate argument to sway her stubborn ally. "Which is why I must surrender the field, as no lady would engage in such nefarious enterprises."

"Tell me, Cara, have we met with success?" His question struck a direct hit to her conscience. "Has your reluctant groom restored your honor?"

"Not quite, I am afraid." And as much as she would have preferred to avoid his question, because of his assistance, she believed she owed her co-conspirator an answer. "Nevertheless, I anticipate he will, soon."

"Then may I make a suggestion?"

"By all means."

"Your chosen suitor may not be swayed by harmless waltzes and a reliable escort to supper."

A dark sense of foreboding settled as a cold chill in her chest, but Cara ignored the annoying sensation. "I do not follow."

"Might I tempt you with an impromptu tour of the Atherton's garden, where we can strategize in private?" Because the music had ceased, Jason leaned close to whisper in her ear. "You see our ruse may require a more intense courtship."

∾

DESPITE THE FACT that he considered Jason an ally, of sorts, Lance struggled to suppress the jealousy raging within him as the blonde giant led Cara to the terrace doors, and Alex's subtle flinch declared that he was not alone in his discomfit. Though Collingwood's actions resembled their plan, to the letter, their plot gave Lance no joy.

In an instant, he recalled his part to play in the Atherton ballroom, so he returned Alex to the relative comfort of the Brethren and prepared for the next scene in the hastily sketched drama. Once cloistered amid the security of their childhood friends, he inhaled and broached the conversation he had rehearsed all afternoon.

"You look quite fetching this evening, Alex." Lance could have laughed when she blinked in surprise. "Tell me truly, have you set your sights on a particular gentleman this season."

"I beg your pardon?" She worried her bottom lip and shifted her weight. "I know not what you ask."

"Oh, give over. Which lucky chap has claimed your attention?" Even as he said the words, Lance marveled at his circumstances, which had devolved to a level that reduced him to a discussion of male and female relationships and left a foul taste in his mouth. "Is he a member of the peerage or branch of the military?"

"Well, I had thought one candidate, in particular, might fit my requirements for a suitable husband." With her gaze fixed on the terrace doors, Alex furrowed her brow and wrung her fingers. "But now I am not so certain of his devotion."

"Oh?" He adopted his most sympathetic demeanor. "Has something changed in that respect?"

"I wish I knew." She sighed. "Are men not constant where their affections are concerned? I mean—my brother has often told me such, just as he claims all women are fickle."

"Ah, well who am I to gainsay Damian?" Lance rocked on his heels. "And he is correct, in part."

"He is?" At last, he captured her full attention. "How so?"

"It is a simple matter of distinction."

"Please, explain." Alex inclined her head. "Because I would dearly love to understand my potential beau."

"As you wish." He tugged on his cravat. "You see, in the games people play, regarding my fellow bachelors, the ultimate goal is everything when it comes to the fairer sex."

"I do not follow." She narrowed her stare. "What is the ultimate goal?"

"How can I put this without being crude?" He tapped a finger to his chin. "As I would not shock your delicate nature."

"But we are old friends, so you need not mince words." Alex rested her hand to his arm. "Pray, continue."

"If you insist." It was time to bait the hook. "When a man sets his mind on a particular lady, nothing will dissuade him until he has her."

"That does not sound so nefarious." Alex giggled. "My goodness, you had me worried for a minute."

"Ah, but I am not finished." Lance cast his line. "As I mentioned, the primary objective is of utmost importance. If a man desires nothing more than a companion for the night, then once he catches his dove, there ends the pursuit, and he moves to the next conquest."

"Oh, my." Alex's mouth fell agape. "How dreadful for the dove."

"Hardly, my dear friend." Lance chuckled, as he realized it had dawned on her that she might have misconstrued

Jason's interest, which is exactly what he had hoped to achieve. "As mutual comprehension on both parts keeps the field level."

"And what if the dove mistakes her pursuer's intent?" She inched closer and glanced left and then right. "What if the lady believes her suitor seeks the latter, more permanent arrangement, as opposed to the former? How is she to know the difference?"

Bloody hell, Lance had not anticipated such in-depth questioning. In a flash, he searched his mind for a convincing response and seized on the obvious solution. How would he have courted Cara, had he not been burdened with guilt in relation to his cousin's death and had she not gifted him her virtue while he convalesced?

"She holds his undivided attention, to the detriment of all else." He could not help but smile, as he envisioned his Cara. For as long as he could remember, he had always been her champion. "And he makes no improper advances on her person, as he would protect his future wife's honor with his life. For him, she is—"

"Forgive my interruption, but may I ask a personal question?" Again, Alex scanned the immediate vicinity. "Given that we are as brother and sister, I feel I may be blunt. Just how do you define 'improper advances,' in regard to courtship?"

"Alex." Lance shuffled his feet and fought to suppress a grin. "Has someone taken liberties with your reputation?"

"Oh—no." She opened her mouth and then closed it. "It is just that I should like, very much, to know what constitutes inappropriate conduct, should anyone attempt such ill-mannered and bold behavior. And with your invaluable counsel, I should guard my virtue with unrestrained fervor."

"Well, in that case, I would argue anything beyond a

polite kiss on your gloved hand is tantamount to an egregious breach of decorum." Given her expression, he made a mental note to discuss the younger Seymour with Collingwood at their next meeting; else Damian might string Jason from the highest yardarm. "Come now, old friend, do tell. There must be some fellow who occupies your thoughts."

"All right." Alex averted her gaze. "There is someone."

"Aha, I knew it. Who is he?" Lance waggled his brows. "You know we must approve of your choice of suitors."

"Yes, I am aware that any potential mate must pass the Brethren test," she replied in a somber voice. "But I would not reveal his identity until I am assured of his devotion, else you may scare him away."

"Then why the long face?" While Lance hated to see the fieriest female of their family so deflated, he reminded himself of her participation in Cara's scheme and stayed the course. "Spill it."

"I remain, as yet, undecided." Alex lifted her chin and looked him straight in the eye. "But you may rest assured you will be the first to know when I have set my cap."

"I am delighted to hear it." He cocked his head and revisited his script. "In the meantime, I suppose we shall have to entertain ourselves with Cara's campaign."

The usually stalwart Lady Alex's jaw dropped. "Cara's campaign?"

"Oh, yes." For a subsequent few seconds, he focused his energy on the simple process of breathing, because the next sentence he uttered would, were he unaware of the truth, have killed him. "It is evident she is quite taken with Captain Collingwood."

"You believe so?" She compressed her lips. "And you are all right with that?"

"Of course." Lance forced a smile. "Why would I object?"

"I do not know." The poor darling appeared on the brink of an apoplectic fit. "I thought perhaps you might not think him adequate."

"On the contrary. He sailed the *Demetrius* and brought her home, safe and sound." He clucked his tongue. "I should name my firstborn for him."

"Is that how you really feel?" With palpable shock, she swallowed hard. "I thought you admired Cara."

"Oh, she and I will always enjoy a convivial relationship, but I have known for some time I would eventually relinquish her companionship to her chosen partner." Lance stifled a snort of laughter, as Alex seemed on the verge of losing her supper. "After all, she could not marry me, for we are as siblings."

"But, you do not think Jas—I mean, Captain Collingwood is serious in his engagement?" Pale and visibly shaken, she pressed a hand to her throat. "That is, what I intended to ask is how do you know he wishes to marry her?"

"I am fairly certain of his regard." In light of her plot, Alex's actions undermined her purpose, countermanding Cara's aim to make Lance jealous. Instead of encouraging his line of thought, she questioned his assertion. "And I have it on good authority."

"How marvelous for Cara." She rubbed the back of her neck. "On what do you base your assessment?"

"Men talk." The ghosts of Brethren past were probably turning over in their graves. "We share our passionate pursuits."

"You do?" she inquired with avid interest.

"Indeed, as much as women." Now that hurt.

"And Jason desires a lifelong commitment with Cara?"

"He has indicated as much." It did not escape him that she referred to her love by his given name. "Daresay a wedding garland shall soon list in the *Intrepid*'s rigging."

"Perhaps you misunderstand," Alex blurted. "Your acquaintance with him is brief. You only just met."

"Actually, I have known Collingwood since we were midshipmen aboard the *Perseus*." He pointed for emphasis. "And he has commanded my ship, which is akin to sharing my ladybird."

"Lance." Was it his imagination, or did a blush stain her cheeks?

"What?" He chuckled. "You did inquire."

"Never mind. Just tell me about Jason. What has he said in regard to Cara—that is, if you feel you can confide in me?" In haste, she added, "I only ask out of concern for her welfare."

"Of course you do."

"She is one of my best friends."

"I do not doubt it."

"I assure you, I am in earnest."

"I know just how you feel."

"We are practically sisters."

Now it was time to reel in his catch. "Well, if you promise to keep this a secret—"

"Tell me." Alex glanced from side to side, and then leaned near. "What did he say?"

His cause required a potent oratory, one that would haunt her sleep, if she managed to quiet her fears, at all. Lance might have regretted his actions, if he had not endured so many restless nights himself of late. In vain, he searched for a convincing argument. At the end of his tether, familiar praise echoed in his ears. It was an enthusiastic approbation he once declared in regard to Cara.

"Over my best brandy, Collingwood divulged a deep and abiding appreciation for Cara. He feels she is unlike any woman he has ever known and is besotted. Her beauty, her poise, is beyond compare. Upon entering a room, she quite takes his breath away. In short, she is every man's fantasy." He wrinkled his nose and fretted that the next part might stick in his throat. "I believe Jason means to offer for her."

Alex gasped and covered her mouth. In a flash, she struggled to compose herself. A war of emotions besieged her once whimsical expression and quelled his urge to comfort her.

When she teetered precariously, Lance lent support. "Are you ill, my dear?"

"I am fine," she insisted. Though she averted her gaze, he caught a glimpse of the pain etched in her stare. "But I would like a breath of fresh air. Would you be so kind as to escort me into the garden?"

"Certainly." He sketched a bow and extended an arm. "Shall we adjourn to the terrace?"

The cool November air kissed his heated flesh, as he slipped out of his coat and draped it over Alex's shoulders. After a few minutes, his vision adjusted to the silvery veil of moonlight on the flagged surface.

To his immense relief, he spotted Jason and Cara seated, shoulder-to-shoulder, on a stone bench in the rose garden, and it appeared they did nothing more than share conversation. And then Alex flinched at his side, and he discovered her peering in the opposite direction.

Beneath a large oak, partially shielded by thinning foliage, he could barely discern the unmistakable silhouettes of two lovers engaged in a tryst. To the emotionally charged, untrained eye, the figures could pass for Jason and Cara. As the lovers embraced in an animated clinch, Alex emitted something between a sob and a sigh.

"Lance."

"Yes?"

"I wish to return to the ball."

CHAPTER SEVENTEEN

"*Y*ou are awfully quiet this morning, Alex." Cara poured a cup of tea and passed it to Rebecca. "Is everything all right?"

Since Sabrina's confinement, and subsequent isolation by Everett, the back parlor of the Douglas townhouse had become the new war room. After setting the porcelain pot on the tray, she grasped a plate piled high with sweets and tempted her friend with her favorite scone.

"No, thank you," Alex replied in an icy tone, which sent a shiver down Cara's spine. "And I am quite fine."

"Are you sure?" Caroline frowned, as she swiped a square of shortbread. "You look a tad peaked."

"And your eyes are puffy." Rebecca wrinkled her nose. "Have you been crying?"

"You seem a bit out of sorts, too." Elaine cast a sympathetic expression. "Are you unwell?"

"Why is everyone so concerned with the state of my health?" Alex grabbed a pillow and punched it. "And it matters not how I feel, now that my captain has lost interest."

"What?" Cara choked and sputtered, splashing tea on her dress. "You can't be serious."

"Oh, please." Alex rolled her eyes, folded her arms, and huffed. "Do not act the innocent."

"I beg your pardon?" Cara almost fell out of her chair. Without doubt, Alex was angry, but Cara could not fathom why. "Just what do you imply?"

"Calm yourselves, sisters. Has something happened?" Rebecca inquired of Alex. "Because you gave us the impression your captain was just that—yours. And we know Cara's affections lie firmly planted in Lance's garden."

"So what has changed?" Elaine asked in a small voice.

A knock silenced what Cara suspected was shaping up to be an imposing tempest. "Come."

"Am I late?" Before the butler could announce her presence, Sabrina shoved her way into the room and shut the door in the poor servant's face. "I had to compose a suitable excuse to throw Everett off my scent."

"Little sister, shame on you." Cara couldn't help but giggle. "If he finds out you lied, he will heat your posterior."

"Oh, let him. I find I quite favor spankings when my shameless lord is the task master." Sabrina ignored the gasps of surprise, pushed an ottoman into the mix, glanced at the two teapots, and queried, "Which one is chamomile?"

"The purple flowers," Cara replied, quick as a wink. "So what did you tell Everett?"

"That Mama had a problem of a female nature, and she requested I accompany her to the physician. Do take note, that sort of excuse always works." Sabrina settled her skirts and narrowed her stare. "Rebecca, will you pass the shortbread? Although I breakfasted this morning, I am absolutely famished. Now, where were we?"

"We were just assessing the most recent developments.

Take a deep breath, dearest," Caroline said to Alex, as she inched to the edge of her seat. "What occurred last night, at the ball?"

"Did you not enjoy yourself at the Atherton's gala?" Sabrina shoved a treat into her mouth. "It is one of the premier fetes of the season."

"An excellent inquiry, Brie." Alex pinned Cara with an angry glare. "But I believe the more important question is did your elder sibling enjoy herself?"

"Actually, I did not." In that moment, Cara recalled the fact that Lance had not once partnered her in a dance, and she frowned. "However, it was an interesting evening."

"So I would wager." Alex sniffed.

"All right, that is enough." With a sigh of frustration, Cara set her cup on the tray. "Out with it."

Alex flicked a stray lock from her forehead. "Out with what?"

"Whatever has you so perturbed?" Cara compressed her lips.

"Do I appear perturbed?" Alex averted her gaze.

"Actually, you seem mad as a hornet's nest." Rebecca arched a brow. "One we are too wise to beat with a stick."

At that instant, Alex bounded out of her chair, marched around the coffee table, and stopped directly before Cara. Noting her friend's fists, Cara reclined on the sofa.

"You kissed Jason in the garden last night," Alex declared.

"I beg your pardon?" Cara did not know what she expected her friend to say, but that was not it. "I did no such thing."

"Do not dare deny it." Alex pointed a finger. "I saw you."

Confused, Cara searched her memory for some reasonable explanation. "Alex, I swear—"

"Alex, I swear." The younger Seymour stomped a foot. "Do you take me for a fool? I suppose I imagined it, and you did not accompany Jason into the Atherton's garden."

"No." Cara peered at Sabrina, then Caroline, then Rebecca, then Elaine, and then Alex. "I admit we ventured into the garden, but we never kissed."

With something between a sob and a sigh, Alex stated, "You were under an oak tree, and—"

"You are wrong." Cara shook her head. "Jason and I shared a stone bench near a rose-covered pergola, bereft of blooms."

As her shoulders drooped, Alex retreated. "But—I saw you."

"I have no doubt you witnessed a tryst, but it was neither Jason nor I." Cara exhaled in relief, as her friend's ire appeared to dissipate. "Just as you remain devoted to your captain, I love Lance."

"Oh, Cara. I apologize, but I am so upset. Jason all but ignored me last night." Alex twined her fingers with Cara's and sat on the sofa. "Why did you venture into the rose garden?"

"Because I needed privacy to end our plot." Given her friend's tremulous state, Cara chose her words with care. "I explained I was no longer in need of his assistance."

"You did?" Caroline glanced at Rebecca and then pinned Cara with an expression of utter befuddlement. "Whatever possessed you to do such a thing?"

"Has Lance proposed?" Elaine bounced with unveiled enthusiasm. "May I stand with you at your wedding?"

"Of course." Cara nodded. "But Lance has yet to make an offer, so let us not put the cart before the horse. And

Alex's estimable captain refused my request to cease our arrangement."

"What?" Alex furrowed her brow. "I do not understand."

"Jason is determined to aid my cause, so he could not possibly have any interest in me." Cara mulled the events of the previous evening. "But he believes a change in tack would be more effective."

"How so?" Caroline asked. "And what does he have in mind?"

"Well, he surmises the reason we have not met with success is because his courtship, up to now, has been largely unconvincing." Cara squeezed Alex's hand. "He also insists it has been too insubstantial to rouse a sufficient response from Lance."

"Have you gone mad?" Brie inhaled sharply. "You revealed the identity of your intended?"

"No." Cara checked her tone and took a second to compose herself. "I am not daft, and I spoke in the general sense."

"So the course of your conversation dealt with his suit in the abstract?" Rebecca inquired.

"Yes." But Cara did not admit the whole truth, because Alex was correct. Something about Jason's demeanor had seemed almost predatory. "How else would I refer to it?"

"I do not know." Alex shrugged. "While I am loathe to mention the possibility, I was wondering if Jason could be forming a sincere attachment to you."

It was a statement, not a question.

"You must be crazy to suggest such insanity." Yet Alex had given voice to Cara's precise thoughts. "Captain Collingwood is unquestionably yours to command. The man adores you."

"I am no longer assured of his regard." Alex stood and paced before the fireplace. "Though I cannot say exactly what has changed, Jason acted out of character at the Atherton's. He was a stranger to me. And from what I gather, Lance and Jason have become close friends. In fact, Lance intimated he plans to name his firstborn for Jason."

"I think you put too much stock in polite conversation." Since Lance had long since declared his intent to name his heir for Thomas, Cara remained unconvinced of Alex's assertion. "In any case, what does it have to do with me?"

"Lance told me Jason speaks very highly of you." Alex halted and appeared on the verge of tears. "Apparently, Jason holds you in great esteem."

A sneaking suspicion formed in Cara's brain. "But that does not mean—"

"Lance claims Jason is besotted with you—those were his words." Alex sobbed. "That you are unlike any woman Jason has ever known."

Cara reflected on Jason's altered behavior and shuddered. At the Atherton's ball, when they danced, he had held her so close she almost could not breathe. Later, when they sat beside each other in the rose garden, he had brushed his hand across her thigh, and she had almost revisited her supper. Then, she had reasoned it indicated nothing more than familiarity, born of the process of their mock courtship, whereupon Jason had grown comfortable in her presence. Never had it occurred to her that the blonde giant might be campaigning, in truth.

"Cara, what are you thinking?" Alex queried in a somber tone.

"Nothing." She lied.

"Telling falsehoods is not your forte." Alex cast a

lopsided grin. "And you could never fool me, given that your face is white as a sheet."

"Oh, dear." Caroline hugged her belly.

Covered in gooseflesh from top to toe, Cara rubbed her forearms. "Now that you mention it, something did happen last night."

"Spare no detail." Alex all but ran to the sofa and plopped beside Cara. "I will have the whole nasty affair, or I shall scream."

"Which will solve nothing," Rebecca admonished. "Take it slow, Cara."

"This is dreadful." Cara tapped a finger to her chin. "And I know not where to start."

"Try the beginning." Alex inched closer. "It always works for me."

Cara bit her lip. "Jason was different at the ball."

"How so?" Brie prompted.

In her mind, Cara replayed a troubling scene. "Well, there was something in the way he held me—when we danced."

"Did he thrust his hips to yours?" Alex pressed her clasped hands to her chest.

Swimming in unease, Cara swallowed hard. "Yes."

Alex gasped. "Was he—did you feel his—oh, you know what I am asking"

"I get your meaning." Cara knew only too well. "And the answer is no."

"Are you sure?" Alex opened and then closed her mouth. "Would you have known if you felt it?"

"Definitely." Cara nodded. "Lance always gets that way when we waltz."

"Ugh." Sabrina wrinkled her nose and frowned. "That

is far more than I wish to know about a man who is, for all intents and purposes, a brother."

"I, for one, am fascinated." Elaine rested her elbows to her knees. "To what do you refer?"

"That is a topic for a later discussion," Caroline replied. "When you have set your cap for a particular gentleman."

"Perhaps I have already selected my candidate." Elaine averted her gaze. "And he is not a member of the Brethren."

"What?" the ladies declared in unison.

"Sisters, focus, please. Once I have married Lance, and Alex has wedded Jason, we can aid Elaine in her pursuit." Cara rolled her eyes. "Now then, where was I? Oh, yes. When Jason and I were in the garden—"

"He kissed you," Alex asserted.

"No." Cara groaned. "Will you let me finish?"

"Then what happened?" Alex shouted.

"All right." For good or ill, Cara owed her lifelong friend unvarnished honesty. She counted to three and blurted, "He put his hand on my thigh."

Alex shrieked and clutched her throat.

"Now you catch my drift." Cara tucked a wayward tendril behind her ear. "I thought it was innocent, but given what you have told me, I am not so certain."

"I do not believe it. My beautiful captain wants you." Alex slapped a fist to a palm. *"Oh, I will kill him!"*

"Easy, dearest." Caroline grimaced. "You are jumping to conclusions."

"And why should I not?" Alex's usually carefree visage flushed red as a tomato. "Jason is jumping on Cara."

"Captain Collingwood has done no such thing." Rebecca studied the hem of her sleeve. "But something is amiss."

"Well that is the understatement of the year." Alex humphed, leapt from the sofa, and resumed pacing the floor. "He said I had fine eyes. I am going to punch him so hard he will resemble a sweep who has cleaned one too many chimneys."

"Becca, what troubles you?" In light of the former spy's distinguished service to the Crown, Cara trusted Rebecca's instincts. "Do you suspect Jason is sincere in his affection?"

"I am uncertain." Rebecca rubbed the back of her neck. "But we would be unwise not to take note of his new tack, as I think we are missing important pieces of a much broader picture. And I would caution you not to overreact, until we gather more intelligence."

"Oh, how intriguing you make it sound," Elaine gushed. "Would that my own courtship could be so fascinating. Do not be angry, Alex."

"I am not angry, I am bloody furious. The devil himself would flee in the face of my wrath." Alex bared her teeth, and her nostrils flared. "Just wait till I get my hands on Jason, and hell will freeze before he puts his on me again."

"Alex, you are weaving unsustainable conclusions from whole cloth." Swamped by a mixture of confusion and guilt, Cara pondered how Lance would react should he learn of his competition. "Please, do not let emotion cloud your judgment, else you may do something you live to regret."

"He touched you." Alex shrieked. "That is enough, in my humble estimation, as he has no business conducting himself in such vulgar fashion with anyone but me."

"But his good opinion means little to me beyond friendship." Cara rued the day she enlisted Jason's aid, because his involvement in her scheme resulted in injury, however imagined, to Alex. "I am so sorry you are hurt, Alex. Never would I consciously cause you pain."

"But you are blameless, Cara." Without warning, Alex

marched straight to Cara and hugged her. "You are my sister as I am yours, and I know you would never play me false."

"I am grateful for your confidence." Cara held Alex at arm's length. "And as I stand here today, I vow no man, Brethren or otherwise, shall ever come between us."

Alex dipped her chin. "And I the same."

"Crisis averted," Rebecca declared. "And not a moment too soon, as now we must strategize."

"What do you recommend?" Elaine asked. "And can I be of assistance?"

"A lovely gesture, my dear." Rebecca smiled. "But I think not, as the solution does not require your participation."

"Give over, Becca." Sabrina swiped the last piece of shortbread.

"In instances such as these, the simplest answer is always best." Rebecca lowered her chin and caught Cara in a lethal stare. "You know what must needs."

"I accept Lance's proposal, even if I must broach the subject, myself." Cara squeezed Alex's fingers. "And you reclaim your Captain Collingwood."

While the ladies prepared what Cara deemed a premature victory toast of tepid tea, she could not escape the dark sense of foreboding that traipsed her spine. Peering out the window, she wondered how something that should have been so straightforward for two lifelong friends had morphed into a complicated mess, and would she ever get Lance to the altar?

PEERING OUT THE WINDOW, Lance wondered how something that should have been so straightforward for two lifelong friends had morphed into a complicated mess, and would he ever get Cara to the altar?

"Well, I would say last night was a rousing success," Jason stated in his booming baritone. "At least, for my part."

It was late in the morning, and after returning from the Atherton's ball, he had offered Jason accommodations, which enabled them the opportunity to strategize. Sitting at the head of the table in the dining room at Raynesford House, Lance speared a morsel of meat pie, raised it to his lips, and paused. "Brother, you do not know the half of it."

"So what is next on the agenda?" Jason stretched his arms and yawned. "And you never told me, how did Alex take my sudden change of heart?"

"For now, I recommend we stay the course." Shuffling the scrambled eggs on his plate, Lance smiled, as he recalled Alex's melancholy demeanor when she spied what she believed were Jason and Cara engaged in a tryst. "And she swallowed it hook, line, and sinker."

"Wonderful." Jason snickered. "Just what my little darling deserves."

"And my Cara?" Lance braced himself against a welling tide of jealousy. "Was she receptive to your advances?"

"To a degree—you should have seen her. I grazed her thigh with the back of my hand, and I thought she was going to jump out of her skin." Jason snorted. "I swear, for a minute it appeared she was about to revisit her supper all over my new coat."

Lance hadn't realized he was holding his breath until he almost fainted. He did not want Cara to welcome Jason's attention, not that he presumed she would. But how unfair was it that although he knew her interest in Jason was a ruse, Lance was still anxious? "The important thing is you dissuaded her from ending your agreement."

"Well, not exactly." Jason averted his gaze. "But I did try."

"I beg your pardon?" Lance set down his fork. "Are you or are you not still engaged in a mock courtship with Miss Douglas?"

"You would think the answer to your query quite simple, yet it is difficult to assess with any measure of certainty." Jason shrugged. "We sort of left the situation unresolved."

"I do not follow." Lance narrowed his stare. "What do you mean you left the situation unresolved?"

"Cara asked me to cease my suit." Jason tugged his cravat. "And I politely ignored her request."

"The devil you say." Lance raked his fingers through his hair. "Did she elaborate on her reasons?"

"I assure you, I am quite serious, and she did not share her motivations." Jason furrowed his brow. "But Cara admitted she is prepared to settle for less in regard to her reluctant champion, so I believe she would be more receptive to your proposal."

"She declared as much?" Based on Collingwood's assertion, Lance could have danced a merry jig. "You are not mistaken?"

"Indeed." Jason dipped his chin. "You may rely on me."

"Excellent." Lance drew the napkin from his lap, dabbed the corners of his mouth, and tossed the cloth on the table. "Then our pursuits are at an end, for we have met my goal."

"Hold on there, friend. I have a score to settle with Alex, and until I exact proper recompense for her shenanigans, we will stay the course, as you insisted."

"But I need to secure Cara's acceptance—soon." Lance calculated the days required to secure a license, publish the banns, and plan a suitable ceremony without piquing the *ton's* curiosity.

"What are you not telling me?" Jason inquired in a low voice.

"It is none of your concern." Lance resolved to contact his solicitor, at once. "In light of our—"

"Oh, no." Jason sputtered and scratched his temple. "Did you compromise Miss Douglas, in truth?"

Unwilling to compound the damage to Cara's reputation, Lance considered his response with great care. "Well, it was not my intent—"

"I do not believe it." With mouth agape, Jason eased back in his chair. "Are we talking a few licentious kisses or a full scale seduction?"

Conscious of the footmen within earshot, Lance asked, "Are you finished with breakfast?"

Jason nodded. "I am."

"My study." Lance pushed from the table and stood. "Now."

Lance strode into the hall and turned right, with Jason in his wake. At the foyer, he veered left. When he gained the relative privacy of his domain, he faced his ally. "The situation is such that I am concerned Cara may be in a delicate condition."

"Hell and the Reaper." Jason blinked. "Is she increasing?"

"I do not know," Lance admitted. "Although she denies it."

"But the possibility exists." It was a statement, not a question.

"Aye," Lance said with reluctance.

"Good God, man, what were you thinking?"

"Must I state the obvious?" Lance rested hands on hips and shifted his weight. "I was not thinking."

"Well there's a revelation." Jason whistled in monotone. "Heaven help you if Admiral Douglas discovers what you have done. He will cut off your head and string it from the nearest yardarm."

"I should be so lucky." Lance shuddered. "As that is not the part of my anatomy I figure he will remove first."

"Ouch." Jason grimaced. "Did you have to say that? The mere thought gives me collywobbles."

"Can you be serious for an instant?" Lance pressed a clenched fist to his lips. "The one thing still puzzling me is Cara's reason for rejecting my proposal, thus compelling her charade. Duplicity is not her forte, and it is not her character. I must believe her motivation is, in her mind, a noble cause."

"You know, I have mulled the situation myself." Jason rubbed the back of his neck and frowned. "As you have been friends since the cradle, and your relationship extends beyond innocence, why did she throw you over?"

"I haven't the faintest notion." Lance scratched his cheek and for the umpteenth time attempted to decipher Cara's actions. "Must confess I presumed she would welcome my suit."

"I suppose you did it up grand? On bended knee, you presented her with a bouquet of roses and proclaimed everlasting adoration and all that drivel?" Jason rolled his eyes. "Women live for such fluff and fancy."

Lance shuffled his feet. "Well, not exactly."

"Oh?" Jason opened and then closed his mouth. "Just what did you do?"

"Given our history and my unique understanding of Cara, I believed the matter straightforward." In a flash, the weight of the world nestled on his shoulders, and Lance sighed. "I simply presented every logical argument necessitating our betrothal."

"You did what?" Jason tripped on the edge of the rug and almost fell, face first, into a chair. As he righted himself, he asked, "Are you mad?"

"Collingwood, I do not suppose you can comprehend my actions, given your brief acquaintance with Miss Douglas, but Cara is an uncommonly level-headed woman." It rankled Lance that Jason presumed to know Cara better than a lifelong friend. "Relying on her intelligence and conviction, I composed an impromptu but convincing explanation of our situation, knowing full well she required nothing more."

"And yet she turned you down." Jason arched a brow.

"Believe me, I was just as surprised." Lance huffed a breath in frustration. "Never did I anticipate rejection."

"You think me surprised that Cara rejected you after what you just divulged." Jason rested a palm to his belly and vented boisterous laughter. "Bloody hell, man, I am nothing more than a sailor, and even I know the fairer sex lives in heightened expectation of such an event. You can't ask a lady to marry you as if you were doing nothing more than writing a report for the Admiral. At least, not if you want her to accept you."

"But Cara is not like other women." Lance folded his arms. "She does not demand such humiliating frippery, and we did not embark on a proper courtship, so I cannot be faulted for improvising."

"Do you imply you never would have proposed had you not compromised her?" Jason appeared flummoxed.

Lance gazed at the floor. "You are correct."

"Forgive me, brother, but you make about as much sense as a berserk mule," Jason said in an uncertain tone.

"I beg your pardon?" Lance snapped to attention. "Do you claim some special insight into my predicament because you sailed my ship and availed yourself of my hospitality?"

"I need no such advantage." Jason pulled on his ear and crossed his legs. "Because your argument holds no water."

"What do you know of it?" Lance scowled. "You spout witty quips and toy with Alex's affections, while I seek a permanent commitment."

"Leave Lady Alex out of this, as I will deal with her a far sight better than you have managed Miss Douglas." Jason smirked. "Now then, you expect me to believe you willingly ruined a woman you claim is a lifelong friend, someone for whom you care, on the spur of the moment? That you have not lusted after her since you were a randy young lad who just discovered a rather beneficial quality of soap while bathing?"

"What is your point?" Lance inquired through gritted teeth.

"There is more to this scenario than you admit." Jason thrust his chin. "So what are you hiding?"

"I have nothing to hide." Now Jason's tack had Lance confused. "I have thoroughly compromised Cara, and she refuses to marry me."

"But you would not have taken her were there not some unrequited passions involved."

"There were none." Of course, Lance lied.

"Then she slighted you as a child." Jason pinned him with an inquisitive stare. "You have never forgiven her."

"That is preposterous."

"Perhaps you were angry with the Admiral?"

"Not by a long chalk."

"Were you foxed?"

"The fact is she seduced me." Lance bit his tongue against further spontaneous confessions.

The study grew silent as a tomb.

"Now I am befuddled." Jason stood, walked to the side table, grabbed the crystal decanter, and poured a brandy. "And I need a drink."

"Make it two." Yes, it was early, but Lance hadn't given a damn. In that instant, he needed a healthy dose of liquid courage. "And I would have your word as a gentleman, you will never divulge my secret to anyone as long as you live."

"You have my solemn vow, if you reciprocate." Jason handed Lance a glass. "You know, in some respects, you and I are in the same boat."

"How so?" Lance resituated his waistcoat and adjusted the lace trim of his sleeves.

"Alex has charged me with the force and determination of an entire brigade. She has coveted my sword as if going into battle." Jason resettled in the overstuffed chair near the hearth. "What on earth makes the Brethren women so bold?"

"Careful, brother." Lance chuckled and shook his head. "Else Damian will feed your most prized protuberance to the fishes."

"Again with the Jolly Roger jokes." Jason winced. "I told you my intentions are honorable, where Alex is concerned. And one thing is certain. You may take some comfort in the knowledge that Cara would not have given herself to you if she did not want you, and since women require commitment of the heart to share their bodies, unless they are a doxy, you may also assume she cares for you."

In that moment, Lance froze.

"What is it?" Jason shifted his weight. "What did I say?"

It was as though he had plunged into the icy waters of the Baltic. A shiver of awareness traipsed his spine, and Lance shuddered. "I had not thought of it that way."

In his brain, the inquisition commenced in rapid succession.

Was it possible?

Did Cara love him?

Was that what he missed?

If so, why the charade?

Why had she not told him?

"How did you think of it?" Jason asked.

"I do not know." Lance needed advice, and he knew just where to seek counsel. "I guess I did not consider the implications."

"But you had to have noticed something. Cara must have hinted at her affection."

"We have been friends all our lives." Lance checked the mantel clock. If he was lucky, he could gain valuable guidance at White's. "Of course I knew she cared for me."

"Hold on, old boy. I am not referring to friendship."

"Blister it, Jason. I swear I never knew Cara saw me as anything more than a friend until she stripped at the foot of my bed."

"She stripped? *Miss Perfect?*" Jason looked his shock. "Were there veils?"

"Forget I said that." Lance could have slit his own throat.

"Not a chance." Jason grinned. "Was there music?"

"Shut up."

"Did she dance?" Jason waggled his brows. "And is she indeed perfect?"

"Collingwood!"

"All right." Jason held up both hands in mock surren-

der. "I concede, Raynesford. I just can't imagine our
demure Miss Douglas enacting an impersonation of
Bathsheba—though I am doing my best to picture it in my
head."

"One more word about that, and you are a dead man."

"Calm yourself, Lance." Again, Jason laughed. "As I
have already promised, you have my word, as a gentleman, I
will not speak of it again, though I may dream of it. So what
is the plan for this evening?"

"As you require, we stay the course." Lance grasped a
pen from the inkstand and a sheet of parchment. Sketching
a directive to his solicitor, he said, "You continue your
pursuit of Cara, and I shall chase Alex, but this is the last
night of our charade."

LATER THAT AFTERNOON, Lance walked through the reading
room at White's. Navigating the sea of high-back chairs, he
nodded acknowledgements to the various members of his
set and surreptitiously ambled toward the rear wall. Six
great men, friends all, noted his arrival. To his left gathered
the bachelors: Dalton, Damian, and Blake. To his right
huddled the husbands: Trevor, Dirk, and Everett.

At the banks of his Rubicon, Lance realized he was
about to make a declaration from which there would be no
retreat. While he dreaded the implications of his actions,
and the relentless ribbing that would, no doubt, ensue, he
wanted Cara more than he valued his pride.

When Dalton waved a greeting, Lance dipped his chin
in blithe salute, inhaled a deep breath, and steered for his
quarry in the opposite direction. Yes, Lance had made his
stand, which had not escaped notice, as evidenced when

Blake, shock investing his features, leapt to the fore, and Damian, ever the voice of reason, quickly yanked him to his seat.

"Trevor. Everett. Dirk." He hoped his attempt to appear nonplussed was convincing, because he was damn near quaking in his Hessians. "How are you this fine day?"

"Lance. Good to see you." Trevor sported a wide grin, to which Lance would've taken exception under better circumstances. "Do you wish to join us?"

"If I may." Lance swallowed hard and shuffled his feet. "And I am not interrupting anything of significance."

"Nonsense." Dirk smiled. "Pull up a chair and weigh your anchor."

"Will you have a brandy, Raynesford?" Everett motioned for a refill.

"I believe I shall pass." Having polished off a bottle of his best stock in anticipation of the impending accidental meeting, Lance shook his head, as he clung to what little remained of his faculties. He reclined and tried to relax. Just as quick, he reversed course, leaned forward, and propped elbows to knees. Then he stretched tall and folded his arms in front of him.

"What is it?" Dirk inquired. "What troubles you, old friend?"

"As if we cannot guess," said Everett, as he glanced at Trevor. "And I would wager you have muddied your rudder where a certain female is concerned."

"Bloody hell." Lance rested his chin in his palm. "Am I that obvious?"

"Oh, brother." Everett chuckled. "Were you wearing skirts, I should prepare to listen with mock enthusiasm as you bemoan the increasing width of your waistline."

"Or the unfairness of morning sickness," Dirk added.

"Garters." Trevor rolled his eyes. "Caroline swears they were invented by the French to torture our women."

"And thereby torture us as we suffer their complaints." Everett shook his head. "Women. Can't live with them—"

"—Can't make heirs without them." Trevor raised his glass in toast.

"Damn, Lockwood." Everett slapped a hand to his thigh. "But I like that."

"Am I not witty?" Trevor clipped the end of a cigar. "I just thought of it."

"You are too clever by half." Dirk chuckled.

Trevor nodded once. "Praise, indeed."

The three men erupted in uncontrollable laughter, and Lance wondered if fate intended the same destiny for him. In that case, his friends seemed genuinely happy, so he resolved to push forward with his plan.

"Brothers, while I am loathe to halt your play, I must impose on your cordiality." Lance tugged at his cravat. "My situation is dire, and I must act in haste."

"Of course, Lance." Trevor poked Everett in the ribs, and Sabrina's husband ceased his incessant chuckling. "How can we be of service?"

"Well." As nerves got the best of him, his rehearsed oratory evaporated in a hairsbreadth of a second. "I find myself in need of your insight."

"To what purpose?" Everett queried, with an arched brow.

"I have a problem." Lance stretched his booted feet and scrutinized the shine.

"All right." Trevor scratched his chin and grinned. "Not faring any better since last we spoke of your lady?"

Lance froze. "What makes you think this involves a woman?"

"Oh, brother." Trevor shrugged. "I have spent too many days behind the look you are sporting."

"He's got it bad." Dirk chortled. "It is sad to watch another man fall prey to perfume and petticoats."

"He does, indeed." Trevor nodded his agreement. "Yet, in the end, I suppose it happens to us all, if we are lucky. And you must admit it is worth the effort. Don't know what I would do without Caroline, little Welton, and the one on the way."

"Tell me about it." Dirk pointed for emphasis. "I am nothing without my Becca."

"I know precisely what you mean." Everett wrinkled his nose. "Can't imagine my life absent Sabrina—even if she does drive me crazy from time to time. But if you ever confess as much to our wives, we will kill you, because although it is perfectly acceptable to enjoy your marriage, it is never wise to admit such lunacy to your mate."

"Oh, I say." Lance gulped. "You may rely on me, as I hope to join your set."

"So." Trevor cast Lance a quizzical stare. "What seems to be the quandary, aside from the uncooperative Miss Douglas?"

"Miss Douglas? You are courting Cara?" Dirk choked and almost spilt his brandy. "But she is like a sister to us."

"Not to me," Lance replied, quick as a wink. "And I would know what would cause a prospective bride, who truly cares for a man, to refuse his offer of marriage, in your collective opinion?"

"Upon my word, Rebecca told me there was more than friendship between you two, but I thought her spy instincts at full sail." Dirk downed the contents of his snifter and signaled for a refill. "I never suspected you."

"Do you not remember our conversation at the Douglas

dinner party, at the start of the winter season? You had your answer then." Caroline's husband narrowed his stare and smirked. To Everett, Trevor said, "And I believe he ignored our sage advice, Markham."

"More's the pity." Everett sat upright. "Because we are, for all intents and purposes, experts in our field, and we could have spared you endless torment, if only you had heeded our warning."

"Brothers, I have slept since then." Lance searched his memory but recalled only bits and pieces of their exchange, none of which made any sense. "I swear, I cannot recollect your recommendation."

"My fellow leg-shackled sympathizers, and veterans of three wicked tours of duty, what is the one statement guaranteed to right all wrongs in the merciless brand of warfare society has the unmitigated audacity to call courtship?" Trevor asked with a snort and a countenance of unutterable supremacy.

In unison, Everett and Dirk stated, "A declaration."

"You can't be serious." Lance squirmed as he pondered the prospect, as no member of the male sex worth his salt willingly professed such maudlin sentiment. "Is there not an easier solution? Perhaps, a gift, of some sort, that would suffice? Money is no object."

"You might think so—but, no," Everett said with grim finality. "Yet I would caution you not to avoid what could be described as the single most important achievement of your life."

Confused, Lance paused to examine their logic. "How so?"

"It is a singular phrase uttered in a seemingly nondescript fragment of time that could define your future, for good or ill, in ways you cannot imagine, until you take that step." Trevor cast a ghost of a smile. "However, were I you, I would not miss the chance for anything."

"Brothers, you have lost me." Nagging guilt resurfaced with a vengeance, as Lance thought of Thomas. Had his cousin survived, Cara would have married him, because the original heir to the marquessate of Raynesford was the better man. So Lance owed his happiness to the untimely demise of his best friend. "Why should I attempt such madness?"

"Because to seize the ultimate prize, you must bet it all without promise of success." With his brow a mass of furrows, Dirk pinned Lance with a potent stare. "You see although I existed in the world prior to meeting *L'araignee*, I did not truly live until Rebecca set foot aboard the *Gawain*. And when I thought I had lost her to Varringdale's treachery, I could not comprehend my future without her in it."

"Damn nasty affair, brother. But I get your meaning." Trevor averted his gaze. "When Cavalier threw Caroline from the *Black Morass* into the Thames, I vowed I would not leave the river if I could not save her, because I am a man if only I can count her as my woman."

"And although my countess was not threatened to such degree, I cannot convey the depth of my despair when I returned to Beaumaris and discovered her gone. Yes, I had the money, the estate, and the title, but they meant nothing without my wife." Everett paused, sighed, and swallowed hard. "Love makes you feel you can conquer the world, if only to deliver the spoils to the lady who holds your heart and have her share your devotion, in kind. It is a priceless treasure, unparalleled in its fragility and its strength, if you can claim it."

"Therein lies the risk, as it is the most courageous advance you will ever make, but it is worth the effort. Given my lady spy's instincts, it is safe to assert that Cara cares for you, so you may be assured of her affection." A peaceful but poignant calm fell over the group, and Dirk checked his timepiece. "Gentlemen, Becca should rouse from her nap in the next half hour. I believe I will go home and make love to my wife, until dinner."

"That is an excellent notion, Wainsbrough. Likewise, our topic has moved me." Everett stood. "I miss my Brie and would do the same."

"And our discussion has worked on me in similar fashion. I should hug my son, kiss my bride, and share her bath." Trevor rose from his chair and halted. Resting a hand on Lance's shoulder, he said, "My friend, you know what must needs. Now go to it."

CHAPTER EIGHTEEN

*A*s Cara ran through the trees, a low-lying branch snagged her hair, and she shrieked. The black night enveloped her in matching melancholia, as clouds shrouded the moon's silvery glow. Hiking her skirts in a most unladylike fashion, she wound her way deeper into the gardens of the Huxley's palatial estate located just outside London proper.

With her heart beating a rapid salvo in her chest, her pulse raced. As she fought panic and persistent nausea, she struggled to breathe, and the chilly wind stung her face as she fled.

For a moment, she sheltered beneath the canopy of a large oak and trained her ear for any sign of her tormentor. The absence of footfalls gave her hope that her persistent pursuer had ceased the chase. To be sure, she took two tentative steps. When an unknown assailant grabbed her from behind, Cara tried to scream, but a hand over her mouth muffled her call of alarm.

"*Shh.* It is Alex."

For a few seconds, Cara mumbled incoherently until she

found the good sense to pull free. "What on earth are you about?" she whispered.

"Evading Lance," Alex answered in a hushed tone. "I swear he has gone insane. And you?"

"Fleeing Jason," Cara replied. "And I believe he suffers the same malady."

Just then, Cara's name carried on the wind, and she threw her arms about Alex's shoulders. "I beg you, shield me from the lunacy."

"It is Jason," Alex said in a low voice.

"I know." At the thought of facing more of his amorous but unwelcome attention, Cara inhaled a shaky breath and shivered. "Quick—we must hide."

"We will do no such thing." Alex wrenched loose and turned in the direction of Jason's call. "He has been avoiding me all evening, and I am more than ready to enact a scene in the privacy of the garden."

At that very instant, Alex's name danced on the breeze as a flirty summons, and she reversed course and flung herself at Cara. "It is Lance. Please, do not let him find me."

"Where can we go?" Cara glanced left and then right. "I am not acquainted with the Huxley's grounds."

Lightning flashed, and the ominous rumble of thunder soon followed. Amid nature's herald of impending doom, familiar voices grew near, and Cara and Alex hunkered behind a thick hedge. Cara pressed a finger to Alex's lips, and a few tense minutes passed, as Cara feared discovery.

"Lance? Is that you?"

"Jason, what are you doing out here?"

"I was searching for Cara," Jason stated.

"What a coincidence, as I am looking for Alex," Lance replied.

"I believe I heard the dinner bell. Perhaps they have adjourned to the dining room."

Cara stared toward the heavens as another impressive bolt bathed the foliage in staccato blasts of bright silver, before the successive resounding boom rattled the earth beneath her feet.

"Oh, no. Not that," she whispered. As if Mother Nature had read her thoughts, a single drop of rain splashed on her forehead, which soon swelled into a torrential downpour.

"This is dreadful." Alex nudged closer. "We will be soaked to the skin if we do not get inside."

Cara peered over the edge of the thorny barrier. "I think they are gone."

"Then by all means, let us get indoors." Alex grasped Cara's hand and pulled her upright.

Racing against the deluge, with Alex in tow, Cara ran first for a side entrance but discovered it locked, so she veered toward the main ballroom doors. By the time she and Alex returned to the gala, they were drenched.

A footman bowed and then his mouth fell agape, which led Cara to suspect she must have looked frightfully awful. In search of her parents, she scanned Huxley Hall. After what seemed an eternity, Cara located the dining room.

Focused on her task, she all but ignored the ever-increasing whispers, lilting giggles, and glances of astonishment as she navigated a sea of elegantly bedecked tables. At long last, she found the Brethren gathered for dinner and made a beeline for her friends.

As she approached, Lance jumped to his feet, shrugged out of his coat, and draped it about her shoulders. "Are you trying to incite a riot?"

"What?" It was then she checked her appearance and almost swooned.

Her fashionable—but wet—gown of *eau de Nil* silk clung to her body like a second skin and was virtually transparent. Even her chemise left little to the imagination.

"Just what in bloody hell are you about?" Jason scowled, doffed his coat, and covered Alex. "Have you no shame?"

"We wandered into the gardens, lost our way, and were caught in the storm. By the time we identified the path that returned us to the house, we were soaked." Cara shuddered and tucked a stray lock of hair behind her ear. "It is not my fault the Huxley's grounds are so vast."

"You had no business taking an unchaperoned tour, at this hour, in unfamiliar surroundings." Lance grabbed Cara by the elbow and escorted her to a chair. "Collingwood and I searched everywhere for you."

"Really?" With an exaggerated bounce, Alex plopped into the seat opposite Cara. "Strange that we did not see you."

Cara sneezed, snatched a napkin, and dabbed her nose. "I fear I may have caught a cold."

"What the devil is going on here?" her father inquired, and Cara slumped in mortification.

"Oh, Papa. I am so sorry." Cara lowered her chin. "Can we please go home?"

"Mark, send for the coach." Her mother cast a sympathetic expression. "I will fetch you a cup of tea. It will soothe your throat and keep the chill at bay until we can get you out of that wet gown. Alex can stay with us and sleep in Sabrina's old room."

"Are you ill, my dear?" Lance clasped Cara's hand in his. "What can I do to make it better?"

For a few seconds, Cara pondered his query and could summon no viable solution to her predicament. And her affliction extended a vast deal beyond a runny nose. Myriad emotions assailed her senses and piqued her nerves. Drowning in a lethal mix of humiliation, embarrassment, and remorse, Cara wished she could return to the past and undo the actions that had set in motion the end of her friendship with Lance.

In the past few weeks, she had lied to those she cherished most and pretended an attachment to a man she held in high esteem, in order to lure the attention of her hero. Worse, after her first failed attempt at seduction, she had behaved like a harlot and given her body to Lance on the desk in Lord Chomley's study.

And for what?

Love?

But how could she cultivate a lifelong commitment from a field comprised of subterfuge and deceit?

Of the Douglas sisters, she had always been known as the graceful one, a true credit to her sex. Miss Perfect. The ultimate embodiment of feminine deportment, she could always be relied upon to follow societal dictates. And yet she had just walked through the Huxley's dining room in a state of near nudity, in full view of the ton.

No wonder the footman had stared.

Oblivious to everything save the beat of her own heart, Cara considered to what she had reduced herself, in an effort to win the husband of her choice. In essence, she had betrayed every aspect of her character, had abandoned each facet of her personality, and had transformed into a foreign creature even she did not recognize.

No wonder she had foundered.

"Cara, are you all right?" Lance drew imaginary circles on her palm. "You do not look so well."

Again she sneezed, and from his waistcoat pocket he pulled an embroidered handkerchief, almost identical to the one tucked in the bodice of her ruined gown. "Thank you."

"I can't bear to see you suffer." He pressed a clenched fist to his mouth and studied her with unfettered interest.

"Please, do not worry." She had always thought it difficult to be elegant and blow her nose at the same time, so she tried to recover some of her famed deportment as she sniffled with delicacy. "I shall be fine as fippence in the morning."

For a scarce second, hope bloomed, but it died in the wake of the realization that Lance had been chasing Alex through the ballrooms the last few nights. As far as Cara could tell, she had squandered her golden opportunity. Her hero had proposed on more than one occasion—and she had refused him out of pride, so she had no one to blame but herself. In the end, all she wanted was his happiness, even if it meant he married someone else. And who better to take her place than another of her oldest friends.

"Cara, we need to talk." Lance traced the curve of her cheek and smiled. "There is so much—"

"Here is your tea, dearest." Her mother held a cup and saucer. "Drink it quickly."

"Yes, Mama." Cara gulped the steaming brew, which scalded her tongue, and she choked.

"Oh, and there's your father." She clapped her hands. "Come, girls. Let us get you home and into a hot bath."

Cara set the cup on the table and gasped when Lance clutched her forearms and lifted her from the chair. In a scandalous display of affection, which incited a fresh spate of hushed murmurs from the crowd, he pressed his lips to her temple and whispered, "Get some rest. I will see you tomorrow night, at your birthday celebration."

"I forgot about that." Another year as a spinster and,

Cara mused, a permanent fixture on the shelf, as the next generation's Lady Stanhope. Overwhelmed by a dark sense of foreboding, she struggled to hold the tears at bay.

When she lowered her head, he cupped her chin and brought her gaze to his. "Everything is going to be all right, Cara. I promise, it is over."

As the family coach teetered along the streets of London, his final words echoed in her brain. Though Lance had said nothing specific, she was certain he intended to declare himself enamored of Alex and to secure Cara's permission to offer for their mutual friend. How like her hero to smooth the waters preceding his nuptials.

Her ruse must have worked better than she thought. Perhaps he assumed she would wed Jason. She was prepared to allow Lance to labor under that mistaken assumption—until he was happily betrothed to Alex. Then she would concoct a suitable story to explain how she would not marry Captain Collingwood and save his reputation, as he had done nothing wrong.

"You have had a rather difficult season, thus far, my dear." Her father smiled and shook his head. "This is your second cold. I believe I shall send for Dr. Handley. Perhaps a tonic will improve your constitution."

"Nonsense." Her mother huffed a breath. "What Cara needs is a hot bath and a good night's rest, not some potion in a bottle."

The equipage halted before the family townhome on Upper Brooke Street not a minute too soon, because her calm façade fractured, little by little, as the future she had planned crumbled to pieces.

"Thank you, Papa," Cara said, as he handed her to the sidewalk.

"Upstairs, this instant."

"Yes, Mama." As a dutiful daughter, Cara obeyed without complaint.

Half an hour later, she sank into the bath positioned near the hearth. Curls of steam rose from the surface of the water in a delicate dance, and the subtle scent of lilac teased her nose, but she found no comfort in the familiar fragrance.

Tomorrow was her birthday, which marked the start of an annual mass exodus, as the ton journeyed to their country estates for the holidays. It was her favorite time of year, but the celebrations brought her no joy. How sad it was to recall the determination with which she had embarked on the Little Season.

As a naïve debutante, she had envisioned jolly festivities with toasts to her future happiness as Lance's wife. Instead, there would be only the customary best wishes for her continued good health.

"It is over," she said to no one.

At long last, Cara succumbed to the heartbreak eating at her insides. Emitting a soft sob, she bent her legs, wrapped her arms beneath her thighs, set her forehead to her knees, and wept.

"I SWEAR Cara and Alex looked like a couple of drowned rats." Jason threw his head back, pressed a palm to his belly, and howled with laughter. "Can you believe our good fortune? They got caught in the rain."

Lance settled into the leather chair behind the desk in his study, and an untouched balloon of brandy rested in his hand. While his friend continued to rumble with mirth, Lance enjoyed no such compulsion. The image of Cara, shrouded in sorrow—in defeat—loomed before him, as a haunting visage, and how he ached for her.

"Daresay things could not have gone better had we planned it." Jason roared with unrestrained hilarity. "The gods smile upon us."

Mesmerized by the gentle flicker of flames in the hearth, Lance reflected on his present circumstances and found no humor. Instead, he struggled with a cold emptiness he had not experienced since Thomas died, and a singular phrase echoed in his ears. "It is over."

"I beg your pardon?" In an instant, Jason quieted. "What did you say?"

"As I remarked earlier, our scheme is ended." Again, Lance envisioned his lady and frowned. "I intend to propose to Cara tomorrow night."

Jason sobered. "Is that the way the wind blows?"

"Aye." Lance nodded once.

"Until this moment, I may have doubted you." Jason stood. "But you are serious."

"Indeed." Of course, Lance second-guessed himself at every turn, because he had no clue how he would respond should Cara reject him, but he saw no need to share that bit of information. "In fact, I never should have allowed the situation to progress so far."

"You kissed Cara in the Huxley's dining room, prior to her departure." Jason cast a devilish grin and waggled his brows. "By societal standards, you committed a scandalous display of affection, friend. I would not want to be near when the admiral discovers your dalliance."

"He will not care and neither will the *ton* when our betrothal is announced." At least, that is what Lance hoped, but he was not half so confident of his position. "But I could not let Cara leave like that."

Jason scratched his temple. "Like—what?"

"Thinking I did not care for her." He revisited the discussion with the Brethren husbands and grimaced. "Never have I seen her so downcast. It was as if she had lost her best friend."

Jason untied his cravat. "Well, what did you expect her to believe, as that is precisely the impression we attempted to portray since you started chasing Alex."

"Yes, I know." In need of distraction, Lance stood, walked to the fireplace, and checked the time on the mantel clock. "But Cara was never supposed to get hurt."

"Bloody hell." Jason clucked his tongue. "You really are done for, are you not?"

"To what do you refer?" How he wished he could return to the past and undo the actions that had set in motion his current quandary.

"You know, I suspected as much, but even I had not guessed the depth of your regard." Jason narrowed his stare and whistled in monotone. "You are thoroughly besotted, head over heels in love with Miss Cara Douglas."

"Don't be ridiculous." Lance clasped his hands behind his back and paced before the hearth. "I will admit I am very fond of her."

"Of course, you are."

"As we have been friends for years, I have no doubt she will make an excellent marchioness."

"Of course, she will."

"She comes from a respected family, and I would be a fool to overlook her connections."

"Of course, you would."

"Blast it all, Collingwood." Lance folded his arms and faced his tormentor. "Stop being so deuced agreeable."

"Do not rip at me, my friend." With a cat-that-ate-the-canary grin, Jason reclined in his chair. "I merely concur with your protestations."

Lance scowled. "Then I take exception to your tone."

Jason burst into laughter, sat upright, and rested elbows to knees. "Of course, you do, but tell me something anyway. Why do you try so hard to convince me that you do not love Cara when your every action speaks otherwise? According to Alex, all Brethren marry for love. Why should you be any different?"

Never had Lance shared his burden—his guilt—in relation to his cousin's death, with anyone, because he dreaded the upbraiding that would, no doubt, ensue. In short, he was a coward of the worst sort, refusing to confront his misdeeds. Then again, it was nothing less than he deserved. "It is a long story."

"I am rather fond of long stories." Jason refilled his brandy balloon and offered a mock toast. "And the night is young."

For a few seconds, Lance studied the fair-haired man he had once considered his enemy. Given Jason's brief affiliation with the Brethren, and the fact that he never knew Thomas, he might be just the person to confirm Lance's guilt, once and for all. As Lance gazed into the glass of liquid courage, he decided it was past due to throw caution to the wind. "It has to do with Thomas, the original heir to the marquessate of Raynesford."

"Your cousin?" Jason furrowed his brow and rubbed his chin. "The one who drowned?"

Lance opened and then closed his mouth. "You know the story?"

"Aye." Jason nodded. "Alex told me of it."

Lance compressed his lips. "Then you know of my shame."

"I apologize, friend." Jason shook his head. "But there you have lost me."

"I let Thomas die." Spearing his fingers through his hair, Lance inhaled a deep breath and rolled his shoulders. "I should be in the grave—not him."

"Wait a minute." Jason splayed his hands and retreated a step. "Calm yourself, man."

"I do not want to be calm." Memories flashed a staccato assault to his consciousness, forming a morbid tapestry. "He was a brother to me, and I stood idly as he perished."

Collingwood shifted his weight. "Easy, Raynesford. You are not—"

"Do not call me that," he said through gritted teeth. "It was his birthright—not mine."

"Hold hard, brother." Jason wrinkled his nose and shuffled his feet. "You make it sound as if you wanted Thomas dead, as if you killed him. However, Alex relayed the events of that sad day, in detail, so I know such is not the case. It was his idea to miss class and skate on the pond. When the worst happened, you nearly drowned trying to save your cousin and almost expired of pneumonia, thereafter. How can you blame yourself for his demise?"

"I should have...done...something." Lance searched in vain for a plausible argument. "I should have found a way to rescue him."

"Could you be more specific?" Jason cleared his throat and gazed at the floor. "Given that you were a child of the same age, at the time of the incident, and trapped in the same ice-covered pond, after you attempted to free your cousin, tell me what you could have possibly done differently to change the outcome?"

The ticking of the mantel clock filled the study.

Tears stung his eyes as Lance fought to form a response.

If only he had not fallen through the ice, he might have saved Thomas. Perhaps he should have sounded the alarm and summoned a teacher. Or maybe he should have stayed on the banks and attempted to fashion a makeshift rope from the vegetation.

"You can second-guess yourself into oblivion, my friend, but it will not bring back Thomas," Jason stated in a low voice. "But I would ask, were you killed that day, and your cousin standing here, drowning in guilt, what would you say to him? How would you want him to go on without you?"

"That is easy." Lance dragged his shirtsleeve across his face. "I would tell him to live his life for both of us, to marry and have a house filled with children. I would want for him all the things I wanted for myself and more."

"Then does it not stand to reason Thomas would want the same for you?" Jason pointed for emphasis. "Or was he a selfish, mean-spirited bastard?"

"Careful, Collingwood." Anger charged every nerve. "I would run through bigger men than you for such insult."

"Forgive the offense, as none was intended," Jason replied with a casual wave. "Pray, continue."

"As a lad, Thomas was never without a smile or a mischievous caper." Lance could not help but grin as he reminisced fonder times. "Had my posterior heated more times than I can count as a result of his pranks."

"Sounds like quite a gadling."

"Oh, he was handful." Lance resituated a chair beside Jason's, weighed his anchor, and chuckled. "He thought nothing of skipping Latin to play in the woods near Eton." He chuckled and shook his head. "Thomas had a particular dislike for the dead language. Although, if I remember correctly, he was a devil of a poet."

"Really? A romantic, too?"

"Aye. We both had wicked crushes on—" Lance swallowed hard.

"You both had crushes on Cara, did you not?"

And there it was, the source of his conundrum, plainly spoken, out in the open, at last.

"I think I understand your perspective." Jason massaged the back of his neck. "In a sense, you view your relationship with Cara as a betrayal of your cousin's memory?"

"Because I survived that day, which in and of itself was an incredible gift, I inherited his title, and all its trappings, so I do not believe I have the right to expect anything else."

"Lance, may I speak freely?"

He arched a brow. "When have you not?"

"Point taken. Allow me to submit, since I am not one of your lifelong companions, and not likely to tell you what you want to hear, that I have witnessed more sensible rationale in a berserk mule." Jason added, "Though you may be as stubborn."

"Go to hell," Lance spat.

"I may in time, however, at the moment my pleasure in life is to cause you no end of torment." Jason chucked Lance's shoulder. "At least, until you accept the folly of your logic. Do you really believe the nonsense you spout?"

"Consider my situation. I survived the incident, which claimed my best friend's life. I hold his peerage and now, after a series of unplanned and unexpected events, stand to marry the woman we both adored from afar." Lance downed the contents of his glass and frowned. "How am I supposed to feel?"

"Overjoyed? In love?" Jason shrugged. "Aroused beyond all imagination?"

Lance emitted a groan in frustration. "I am being serious, and you are making jokes."

"Ah, but you mistake me, friend. I am serious. If Thomas were half the person you claim, then you should know, were he alive, he would be the happiest for you."

"It is easy to say that when I am here, and Thomas is dead."

"And so should you be, as you have one leg in the grave. I would wager Thomas would not approve of your extended mourning." Jason stood, stretched his back, and yawned. "I am for Bedfordshire, but I would leave you something to ponder. Guilt is a powerful emotion, brother. It numbs your senses and impairs your vision, shrouding your reality in a dense cloud of regret, which further impedes your capacity to reap the rewards of life. Would you condemn your lady to the same fate? In regard to Thomas's death, Cara is blameless, yet your actions punish her, as well."

Hours later, as Lance sat before the fireplace, Jason's words echoed in his brain, again and again, as a taunting refrain. The mantel clock sounded the hour, and soon the sun would rise. Lance retrieved a candle and, with a purposeful stride, exited his study. In a matter of seconds, he crossed the foyer and skipped up the stairs. At the landing, he halted.

The vast gallery, a sea of Prescotts past, bespoke a rich heritage of military prowess, male pride, and the spirited ladies who claimed their hearts. He paused at the portrait of his cousin before he realized he had moved.

With wild curls jutting in all directions, in defiance of fashion, a garish red short coat, an impish grin, and his favorite hound sitting at his feet, Thomas seemed to gaze at Lance. Painted when his cousin was the tender age of three and ten, it was the last artwork commissioned of the original heir to the marquessate of Raynesford.

Lance smiled.

As lads, they bore strong resemblance, so much that many in the *ton* had speculated as to Lance's true parentage. They had shared a common height, comparable carriage, and matching lopsided grins. The only physical trait that distinguished them was their eyes. Lance sported emerald green and Thomas a vivid blue.

But it was their personalities that truly set them apart. In short, Lance and Thomas were diametrical opposites. Whereas he always played by the rules, and walked the straight and narrow path, Thomas lived on the edge— always flouting the limits of good society.

Lance liked to think they had struck a fine balance. While he provided discipline, tempering his cousin's outlandish antics, Thomas brought a little color into his world, if not his backside.

And if Thomas could see him now, Lance knew his cousin would be disappointed. Ever the rebel, Thomas would take Lance to task for being so bloody noble. Jason, god bless him, was right.

Lance had been living in the past for too long, carrying burdens that existed only in his mind. And as clouds veil the bright rays of sunlight, shrouding the earth in grey gloom, he had enveloped his own destiny in the oppressive shadow of guilt.

"If you can hear me, brother, know that I am so sorry if I have caused you additional pain, and how I wish you were here. Please, be at peace, as I believe I have found it, at last."

In that instant, the weight of the world, so long perched on his shoulders, seemed to evaporate, and Lance exhaled a sigh of relief. It was high time he picked up the reins of his life and rode hell bent for leather toward the future.

And his future was Cara.

CHAPTER NINETEEN

*T*he sun shone brightly on the anniversary of her birth, in sharp contrast to Cara's mood, as she had shed a river of tears mourning the future she had planned with Lance. When the first members of her odd extended family arrived promptly at eight, she positioned herself beside her mother.

"Good evening, Alex." She exchanged a peck on the cheek with her erstwhile ally.

"Happy Birthday." Alex's smile morphed into a frown. "Oh, my. But your face is puffy. You must have a terrible cold."

"Yet you remain the loveliest of ladies." Damian clicked his heels, bowed, and offered a beautifully wrapped package. "I have come to pay homage to your beauty, my dear Cara."

"Ignore him." Alex rolled her eyes and smacked her brother on the arm. "I believe his new ladybird has a fondness for Shakespeare. He has been spouting all manner of useless drivel for the past fortnight."

Damian stood tall and adopted a mock pout. "Now I resent that, Alex. Really I do."

"There she is." With arms splayed wide in welcome, Sabrina waddled across the threshold. "Cara, I have missed you so. Why have you not visited me?"

"I would have, dearest, but Everett said you needed your rest." Cara bent to make allowance for Brie's well-rounded belly. "And how is my little niece or nephew coming along?"

"Oh, I am doing fine, as is the babe. You mustn't worry about us." Sabrina hugged Cara and whispered in her ear, "What happened with Lance? You must tell me everything."

"Hello, sister." Everett smiled at Cara as he embraced Sabrina from behind and patted her most protuberant part. "Is my wife not the most beautiful creature of our existence? And look at the size of her. Daresay my son is going to be as hale and hearty as his father."

"You are quite the proud papa, Everett." Cara laughed. "Thank you allowing my sister to join us."

"Allowing?" Sabrina humphed. "He does not allow me to do anything. I decide where I go and do not go."

"Of course, you do, darling." Everett winked at Cara, kissed the top of his Brie's head, and gently ushered her into the foyer.

"Felicitations on your birthday." Rebecca presented Cara with a beribboned parcel. "And I hope to hear additional good news, tonight."

"What additional news?" Dirk inquired, with a perplexed expression.

"It is none of your affair," Becca replied, with a wink.

"Then let us find you a comfortable chair, darling." Dirk gave his wife a gentle nudge. "I would not have you overtire yourself."

"Now there is the prettiest birthday girl in London."

Blake strolled into the foyer, with Dalton in tow, carrying a wrapped gift.

"Why you grow more beautiful with each passing year." Dalton placed a chaste kiss to her forehead.

Blake followed suit in similar fashion. "Tell me, my dear, when are you going to stop holding half the men of our set in suspense?"

Cara shuffled her feet. "I beg your pardon?"

Dalton cocked his head and cast a mischievous, lopsided grin. "What he wants to know is when you are going to settle down and marry some lucky but undeserving chap?"

"Perhaps she has already made her selection." Trevor escorted Caroline across the threshold. "And she keeps it a secret."

"Do not tease her, Trevor." Caroline elbowed her husband in the ribs. "And all women have secrets."

"Some more than others," Lance replied, as Elaine clutched his arm.

"I hold no store." In an effort to conceal her shaking hands, Cara smoothed the skirts of her emerald velvet gown, and reminded herself she had nothing to fear. For better or worse, her course was fixed, and she would not deviate from her plan. "Do not feel you must stand on formality, as there are refreshments in the drawing room."

"Happy birthday, sister." Elaine bounced with unconcealed excitement. "Are we the last to arrive?"

"Indeed." Cara nodded. "But we are family, so punctuality is of no concern."

"Then, if you do not object, I should like to see Sabrina, as it has been ages since we last met." Elaine arched a brow. "I believe Everett would deny Napoleon entrance were the general to show up on his doorstep and beg an audience."

"I would wager you are correct." Cara could not help but

giggle. "But it is only because he loves her, so I cannot fault his behavior."

"Ah, love can turn the most sane man into a blithering idiot." Jason smirked. "Happy birthday, my dear Miss Douglas. May I introduce a friend?"

As only Lance loomed in Jason's wake, Cara blinked in confusion. "I believe we have already met—twenty-six years ago, today."

"That may be, but do you really know him?" Jason asked.

"As well as I know myself." Cara mustered a smile, even as her heart fractured. "Good evening, Lance. I am honored by your presence."

"I would not miss the celebration of your birth for the world." Lance inclined his head, searched her eyes, and cupped her cheek. "Are you feeling better? No ill effects from the impromptu bath in the Huxley's garden?"

"I am quite well, I assure you." Cara shivered beneath his touch, but his levity put her at ease. "Do not be concerned on my account."

"I have a gift in homage to your beauty." He leaned close and in a low voice said, "But I would prefer to give it to you in more private surroundings."

"I am sure that is not necessary." How she ached, as reality beckoned with a vengeance. "Your attendance is my boon, my hero."

"As we are all present, shall we gather in the drawing room?" Her father slapped Lance on the back. "So glad to see your improvement, my boy."

While Lance chatted with her parents, Cara grabbed Jason by the elbow. In a hushed tone, she said, "I must speak with you."

With a brow arched in question, Jason dipped his chin. "Of course."

"Come with me." Cara glanced over her shoulder and then steered him down a side hall. After a quick check to ensure their privacy, she drew Collingwood into the small alcove just outside her father's study.

"Captain, you have been so kind, and I shall always be grateful for your assistance." A shiver coursed her spine, and she inhaled a deep breath and recalled her well-rehearsed speech. "I owe you a debt I fear I can never repay."

"Forgive me, Miss Douglas." He appeared perplexed. "What are you about?"

"It concerns our arrangement." If she stopped now, she might never resolve her predicament, and she had to put an end to the insanity. "I am no longer in need of your services."

"Ah, your reluctant suitor has come to his senses, at last." Jason grinned and squeezed her fingers. "Somehow, I knew he would not disappoint you."

"As much as I wish it were so, I must confess the opposite is true." A dull ache weighed heavy in her chest, yet Cara persevered. "My suitor is no more."

"What?" Jason blinked and sputtered. "But—you must be mistaken. I do not understand."

"My beau has quit his campaign. It seems he has lost interest, at least, in me." Hers was a humiliating admission, and Cara gazed at her clasped hands. "Therefore, you are free to continue your courtship of Alex, unfettered. You will make a wonderful husband."

"Wait a minute." Jason rolled his eyes. "I do not believe this is happening. Are you telling me your hesitant hero has declined to marry you—that you have conferred with him directly, and he has refused you?"

"Not exactly—"

"Then you have not spoken with him?"

"No."

"You know, war is much simpler than this game we play." Jason sighed. "Cara, regardless of your deductions, and evidence to the contrary, for which I must own part of the blame, your conclusion is woven of whole cloth."

"Jason, I know a vast deal more than you when it comes to my intended." She compressed her lips. "Well, my former intended."

"How did I end up in this position, dispensing advice to the lovelorn?" He groaned. "I should have stayed in the navy."

"Please, if I may be frank, you must not think me ungracious, as I appreciate all you have done to aid my ill-fated campaign." Just how many fractures could her heart withstand, she mused. "But I have to accept the reality of my situation. The man for whom I set my cap does not want me, and it is past time I move on with my life."

"Cara, you are so very wrong." Jason stood and paced the hall. Then he paused. "Promise me something?"

Despite her better judgment, she replied, "It depends on what you ask of me."

"Give me your word, as a lady, that you will meet your prospective groom, and allow him the opportunity to explain himself. On my honor, I vow you will be glad of it." Jason repositioned himself beside her. "He is in earnest."

"You know." It was a statement, not a question.

He opened and then closed his mouth. "Aye."

Now her shame was complete. "How did you guess?"

"We inadvertently discovered your plot after Lance

threatened to kill me, when he thought you ill-used." Her erstwhile ally chuckled. "And we consumed an impressive amount of brandy in commiseration of our folly."

"So Lance knows everything?"

"Unfortunately, yes." Jason tugged his cravat. "It was that or a dawn appointment at Paddington Green."

"Oh, dear." The once confusing pieces of the puzzle suddenly made sense. "And your behavior, of late? You were trying to make Alex jealous."

His features hardened. "Indeed."

If she had ruined Alex's chances with Collingwood, Cara would never forgive herself. "But—why?"

"Because she lied to me." Jason folded his arms and snickered. "I had thought to offer for her, but now I am unsure she possesses the qualities I require in a wife."

"But I demanded she keep my secret, so you must not punish Alex for my indiscretion," Cara explained. "Her only thought was to help me. Is that not worth something?"

"Given our relationship, Alex should have confided in me." His harsh expression conveyed a world of angst and testified to the depth of his hurt. "She could have had faith in me."

"And yet I forbid her from sharing the truth, so I, alone, am to blame for her duplicity." At last, the damn burst, and the tears flowed. "I am so sorry, Captain. If you are angry with anyone, be angry with me."

"Dearest Cara, I understand the noble motives behind your enterprise. Please, do not cry." Jason produced a handkerchief, cupped her chin, and blotted her cheeks, with care. "And Lady Alex will suffer her day of reckoning, if she hopes to have a future with me. But, at this moment, there are more pressing matters to be settled between you and Lance."

"I dread the prospect." Cara hiccuped.

"You need to speak with him." Jason clutched her hand in his and brought her knuckles to his lips.

"Captain, you should not—"

"What in bloody hell is going on here?" As a manifestation of her final downfall, Cara's father dominated the hall, with his chin hovering at dangerous heights, hands on hips, and a narrow stare that left Cara shivering in her slippers.

In an instant, she recognized the imperious posture and the lethal anger it bespoke, because she had seen that stance on occasions too numerous to count. But his ire had only been provoked by Sabrina's most grievous infractions. Never had Cara been subjected to such wrath.

"Papa, it is not what you think."

"In my study—now." Her father pointed for emphasis, as if she were unfamiliar with her surroundings.

Without hesitation, Cara stood. "Yes, sir."

"I should return to the drawing room," Jason stated. "I shall leave—"

"You, too," the Admiral replied.

"Of course, Admiral." Jason tugged his collar and cleared his throat. "I should be happy to accommodate you."

"You will cooperate, or I shall hang you from the *Intrepid's* highest yardarm," he declared through clenched teeth.

Marching as a dutiful daughter, with Jason in tow, into the Brethren's strategic domain, Cara seized upon limitless excuses to account for her behavior, none of which possessed sufficient gloss to save her posterior, in her estimation.

The subtle aroma of cigar smoke teased her nose, and before her sat eight high back chairs, one for each knight of the ancient order, situated in a wide arc in the middle of the cavernous room. In pride of place rested her father's hand-tooled, antique mahogany desk. It was an arrangement meant to convey eminence and intimidation, at once, and the effect was not lost on her.

When the bolt slide home, with an ominous click that seemed to reverberate off the walls, Cara almost swooned. That her sire had locked the door portended dire consequences, and no interruption, however impassioned, could save her.

"Have a seat." Her father poured himself a brandy.

"Papa, you are making a terrible—"

"I said *sit down*."

"Please, do not incite him further," Jason whispered and quickly perched in obeisance of her father's command.

Without further delay, she clamped her mouth shut and followed suit. When her sire assumed his customary position, steepling his hands atop the leather blotter, she gulped.

"Cara Felicity Douglas, I cannot begin to imagine what would possess you to disgrace this house, your family, and yourself with such deplorable behavior." He then seared Jason with a fiery glare. "And you dare come into my home and defile my daughter in my presence. *By God, I will not have it!*" The last was said as he pounded his fist on the desk, enunciating each syllable.

"Father, please." In defiance of all measures of self-preservation, Cara stood and approached the edge of the desk. "You are making a dreadful mistake."

"Young lady, you—"

"Am I to have no say?" Cara would not be silenced. She had claimed too many victims in her failed campaign to win Lance, and she was determined to spare Jason any additional repercussions. "Will you judge me without cause?"

"All right." He arched a brow and frowned. "You may have the floor."

Now that she had her sire's attention, Cara was not sure she wanted it. She took a minute to compose herself and considered her words. When faced with similar circumstances, Sabrina, unabashed and unapologetic, always charged the field. In the end, she opted for the truth—to some extent.

"Papa, despite what you observed, nothing illicit or improper occurred between myself and Captain Collingwood." She inhaled a shaky breath. "I was merely thanking him for his assistance in a difficult matter, and he is all that is noble and kind. He is an honorable man, and you do him a grave disservice with your accusations, for they are unfounded."

"If I am proven wrong, then he shall enjoy my utmost regret," her father stated, in monotone, which conveyed his skepticism.

"And if I have brought shame on our family, then I, alone, am responsible." How much more she could withstand, she did not know or care. "But I seek to make reparations, and I will endeavor to restore your good opinion."

Her father propped an elbow on the armrest of his chair and rested his chin in his hand. After what seemed an interminable silence, during which he appeared to weigh her impromptu oratory, he inclined his head. "Well, Collingwood. Have you anything to add to my daughter's heartfelt plea?"

"Miss Douglas speaks the truth, sir." Jason shifted in his seat. "Could not have said it better, though I am humbled by her praise."

"You make an impassioned argument, my dear." Her father rubbed the back of his neck and sighed. "But I have to wonder how much of this charming display is influenced by engaged affections."

"Sir, if I may, you read too much into the situation," Jason proclaimed.

To wit her sire impaled Captain Collingwood with a potent stare.

"Sorry." Jason choked and crossed his legs. "Perhaps I should just sit here and remain quiet."

"An excellent notion." Her father gave her his full attention, and she shrank beneath his scrutiny. "Cara, of the fruit of my loins, you have always been the sensible one. While the constancy of my concern for your sister never wavered, because she seemed destined for trouble, I have never fretted for you. I had thought you a woman of uncommon intelligence, not only because you are my daughter, but because you have merited such opinion by the steadfastness of your behavior."

"Papa, you must believe me, as nothing untoward occurred between Captain Collingwood and I." Everything in his demeanor, from the tone of his voice to the blank emptiness of his gaze, bespoke disappointment. If any portion of her heart remained whole, it shattered in that instant. "Despite the familiar sobriquet by which I am known throughout the *ton*, I am not perfect. I am human and, therefore, fallible. But in this situation, Jason is innocent. You must not punish him for my shortcomings."

"Well said, my dear, but I expected nothing less." Her sire cast a half smile that did not fool her for a second. "You see there was a time when I was fully prepared to place my children's happiness above the *ton's* good opinion. When faced with similar circumstances regarding your sister, I indulged her stubborn streak, as she decided whether or not to marry Everett, and I lived to regret it."

"Father, no." Gooseflesh covered her from top to toe. "You would not force me to wed. I will never—"

"Silence." Her father downed his brandy and speared his fingers through his gray hair. "I am not inclined to repeat what I feel was a grievous mistake on my part, especially in light of the wonderful match Sabrina enjoys with Lord Markham."

Cara glanced at Jason, and he peered at her. In unison, they blinked.

"But I do not love Captain Collingwood," she responded, in desperation.

"Then you should not have engaged in improper advances on his person." Her father snatched a pen from an inkwell and a sheet of parchment. As he made notations, he said, "I shall meet with my solicitors in the morning. Captain Collingwood, you have a choice to make. Either you announce with sufficient enthusiasm your engagement this evening, at Cara's birthday celebration, or you will meet me at dawn, with your second, as I demand satisfaction, one way or the other."

IN NERVOUS ANTICIPATION, Lance twittered his thumbs and assumed a position near the double doors leading into the drawing room. Beyond the entrance, a spirited discussion commenced, lauding the tenets of naval warfare, with Everett playing the devil's advocate, a role he often adopted as the only Nautionnier Knight without a commissioned vessel.

Several minutes had passed since he spied Admiral Douglas in the hall, headed in the general direction of the study. So where were Cara and Jason?

The dinner bell sounded.

As his odd extended family ceased their verbal jousting and filed into the dining room, Lance lingered in their wake. It was not until he had claimed his usual seat that Admiral Douglas, Jason, and Cara walked into the dining room.

To the casual observer, nothing might have seemed strange or extraordinary. But he was no casual observer, so he could not overlook the profuse perspiration on Collingwood's brow, the pale expression Cara sported, or the granite-like set of Admiral Douglas's jaw.

"Is everything all right, Mark?" Cara's mother inquired.

"Everything is fine, Amanda." Admiral Douglas nodded once. To the butler, he barked, "You may serve dinner."

Confident of his plans, and his eventual success, Lance savored the six-course meal, scarcely noting neither Jason nor Cara appeared to have much of an appetite. When a servant steered a tea trolley, bearing a three-tiered cake decorated with roses of rich marzipan, to the sideboard, Lance envisioned future celebrations heralding the birth of his heir.

While toasts were made to Cara's beauty, continued health, and long life, Lance raised his glass and added a personal, albeit silent, wish for a rousing wedding night.

"Shall we adjourn to the drawing room?" Lady Amanda covered her plate with her napkin and stood. "Cara must be anxious to open her gifts."

"I would wager she favors my selection best." Blake winked.

"I beg your pardon?" Caroline snorted. "I chose her present."

"But I paid for it." Blake grinned.

"Do not upset my wife, brother." Trevor chucked Blake's shoulder. "Else I will box your ears."

"I should very much like to see that," Everett remarked with a chuckle.

"Oh, shut up." Blake elbowed Everett. "Landlubber."

"Now I resent that, Blake." Everett scowled.

"But I do not," Sabrina replied, with an air of whimsy. "As I prefer you to sleep at home, my shameless lord. And I want a rather large family to secure the Markham lineage, so you shall be too busy to sail for the Crown."

"My saucy Sabrina, it will be my pleasure to accommodate you." Right there, in front of everyone, Everett kissed his wife.

"Must you do that here?" Blake wrinkled his nose.

"Mama, I require a moment to compose myself." Cara smoothed a stray curl. "The evening has been quite overwhelming."

"Are you unwell, my dear?" Lady Amanda frowned. "Perhaps your father was right, and I should send for the doctor."

"No, I am not ill." Cara shook her head. "I just need a bit of privacy, and I promise to join you shortly."

"All right, but do not tarry." Lady Amanda wagged a finger. "It is discourteous to keep our guests waiting."

Lance counted to three before following Cara, after she veered in the opposite direction of the crowd. He had just stepped into the hallway, when Jason all but attacked him. "What in bloody hell—"

"*Shh.*" Wild-eyed, Jason glanced left and then right and dragged Lance into the morning room. "We need to talk."

"What is it?" Lance wrenched free. "What has happened?"

"Admiral Douglas *happened*." Collingwood wiped his brow and groaned. "I am in a fine mess, thanks to you."

"I do not follow." Perplexed, Lance listened with great care, digesting every revelation of the showdown in Admiral Douglas's study. "Hell and the Reaper. What were you doing with Cara?"

"Is that really of importance?"

"Sorry." Lance exhaled in exasperation. "But I have a precise strategy, and it does not involve a hasty engagement. I had hoped to broach the subject tonight and secure her response tomorrow."

"Might I suggest you alter your plan?" Jason rested hands on hips. "You have to act, else you may lose your ladylove, because Admiral Douglas made his position crystal clear. Either I announce our betrothal this evening, or I will not live to see the morn."

"All right." Lance assessed his predicament and mulled the possibilities. "Do me a favor. Bring me the parcel with the pale blue wrapping and the lavender bow, and be quick about it."

"Aye." Jason all but ran down the hall. Less than a minute later, he returned with the requisite item. "Good luck, brother."

Lance continued to the rear of the elegant townhome but found no sign of Cara. His pulse raced, and his palms dampened, as he crossed the morning room and exited the French doors leading to the garden. After a brief searched yielded no hint of his intended, he returned to the house and turned left at the side hall. At long last, he located his wayward bride-to-be in the back parlor, sitting on the floor before the hearth.

Just as he prepared to reveal his presence, she sighed heavily, slipped her hand beneath the neckline of her gown, and drew an item, which he recognized in an instant, from her bodice.

"It is time to let you go, my hero." With a sob, she pressed the cotton square to her cheek, and then she tossed the embroidered gentleman's accouterment into the flames.

"Oh, I say. That was one of my good handkerchiefs."

"Lance?" Cara gasped and jumped to her feet. "What are you doing here?"

"I have come to compose a suitable proposal for the woman who has claimed my heart. But I am not sure she will be swayed by the customary request." He arched a brow in question. "Perhaps you can help me?"

"I suppose I can." Cara bit her lip. After a few seconds, she gazed at him with a sorrowful expression. "Is she what you want?"

Oh yes. "She is everything to me."

"Then tell her so." She smiled, but a subtle shiver betrayed her true state.

"Men are not very good with particulars, my dear," he said softly. "Any suggestions?"

"You should declare your love, as she will need that to make her decision." Cara peered at the floor. "Explain how you have watched her grow into a charming young lady, and so much more, and you want her as your partner, your lover, and the mother of your children. Proclaim her the embodiment of your dreams. Then you need only say, 'Alex, will you marry me?'"

"That sounds perfect." Lance detected the briefest hint of a plaintive cry as Cara gave him her back. "Except I require one minor alteration."

"Oh?" Now she trembled violently. "What did I miss?"

"Her name is not Alex." He approached from behind,

hugged her at the waist, and whispered in her ear, "My lady has been, is now, and always will be you, Cara."

"But I thought—"

"You thought wrong, love." He turned her in his arms but kept her close. "For two people who have been lifelong friends, we have mucked up what should have been a rather simple affair. And yet I must shoulder the greater portion of the blame, as I should have known you loved me, as I love you, when you performed that oh-so-sumptuous dance at the foot of my bed. You are the marrying sort, so you never would have gifted me your maidenhead without first committing your heart."

"Please, do not speak of that day." Cara buried her face in his chest. "I am so ashamed."

"Why would you be ashamed?" He chuckled and gave her a playful squeeze. "You were quite the seductress, and I desperately hope to see that side of you again—on our honeymoon."

"That will never happen." She wiggled and squirmed in his embrace, until he released her.

"And why not?" Somehow he knew she would not cooperate. "We belong together."

"I recall a time when you argued otherwise. Do you remember what you said to me that afternoon, because I will never forget it." Her chin quivered, as tears welled. "'I will never be your husband.' Those were your precise words. Would that I had listened to you."

"Darling Cara, I was injured, drugged, frustrated, and angry. And I would assert, however late, I was also grievously mistaken about us, but never have I claimed to possess above average intelligence." Lance cupped her cheek. "Marry me. You know we belong together."

"I once thought you wanted me, but I no longer know

how to believe you." Cara frowned. "And I will not enter a union based on some misguided notion of chivalry. Do you not understand? I seek only to make things easy for you."

"Oh, yes. About as easy as peeling a turtle—which reminds me." With a grand flourish, he presented her the beribboned parcel. "Open your gift, as it may sway you in my favor."

"I fail to see how any token—"

"Bloody hell, you are a stubborn woman. Then again, I know you as I know myself, and once you seize upon an idea you will not relinquish it without a fight." Lance could not help but laugh at the irony. "So, if I am to convince you that I am in earnest, I must change my tack, sugar kisses."

"Do not call me that." She pouted.

"But I thought you liked it. Here—" He thrust the wrapped box into her hands. "Hold your present. There's a good girl."

Without warning, he bent and hauled her over his shoulder as a sack of wheat.

"*Lance.*" Cara shrieked. "Put me down this instant."

"Not a chance, and be still, else my bum leg may land us both on the floor in a terrible tumble." His injured limb smarted under the additional weight, be he did not care. Limping to the door, he smacked her bottom when she pummeled his back with a fist. "Watch your head, darling."

"Have you lost your mind?" His bride-to-be shifted in his grasp. "What are you doing?"

In the hall, he veered right and set a course for the family gathering and a date with destiny. "What I should have done a long time ago."

CHAPTER TWENTY

*C*ara's shouts of alarm brought everyone to their feet when Lance strode into the drawing room. Without fear or hesitation, he marched to the one person with sufficient power to terminate his campaign.

With an expression of utter shock, Admiral Douglas asked, "What is the meaning of this?"

"Papa, make him put me down—*Ooh!*" She shrieked when Lance again spanked her bottom.

"Sir, consider this my formal petition for Cara's hand." As his sails caught wind, Lance gained renewed determination. "She loves me, and I love her. I will marry her, one way or another, but I would prefer to have your blessing."

"It is not true." Resting her palms to the small of his back, Cara braced herself. "He does not love me. His offer is born of the mistaken assumption that he ruined me, but I gave myself to him, of my own volition."

The room fell silent as a tomb.

With Lady Amanda at his side, Admiral Douglas looked to be on the verge of an apoplectic fit. With a dumbfounded visage, the admiral pointed to Jason. "But I thought he—"

"You thought wrong." Lance gulped as he prepared to seal his fate. "And if you must know, I have well and truly compromised your daughter."

The admiral dropped his glass of brandy.

"Bloody hell," Dirk, Damian, Blake, Jason, Dalton, Everett, and Trevor swore in unison, as they retreated behind the line of fire.

"Do not listen to her, Papa." Sabrina edged to the fore, grabbed her father's wrist, and wrenched him to face her. "Despite what she says, Cara loves Lance. She told me so, herself. That is why she seduced him."

A chorus of gasps, some in surprise, some in horror, and others still in amusement, formed an awkward ensemble.

"Sabrina Francis." Everett shifted his weight. "Were you involved in the shenanigans?"

To wit Brie shrugged. "I was only trying to help."

"I will deal with you later." Everett tucked his bride into the crook of his arm. "I apologize for the interference, Admiral."

"Ah, that reminds me. Brothers, you played me false." Lance glared at the Brethren husbands. "I declared myself, and yet she refused my proposal, so you should check your advice to the next unsuspecting dolt that wades into the shark-infested waters known as courtship."

"What is this?" Rebecca compressed her lips. "Dirk, did you meddle in their affairs?"

With nary a word, Dirk grabbed Rebecca and gave her a sound kiss.

"You are shameless." Rebecca blushed.

"I am in love." Dirk rocked on his heels. "And men so afflicted know no shame."

"Ignore them, Papa." Cara squirmed in an attempt to

break free, but Lance tightened his hold. "I need no husband, as I never—"

"Sir, this is not how I would have your daughter, but she has left me no choice by rejecting my repeated offers of marriage, out of some misplaced belief that she does me a service." Lance swallowed hard. "I mean no offense."

The admiral bared his teeth. "Be that as it may, I will not—"

"Let her go, Mark." Lady Amanda smiled and wiped a tear from her eye. "It is evident Cara has made her choice."

After another painfully protracted silence, Admiral Douglas shook his head and sighed. "What are your intentions?"

Beneath such vehement scrutiny, lesser men would have faltered, but Lance would not waver an inch. "With your permission, I will take Cara home and persuade her to accept me."

"Oh, this just keeps getting better." The admiral glanced right and then left, snatched the decanter of brandy from the trolley, and drank directly from the bottle. Then he wiped his mouth on his coat sleeve and inquired, "I do not imagine her virtue is in peril?"

"She has already gifted me her virtue," Lance responded without hesitation. "Again, sir, I mean no disrespect, but it was beyond my control. She took me while I was still abed with a broken leg."

Lady Amanda inhaled sharply and clutched her throat.

To a lesser extent, feminine giggles and male chuckles formed a concert of amusement.

"She took you?" The admiral teetered.

"Papa, I can explain." Cara groaned. "It was—"

"Oh, no. Please, no more." The admiral splayed his palms. "I will speak with my solicitors in the morning and have the contracts drawn, so you will have her home, by noon, and be prepared to sign the documents." And then he lowered his chin. "Be prompt, my boy. Despite the tenure of our acquaintance, trust me, you do not want me to come after you."

"Aye, aye, sir." With a mock salute, Lance clicked his heels. "Upon my word, I will not fail you."

∽

"Papa. Mama, you must help me." Cara reached for anything to forestall her captor, as Lance carried her from her family home. "Do not let him take me."

Standing as a united front, her parents waved farewell.

When Lance shoved her inside his town coach, she scrambled for the opposite door to freedom, but her tormentor grabbed a fistful of her skirts and held her prisoner.

"Lance, let me go."

"Not a chance."

"I will not yield."

"Yes you will." Lance settled her in his lap and nipped the crest of her ear. "And you are going to enjoy every minute of it, but I would wager I am going to enjoy it most."

"You make no sense." In panic, Cara searched her surroundings for a means of escape. "First you rejected me, then you proposed an honor-driven union, then you courted Alex, and now you claim otherwise. What am I supposed to believe?"

"Point taken, darling." Lance chuckled and smiled, his wolf's smile. "That is why I am taking you home, where-upon I will seduce you in every way possible, until you beg me to marry you. When next the sun rises, there will be no more secrets between us. I will know all the intimate details of your existence, and you shall know mine. Then I will do the honorable by you and make you my wife."

"Beg, indeed." Cara snorted and shoved the wrapped parcel at him. "And you should take back your gift, as I want nothing from you."

"Oh, that particular item is merely a loan, as I would never part with it." He nuzzled her temple. "Will you not open the box?"

"No." Mustering her last vestiges of courage, she folded her arms in defiance. "I will fight you, I swear I will."

"No need to make it interesting, love." He trailed his nose along her jawline. "I am quite aroused, already."

"You are relishing this, are you not?" How could she evade what he presumed was their inevitable fate?

He smirked. "Indubitably."

"And I thought we were friends." She glared at him.

"My dear, we are a vast deal more than that, and you know it." Lance kissed her cheek, and she shivered.

The coach slowed to a halt before Raynesford House, and Cara almost swooned. The bane of her existence shuffled her to his side and leapt from the equipage before the footmen could assume their stations in the portico.

"Lance, please do not do this." She remained firmly rooted in the squabs.

"Pick up your present, darling." He clasped her hand in his and pressed his lips to her knuckles. "That's my girl."

When she retrieved the package, he wrenched her by the wrist, bent, and once again flung her over his shoulder. Despite her protests, she ended up in the same humiliating position.

"I can walk, you know," she said, with her bottom in the air.

"You have not seemed so inclined." The amusement in his voice caught her off guard. "Besides, I like it better this way."

"Well, I do not." She smacked his rear.

He responded, in kind. "You should have thought of that when you refused my proposal."

Cara cursed the searing burn of a blush as he navigated the entrance stairs.

"Good evening, your lordship." Her shame tripled at the butler's greeting.

"Good evening, Banks. Wish me merry, because Miss Douglas is going to be my wife." Lance rotated to afford Cara a view of the distinguished manservant. "Say hello to your new mistress."

The butler bowed. "On behalf of the entire household, I wish you great joy, Miss Douglas."

"Say goodnight, darling," Lance said as he crossed the marbled foyer.

"Goodnight, darling." It was only when Banks covered his mouth and nodded, that Cara realized her error. She was not sure what she had expected, but the butler closed the front door and went about his business, as if the sight of his master conveying a woman to his bedchamber in full view of the staff was an everyday occurrence.

Due to his injured limb, Lance carried Cara upstairs at an interminable pace, and she prayed they made it in one piece. But as it dawned on her that they neared his private apartments, she composed a speech she hoped would spare her further heartache.

Returning to the scene of the crime brought her pangs of remorse mixed with guilt. When her hero shut the door, turned the key, and locked her inside his domain, fear set in with a vengeance. But to her surprise, he bent and stood her upright.

"Now, before we commence the test of wills, I would have you open your birthday present."

"Lance, I would not—"

"For the love of all creation, *open the bloody box*." He tugged the folds of his cravat, drew the yard-length of fine linen from his neck and tossed the strip of cloth to the floor. "If you are not convinced of my affection, even after you have seen what is inside, then I will release you."

"Have I your word, as a gentleman?" Skeptical that an inanimate object could change her mind, she pulled the bow from the parcel.

"I will summon the coach, myself, and return you to your family." He doffed his coat and waistcoat. "Open it —now."

Quivering beneath his uncharacteristic loss of temper, Cara tore the blue paper and lifted the lid. Her ears rang, her heart pounded in her chest, her knees buckled, and she sank to the floor.

In her tremulous grasp, nestled in a bed of white cotton, rested a familiar wooden figurine. Although the paint had long since worn away, from countless rubbing, no doubt, and the surface was smooth, the shape was unmistakable, and she recognized it in an instant. It was the little turtle she had given him all those years ago.

The night he almost died.

The night they shared their first kiss.

"You still have it?" The implication was unequivocal, the meaning irrefutable, and her mind struggled to embrace his silent pledge even as her heart rejoiced.

"Of course." He sat beside her.

"But—why?" She traced the lines and curves of one of

her most cherished collectibles.

"Perhaps for the same reason you kept my handker-chief." Lance inclined his head and winked. "The one I gave you in Hyde Park, when I taught you to ride and claimed a kiss in payment for services gladly rendered."

"You remember?" she asked, in a ghost of a whisper.

"Dearest and loveliest Cara, I forget nothing where you are concerned." He removed the turtle from the box, placed it in her palm, and closed his hand over hers. "Wherever I have traveled, however far, whatever I have done, however perilous, whomever I have faced, whether friend or foe, I have never been alone, as you have always been with me—in my heart."

With something between a sob and a sigh, Cara lunged, knocking Lance backwards. Sprawled atop him, she kissed her knight with all she had and for all she was worth. Comforting warmth eased the tension investing her nerves, and her skin tingled. Her hero's modest but monumental gesture was exactly what she needed to accept his proposal of marriage.

And it had to happen just like that.

It could not have been rehearsed, could not have been planned. It could not have been a best guess or a shot in the dark. Though the journey had been long and painful, in the end, she had to admit it was well worth the wait.

"You are wearing too many clothes, sweetness." Lance rolled her to her side. "And you have yet to formally accept my offer of marriage."

"Did I miss something?" She scored her fingers to the back of his neck. "Because you did not ask the question, at least, not tonight."

"Ah, my lady is displeased?" He rubbed his nose to hers, stood, hauled her from the floor, and clutched her hands in his. "Darling, were my legs capable, I would kneel before you. But my injury still smarts, and I would walk down the aisle with you, on our wedding day. So, tell me true, Miss Cara Felicity Douglas. Will you marry me?"

She shrugged. "It depends."

"On what?" He narrowed his stare and looked on her as a warrior preparing to lay siege to his latest conquest.

"The inducement." She kicked off her slippers and gave him her back. "Can you help me out of my gown?"

"Now that is an offer I dare not refuse." As Lance unlaced her dress, he trailed his tongue along the skin at the nape of her neck. "You know, the Brethren husbands advised me that, as an aphrodisiac, love is *sans pareil*, and I am inclined to agree, as I may be erect until the New Year."

"How romantic." Wearing only her chemise, Cara giggled, unfastened his shirt, slipped it from his shoulders, and dropped it to the floor.

"Sugar kisses wants romance?" He removed his Hessians and then unhooked his breeches. "How about this? I want to lick my favorite wine from your nipples, and sip champagne from your navel, until you scream with pleasure."

"That will do nicely, my hero." Without hesitation or shame, she whisked the chemise over her head in a single fluid movement. In a vague sense of *déjà vu*, she recalled the first time she had stood naked but proud in his bedchamber, when her hopes had been based on a girl's fancy. Now, her actions bespoke the love and devotion of a woman, and she decided his gesture merited more than a one-word affirmation. The answer, when it came to her, seemed so obvious. "With my body, I thee worship."

Lance sent the breeches to join the discarded garments and then splayed his hands. "With my heart, I thee adore."

Cara all but ran into his embrace. "From this day forward you shall not walk alone."

He rested his forehead to hers. "My heart will be your shelter."

"And my arms will be your home." She smiled.

"So you will marry me?" he asked, with a boyish grin.

"I believe you promised my father that you would convince me to accept your suit, and I am prepared for the assault, my lusty lord." Cara retreated and then climbed into bed. Reclining amid the pillows, she struck a seductive pose. "Persuade me."

THE SUN SHONE bright on the crisp December day that Cara married Lance, at St. George's Church in Hanover Square. Despite the impending holidays, the ton turned out *en masse* to witness the wedding of Miss Cara Felicity Douglas to Lance Fortescue Prescott, sixth marquess of Raynesford.

With Jason at his side, Lance looked on in pride as his bride, escorted by her father, made a spectacular entrance and held all in attendance enrapt as she walked the aisle.

Before the archbishop, they took their vows, and he could not suppress a grin as Cara repeated the very portion of the ceremony with which she had accepted his proposal, that memorable night in his bedchamber. And the charming flush in her cheeks told him she knew exactly what he was thinking.

After running a gauntlet of well-wishers outside the church, they repaired to Raynesford House for the wedding breakfast, where champagne flowed, and the happy couple were toasted and roasted.

"So Jason was never interested in Cara?" Blake

scratched the back of his head and glanced at Damian, who merely shrugged.

"No." Lance chuckled. "He was only helping my wife catch my attention."

"Rebecca told me there was something going on between those two long before Jason entered the picture." Dirk rolled his eyes. "Her spy instincts, you know."

"Bloody hell." Dalton tossed his familiar lucky coin. "If she ever imparts such vital information about me, I would know it, so I might run in the opposite direction."

"Sooner or later, it happens to all of us." Trevor rocked on his heels. "You will not escape the preacher's noose."

"Well I opt for later." Damian elbowed Blake. "What say you, brother? Time to chase some skirts."

"So, have you spoken to Alex?" Lance bit his tongue when Collingwood scowled.

"No." Jason peered at the lady in question. "And I do not intend to until I can do so without losing my temper, else I might say something I regret."

"Do not be too hard on her. From what Cara imparted, Alex's heart was in the right place." Lance checked his time-piece. "Brothers, I have done the pretty, long enough. I have an important engagement with my bride, so if there are no objections, I shall search out my wife."

"Go to it, man." Everett raised his glass. "Take comfort in the fact that you will not have to run her aground, as I did with her sister."

"Oh, I say." Trevor thrust his chin. "Caroline and I almost broke the bunk in my cabin."

"There is nothing like your wedding night." Dirk slapped Lance on the back. "My Becca practically attacked me, and I still have the scars to prove it, but it hurt so good."

In the wake of such bawdy thoughts, he located Cara

surrounded by the Brethren women. After making their excuses, he steered her to a corner of the chasmal ballroom and sheltered behind a vase filled with hothouse roses.

"What is it?" She frowned and adjusted his cravat. "Is something wrong?"

"Today? Of course, not." He traced the delicate pattern of Alençon lace, from which her gown was fashioned, and lingered dangerously near her décolletage. "I thought we might make our escape."

"I see." She cast him a flirty smile, which warmed him to his toes. "What did you have in mind, my hero?"

"A strategic tack." Lance scanned the crowd and cupped her cheek. "As I fear we will never make it out of here if we stay together."

"So you suggest we divide and conquer?" Cara pressed her lips to his palm.

"Precisely." He hugged her close at the waist and kissed her forehead. "You exit the main doors, and I will leave via the terrace and re-enter the house through the back parlor."

"All right." She clucked her tongue. "Sounds like a very smart plan."

"Do not tarry, lady mine." With great reluctance, he released her. "As I shall await you in our bedchamber."

"Until then, my lusty lord." She pinched his bottom, and his Jolly Roger saluted.

It took him a few minutes to wind his way through the crush of revelers, but Lance was a man on a mission, and he hoped he would make it to his apartments before Cara. So he was surprised to find her in the gallery when he stepped onto the landing at the top of the grand staircase.

"What are you doing?" For the briefest moment, a nagging thought entered his brain. Did she covet unrequited feelings for Thomas?

"I was just thinking." She stared at his beloved cousin's portrait. "The one thing that would have made this day even better would have been if Thomas were here."

"I know." Lance snaked an arm about her waist and rested his chin atop her head. The pangs of guilt returned as he realized he had spared nary a thought for his cousin in the week preceding his marriage. "I miss him, too."

"He would no doubt have teased me endlessly." She giggled and covered his hand with hers.

He frowned. "Why is that?"

"Because, even as children, he knew I harbored a wicked crush on you," she declared with a wistful sigh. "Oh, he was a mischievous gadling."

"How could he know?" Confused, Lance turned her in his embrace. "Are you certain?"

"Yes." Cara grinned, averted her gaze, and fingered a mother-of-pearl button on his coat. "He caught me spying on you, one summer at Pembroke, while you were bathing in the pond."

"Well are you not the naughty minx?" Of course, he would not divulge the fact that Thomas had discovered Lance, in similar circumstances—doing the same thing. Lance burst into laughter at the absurdity of it all.

"Stop it." She pouted. "I was a young girl, and you must admit our bodies are very different. It is only natural that I would be curious."

"You have quite the wild streak, sugar kisses." He bent his head but halted. "Wait a minute. When did this happen?"

"You mean the first time?" she asked, with an expression of cherubic innocence.

"I beg your pardon?" He opened his mouth and then

closed it. "The first time? There were more than one instances?"

"I like watching you." She shrugged. "I always have, and I expect that will never change."

"You are the vixen." He grinned and dropped his hands to the twin swells of her bottom. "Who would have thought it?"

"I will take that as a compliment." She kissed his cheek. "You know, I secured his silence by not revealing his infatuation with my sister. He had composed an ode to her beauty."

"Thomas was infatuated with Sabrina?" But Lance had believed Thomas loved Cara. "Are you sure?"

"Indeed." She inclined her head and peered at the ceiling. "It was the summer Brie fell from that old oak tree, near the orangery at Sandgate, and broke her ankle. I discovered him reciting poetry, and poor Sabrina appeared on the verge of revisiting her lunch, but she was a captive audience, as Thomas had taken her crutches."

"Why that sly dog." It was the very same year Thomas had professed his undying devotion to Cara. His cousin had thought it comical they shared the same taste in the fairer sex, and he had ribbed Lance mercilessly, taunting him with the prospect of Cara wedding another. In hindsight, it was obvious Thomas meant to rile Lance with his declaration—nothing more.

"Bloody hell." He emitted a self-deprecating snort and rolled his eyes. "I do not believe it."

"But I speak the truth." She snuggled close and gave him a squeeze.

"Oh, I do not doubt you, my lovely wife." The weight of the world, so long inhabiting his shoulders, seemed to vanish in a flash. "Our dear Thomas has been gone these sixteen years, and yet again I find myself on the wrong end of one of his pranks. Somewhere, I know he is enjoying a good belly laugh."

Cara furrowed her brow. "I do not follow."

"It does not signify." Lance studied the portrait of his cousin. *Well played, my friend.* "One day, when we have nothing more important to do, I will tell you the whole of it. Right now, I want to get you out of that dress and into our bed."

Hours later, Cara slipped from the bed, walked to the washstand, poured water in the basin, wet a towel, and wiped the sticky wine residue from her breasts.

"Now tell me that was not fun." Naked, Lance rolled the trolley, bearing an array of covered dishes, from the sitting room into his chamber. "And there is champagne for the encore, sugar kisses."

"You, sir, are a barbarian." She grabbed his silk robe from a peg and draped it over her shoulders.

"Complaining?" he asked, with a narrow stare, as he checked the condition of their meal. "How strange. I did not order cherry compote for dessert, but we have a large portion of it."

"Never, as I rather prefer your particular brand of ravishment, my hero." She came to stand behind him, wrapped her arms about his waist, and hugged him. "What I had not anticipated was all the noise. You make a startling ruckus in the throes of passion."

"You are one to talk." Lance scoffed. "And you snore."

"I do not." Retreating a step, she slapped his bare bottom. "What a horrid thing to say."

"Reminds me of old Willie Boyle, from my years as a midshipman." He chuckled and caught her in a devil of a clinch. "The man could rattle the timbers, and you could give him a run for his money."

How amazed she was at Lance's transformation since he signed the wedding contract, in her father's study. If she had any second thoughts concerning their betrothal, his behavior leading up to their wedding ceremony erased them.

"That, sir, is unforgivable." Cara humphed. "Perhaps I shall sleep in my chambers, tonight."

"Not a chance." He cast a lopsided grin and rubbed his back. "I am still smarting from the confines of your bed."

Ah, the previous night had been a singular success, when her erstwhile reluctant knight climbed the trellis outside the window of her former quarters at her family's townhouse and shared her final eve as a spinster, in her old room. With Lance beside her, she had enjoyed the first restful slumber since he returned, injured, from his voyage. She had drifted off cataloguing all the hopes she had for their future.

"Poor darling." She shimmied and dropped the robe to the floor. "Come back to bed, and I shall soothe your aches. And bring the cherry compote, as you are not the only one with fantasies."

Lance burst into laughter.

How she had dreamed of the love that shimmered in his eyes, as he gazed upon her now.

She dreamed of the children they would bring into their world, of the family they would endeavor to create.

As she drew him near and set her lips to his, one sweet refrain sang in her head.

It was time to live the dream.

EPILOGUE

*S*ince the disastrous invasion of Russia, the past
June, rumors circulated throughout the Continent
that Napoleon, and the bulk of the French army in Eastern
Europe, would soon retreat. Hoping to seize the opportunity to attack, Wellington summoned his officers to Cadiz,
reorganized the war effort, and called for supplies and troop
reinforcements.

To his displeasure, Lance studied the embossed parchment, which signaled his reinstatement to full duty, and
read it for the third time. It was the only thing that could
instigate his premature return to London from Sandgate
Manor, his ancestral pile in Southampton, shortly after the
holidays.

"Your trunks are loaded, darling." Wearing a tan merino
pelisse trimmed in ermine, Cara stood, pretty as a picture, in
the doorway of his study. "We await your presence."

Prior to their marriage, he had always admired her
understated elegance, in secret. Now that she was his, and
he was hers, he could ogle her to his heart's content, which

he did at every opportunity. The mere sight of her brought a smile to his face. "I will be right there, sugar kisses."

Rolling his maps, charts, and orders into a tight bundle, he checked and rechecked his Letters of Marque. After another cursory survey to ensure he had overlooked nothing, he crossed the room and claimed a quick kiss before following his bride down the hall.

"Elaine has a cold and has decided to remain at home." Cara peered over her shoulder and winked. "So it will be just the two of us in the coach."

"Alone in a confined space, with only my charming Cara for company?" Lance clucked his tongue. "There is a god."

"Shameless." She giggled.

"I am in love." As he contemplated the gentle sway of her hips, he considered the logistics and calculated how many ways he could take his wife before they arrived at Deptford. "And as Dirk remarked, quite accurately, I might add, at your birthday celebration, men in love know no shame."

"And are you so afflicted?" she inquired, with a flirty lilt in her voice, which scored a direct hit to his loins.

"Do you doubt me?" He hastened his step, as they crossed the threshold.

"Never." She licked her lips, as he handed her into the equipage and then settled into the squabs beside her. "And more's the pity, for I share your burden."

No sooner had they passed the gates of Raynesford House than she pulled down the shade, and he followed suit. And then he turned—right into her kiss. Several heated, desperate, achingly sweet minutes later, and they arrived in Deptford.

As Cara situated her skirts and adjusted her pelisse, he re-hooked his breeches, fastened his coat, and speared his fingers through his hair. "Another fantasy realized, my lady wife."

"Oh?" She smoothed a wayward curl. "You never mentioned a particular fondness for coach travel."

"I only just discovered it." And then he noted the hem of her dress caught on her garter. "You missed something."

With their clothes righted, Lance and Cara descended the coach and walked to the berth where the *Demetrius* anchored.

The decks were alive with the activity one would expect of a ship preparing for a long journey. Sailors danced in the ratlines, loaded cargo, and sang ribald shanties as they worked. To his surprise, his lady remained in his wake, as he ascended the gangplank.

"Careful with the Captain's trunks, as I packed them beautifully." She directed his men as though her position of chatelaine extended to his rig. "And I must speak with the cook about the Captain's favorite dishes."

"Morning, Cap'n." On the quarterdeck, Scotty saluted. "That is a live cannon you married."

"Tell me about it." Lance arranged his maps, reached into his pocket to retrieve his watch, and found a folded piece of parchment, bearing an instantly recognizable script, and he unfolded the letter.

To My Most Cherished Husband,

By the time you read this missive, I will be at Raynesford House, and you will be somewhere on the deep blue sea. I have returned the little turtle to your personal belongings and claimed a handkerchief, in kind, which I shall tuck in my bodice, over my heart, until you are home, and your lips take its place. Please know that I am so proud of you and your service to the Crown, even though it takes you from me, and I miss you, already.

All my love,
Your Cara

When his knees buckled, Lance grasped the rail for support. A stark emptiness spread in his chest, at the prospect of spending the next few weeks without what he considered his exceedingly better half. With Cara at his side, he felt invincible.

What was it Everett said?

Love makes you feel you can conquer the world, if only to deliver the spoils to the lady who holds your heart and have her share your devotion.

For Lance, truer words were never spoken.

All too soon, the mighty ships of the Brethren of the Coast cast off, one at a time, forming an impressive line of British military prowess. And yet, for him, the sight held no joy, because he could not bear to part from his wife.

And then it hit him. A marvel of brilliance dawned in his brain, which would solve his quandary and ease his torment. He could take Cara with him. But the logistics of such madness presented a whole new host of problems, and by the time he located his bride on the docks, anticipating his farewell, he had reversed course.

"Well, my dear, the tide awaits no man." He drew her into his arms. "I suppose this is goodbye."

"You will be careful, my hero." Cara lowered her gaze and smoothed the folds of his many-caped greatcoat. And although she was clearly trying to be brave, her quivering chin bespoke her tremulous state. "If you do not return, safe and sound, hale and whole, I will never forgive you."

"Oh, love, I shall miss you every second, of every minute, of every hour, of every day we are apart." Lance cupped her cheek and bent his head, in preparation for a kiss, but Cara stayed him.

"You could take me with you." She pressed her hands to his chest. "I packed a trunk—it is very small and will take little space, such that you will scarcely notice my presence."

His bride spoke so fast; he could not get a word in edgewise.

Lance burst into laughter.

"Please, I cannot be without you." Cara all but bounced in his embrace. "I thought I could do it, but I cannot. I promise, I shall obey your every command and will be as quiet as a mouse."

"Snoring, aside." He rested his forehead to hers. "Will you not be afraid?"

"What have I to fear when we are together?" She rubbed her nose to his. "I beg you, do not leave me alone."

He pretended to give the matter due consideration. "Tell me, darling, are you familiar with Botticelli's *Birth of Venus*?"

"Yes." Confusion invested his bride's features. "I know the painting quite well."

"Then I should like, very much, to see your impersonation." Lance kissed the crest of her ear and whispered, "In my bunk."

And then he swooped, flung his lady over his shoulder, and shouted at a sailor, "You there, fetch my wife's trunk, and be quick about it." Amid a chorus of bawdy hoots and hollers, Lance carried Cara aboard the *Demetrius*.

PERCHED ON THE DOCKS, Lady Alexandra Seymour waved at Lance and Cara, as they set sail with the Brethren fleet—save one. The *Intrepid*, Jason's powerful vessel, had been moved to Plymouth for a final refitting, and she had over-heard Admiral Douglas ordering her captain to prepare to join his crew. If she were going to catch the husband of her dreams, she would have to work fast.

To her infinite frustration, her intended showed no incli-nation to cooperate. Since Cara's birthday celebration, when Alex's part in the plot to bring Lance to the altar was revealed, Jason had not spoken to her.

Swallowing her pride, because she valued Jason more, she had apologized to her erstwhile fervent suitor, but he remained unmoved, which left her befuddled and teetering on the brink of heartbreak. She had expected him to accept her sincere expression of regret, to declare his undying devotion, and to propose.

That had not happened.

Instead, he resisted her every attempt to make amends, and how she ached for him. Casting a side-glance at her wayward captain, Alex began to rethink her strategy.

Lingering in the wake of her odd extended family, she dallied until Admiral Douglas departed and then approached her connubial conquest.

Skimming her tongue across her lips, something that never failed to catch his attention—or any man, for that matter, Alex inclined her head and smiled. "Good morning, Jason."

He nodded once. "Lady Alexandra."

His formal address sent a chill of dread down her spine, and she flinched. When his heated gaze dropped to her mouth, her confidence soared.

"So, Captain of my heart, may I offer you a seat in my coach, as we return to London?" With victory in reach, she took a step in his direction, closing the distance between them. "There is plenty of room, given I journey alone and would be most grateful for your company."

"But I am for Plymouth." With features like granite, and his arms folded imperiously in front of him, Jason impaled her with his stare. "And you may go to the devil."

ABOUT BARBARA DEVLIN

A proud Latina, USA Today bestselling author Barbara Devlin was born a storyteller, but it was a weeklong vacation to Bethany Beach, Delaware that forever changed her life. The little house her parents rented had a collection of books by Kathleen Woodiwiss, which exposed Barbara to the world of romance, and *Shanna* remains a personal favorite.

Barbara writes heartfelt historical romances that feature not so perfect heroes who may know how to seduce a woman but know nothing of marriage. And she prefers feisty but smart heroines who sometimes save the hero before they find their happily ever after.

Barbara is a disabled-in-the-line-of-duty retired police officer, and she earned an MA in English and continued a course of study for a Doctorate in Literature and Rhetoric. She happily considered herself an exceedingly eccentric English professor, until success in Indie publishing lured her into writing, full-time, featuring her fictional knight-hood, the Brethren of the Coast.

Connect with Barbara Devlin at BarbaraDevlin.com, where you can sign up for her newsletter, The Knightly News.

ALSO BY BARBARA DEVLIN

BRETHREN OF THE COAST

Loving Lieutenant Douglas

Enter the Brethren

My Lady, the Spy

The Most Unlikely Lady

One-Knight Stand

Captain of Her Heart

The Lucky One

Love with an Improper Stranger

To Catch a Fallen Spy

Hold Me, Thrill Me, Kiss Me

The Duke Wears Nada

A Very Brethren Christmas

Owner of a Lonely Heart

BRETHREN ORIGINS

Arucard

Demetrius

Aristide

Morgan

Geoffrey

PIRATES OF THE COAST

The Black Morass

The Iron Corsair

The Buccaneer

The Stablemaster's Daughter

The Marooner

Once Upon a Christmas Knight

The Reaper

WORLD OF DE WOLFE PACK

Lone Wolfe

The Big Bad De Wolfe

Tall, Dark & De Wolfe

MAGICK TRILOGY

Magick, Straight Up

A Taste of Magick

Magick in the Air

PIRATES OF BRITANNIA

The Blood Reaver

THE MAD MATCHMAKING MEN OF WATERLOO

The Accidental Duke

The Accidental Groom